EVERY *Graceful*
FANCY

EVERY *Graceful* FANCY

Dickens Inn

Volume Five

a novel

Anita Stansfield

Covenant Communications, Inc.

Cover image *Swans* © DenisTangney, Jr., courtesy of iStockphoto.com; *Blank Sign* © xyno, courtesy of iStockphoto.com.

Cover design © 2010 by Covenant Communications, Inc.

Published by Covenant Communications, Inc.
American Fork, Utah

Printed in United States of America
First Printing: November 2010

16 15 14 13 12 11 10   10 9 8 7 6 5 4 3 2 1

ISBN: 978-1-60861-121-8

CHAPTER 1

Anaconda, Montana

Autumn could be cold in Anaconda, but Chas was still surprised at the bite in the September wind as she unloaded groceries from the heavily weighed-down cart into the back of her SUV. She knew there would likely be some pleasant autumn days before the full onset of the typical early winter, but today it felt like winter had come early. Glad to be in the vehicle with the heater on, she sat there for a minute and rubbed her hands in front of the vent before she put her gloves back on and drove out of the parking lot. She stopped at the bakery to pick up her usual large order, and took a minute to chat with her dear friend Jodi, who was the manager. Before leaving the bakery, she called her husband as usual from her cell phone to let him know she would soon be arriving. He'd been watching their two children while she did the errands and shopping, but having him help unload it all and put it away made the chore much more bearable. The amount of groceries it took to run a bed-and-breakfast could sometimes be daunting.

Chas never pulled into the little parking lot of her business-slash-home without looking up to admire the beautiful Victorian mansion where she had been raised by her maternal grandmother. It had been old and falling apart at that time, but after Chas had lost her first husband in a military training accident, and then her baby due to a heart defect, she had put all of her energy into seeing the home restored and remodeled into a bed-and-breakfast that would provide a viable income for the two women. Chas had cared for Granny until she'd passed away, which was only a matter of weeks after Jackson had come to stay at the inn and had fallen in love with both of them.

Jackson Leeds was a former FBI agent and an ex-Marine, with a deeply troubled past and more struggles chalked up in his life than the average ten men. But he'd come through brilliantly, and now he and Chas were happily married and living the American dream. The crown jewel of that dream for them was having the gospel as a part of their lives, something that Chas considered to be a miracle. They had been sealed as a family in the temple in February, and every day they knelt together and thanked their Heavenly Father for the reality that they would all be together forever, no matter what else happened.

Attached to the restored mansion, which was built in 1870, was a family home that had been recently built. When Chas had been single—or newly married—living in the inn had not been a problem. But when it came to raising a family, they needed the space and privacy for children to play and be noisy without disturbing their guests. Now the kitchen doors connected the new house to the old, and everything was set up to run the business effectively—with the help of a few employees—and to raise a family with every possible comfort.

Jackson met Chas at the door with a kiss, then he quickly went back inside to get a jacket, surprised by the cold. He assured her the children were playing in the area of their home that was completely baby-proofed, and he handed her the cordless phone that someone always had to be available to answer. It was the main line to the inn, and it was also the line that guests could call from their rooms if they needed something. Chas traded her coat for an apron and put the phone in one of the pockets while Jackson carried the remainder of their supplies through the biting wind that had to be endured between the car and the door of the inn. Once everything was inside, much of it had to be carried to the basement to the overflow pantry and freezers. Chas was only too glad to let Jackson do the heavy lifting and the physical labor.

Chas greeted her children while putting food away in both kitchens she divided it between that intended for family use, and the breakfast and snacks provided for their guests. The kids were busy playing in a mass of toys in the common room of the house and hardly noticed her. Charles would turn three in late November, and Isabelle had turned one during the summer. They were very close in age, but since Isabelle had become old enough to walk and play with many of the same toys, the two of them played together relatively well—most of the time. There was often a little tussle over a particular toy, or a toddler wrestling match, but for the most part they were happy, well-behaved children.

The phone in Chas's pocket rang, and she moved away from the noisy children as she answered, "Dickensian Inn." It was immediately evident that the purpose of this call was to make a reservation. Chas hurried to the office of the inn where she could look at the scheduling book. She passed Jackson on her way and signaled to him so that he knew where she would be and that he was in charge of the children.

As Chas sat down in the chair behind the desk, answering questions about the inn and its amenities, she missed Polly more than usual. Of course, Chas saw her best friend every few days, but Polly had also worked at the inn for many years, and she was so great at handling all of the extra little things in the office. Jackson and Chas had managed to cover for Polly by each putting in some extra time, but it had made the days longer and more challenging. Polly was currently taking maternity leave, adjusting to life as the mother of a beautiful little girl with red curly hair, much like Polly's. She would soon be returning to work and bringing the baby with her much of the time. Her husband, Elliott, a former colleague of Jackson's, worked varying shifts as a security guard in the city of Butte, about an hour away.

"Now I noticed," the woman on the other end of the phone said, and Chas focused on the task at hand, "that on your website it says you have weekly and monthly rates."

"That's right," Chas said, intrigued by the possibility of this being something more than a single-night or a weekend guest. A series of unique events and some tender, spiritual moments had prompted Chas and Jackson to encourage, through their advertising, longer stays for potential guests. Their hope was that people might come to the inn in times of need or crisis, which might allow Chas and Jackson the opportunity to make a difference in these people's lives. There was no set formula for such opportunities; they only knew that they needed to be open to the possibility and allow the Lord to choreograph situations that might allow good things to happen. They'd both been very blessed, and they were more than willing to share those blessings with others in need—even if those needs were more spiritual and emotional than monetary. Chas had always taken being an innkeeper very seriously, but now she felt this responsibility even more keenly.

"Are you looking to stay for an extended time?" Chas asked with kind eagerness, wondering what adventure they might have in store. It had been a long time since they'd had any long-term guests.

"It's not for me," the woman said, and her previously congenial tone became mildly defensive. "It's for my daughter. She needs a place to stay for four or five months . . . or so. But I don't want it to just be some second-rate hotel. I want her to be comfortable."

"We can certainly provide that," Chas said, her curiosity growing while she felt a subtle but undeniable warmth that let her know this was one of those moments when they were being given the opportunity to help someone in need, and she needed to do everything she could to facilitate that.

"May I be frank with you, Ms. . . . ."

"Oh, you can call me Chas," she said. "And you're welcome to be candid with me."

"My daughter went and got herself pregnant," the woman said, now sounding angry. Apparently being *frank* meant casting aside any inhibitions about her feelings over the matter. "After everything we've done for her, she does something stupid like this and tries to throw away her whole life. Well, we told her we won't have it. She's going to have this baby and give it up for adoption, and if she can stay somewhere else—somewhere obscure and discreet—until it's over, then we can hope that no one ever finds out. And then she can go back to college and do something worthwhile with her life. I need a place for her to stay where I know she's safe and I don't have to deal with it."

Chas was glad the conversation wasn't face-to-face, which made it easier to cover her astonishment. She said in an even and neutral voice, "We would be happy to have your daughter stay here as long as she needs to."

"It says on the website that breakfast is included in the rate, but that you have other meals available."

"That's right," Chas said. "With advance notice, we're happy to provide three meals a day for a reasonable rate."

"Money isn't a problem. I want my daughter to have every comfort; I just don't want to deal with it." That was the second time she'd said *that*. Chas was absolutely certain this woman did *not* want to deal with her daughter's pregnancy *at all*.

"Do you have a hospital nearby?" this woman asked. Chas wanted to counter the question by saying, *Do you intend to just leave your daughter completely on her own, figuring she can drive herself to the hospital when she goes into labor?*

Instead Chas said politely, "Yes, we do. However, when I had my babies, I saw a doctor in Butte and they were delivered in a hospital there. It's about an hour away."

"That'll be fine," the woman said as if she didn't want any information that wasn't absolutely necessary. "I assume that a maid will make certain the room remains clean."

Chas swallowed carefully, trying to ignore the implication that the room maids might be considered some kind of servant, expected to go above and beyond the call of duty for this woman's possibly spoiled daughter. She took the question at face value and answered it directly. "With the weekly or monthly rate, the bed linens are changed once a week, and the bathroom and room are cleaned thoroughly at the same time. The daily service includes making the bed, clean towels, and a quick surface cleaning of the bathroom."

"That should be fine," the woman said, but she sounded mildly concerned, as if it took some effort to accept it as fine. "It all sounds well enough. I'll be sending Catherine Jane to Butte, and she'll be renting a car. As long as you provide the services you've described, there won't be any need for you to fuss over her. She knows how to be independent."

"Very well," Chas said, again biting her tongue to keep from saying what she *felt* like saying. "Our rooms vary in rate according to their size and features. Do you want to—"

"Give her a good one," the woman said. "Money isn't a problem." That was the second time she'd brought *that* up as well. Apparently money wasn't a problem.

"We'll take very good care of your daughter," Chas said, actually beginning to feel excited to meet Catherine Jane, even though she had no idea what to expect. Hopefully she wouldn't be as abrupt and arrogant as her mother. Chas wondered if she would be expected to call her *Catherine Jane* each time she spoke to her. It was kind of a mouthful. But then, she was accustomed to having a one-syllable name.

Chas learned from the woman's credit card information that her name was Avis Fitzgibbons, and the billing address for the card was in Maine. Catherine Jane would be checking in the day after tomorrow and staying until after "this mess is all cleaned up and cleared away."

As soon as Chas got off the phone she went back into the house to find Jackson fixing some lunch while Charles was hanging on his leg, whining for attention, and Isabelle was in the high chair banging her sippy cup on the tray and yelling just to hear herself yell. It was a typical scene, and Jackson always handled it with a gentle patience that seemed almost out of character for a man who had once believed he'd never have children. He'd been raised by a very bad example of fatherhood, and he'd lived a tough life. The Marines and the FBI were not necessarily conducive to tutoring a man on gentle fatherhood. And yet Jackson was instinctively good at caring for his family.

"I want you to be the father of my children," Chas said loudly.

Jackson turned toward her. "What?"

Chas laughed, then shouted, "I want you to be the father of my children."

"Already done," he said and turned back to the stove to stir the macaroni and cheese.

"I know," Chas said, picking up Charles, then hugging Jackson with the other arm. "I just want you to know that I made a good choice."

He made a comical scoffing sound and kissed her quickly before he handed Isabelle a handful of Cheerios. She quieted down as she concentrated on picking them up one at a time and putting them into her mouth—in a delicate, girl-like way that was much different from the way Charles had eaten Cheerios at her age.

Chas helped Jackson finish up the food preparations and put a simple lunch on the table. They sat down to eat, putting Charles into a second high chair. The children were then given their toddler version of the menu.

It was easy to relax and still keep track of business, since the inn was under good surveillance from the common room of their attached home. They had some small monitors that were fed from security cameras in the main hall and the parking area. A chime would sound in their home if anyone came in or out of the doors of the inn during business hours. These were turned off when they went to bed and the inn was locked up for the night. Guests were given a key to the outside doors to let themselves in and out. At the moment, the office was locked, but Chas had the cordless phone with her and the key to that door around her wrist. If someone came in or called, she could be available to help that person in seconds.

"Guess what?" Chas said after the blessing had been said on the food.

"You're pregnant," Jackson said tonelessly.

"No," she chuckled, "I'm not pregnant. You know very well I'm not."

He chuckled too, and they both smiled at their two children, who were so close together and such a handful that they'd decided to give Chas a little recovery time before trying for another one.

"Okay, what?" he asked.

"You know how we were discussing just the other day that we haven't had any long-term guests at the inn, even though we've advertised great weekly and monthly rates?"

"Yeah, I know," he said. "And I thought that 'home away from home' thing I put on the website was pretty good."

"It was *very* good," Chas said. "I think it worked." Jackson's brows went up and Chas added, "We might just have an opportunity to do what we know the Lord wants us to do with our inn." They shared a tender smile, and she saw his eyes light up with intrigue. They both felt strongly about the spiritual guidance they'd received in regard to making their place of business a place of refuge for people in need, and they knew those needs could come in a thousand different ways.

"I'm on the edge of my seat," Jackson said, even though he was comfortably leaning back in his chair, eating macaroni and cheese with leftover roast beef and green beans.

"A college-aged woman will be staying here through the duration of her pregnancy until she has the baby and gives it up for adoption." Jackson's eyes widened. "Her very wealthy mother wants to know that her needs will be met; other than that she wants nothing to do with it. I get the impression from talking to her on the phone that she's very good at making problems go away with money."

"Wow," Jackson said. "I wouldn't have seen that one coming. How long until this baby comes?"

"She'll need to stay four or five months, I was told. I don't think the mother actually expects us to do anything but house and feed her daughter. Apparently she believes that this girl has gotten herself into trouble, and as long as she has a place to stay and something to eat, she can take care of the rest on her own. She's flying in the day after tomorrow, and she'll be renting a car. Money's not a problem. The mother told me that more than once."

"Wow," Jackson said again.

"So, I don't know about you, Mr. Innkeeper, but I think we need to make some effort to give her a home away from home—and home isn't just a roof over your head."

"Of course," he said easily.

"If our personalities don't mesh well, she may choose to keep more to herself. But we can at least help her get the right medical care, and make certain she's not driving herself to the hospital when the time comes."

"Of course," Jackson said again.

Chas thought about her conversation with Mrs. Fitzgibbons and felt astonished all over again. "I have difficulty imagining how a mother can be so . . . cold . . . about something like this. Even when children make mistakes, I would think they need a parent's love and support more than ever. It's like she's just . . . writing her off by giving me a credit card number. I can understand the need for going away to have a baby under the circumstances. It would be easier than having to explain to nosy neighbors and relatives, and it would be easier to put it behind if everybody didn't know about it. But . . . it's not the situation that bothers me. I'm glad we can provide a place for someone like her to stay. It's the mother's attitude about it that bugs me."

"Yeah, it's hard to understand," Jackson said. "We'll just have to do our best to make up for that."

"Yes, we will," Chas said and actually felt excited for Catherine Jane Fitzgibbons to arrive.

That evening Jackson watched the children so that Chas could go visit Polly and her new baby. Elliott was working a swing shift and Polly appreciated the company during the long evening while her husband was gone. Chas loved holding little Autumn and playing with her wispy red hair, and she also loved giving her back to Polly for all the serious care. She had two babies of her own at home that kept her way too busy to make her want another one just yet.

Chas told Polly about the forthcoming adventure of a long-term guest. Polly loved people, and she was very good at making them feel welcome and comfortable. She too was looking forward to the opportunity to get to know this Catherine Jane.

"I hope she's not snooty like her mother," Polly said. "I'm not sure I'd have much to talk about with a snooty person." She chuckled. "Mostly because a snooty person would probably be too snooty to talk to *me.*"

"We'll just give her the benefit of the doubt and do our best to make her feel welcome. And the timing is perfect, because she's arriving the day after tomorrow, and that's the day you're coming back to work. Boy, am I glad you're coming back to work!" she proclaimed with mock exhaustion. "We've managed, but the paperwork is seriously backing up, and Jackson and I are getting worn out trying to be *three* people between us, especially with taking care of those kids. They're exhausting sometimes."

"Well . . . duh!" Polly said. "I don't know how you had them so close together. I'm bone-tired with just one."

"Not too exhausted to come back to work, I hope."

"No, I'm ready—especially since I can bring Autumn with me. I'm glad that I had the chance to help with your babies, and that you have the office set up to accommodate a child."

"Oh, we'll manage just fine," Chas said. "I'm glad to have your help, *and* your company. And I'm especially glad that running an inn is a job that can be worked around children. Autumn needs her parents around as much as possible."

They talked about how Autumn could be watched in the house with the other children as she got older, during the hours that Polly needed to work and Elliott wasn't available to help with her. All in all, they figured it would be rare for Polly to actually need to hire a sitter;

Chas knew she was eternally indebted for all of the babysitting that Polly had done for her. Since they were all like family, it was a great arrangement and they were glad for it.

Chas returned home later than she'd planned and found Jackson in the common room reading. The kitchen was clean, and the children had been bathed and put to bed. She plopped down on the couch beside him and said, "You're the best."

"Hey, I have a posh job . . . thanks to you. Since you hired me to be an innkeeper, it's much less complicated and has better hours than the FBI. I've got plenty of time to do dishes and be a daddy." He leaned toward Chas and kissed her. "I especially like that last part. If I were still in the FBI, I would never see my kids." He kissed Chas again. "It's a pretty good life—even with doing the dishes now and then."

"Amen," she said and kissed him so fervidly that he set aside his book and took her in his arms. She smiled at him. "Yeah, it's a pretty good life."

* * * * *

Catherine Jane Fitzgibbons discreetly wiped away a couple of tears as the plane landed in Butte, Montana. She was glad to be in business class for the sake of space and comfort, and glad that the seat next to her had been unoccupied during the flight. Being discreet was easier with no one close by. She'd had to go to the lavatory twice to throw up during the flight, and having no one beside her had made it easier to get there quickly. The nausea of her pregnancy was still plaguing her almost continually, even though she'd been told that most women felt relief from those symptoms once they were this far along.

Catherine felt drained by the time she had gathered her luggage and loaded it into a rented car. But at least she'd been able to get something decent to eat in the airport, which had eased her nausea somewhat. Her mother had arranged everything very neatly, but Catherine had no idea what to expect, and the unexpected only contributed to the continual uneasiness she'd felt since trauma had struck her life. She got the address for the inn out of her purse and programmed it into the navigation system in the vehicle, then headed toward Anaconda, where she would become a temporary resident. She felt more afraid than she dared admit. Her mother had said the woman on the phone was kind, but that didn't mean anything. She said the inn was lovely, with atmosphere, and very comfortable. It had good ratings on the website. But what good was that for Catherine when she was facing such a heartbreaking event in her life—alone? She could well imagine herself holed up in a beautiful hotel room for months, except for when she got out to wander around a relatively small town. But it was too cold to do too much of that.

Catherine was grateful for good weather as she drove, and she had no trouble finding the Dickensian Inn. Some hope trickled into her concerns as she caught sight of the beautiful inn. It was breathtaking, but it also had a good feeling about it—even from the outside. She parked and sat in the car for a minute, just looking up at the third-story eaves of the Victorian mansion. Then she took a deep breath and got out of the car to face the next step in this unforeseen adventure. She swung her big purse over her shoulder and unlocked the trunk, but before she could lift out the first bag, a man appeared at her side. He was nice looking, in his late forties she guessed, with prematurely gray hair.

"Let me get those for you," he said and easily lifted both suitcases from the trunk.

She was so utterly exhausted that her relief was inexpressible. She simply said, "Thank you so much!"

"You're welcome," he said. "I'm Jackson," he added, setting one of the bags at his feet to offer her his hand. She shook it, and he added, "My wife and I run the inn. And since we have only one guest checking in today, I know which room to take these to."

"Thank you," she said and followed him up the steps of the big porch at the front of the inn.

"You're Catherine?" he asked, as if to be sure.

"Yes," she said, "but I prefer Kate."

"Welcome to the Dickensian Inn, Kate," he said as she walked through the door. The good feeling she'd had increased immediately, as if a literal warmth rushed over her—more than just the fact that the temperature was much warmer in here than outside. He motioned down the hall and said, "The office is there. Someone will help you get checked in."

"Thank you," she said, and he went up the elegant staircase with her luggage. *What a nice man,* she thought. Perhaps this experience would be tolerable after all.

* * * * *

Chas felt almost giddy when Polly arrived at the inn for her first day of work since Autumn had been born. Chas had already set up the little portable, soft-sided crib that she'd used for her own babies in the office. It also served as a playpen until they got as old as Isabelle and were too impatient to be so restricted. Polly settled in within minutes, and the baby slept while she got down to business and assessed the damage after her many weeks of absence. Chas visited with her for a few minutes before she went to the kitchen to prepare breakfast for the one couple that had stayed the previous night at the inn. They'd requested breakfast at ten o'clock since they'd wanted to have the rare opportunity to sleep late. Michelle, a long-time employee of the inn, did breakfast most mornings, but today was her day off, so Chas was covering for her. It used to be the other way around. Chas had personally fixed breakfast for her guests almost every day for years. But she was a mother now, and she had more important ways to spend her time. Michelle did a wonderful job, and the two girls that came in to clean rooms as needed were also competent and reliable. With Polly back at work and Jackson continuing to do certain aspects of the business and paperwork that he preferred to handle, as well as any ongoing maintenance, the inn ran smoothly, and guests always left feeling satisfied with their visit and were often complimentary about how fine it had been.

When she was finished serving breakfast and had put the kitchen of the inn in order, Chas took over with the children so that Jackson could do some things that needed his attention outside. He came in for lunch, then went back out. After the children went down for their naps, Chas took the baby monitors with her to the office so she could hold Polly's baby while Polly did her work. Autumn was asleep and would surely sleep fine without Chas's help, but she declared—not for the first time—that there was nothing like holding an infant. Her own babies were so big and wiggly now. They would never tolerate this kind of snuggling, and they never fell asleep in Chas's arms.

When they heard the front door open and Jackson talking to a woman in the hall, Chas whispered, "Oh, I bet that's her." She glanced at the clock. "Right on time, I think."

A woman appeared in the doorway of the office a moment later, and Chas was immediately struck by her refined beauty. Her dark auburn hair was thick and wavy and pulled up on the top and back on the sides with matching clips. She looked more mature than Chas suspected her age to be, since she'd been going to college before this unexpected pregnancy.

"Hi," Chas said. "I think you just met my husband. I'm Chas. I'd get up but I'm busy, as you can see."

"Oh, she's beautiful," the guest said, able to guess the gender from the pink bow in the baby's hair that was impossible to miss. "How old is she?"

Chas considered the fact that this woman was pregnant and planning to give the baby away. She wondered if it was hard for her to see a baby. But she took the question at face value. "She's about six weeks, but she's not mine. This is Polly; she manages a lot of the office work here."

"Hello," both women said.

"Autumn is Polly's baby," Chas said. "I have two children, but they're asleep at the moment, so I'm enjoying this one. You must be Catherine."

"Yes," she said, "but I prefer Kate."

"Then Kate it is," Chas said.

Polly said, "There really isn't anything to do except give you the key to your room. Your mother took care of all the payment information."

"All right then," Kate said. "I'll just—"

"I'll show you where it's at," Chas said, reluctantly putting the baby into the portable crib. Autumn wiggled a little, then settled back into contented sleep. Chas took the key from Polly and smiled at Kate. "Just follow me." On her way up the hall she explained the usual amenities. Internet in the parlor, magazines and newspapers in the dining room, and a snack fridge that always had complimentary sandwiches, snacks, and cold beverages.

"Your mother asked that we provide three meals a day for you, which is not a problem since I'm always fixing food for the family."

"I don't want to be a bother," Kate said.

"It's no bother, really. Although I can't promise that every meal will be exciting. We do things pretty simply around here."

"I like that," Kate said, pausing at the bottom of the stairs. "It's a beautiful inn. There's a wonderful feeling here."

"Thank you," Chas said with pride. "The house was built in 1870 by my great-great-grandparents. My grandmother and I oversaw the restoration. It's been wonderful to share its beauty with others." As they headed up the stairs, Chas added, "We have an elevator if the stairs are ever too much for you. I want you to be comfortable during your pregnancy. Back to the food—there are some nice places to eat here in town, and I'm sure you'll want to get out some. Just let me know each morning at breakfast if you won't be having lunch or dinner here. Otherwise I'll plan on you."

"You're very kind," Kate said.

"We're glad to have you here." Chas explained that one of the staff always carried a cordless phone, and if she needed anything or had a problem, she only needed to dial from her room and someone would answer. They established nine o'clock as the time that Kate would prefer to have breakfast each morning, and Chas told her that her meals would be served in the dining room, but if she ever wanted them brought to her room, she only had to call and ask. She asked Kate if she had any food allergies or if there was anything she just didn't like so that Chas could keep it in mind. Kate assured her that she was fine with anything, and Chas added, "Not that I get too fancy or weird, but I don't want to gross you out if you have an aversion to something."

"I like just about anything," Kate said. "Thank you."

On the second floor they stopped at a door with a little plaque that read, *The Nickleby*. "The rooms are named for Dickens characters," Chas explained. "This one is spacious and it has a jetted tub. I hope you'll be comfortable here."

"I'm sure I will be," Kate said. Chas opened the door, and Kate let out a pleasant gasp. "Oh, it's lovely!"

"Is there anything I can get you right now, Kate? Are you hungry? I'd be happy to bring something up."

"No, thank you. I got something at the airport."

"I know how it feels to be pregnant and not have something in your stomach all the time. Please make yourself at home and help yourself to those snacks as much as you'd like. If you need something that you can't find, please call."

"Thank you so much," Kate said with such sincerity that Chas felt touched. Recalling her mother's attitude about all of this, she could imagine that a little kindness meant a great deal to this woman. Chas was relieved that Kate apparently had very little in common with her mother—at least as far as her attitude went. So far so good.

"You're very welcome," Chas said. "I'll have dinner for you in the guest dining room at six."

"Thank you," Kate said again, and Chas left her alone.

Once the door was closed, Kate took a few minutes to go slowly around the perimeter of the room, taking in the beautiful details of the furnishings and decor. Everything was fine and lovely. She noted that some of the furniture was probably original to the era of the house, and other pieces were excellent replicas. She took in the view from the window and discovered that it looked out over the street; there were many trees, and she found it pleasant. She kicked off her shoes, tossed her jacket, and lay back on the bed, sighing to feel its quality beneath her back. Her anxiety melted away, and for the first time since her mother had discovered the truth, she actually felt like she was going to survive this ordeal.

CHAPTER 2

Kate felt so relaxed that she could have fallen asleep right then and there, until she was reminded that pregnancy required more frequent trips to the bathroom. She groaned as she got up, but when she saw the gorgeous bathroom with the large jetted tub, she immediately started running water for a bath. While she was soaking up to her chin, the events that had brought her to this moment trickled into her mind, provoking tears that spilled down her face. The timing of her parents' lengthy stay in Europe had been perfect, giving her the house all to herself while she'd struggled to adjust to what had happened to her.

But their return had been inevitable, and their reactions at their discovery of her pregnancy had gone much worse than she'd ever imagined. Her father had said practically nothing. He'd just looked disappointed and sad. Her mother had flown into a rage unlike anything Kate had ever seen or believed possible. In spite of the dramatic differences in her and her mother's personalities, and Kate's preference to keep a distance from her mother, she still never would have foreseen such irrational anger—without even a hint of love or concern. Even if Kate had made a mistake, she would have hoped that her parents could muster up some kindness toward helping her face its consequences. But she *hadn't* made a mistake. She'd done nothing wrong.

Kate at least felt grateful that her mother hadn't kicked her out on the streets. She reminded herself that her mother's version of love was providing a safe and comfortable place for her to get through this ordeal. She clung to that thought and forced memories of her mother's anger and her father's disappointment out of her mind. Instead she concentrated on the luxurious experience of the moment—and the safety and comfort of her surroundings.

Following her bath, Kate went straight to bed and crawled between the crisp, cream-colored sheets to take a nap. Before she fell asleep she set the alarm so she wouldn't miss supper. She woke to the alarm, surprised at how deeply she'd been sleeping. But then, she'd been abnormally tired even before she'd been confronted with the results of a home pregnancy test.

Her need to use the bathroom urged her out of bed. Once she was upright, the nausea reminded her that she'd gone too many hours without eating. She rummaged through the collection of individually wrapped snacks in her luggage and grabbed a little packet of crackers that would keep her from throwing up before she made it to the dining room. She left her room at two minutes to six, certain she looked as bad as she felt, but not really caring. The people who ran the inn had been very kind, and she didn't take them for the type of people who cared about appearances. There was no one else she needed to impress, or even interact with. Her biggest challenge over the coming months would probably be boredom.

Kate entered the guest dining room that she'd only gotten a peek at earlier. There were several small tables with two chairs at each one, perfect for serving meals to single guests or couples at a place such as this. She could hear some productive noises coming from the nearby kitchen and sat down. A moment later Chas appeared, wearing an apron and a bright smile.

"Oh, you're here. How are you feeling?"

Kate shrugged. "Pregnant," she said with a chuckle. It was the simplest explanation she could give without lying to say that she felt fine.

"I certainly understand," Chas said. "About your supper—I wanted to give you some options . . . about where to eat it, at least. I'm happy to serve it here if you prefer being alone, but . . . if not, I want you to know that you're welcome to eat with our family. We live in a house attached to the inn, so it's right through there." She pointed toward the kitchen. "Our kids can be kind of noisy, so maybe you would prefer peace and quiet. I just wanted you to know that it's an option."

"I would love to join you," Kate said. She only preferred being alone when the other choice was being with her parents. As it was, her recent interaction with them was the only time she *hadn't* been alone for several weeks. "But I don't want to impose. Perhaps *you* would prefer that I *not* join you."

"I wouldn't have offered if that were the case," Chas said. "And Jackson agrees. Come along." She motioned with her arm, and Kate followed her. "You have to bear in mind that the inn is kept meticulously clean, but the house is meant to be lived in. With young children, it's rarely tidy."

"Lived in sounds nice," Kate said, thinking of the mausoleum-like atmosphere of her parents' home.

Chas felt pleased that Kate had accepted her invitation. She'd discussed it with Jackson, and they both agreed strongly that they should make a concerted effort to help this young woman feel comfortable, which might open up more of an opportunity to help her through this. Chas was fine with bringing a stranger into her slightly messy and cluttered home. The lived-in look was something she actually took pride in. As she'd explained to Kate, the house and the inn served different purposes. The house was clean, albeit somewhat disorderly, but she never wanted her family—or guests—to feel anything less than at home.

Kate immediately loved the atmosphere of the large living area of Chas's home. It reminded her of the homes of a couple of friends from her youth. She'd loved going there, feeling like she could occasionally be part of a normal family experience. The room had clearly been designed for family togetherness. The kitchen and dining area merged gracefully into a living section with large, comfy sofas and a well-equipped entertainment center. Two young children were playing among scattered toys, while soft music played. Jackson was in the kitchen, doing something at the stove. Kate noticed the table was set for three, and two high chairs sat next to it. Chas had already predicted that Kate would join them, or had at least been hopeful. Kate felt more touched by that than she could express.

"Have a seat," Chas said. "We're ready to put it on the table."

"Hello again, Kate," Jackson said, smiling toward her.

"Hello," she said. "May I help with something?"

"No, just relax," Chas said, motioning her toward a chair at the dining table. "You must be exhausted. We've got this down to a system."

Kate sat on the chair Chas had indicated. Within about three minutes Jackson and Chas had both children in high chairs, with bibs on and hands washed, and they had set out serving dishes of hot food on the table.

"We always bless the food," Chas said, and the older of the two children folded his arms rather comically. Kate followed the example of the adults and bowed her head, listening as Jackson offered a blessing. That too reminded her of being in friends' homes, although she'd never heard a prayer quite like this spoken over a meal. It was brief but profound, and in it Jackson expressed thanks to God for having Kate in their home. It was difficult for Kate to blink back the tears and be able to lift her head and smile at her hosts once the amen had been spoken.

While they were passing around the dishes of baked chicken, rice pilaf, a cooked vegetable, and a green salad, Kate asked about the children.

"Charles will be three at the end of November," Chas said. "Technically he was named after me, since my name is actually the abbreviation for Charles."

"There must be a story behind that," Kate said, watching Jackson and Chas each prepare a little dish of food in bite-sized pieces for the children.

"Yes, actually, there is. My grandmother had a passion for Charles Dickens, hence the theme of the inn. When I was born, she'd been hoping for a boy so she could name him after her hero. When she got me, she abbreviated the name so it could work for a girl. When we had a son, we just felt the name Charles was right."

"It's a very fine name," Kate said as if she were saying it to Charles. He offered her a funny grin that made her laugh. She said to Chas, "You said your grandmother gave you the name. I assume your parents were all right with that."

"My father wasn't around," Chas said, "and my mother had a weak heart; she died giving birth to me. It was just me and my grandmother. It sounds very tragic, but since I never knew my parents, I never really minded. Granny was an amazing woman who raised me well."

"Amen to that," Jackson said.

"You knew her?" Kate asked.

"Not for as long as I would have liked," Jackson said. "But long enough for her to have a great impact on me."

"I'd like to hear more about that," Kate said, realizing that the meal was truly delicious. She told them so, then asked about Charles's little sister. Both of the children had adorable faces and dark, thick hair. Since Chas's hair was medium brown, Kate suspected that Jackson had been dark before going prematurely gray.

"Isabelle turned one during the summer," Chas said. "The most amazing thing about her is that she's alive." Kate focused more fully on Chas. Since she didn't seem the type to be overly dramatic, she wondered about such a comment. "A genetic heart defect runs in my family. That's why I'm the only child of an only child of an only child. As I mentioned, my mother had a weak heart. I actually had a baby die of the same problem years ago. Anyway, they picked up on the ultrasound that something was wrong with Isabelle's heart. But we were able to go to Utah where they have some amazing medical care for children. She had open-heart surgery right after she was delivered C-section. And as you can see, she's doing fine."

"That's quite a life you've lived, Isabelle," Kate said to her. The little girl just stared at Kate as if she were an alien, but it provoked laughter from the adults.

They ate in silence for a minute or so, then Kate said, "Your home is lovely. Of course, the inn is remarkable, but your home is lovely as well. There's a good feeling here."

"Thank you," Chas said. "And I'm glad you noticed . . . the good feeling. I think that's the most important thing a home can have."

"I would have to agree," Kate said. Her thoughts rushed to the absence of any positive feeling in her home, *ever!* She pushed her thoughts back to the present by saying, "Is it too nosy of me to ask how the two of you met?"

"No, of course not," Chas said. She pointed her fork at her husband. "Your turn to talk. You love this story."

"But you tell it with more detail."

"Just tell it. Kate and I have months to catch up on the details."

Kate appreciated the reference to being here for months. She didn't have to wonder if Chas and Jackson knew the situation, but she preferred having such things addressed directly.

"Okay," Jackson said with a smile toward Kate, "I was living in Virginia and working for the FBI."

"Really?" Kate asked, intrigued.

"A shooting incident occurred that required some investigation and some administrative leave. I wanted to get some distance from it, so I got online to find a bed-and-breakfast in some remote part of the country. In my search, the Dickens theme intrigued me because his work had left quite an impression on me in my youth. I arrived the Sunday before Thanksgiving in a blizzard, and . . . the rest is history." He put a bite of chicken into his mouth as if that would prevent him from having to share anything further.

"And how long ago was that?" Kate asked.

"We're coming up on five years . . . since we met," Chas said.

"And now you have this lovely family," Kate said, taking in the whole picture of these kind people, their beautiful children, and their feel-good home. She wondered if it could ever be possible for her to have such a life—such a marvelously simple life. Given her present situation, the likelihood seemed lower than it would have six months ago. But she couldn't think about that right now. When she came out of the other end of this tunnel, she could reevaluate and move on. Right now, she would enjoy the opportunity to observe a *real* family in action. She wondered if they were always this congenial with each other, or if they were just on their best behavior for company. She wasn't sure whether they would continue to invite her to actually share meals at their table, but she hoped they would. Surely no one could keep up their best behavior for as long as she would be staying here. The cynical, hardened part of Kate believed that no family could be the way this one appeared to be at the moment. Her life's experience had been tainted by her own upbringing. She didn't have to question that. The hopeful, optimistic part of Kate wanted desperately to believe that such a home could be within the reach of anyone willing to make it happen—even someone previously tainted.

"Yes, we do," Chas said. "Although we've certainly had some bumps along the way."

"I think you should save the conversation about the bumps until Kate settles in a little more," Jackson said.

"I'll look forward to it," Kate said, surprised to see that Jackson didn't seem to mind having his wife talk about *the bumps* with someone who was still mostly a stranger.

"I think it's your turn now," Jackson said to Kate. "Tell us about yourself."

Kate looked down and straightened her napkin on her lap. "I know you're both well aware of my reasons for being here."

"Yes," Jackson said, "but your present situation tells us nothing about *you.*"

Kate looked up at him abruptly, astonished. She looked at Chas and saw a silent affirmation of the statement. In the back of her mind she heard contradicting echoes of her mother screaming at her, telling her that this mess she'd gotten herself into was a clear indication of her character, or rather the lack of it.

"We all meet challenges in life," Chas said. Even the way it was called a *challenge* and not a *mistake* soothed Kate. She'd spent less than half an hour with these people and she wanted to jump out of her chair and hug them both. She'd spent her life thinking that there was *no one* out there who was like her, no place where she could feel truly comfortable. She'd felt more comfortable in her friends' homes than her own, and even more so among friends she'd made at college. But in every case there was something missing that Chas and Jackson seemed to have—even if she couldn't quite define it.

"Some of us more than others," Jackson said. "I've got about twenty-six years I'd like to just erase. Well," he chuckled, "there are other years I'd like to erase, too, but my childhood wasn't really *my* responsibility. The first twenty-six years *after* I became an adult were kind of a mess."

While Kate was wondering how to share something about herself without having a complete emotional outburst, Chas said, "You're from Maine. Is that where you've always lived?"

"Until I went to college in Boston, yes."

"And what were you studying?" Jackson asked.

"I want to teach elementary school," Kate said. "I love working with children; I always have."

"That's wonderful!" Chas said. "I think *good* teachers are always something we need more of."

Kate thought of the years' worth of demeaning things her mother had said about lowering herself to such a profession, and it became more difficult to hold back that emotional outburst. Noting how comfortable she felt, combined with the fact that she would be under the same roof with these people for months, she cleared her throat and impulsively ventured to get something out of the way. "Listen," she said, "there's something I need to say, and then I can stop dreading it. I don't know exactly what my mother told you, but I do know my mother is abrasive when she's at her best. I want to apologize if she was unkind or rude, and I hope you won't think that I'm anything like her, because I'm not."

"We would never judge you by anything but what we come to know for ourselves," Chas said.

"Yes," Kate glanced at both of them, "that's evident. You've been very kind—more so than I expected. I just want you to know that whatever my mother said, you don't need to feel like you have to take responsibility for me while I'm here."

Their silence implied they were trying to decide what she meant exactly. "Kate," Chas said gently, "do you believe your mother would somehow . . . what . . . bribe us to be kind to you? Or to offer more than the actual services we usually provide?"

Kate nodded and fought her urge to cry. "It wouldn't be the first time." She chuckled tensely and couldn't keep a couple of tears from escaping. She wiped them away quickly. "You know those jokes about mothers paying other children to be their child's friend? My mother is like that. She believes I'm completely incompetent and incapable."

"Kate," Chas said again, putting a hand over hers on the table, "your mother told us you were pregnant and you would be staying here until you could have the baby and place it for adoption. She asked about meals. She asked about local medical care. I assured her that we would see that you had your needs met. That is all. We just . . . didn't like the idea of you eating your meals all alone for the next few months . . . or however long it will be . . . and we figured you could use some support at a time like this. It's as simple as that. We don't want to be pushy. We just want you to know that . . . somebody cares. We really do."

"But . . . how could you? You don't even know me."

"We know that no one should be completely alone at such a time, and we're glad to do whatever we can to help." While Kate was wondering how to respond, Chas added, "Which brings me to something that I just feel I need to ask. I was wondering if I can help you find a doctor, and if there's anything else you need help with—anything at all."

"I would welcome advice on a doctor," Kate said. "I was going to get online tomorrow and start looking, but if you have a personal recommendation, that would be all the better."

"The clinic I went to was very good. In the morning I'll give you the number, and you can make an appointment. I'd be happy to drive you there, the first time at least."

"That would be *so* wonderful, thank you." Kate resisted the urge to divulge the full depth of what this meant to her because she knew that doing so would not only be awkward, it would likely also cause her to gush with tears. Instead she smiled and said, "Your kindness means a great deal to me."

"We're glad to help," Jackson said. "Please don't be afraid to ask one of us if you need something, and we'll do what we can."

Kate smiled and nodded, grateful when Charles became suddenly impatient to get out of his high chair. They all couldn't help but laugh when he threw his bowl on the floor as a declaration that he was finished.

"Don't encourage him," Jackson said as he grabbed some paper towels to clean up the mess, and Chas grabbed a washcloth to wash the little boy's hands and face before she got him out of the chair and set him free to play.

The remainder of the meal was filled with small talk, mostly focusing on the babies and their antics. Kate insisted that she help clear the table, but after a couple of minutes, Chas insisted that she sit down and relax.

"You're welcome to hang out with us for a while if you'd like," Chas said, "or you can go elsewhere for some peace and quiet and we won't be offended."

Kate sat on one of the sofas and watched the children play while Jackson and Chas got the dishwasher loaded and put the kitchen in order very quickly. She sat and visited, avoiding anything personal, until it was time for them to bathe the children and put them to bed. They both insisted she was still welcome to stay, but she pleaded exhaustion, thanked them once again for their kindness and hospitality, and returned to her lovely room on the second floor of the inn.

Looking out the window at a partial moon, Kate never imagined that this day could have ended so well. This morning she had been dropped off at the curb of the airport by her mother's chauffeur, with her mother's final words ringing in her head. Kate knew she had more or less been banished, sent to some obscure town where no one would know her so that the family wouldn't have to bear the shame. Kate had visualized all possible kinds of scenarios as to what might be waiting in Montana for her, but being warmly welcomed and treated with such kindness by strangers had never occurred to her. With no reason to believe that Jackson and Chas were not sincere in their offer to help her get through this, she began to feel some hope that perhaps surviving this ordeal might be possible.

* * * * *

Kate slept well except for having to get up twice to use the bathroom. The bed was delightfully comfortable, and she loved waking up in the lovely surroundings of her Victorian room. The home she'd grown up in was fine and elegant, and no expense had been spared in its decor. But it had all been done according to her mother's taste. Even when Kate had arrived at an age when girls felt a need to assert their own personality and independence, Avis Fitzgibbons had insisted that *she* would decide on the colors, furnishings, and decor of her daughter's supposedly personal space. But Kate *loved* the decor of this room where she would be living for the time being. She felt at home here, and was truly comfortable.

Once fully awake, Kate reached for her cell phone on the bedside table. Not a single call since she'd left Maine. None of her friends had called for weeks. She'd had very little contact with any of the friends from her youth since she'd gone to college, but she'd made some good friends while living in Boston, and a couple of them had been very supportive since the ordeal that had resulted in her pregnancy. But not one of her friends from either side of her life had so much as called to check on her in weeks. She'd called a few and left messages, saying that she wondered how they were doing and she'd love to talk. But none of them had called her back.

Kate was mostly glad that she hadn't received a call from her mother. She didn't want to talk to her for any reason. But she still thought it was strange for a mother not to make certain that her daughter had arrived safely. She would have liked to have her mother inquire over how she was feeling. But Kate had been efficiently transported to a place that was out of sight and out of mind. And in a different way, she'd always been that way to her father. He would call her in a week or two. He averaged one or two calls a month. He would pretend that nothing was wrong, chat about insignificant things, and they would talk for fewer than ten minutes.

Kate sighed and turned the phone off before she shoved it into a drawer. The less often she checked it for messages, the less likely she was to be disappointed. She then noticed a beautiful, leather-bound book on the same bedside table with the alarm clock and the lamp. She picked it up and opened the cover. *Nicholas Nickleby* by Charles Dickens. Of course; her room was called *The Nickleby.* "How quaint," she said aloud and almost started to read, then she noticed the time and realized she should get something to eat instead.

In the guest dining room, Kate found a table set for one with elegant dishes. She heard sounds from the kitchen, then a young woman, near her own age, came out and smiled. "Hi, I'm Michelle," she said. "I do breakfast most mornings. Chas had some errands but I promised her I'd take very good care of you, and she wanted me to tell you that she'll talk to you when she gets back."

"Thank you," Kate said, disappointed not to see Chas. But she also had to remember not to latch onto this sweet family too strongly and wear out her welcome. Breakfast was delicious, and she told Michelle so more than once. Once finished, Kate took her own dishes to the kitchen, thanked Michelle, and went back to her room where she began to read *Nicholas Nickleby.* She had plenty of time to read long novels, and getting acquainted with the namesake of her room seemed a good place to start. She chuckled aloud when she realized that Nicholas's sister's name was Kate. "Much better than Catherine Jane," she said aloud to no one. She wondered if pregnancy hormones were making her talk to herself, or if it was a culminating result of the life she'd lived.

It took Kate some effort to get into the book and the feel of Dickens's language. She'd read Dickens before, but it had been a long time ago. And she'd only read one or two of his most popular novels. She paused occasionally to ponder the Dickensian theme of the inn and felt a desire to talk more with Chas about that. She found it very quaint—and intriguing.

Nausea prompted by hunger forced Kate away from the book. Knowing it wasn't lunchtime yet, she went downstairs to check out that snack fridge that Chas had told her about. There were a couple of sandwiches wrapped in plastic with a date written on them; they'd been made yesterday and they looked good. There were soft drinks and little bottles of juice, and a number of other odds and ends, including cheese and crackers, fresh fruit and vegetables, and yogurt. Some paper plates and plastic utensils were on top of the little fridge, so Kate loaded up a plate and took it back to her room. She snacked and read until the phone on her bedside table rang, and she noticed that the clock read 11:40.

"How are you?" Chas asked after Kate had picked it up.

"I'm fine, thank you. How are you?"

"I'm very well, thanks. Sorry I missed you this morning. I hope you've found something to keep you busy."

"I'm reading *Nicholas Nickleby,*" Kate declared.

"How delightful!" Chas said, as if it truly were. "Listen, Jackson is willing to tend the kids, Polly's got the inn, and I'm craving Chinese food. Would you like to come along? Or if you'd prefer, I can just make you a fresh sandwich or—"

"It sounds wonderful," Kate said. "I'll be down in five minutes."

Kate hurried to make herself presentable and found Chas leaning in the doorway of the office, chatting with Polly.

"Hello, Kate," Polly said, as if they were old friends. "How's the inn so far?"

"Oh, it's heavenly," Kate said.

"I'm glad to hear it," Chas said. "We aim to please."

"And you go above and beyond the call of duty," Kate said.

"She's like that," Polly said with a smile.

Kate's eye was drawn to the sleeping baby in the little crib before Chas asked, "Shall we go? I promised to bring Polly some takeout."

"I'm ready," Kate said and followed Chas out to the little parking lot where they got into an SUV. "How did you know?" Kate asked.

"Know what?"

"That I was craving Chinese food."

Chas laughed softly. "No, I said that *I* was craving Chinese food."

"Well, I was too," Kate said. "I was actually thinking about looking in the phone book to find a place and go there, but it's never as fun to go alone."

"How true!" Chas said, and pulled out onto the road.

"You know," Kate said, "I really feel like I have to say that you don't need to feel personally responsible for me. I appreciate your kindness more than I can say, but . . . I really know how to be pretty independent."

"I'm sure you do," Chas said. "And I'm sure things will balance and settle after you've been here for a while. I just . . . well, I admit that I felt concerned for you even before you arrived. And I'm glad that we can be straightforward about these things. But . . . I didn't know what to expect. We've had some long-term guests before, some that I didn't feel all that comfortable around. But the truth is that I like you, Kate, and I'm glad to have you here." She turned briefly to smile at Kate, then turned her eyes back to the road. "We'll just take it one day at a time. You promise to tell me if I'm being too pushy or nosy and you need some space, and I promise to tell you if I don't have time to spend with you or I need more time with my family. How does that sound?"

"It sounds perfect," Kate said, "but I insist on buying lunch, for all three of us. And what about Jackson? Does he need takeout too? I'm glad to buy and—"

"No, he's good with some leftovers, which he prefers over Chinese food. And if you really *want* to buy, I won't argue with you, but you shouldn't feel like you have to. I offered."

"I would love to," Kate said.

Before going to the restaurant, Chas gave Kate a quick driving tour of the town, telling her where the most important places were in case she needed to run an errand or get something.

Over sweet-and-sour chicken, fried rice, and egg rolls, Kate asked Chas to tell her more about the inn and its Dickensian theme. She loved hearing stories about Granny, who had talked about the great writer as if they were dear friends. Chas added matter-of-factly, "And since I believe in angels, I wouldn't be surprised if it were true."

Kate just smiled, not sure what to make of such a comment but realizing that she couldn't completely discredit it when it came from someone like Chas. She was just so genuine and confident about her life and who she was. Kate wanted to be more like her.

Following a leisurely visit over lunch, Kate graciously insisted on paying for the meal, and they left with the bag of takeout for Polly. Once they were in the car, Chas told Kate that she needed to make a quick stop that was on the way home. They pulled into the parking lot of a bakery while Chas explained that the manager was a good friend of hers, and the bakery supplied the ongoing needs of the inn so she had to pick up fresh baked goods every two or three days. Kate liked the atmosphere of the bakery, and she wanted to hear more than the brief explanation she got from Chas that her Granny had worked in this bakery when Chas had been a child. She liked Jodi immediately, and enjoyed listening to Chas and Jodi share a brief chat. It occurred to Kate right then that the reason her friendships hadn't lasted was that she'd had the wrong kind of friends. She already felt more bonded with Chas than she had with any friend in her adulthood. A couple of friends had helped her following the ordeal, and they'd been very kind and supportive. But they weren't like Chas. And they were now avoiding her. Either their lives were too busy, or her situation was too uncomfortable. Either way, it was easy to conclude that they weren't really that great of friends. But Chas and Jodi were both grounded women with no pretenses, and their kindness was immediate and genuine. Kate wanted to be a friend like that, knowing that she couldn't expect to *have* friends like that unless she did her part.

Kate helped carry the baked goods out to the car after she told Jodi she was looking forward to getting to know her better. And she really was. The thought surprised her, and she had to acknowledge that every few minutes she was reminded of her ongoing surprise at how much she liked it here in Anaconda, and how grateful she felt to be here as opposed to anywhere else—most especially home with her mother.

Back at the inn, Jackson carried the baked goods into the kitchen of the inn, while Chas took Polly's food to the kitchen of the house. She transferred it from the Styrofoam container to a real plate and warmed it in the microwave. While it was heating, she took some leftovers out of the fridge and fixed a plate for Jackson, which she stuck in the microwave as soon as Polly's food was hot. Kate observed the way Chas took special care in preparing her husband's meal, and the way that he kissed her and thanked her when he came in.

"Did you have a good time?" he asked while he was washing his hands at the kitchen sink.

"Oh, *I* did," Chas said. Jackson smiled, then looked at Kate as if to repeat the question.

"*I* certainly did," she insisted.

"Well, the little bugs are sleeping and I've got it covered, so why don't you two go . . . talk or something. It's what you women do best." He winked at Kate as he said it.

"I'm sure Chas has better things to do with her time than babysit me," Kate said.

"Not at the moment," Chas said. "Innkeeping can be a pretty posh job—some days more than others."

"She's earned some time off," Jackson said.

"In that case," Chas said, "I think we'll go get dessert." Again they shared a quick kiss, then Jackson sat down to eat his lunch, and Kate followed Chas back out to the car after they delivered Polly's lunch to her in the office.

Chas drove to a place that she declared had the best ice cream in town. When they were each eating a small sundae, Chas said, "Can I be completely up front with you, Kate?"

"Of course," Kate said. "I wouldn't want you to be otherwise."

"I hope this doesn't come out sounding strange, but just . . . hear me out."

"All right," Kate said, feeling a little nervous.

"When I made the decision to turn the house into a bed-and-breakfast, it awakened something in me. Before the first guest checked in, something inside of me knew that this was . . . well, call it my life's mission."

"Like your personal calling in life," Kate said. "Finding your authentic self." She'd heard such things discussed more than once in college classes, and even on television talk shows.

"That's right," Chas said.

"I feel that way about teaching children."

"Then you understand."

"I understand the concept."

"So, I've always taken my job seriously. I've always looked at each person coming through the door and felt some responsibility while each was in my care. It might sound silly, because in most cases I don't see these people any more than a few minutes three or four times before they leave. Since Jackson and I were married, he's adapted very naturally to the same idea, and then . . . well . . . we've had some experiences that have made us realize that while most guests will come and go quickly and they may never remember us, there are others that . . . were meant to come here, and that we can make a difference in their lives."

As Kate realized where this was going, an emotional knot began to form in her throat. She just nodded and listened.

"I don't want you to feel like we're seeing you as some opportunity to make you into a charity project or something. It's not like that at all. We don't believe in coincidence, and we believe that things happen for a reason. We specifically started advertising weekly and monthly rates to encourage long-term guests, because we've seen good things happen in people's lives when they've come here. So, the first thing I want you to know is that we are so glad you're here, and we are happy to be in a position to help you through this. The second thing I want to say is that I would have been willing to help you as much as it was appropriate no matter what kind of person you were. I confess that with my impressions of your mother, I had no idea what you might be like, but . . . what I'm really trying to say is that I genuinely enjoy your company, and I'm surprised at how comfortable I feel with you. I know that all probably sounds way too analytical, but I can be like that. I hope it makes some sense."

Kate nodded again. "It does, and . . ." She shrugged. "I *never* expected coming here to be much more than some form of banishment. Already you've made it not only bearable but pleasant, and you've given me some hope that getting through this won't be completely horrid."

Chas smiled. "I'm glad to hear it."

CHAPTER 3

When they returned to the inn, Chas took Kate to the office with her. There was a note from Polly saying that she'd gone home for the day, but she'd taken some paperwork with her to work on there. Chas sat behind the desk and wrote down the name and number of the clinic where she had gone for care during her pregnancies.

"I'm happy to go with you the first time," Chas said, repeating her earlier offer. "Although, if you'd prefer to go alone, I'm certain you can find it and—"

"No, I'd love to have you come with me," Kate said. "I just . . . I feel like I'm taking so much of your time."

"That will all balance out," Chas said. "Obviously, every day won't be like today. As much as lunch, *and dessert,* out with a friend might be my daily preference, I do have a family and a business to run. But I'm more than happy to do this. If you want to call and make the appointment now, we can make sure it's at a time I'm available."

"That would be great," Kate said and sat down to use the phone. "I don't have *anything* to work around, so this shouldn't be too difficult."

Chas opened up the personal calendar where both she and Jackson recorded any appointments or obligations. They kept it in the office so that Polly would know their schedules, since they often had to coordinate certain duties and time in the office.

Chas stayed close by, going over some paperwork that needed her attention, while Kate spoke to the receptionist at the clinic, giving some personal information and setting an appointment for the following week. When she got off the phone, Chas asked, "Have you been to a doctor yet?"

Kate looked mildly uncomfortable, and Chas wondered why. "Not since I discovered I was pregnant," Kate said. "I know I probably should have. Maybe it was some form of denial."

"Well, you're going now. I'm sure everything is fine."

Kate nodded, then admitted that she was tired. She thanked Chas for everything and they shared a hug before Kate went upstairs to rest for a while before supper. Once she was alone, she cried, even though she wasn't certain why. But she'd been doing a great deal of that lately. She was grateful and relieved to be in such a positive environment with supportive and kind people. But her reason for being here was still difficult to accept as real, and she knew her life would never be the same, whatever the outcome might be. She'd never been one to care much what other people thought of her. She'd always had a strong sense of self that had even survived her mother's continual attempts to manipulate Kate toward her way of thinking. But this experience had apparently damaged that to some degree. She didn't want Chas and Jackson to think badly of her. She thought of Polly and Jodi and how kind they had been to her as well. What did they all *really* think of an unmarried, pregnant woman showing up here to remain in hiding until the matter was taken care of?

Thankfully Kate was tired enough that she didn't think about it too long before she fell asleep. She woke up surprised to find it dark, then was even more startled when the time on the clock told her it was far past supper time. Sitting up abruptly, she felt both light-headed and nauseated. She had to lower her head and get her equilibrium before she turned on the light and found some crackers that offered a quick relief to the emptiness in her stomach. She was thinking she should call the phone that she knew Chas or Jackson had with them all the time, then she noticed that a note had been slid beneath her door. She picked it up to read, *I didn't want to disturb you. I can reheat your supper whenever you're ready to eat. Call me or just come into the house. We'll be there. Chas*

Kate pulled herself together and went downstairs and through the kitchen. She found the adjoining door between the two kitchens open and entered to find Jackson breaking up a fight over a toy between the two children, while Chas was picking up plastic animals and tossing them into a basket.

"Oh, hello," Chas said when she saw her. "Did you get some rest?"

"I did, thank you," Kate said.

"Your supper is in the fridge," Chas said. "Sit down and I'll get it as soon as—"

"I can do it," Kate said and hurried to the fridge. She quickly figured out the microwave and had it heating her food before Chas got there. "You don't need to wait on me," Kate added. "In fact, I'd love it if you'd let me help with something . . . with the kids, the house, the inn, anything. I need something to do or I'll go crazy. I realize it all runs just fine without me, but . . . if there's something I can do . . ."

"I'll be thinking," Chas said. "We can talk about it some more tomorrow."

"Okay," Kate said. "Thank you."

Since the family had already eaten, Kate felt a little awkward with the idea of eating by herself while in the same room with everyone else. She asked if it would be okay to just take her plate to her room, and, of course, Chas agreed. Kate ate the delicious meal, took a bath, and went back to bed, glad for the excessive sleepiness of pregnancy that easily lured her mind away from things she didn't want to think about.

* * * * *

The following day, Kate ate breakfast and lunch on her own while Chas was busy. She read and visited some with Polly. She wasn't sure if it was a good idea or not to hold Polly's baby, but she sat in the office with the baby in her arms for nearly an hour, wishing it might be possible to keep her own baby. She could, however, see the wisdom in adoption. Her situation was deplorable, and this child deserved two parents and a stable upbringing. Kate simply wished that she'd been given the opportunity to have a choice. Her mother had immediately stated that this would be the course taken, and Kate relied on her parents' financial support too much to even consider opposing her mother's edict.

Late in the afternoon, Chas asked Kate if she would mind helping with supper. Kate admitted that she knew little to nothing about cooking, but she would be thrilled to learn. Chas graciously gave Kate simple tasks and answered her questions when she didn't know what she was doing. While they were working side by side at the counter, Kate said, "I always wanted to learn how to cook, but my mother considered it demeaning."

Chas let out an astonished chuckle. "Demeaning?"

"That's right," Kate said, appreciating the validation of her own feelings. She'd always believed her mother's ideas were excessive and strange, but it was nice to hear it from someone else. "She truly believes that some people are born to be waited upon, and others are born to be in servitude."

"It's amazing that someone like her could raise a daughter who's so down to earth."

Kate chuckled. "That is more amazing than you could imagine. My mother is *appalled* at my viewpoints on almost everything. It wasn't until I started spending time in the homes of some of my friends in high school that I began to see how strange her ideas really were. Prior to that time, I only spent time with friends my mother chose for me, which, of course, were girls who came from wealthy families that met with my mother's approval. Gradually, I realized that my instinctive desire to be different from my mother was a good thing, but of course my mother only saw it as rebellion. She can't understand why a young lady who wants for nothing would be so determined to lower herself to such an ordinary life. Ordinary is *exactly* what I want."

"Well, you'll get ordinary here," Chas said with a little laugh.

"Yes," Kate said, "but it's an extraordinary kind of ordinary." She looked around. "I like it."

Kate asked questions while she watched Chas prepare an enchilada casserole and a green salad. With the salad in the fridge and the casserole in the oven, they chatted while Chas dealt with the children and Kate rinsed dishes and loaded the dishwasher. That much she *had* learned to do in college, but no one had ever taught her any degree of cooking until today.

"Did you have cooking classes in school?" Chas asked.

"I went to private schools and/or had tutors. My mother made certain that such things as cooking and sewing weren't on my schedule.

She was more concerned about my learning French and Latin." Kate sniggered. "I'm certain Latin will be very useful in teaching first graders and raising a family."

"You want a family, then?"

"Oh, I do," Kate said. She sighed and focused intently on arranging bowls in the dishwasher. "Someday."

"Well, it's funny you brought up sewing, because I was going to ask if you knew anything about that."

"Not a thing," Kate said, straightening up to look right at Chas. She felt intrigued and maybe even excited. "Why?"

"The ladies at my church are doing a project to make things for newborn babies in third-world countries. They need lots of blankets. I brought home a few pieces of fabric that are already cut to the right size. They just need to have the edges stitched on a machine. It's very easy and I could teach you in minutes. It's just . . . tedious. I committed to doing them, but I keep putting them off. They need to be done by next Thursday when a bunch of ladies are meeting at the church to assemble the kits."

Kate's intrigue deepened with such intensity that she almost felt chilled. "I'd love to!" she said.

"Good." Chas smiled. "I'll get the sewing machine out in the morning after breakfast and show you what to do."

"Great!" Kate said, delighted at the prospect of doing something worthwhile with her time.

Kate felt excited when she woke up the next morning. It was the first time in months, maybe longer, that she'd actually had something to look forward to. After breakfast, Chas took Kate into a room in the inn that she said had once been the bedroom she and Jackson had used before they'd built the attached house. Prior to that time, it had been Granny's room for many years. They'd debated turning it into another guest room for rent, but they liked having a room where projects could be done, and there had been times when guests had wanted a room like this where tables could be set up for activities.

"Like what?" Kate asked.

"We had a group of friends stay here that made scrapbooks and other craft projects," Chas said. "And we've had a few weekend family reunion events where they've done similar things."

"Delightful," Kate said, her eye on the sewing machine set on a long table, with folded pieces of fabric nearby.

Chas opened the drapes, and the room became so well lit that she turned off the light. Kate examined the pieces of fleece fabric, printed with colorful designs. There was a pink one with fairies on it, a blue one with teddy bears, and a green one with little comical frogs. The fabric had been cut into large squares, just right to wrap a baby in. Chas explained that the edges simply had to be hemmed on the machine with a particular stitch. Using some fabric scraps, she showed Kate how to run the machine and do the hemming. After Kate had tried it, amazed at her immediate success, Chas handed her one of the blankets and talked her through getting started. She stayed at Kate's side until she'd finished one edge so that Chas could show her how to turn the corner. Chas then left her to it, saying she would check back, and that she would either be in the office or the common room of the house if Kate had a problem or a question. She had to find Chas when the thread broke and the machine needed to be threaded again, then she finished the first blanket and moved on to the second. The next time the thread broke she was able to thread the machine herself. She was slow, but her work was meticulous, and she was amazed at how much she was enjoying such a simple task. And she was sewing! Her mother would be disgusted! She laughed at the thought and kept at it. She finished the second blanket before lunch, and was quickly back to work after eating a sandwich. When the three blankets were completed with Chas's approval, Kate asked, "Can I go to a fabric store and get stuff to make more?"

Chas looked surprised but said, "Of course. I'm sure a place can be found for as many blankets as you would like to make."

"Good," Kate said. Chas was busy with other things, but Kate was fine with that. She was used to being on her own, and it felt good to find the fabric store and explore it for a long while. She easily found the fleece in children's prints, and with the required blanket measurements written down, she quickly figured out how much fabric she wanted. There were so many adorable prints that it was hard to stop. The ladies cutting the fabric for her seemed to catch her spirit of enthusiasm, and they all chatted and laughed together, joined by another customer that one of the ladies helped while the other kept cutting fabric for Kate.

While Kate was out, she did some other shopping to get some odds and ends she needed, and she bought some snacks she could keep in her room to ease her cravings and soothe her nausea. When she returned to the inn, Polly was in the office working, but she saw no sign of Chas or Jackson. She took her personal things up to her room, then it took three trips from the car to bring in the fabric and thread she had purchased, which she took into the project room. Using the first blankets she'd made as a pattern for size, she cut out four more blankets. Her back began to hurt from bending over, so she sat at the sewing machine and got to work hemming while she listened to music on her iPod.

When Chas came in to check on Kate, it startled her, and she popped out her earphones. "How did the shopping go?" Chas asked.

"Great!" Kate said, motioning to the piles of fabric.

Chas was astonished but thrilled, and even more so when Kate pointed out that she'd already completed two more blankets and had started a third.

"It's easy but fun," Kate said. "I might get bored with it eventually, but it's giving me something to do that feels worthwhile."

"I think it's wonderful," Chas said.

Kate ventured to ask a question that she hoped wouldn't be out of line. "You said that ladies from your church were meeting to put these kits together. Is it against the rules for me to go with you? Or . . . maybe you would prefer that I didn't, or—"

"I'd *love* to have you come along!" Chas said. "And anyone is welcome."

"Good," Kate said. "I'd like that very much."

Over the next few days Kate shared her evening meals with the family, usually helping Chas prepare the meal and clean it up, and visiting with them afterward. One of the highlights of spending time with the family was the opportunity to play with the children. They took to her quickly, and Kate loved to join in their play or look through storybooks with them. She tried not to think about giving up the baby she was carrying; instead she focused on a more distant future when she might have a family of her own.

Kate generally ate breakfast and lunch on her own in between reading and sewing and getting all the rest that her body demanded.

She felt entirely comfortable at the Dickensian Inn, and at the moment only dreaded the day when this ordeal would actually be over and she would have to face the fallout from her parents. Until that day came, she was going to enjoy this unexpected reprieve in her life.

On Saturday evening, Chas mentioned that the family would be attending church the following day. She invited Kate to join them, but she declined. "Perhaps another time," Kate said, but she doubted she would ever go. Religion fell into one of the categories of her life that she preferred to avoid due to the way her mother had tainted it. Kate stayed in her pajamas late on Sunday, just reading and relaxing. She spent the evening with Jackson and Chas and the children and went to bed early. On Monday, Kate watched the children for a couple of hours while Jackson and Chas went to an appointment with their accountant. Kate had been around the children enough to feel fairly confident in fulfilling their needs, and she knew Polly was in the office if a problem arose that she couldn't handle. But everything went smoothly, and Kate told them she'd be glad to watch the children whenever they needed a sitter.

"We generally manage juggling the kids back and forth to do what we need," Chas said.

"But how long has it been since you two went on a date?" Kate asked. "You've told me Polly used to watch the kids more, but she's got her own baby now. How about if I watch the kids while the two of you go out? Maybe this weekend?"

"That sounds wonderful," Chas said, and Kate felt gratified with the possibility of doing something for these people who had given her so much in so few days.

On Tuesday Jackson watched the children while Chas drove Kate into Butte for her doctor appointment. They waited quite a while in the waiting room, and Kate felt nervous. Having Chas there to talk to helped immensely. She asked Chas to go in with her when she talked to the doctor, so that she could help Kate remember everything that was said. Chas sat with her through the visit, then went back to the waiting room while the doctor examined Kate to make certain everything was all right. Before they left, they made an appointment for an ultrasound for the following week. Since Kate was more than halfway along, they wanted to make certain that everything was okay.

Back in the car, both women were unusually quiet. To distract herself from her own difficult thoughts, Kate asked, "Are you okay?"

"Sorry," Chas said. "Just . . . memories."

"Of what?"

"I told you about Isabelle's heart problem."

"Yes."

"It was discovered with an ultrasound. I just . . . got thinking about that day. It was a rough one." She smiled toward Kate. "I'm glad to say that it turned out all right."

"Yes, so am I."

"Do you want to know if the baby is a boy or a girl?" Chas asked.

"I don't know," Kate said. "Since it's not really my baby, I think knowing might make it harder. I'm trying to remain emotionally detached."

"I understand," Chas said. "At least I think I do. I can understand why adoption is a good choice, under the circumstances, but it would be very hard." Kate only nodded and changed the subject. They went out for some lunch, then did a little bit of shopping, since Kate had no choice but to resort to maternity clothes now. She found some things she actually liked, and was stunned when she tried them on to see how very pregnant she was looking. The reality still felt difficult to swallow.

They returned to the inn to find the children sleeping and Jackson working in the office. Polly had gone home. Chas greeted her husband, then took the two baby monitors with her to go into the house. Kate took her purchases up to her room, then met Chas in her kitchen. They worked together to prepare a chicken dish that needed to bake a long time in the oven at a low temperature, then they sat down to relax. Kate realized she was *still* being unusually quiet just before Chas asked, "Are you okay?"

"I don't know. It's starting to feel real."

"The baby, you mean?" Chas asked. "It's really a baby?"

"It really is," Kate said. "I'm not sure how to feel." She was amazed once again at how comfortable she'd come to feel with Chas, and she felt grateful to have someone to talk to about these things. Otherwise she felt sure she'd go crazy. "It just all seems so . . . strange."

"Forgive me if I'm being too bold, Kate, but . . . I want to understand what you're going through. I just have to ask . . . if you loved him."

"Who?"

"The father of the baby."

Kate felt utterly astonished, and worse than that, her heart was assaulted with a painful pounding that made it difficult to keep her voice steady. "What did my mother tell you?"

"Almost nothing."

"Okay, but . . . what exactly was this 'almost nothing'?"

"Exactly?" Chas added, and Kate nodded, her stomach smoldering.

"She said you'd 'gone and gotten yourself pregnant.'"

Kate wasn't at all surprised by the comment. She *was* surprised by how sick it made her feel. So much so that she had to say, "Sorry," as she rushed down the hall and into the bathroom. After throwing up her lunch and heaving for a few minutes after that, Kate soaked a clean washcloth with cold water and pressed it over her face, then she poured some mouthwash into a little paper cup. Once she'd spit out the burning liquid, she had to hang her head over the sink for several seconds to get her equilibrium. Balancing her anger toward her mother against the knowledge of her own circumstances, she went back to the common room and sat back down.

"Sorry," she said again. "It comes back to me like that. My mother's attitude doesn't help."

"I understand. At least I'm trying to. It must be hard to feel that she's so judgmental."

"Oh, that's not the half of it," Kate said. She chuckled bitterly and shook her head. "I really try not to speak ill of my mother. I've taken college psychology classes and I've studied every self-help book that I felt drawn to. It seems to be the standard that talking about all the things I hate about my mother only makes me a negative person; it will never change her."

"But . . . isn't there a difference between being able to express what you're feeling, and crossing the line where you wallow in it for the sake of just being negative?"

"That makes sense, I suppose. I just . . . I . . ." Tears came and once again she said, "Sorry. It must be pregnancy."

"That certainly makes a woman more emotional, but you also need to consider that you're going through something difficult."

"The thing is," Kate said. "I . . . I don't really want to talk about this, but . . . you've been so very good to me, and it's evident you're going to be with me throughout the remainder of this pregnancy. I trust you, Chas, and I don't trust easily. I *should* talk about it. That's what the therapist said, but . . . it's hard, because . . . I don't remember."

"Remember what?"

Kate took a deep breath, closed her eyes, and just said it. "I don't remember anything from when I started feeling light-headed at a party until I woke up in my own bed, realizing as soon as I was fully coherent that I had been raped."

Chas was stunned. She'd simply never expected this. From the way Kate's mother had talked, there hadn't been any reason to expect *this*. But Kate would have no idea how close this hit to home for Chas. In fact, this revelation pierced a nerve in Chas that she hadn't even known existed until it suddenly became inflamed.

"I've upset you," Kate said, startling Chas back to the moment.

"No, not at all."

"I can understand why it's uncomfortable to talk about such a thing, but I need you to be straight with me. Frankly, my mother simply didn't believe me. In some ways, I think that's harder than . . . the other."

"She didn't *believe* you?" Chas was too astonished to think straight. "Maybe you'd better tell me everything . . . from the start."

"I went to the hospital immediately, and they called the police. They did all the standard procedures and tests. It was so horrifying. But I made up my mind that I was not going to pretend it hadn't happened, and I wasn't going to be ashamed to talk about it. My friends were very supportive, but the police never found the man who did it. Until he offered me a drink at the party, I'd never seen him before, so I couldn't remember his features terribly well. No one at the party seemed to remember him; either that, or someone was covering for him. So, there were never any actual suspects who could be matched to the DNA. The case was basically dropped. I became paranoid, but the term was almost over at the time and I managed to get through those last few classes and finals—thanks to some friends who let me stay at their place. I never went anywhere alone after dark, and I was always looking over my shoulder. Once the term ended, I packed up and drove home. Fortunately, my parents were in Europe for an extended stay, so I had the house to myself. I was there when I realized I was pregnant."

"You were all alone?" Chas asked, horrified to think of her going through *any* of this alone. She was amazed that Kate could tell this story with no trace of emotion, but she suspected that was just a coping mechanism.

"There were always servants around; I'm almost ashamed to admit that's the way I grew up."

"No need for that."

"So, I wasn't *alone,* but no one was there who actually cared what I was doing or what might be going on. Once I moved from Boston, my friends didn't really keep in touch. Friends from Maine had either left or were busy with their lives. When my parents came back, I told them what had happened. My father just looked disappointed in me; he didn't say much. My mother acted as if I had personally ruined her life. I even showed her the hospital records and the police report. She told me that she didn't doubt I'd gone to them with this story, wanting to cover up my promiscuity and . . . bad behavior."

Chas saw emotion finally come through. Kate shrugged and tears came on in quick abundance. "I still cannot believe," she cried, "that my own mother could read that hospital report . . . and deny evidence that could have never been present if it had just been my . . . bad behavior." She sobbed and wiped at her face. "She called you that very day to make arrangements to ship me off, and . . . you know the rest."

Chas put an arm around Kate and let her cry long and hard. She probably needed it. And it was evident she needed a friend and some moral support more than Chas had ever imagined. When Kate finally calmed down, she apologized and said, "I hate to burden you with this, but . . . I can't deny how grateful I am for you. I don't know what I would do if I couldn't talk to *somebody.*"

"I'm very glad you came here, Kate, and even more glad that we can be friends. We're going to get through this."

Kate regained her composure and thanked Chas for listening before she went up to her room, where she sank into a warm bath and cried again. The doctor visit combined with buying maternity clothes had somewhat served to shock her out of denial. And finally sharing with Chas the truth about her situation had brought it all closer to the surface than it had been since she'd come here.

By the time Kate went down to supper, she felt like she finally had it out of her system, but once the meal was over and cleaned up, she pleaded exhaustion and went back to her room. She went to bed early and cried some more, but she woke up determined to press forward and not wallow in the aspects of this situation that could never be changed.

Kate was more grateful than ever to have a project that required her attention. She worked most of the day on hemming blankets, finding that she'd become very fast at it as the blankets started piling up. Chas checked on her frequently, very impressed with her progress. She commented that they might have to find a way to put together more kits to put the blankets in, and Kate felt intrigued by the possibility of branching out with this project. Chas explained that her church collected and distributed kits for people in areas of the world where there were humanitarian needs. She showed Kate a website that had detailed descriptions of the items needed and strict instructions on how to pack them in plastic bags that could be easily distributed. Kate sat and looked at the website long after Chas left to take care of her family. She imagined what it would be like for a poverty-stricken mother who had nothing with which to care for a new baby. She imagined such a mother getting one of these sweet little kits with a soft, brightly colored blanket, a little nightgown, cloth diapers and pins, soap, and little socks or booties. With those images in her head she went back to work.

The next day Kate went with Chas to her church building where they gathered with several other ladies to assemble the supplies into plastic bags. The ladies were all very kind to Kate, and some of them made a very big fuss over the blankets she'd hemmed. Kate knew that in the grand scheme of this project, her efforts—and the minimal skill it had taken—were very insignificant. But it felt good to be a part of something bigger than herself, something that took her mind off of her own problems. While she and Chas were folding little baby nightgowns that some of the ladies had sewn, Kate asked, "Do you think I could learn to make these?"

"Absolutely," Chas said. "We can get some materials tomorrow and I'll teach you."

"Wonderful," Kate said, and they kept working.

Later the ladies stopped to have what they called a potluck lunch. Kate had never heard of such a thing, but it was delightful. Every lady had brought something from home and stored it in the kitchen of the church while they'd been working. They set out the food and shared everything there while they sat and visited. Kate enjoyed listening to them talk, even though they were obviously part of a religious culture she knew nothing about. But the project they were doing was something with a universal message, and Kate was impressed. No one commented on her pregnancy or asked about it, and she was glad for that. She wasn't sure how she would respond.

The following day, Chas kept her promise, and by afternoon Kate was well on her way to completing a little nightgown. It was easier than she'd expected, even though she had to unpick mistakes several times. But she liked the way her mistakes *could* be picked out and redone. She wished it could be that way with real life.

When Kate became serious about really getting into this project, Chas had Jackson set up two more long tables in the project room, and Kate began filling the room with everything she needed to make her own personal difference in the world. Over the next month, Kate followed the guidelines on the website to assemble many kits of different kinds. She went into town several times to purchase supplies, in some cases ordering the specific items online when she couldn't find those that fit the exact specifications. She had returned her rental car when it became apparent how little she would use it, and there was always one vehicle or another that Chas and Jackson were glad to let her use for her occasional errands. With all the materials purchased, she learned how to make the other types of blankets, and she quickly improved her skills with the little nightgowns. She made dozens of them. The school bags were easy after doing baby gowns, and she made numerous school kits as well as newborn kits. Assembling hygiene kits was easy because they didn't actually require any sewing projects. In each case she boxed up her accomplishments, carefully following the strict instructions, and shipped them to Salt Lake City. She kept a careful tally in a journal she picked up in town. She'd never kept a journal, but this one had meticulous notes on how many items she'd sewn, kits she'd made, and boxes she'd shipped. Occasionally she jotted down some personal notes on how it felt to do this, or her speculations on where the items might end up.

With the weeks passing by, Kate realized she would still be at the inn through the holidays, and she made a point to bring it up at dinner, insisting that Chas and Jackson be completely honest about her presence there. She didn't want to intrude on their holiday celebrations in any way, and she made it clear that she was accustomed to spending Christmas on her own, since she'd done it many times while her parents were traveling or staying with relatives that she had preferred to avoid.

Chas and Jackson were both appalled that Christmas had been treated so trivially in Kate's upbringing, and even more so that Kate would assume they wouldn't be thrilled to have her be a part of their Christmas preparations and celebrations—when the time came.

By the end of October, Kate was more than six months pregnant with a baby that she tried not to think about. She felt it moving and growing inside of her. She'd seen ultrasound images and she'd heard its heartbeat. She'd been told that it appeared to be healthy and right on track with its growth, but she didn't want to know its gender or any more about it than she absolutely had to know in order to give it life. She was far more comfortable providing bare necessities for needy children on the other side of the world somewhere, while a part of her wished that she would never have to leave the temporary oasis she'd found at the Dickensian Inn.

CHAPTER 4

"Is something bugging you?" Jackson asked Chas after they'd said their bedtime prayer together.

"I'm fine," she said and slid beneath the covers, arranging pillows against the headboard so that she could lean against them and read.

"You're lying," Jackson said in a tone that motivated her to turn and look at him, astonished. But it only took a moment for guilt to make her look away. "Something has been bothering you for weeks. I've left you alone about it because . . . well, who am I to make judgments on needing time to mull something over? You said you didn't want to talk about it. But you've had plenty of time, and whatever this is, it's getting worse, not better."

"You're right," she said, "about everything. I figured it would come up eventually, but . . . I guess now is as good a time as any."

Chas set her book on the bedside table, then smoothed the covers over her lap. Jackson spread himself over the bed sideways and leaned on his elbow to look directly at her, planting his head in his hand.

"You know, of course, the reason that Kate is pregnant."

"You know I do. You told me about it a long time ago."

"The thing is . . . you see . . . I . . . ."

"This is about your mother, isn't it," he stated with certainty.

"How did you know?" Chas felt astonished, then realized she shouldn't have been.

"The connection is obvious, Chas, and so is the timing. To tell you the truth, I've wondered if this might come up eventually. Kate's situation has just drawn it to the surface."

"You wondered if *what* might come up eventually?"

"This?" He motioned toward her with his hand. "Remember who you're talking to, Chas. When you come from difficult parentage, eventually you have to face up to it—one way or another—if you want to truly be at peace."

Chas opened her mouth to speak, then closed it again. They had shared a great deal of drama over the difficulties of Jackson's upbringing, and the challenges that had resulted in his life prior to meeting Chas.

While she was still thinking, Jackson said, "Would you expect to sail through life and never *really* stop to ponder the reality of your origins when they're so obviously difficult? You will never convince me that the anger you felt over it when you were a teenager was enough to fully come to terms with the kind of man your father was, and what he did to your mother."

Chas couldn't hold back tears as he voiced the bottom line of what had been troubling her. "How *do* you come to terms with that?" she asked.

"You can start by actually admitting that it's troubling you; that's a good start."

"And what makes you so analytical all of sudden?"

"Not all of a sudden, Chas. You, of all people, should know how much counseling I've been through. But I can't take credit for this. Nolan predicted that this would happen. He's talked to me about it more than once."

"About *what?*" Chas demanded, stunned to think of Jackson and her grandfather discussing something that hadn't even occurred to her until Kate had confessed the truth of her situation.

"He asked me quite some time ago if you had trouble with knowing your father's identity—and his crimes against your mother. At the time I told him I wasn't sure, because I wasn't. He brought it up again more recently. He mentioned that since *he'd* had trouble dealing with it, he suspected a time might come when you would as well."

Chas considered the bizarre relationship she shared with Nolan Stoddard. For the majority of her life, her only connection to family had been Granny—her maternal grandmother. Then, out of nowhere, a few years earlier, her father's father had tracked her down. Nolan had been well aware of his son's crimes, and was appalled by them.

It turned out that Chas's father had been the black sheep of the family—a very *fine* family. And he'd died in prison for what he'd done to Chas's mother. When Nolan lost his wife to death, and his children were all scattered across the country, he'd made the decision to find Chas. They'd quickly grown fond of each other, and now she truly felt like a part of the family—in spite of the ignoble means by which she was actually related to Nolan and his children and grandchildren. But she never would have dreamed, for all of the time she'd spent with her grandfather, that he was secretly concerned about her coming to this day, that he had actually predicted it.

"What did he say?" Chas demanded.

"I already told you what he said. He simply expressed some concern. Which is why—now that it's come up—I think you need to talk to *him*. You never knew your father, but he did. And we *do* know that he struggled a great deal with the way his son hurt so many people—most *especially* your mother. On the other hand, those of us who love you could never regret your existence. It's a paradox if I've ever heard one." Jackson sat up and leaned more toward her. "Call him tomorrow. Have a good talk with him. You know he'll be kind and understanding. And then . . . if you feel like you're still struggling with this, I know a good shrink."

"I don't know that it's as serious as that," Chas insisted.

"Maybe. Maybe not. You know that I will always be here for you, and I'm willing to listen as much as you need to talk, but that doesn't necessarily mean I have the answers."

"You have very good common sense."

"And maybe you'll need more than that. Let's just take it one step at a time."

"Okay," she said and settled farther down into the bed.

Jackson eased beneath the covers and turned off the lamp on the bedside table. He held her close while she could feel him relaxing, but she wondered if she would ever be able to sleep.

Chas woke to daylight and realized that she *had* slept, and if Isabelle had awakened in the night—which she did on occasion—Jackson must have taken care of it. Her most prominent thought as she began her daily routine was that she needed to call her grandfather. A part of her didn't want to, knowing such a conversation could be awkward, if not downright difficult. On the other hand, she knew Jackson was right. Nolan *would* be kind and understanding. And he might know more about the situation than he'd previously told her. Since he'd had to face the fact that his own son had done deplorable things, perhaps it was possible that he could help her face the same thing about the man who had fathered her.

Jackson seemed to know her thoughts when he handed her the phone the moment they were done eating breakfast and said, "Call your grandfather. Arrange a time to meet with him. You'll feel better."

Chas nodded stoically and took the phone in the other room to dial the memorized number. She was hoping to get his answering machine, but he answered with a cheery hello and she had to jump past her pounding heart to try to sound equally cheery. After they had exchanged the usual greetings, she said, "I was wondering if it would be possible for us to get together . . . just the two of us . . . and talk."

"That would be more than all right, honey. Is something bothering you?"

"I guess I've just been thinking a lot about . . . my parents, and . . . how they came to be my parents. Jackson told me you'd predicted this might happen, so you don't need to pretend to be surprised."

"It's a difficult situation," Nolan said. "I'm sure that talking about it might be good for both of us. You tell me when and where, and I'll be there. Do you want me to come to the inn, or—"

"No," she said, "I think I'd like to come to your home . . . if that's okay. Maybe the drive will help me sort through some of my thoughts."

"If that's what you'd like, that will be fine. When can you get away?"

"Anytime, really. Jackson let me know he's available to cover for me—with the inn *and* the kids. Polly will be here through the middle of the day, but Kate's here as well, so—"

"How *is* Kate?" Nolan asked. They'd met a few times when Nolan had come for his usual visits. He knew why she was staying at the inn, but he had no awareness of the reasons for her pregnancy, which were the same reasons this unrest had been stirred up inside of Chas.

"She's doing well," Chas said.

"I'm glad to hear it. Why don't you come today . . . as soon as you can get here. I was going to make my famous vegetable soup for lunch."

"I *love* your famous vegetable soup."

"Then it's a date," he said, and Chas agreed.

Jackson was pleased with her plans, and he made it incredibly easy for her to get away. Chas simply told Polly and Kate that she was going to spend some time with her grandfather and she was on the road before ten A.M. The drive to Butte *did* help her sort through her thoughts—or at least it helped her come up with a way to open up this sensitive topic with this man she'd come to care for so deeply.

Nolan met Chas at the door and hugged her tightly. His embrace had become familiar to her, and being a part of his family had filled something in her that had been missing. But the circumstances were very odd, and it was the oddness they needed to talk about. He was distinguished and handsome for a man his age, and he kept his home in good order in the absence of his deceased wife, a woman he had a shared a lifetime with. Chas had never met her, but she knew her well through stories and photographs.

"How are those great-grandbabies of mine?" he asked, showing her into the front room where they sat down to face each other.

"They're adorable as ever," Chas said, and she took a few minutes to catch him up on their latest antics. She realized then that she found great satisfaction in sharing the joy of her children with someone who loved them as well. He was the only living grandparent on either side of the family that her children had left. She hoped that his good health would hold out and that he would live long enough for her children to really know him.

When the small talk had run down, Nolan leaned toward her and said gently, "Tell me what's troubling you, Chas."

"Maybe it *shouldn't* trouble me," she said, "but lately, I just keep thinking about . . ." tears came with her confession, "about . . . my mother . . . and what she went through to bring me into the world." She reached for a tissue from her purse and pressed it beneath her nose. "I know that the heart condition that took her life in childbirth had nothing to do with the rape, but . . . I guess I just never *really* stopped to consider before now . . . how hard all of it must have been for her."

"Why now?" Nolan asked. She hesitated to answer, and he asked, "Does it have something to do with Kate?" Chas knew her eyes had told him the truth even before she considered how she might answer. "I wondered," he said. "For all of her grace and dignity, she seems a bit . . . traumatized."

"Yes, I suppose she does," Chas said. "The thing is . . . Kate was drugged; she doesn't remember anything. I'm not sure if that would be better or worse."

Chas was amazed at how quickly it became completely comfortable to unload all of her thoughts and feelings regarding this sensitive topic. Nolan listened attentively and made her feel validated in all that she felt. He in turn shared a deeper level of his own feelings regarding the pain his son had caused.

They moved to the kitchen while they talked, and worked together to make his famous soup. They continued to talk while it simmered, and then while they sat across the table and shared lunch. In the end, Chas felt better simply because she felt understood. Her grandfather's empathy and kindness were no small thing. But driving back to the inn, Chas still felt unsettled over the matter.

It started to snow about the time Chas arrived at the inn. She hadn't even bothered to check the weather report, and she was glad to be home on the chance that this storm might turn into something significant. She went in search of her husband, glad to discover that the children were napping and they could talk without interruption. She shared with him the gist of the conversation she'd shared with her grandfather, and the conclusion she'd come to—that she had a long way to go to come to terms with this.

"And I'm sure you will," Jackson said, hugging her tightly. "You know I'm here for you."

"I know," she said, "and I'm grateful."

Charles woke up, with Isabelle following close behind, and the busyness of the day ensued again. Chas continued to ponder all that she had discussed with her grandfather, and how she felt about it, but she just wasn't sure what she was supposed to learn from all that she was feeling.

The snow continued to fall that night and into the following day. Chas was glad not to have any errands that couldn't wait, and she enjoyed the coziness of being safe in her home—and being able to commute to work without actually going outside. But her thoughts continued to hover around her mother, and she prayed that she could come to terms with this and make peace with it.

* * * * *

Kate enjoyed looking through the large windows of the project room, watching snow fall, while Chas helped her box up the most recent kits that were going to Salt Lake City. They were both silent for several minutes. Silence was rare between them, but Kate had come to notice that nearly every time it happened, something had come up regarding the reason that Kate was pregnant. Kate had considered bringing it up and had determined that she and Chas had become too good of friends to ignore such an obvious tension between them. She finally settled on a sentence that would thrust it into the open.

"You have a hard time with what happened to me," Kate said.

Chas looked up, astonished. "Of course I have a hard time with it. It's horrible."

"But . . . it's more than that," Kate said. "Every time anything comes up about it, you get this faraway . . . uncomfortable . . . look on your face. And you get very quiet. I know it's a difficult topic, but . . . you need to be honest with me. If you don't want me to talk about it, then—"

"Oh, no!" Chas said. "It's not that at all! I'm sorry if I gave you the wrong impression. I want you to talk about it as much as you need to. You might need to just keep doing so until you've finally worked it through, and I'm okay with that. It's just that . . ."

"What?" Kate pressed when Chas hesitated.

Kate was surprised at how unsettled Chas became. She moved to a chair and sighed. Kate sat close to her and felt unsettled herself as she considered what Chas might be trying to say.

"I told Jackson what happened to you; I hope you don't consider that breaking a confidence."

"I wouldn't have expected you not to tell him," Kate said. "If I hadn't wanted you to, I would have said so. In fact, I don't really mind people knowing, as long as I don't have to tell them myself."

"I think that makes sense."

"I believe I'd rather have people know the truth than think of me the way my mother thinks of me."

"I could agree with that."

"So, what did Jackson say?" Kate asked.

"Not much. I'm glad you don't mind that I spoke to him because . . . I admit that it's weighed on me, and I felt like I needed to talk to him."

Kate nodded and said, "I understand." But she was still waiting for an explanation.

"Well," Chas began, "first I have to share with you a little bit about myself. I believe in destiny, Kate. More accurately, I believe in God and I believe that He brings people together for a reason."

"Okay," Kate said, "that's not such a stretch."

"Do you believe in God, Kate?"

"I do," she said. "My parents only went to church on special occasions, and mostly for appearances. I've never been comfortable with organized religion for that reason, but I certainly believe in God. There are too many things that could never be explained any other way. Where are you going with this?"

"I don't believe it's a coincidence that you're here with us. I felt that way even before you told me what had happened to you. But . . . considering what happened to you . . ."

"You've been through this?" Kate guessed, astonished.

"Actually, no," Chas said. "But . . . I told you that my mother died giving birth to me."

"Because of her weak heart."

"That's right."

"And I told you that I never knew my father."

"Yes," Kate drawled.

"My conception was a crime, Kate. My father died in prison for what he'd done to my mother." She took a deep breath while Kate couldn't catch hers. "I am the product of a rape."

Kate started to cry and realized that she hadn't cried for weeks. She reached for Chas's hand, and for a full minute neither of them spoke. Chas finally said, "I have thought more about my mother in the weeks since you told me what happened to you than I have for years. I guess your situation has brought it close to home. I can't help . . . wondering how it might have been for her. I almost feel ashamed to think that such an aspect never occurred to me before. When I first found out the truth about my father, I was angry and hurt—but it was a selfish kind of hurt. I never really pondered—not very deeply, anyway—how it was for my mother. That's why I went to my grandfather's yesterday."

Kate felt suddenly enlightened. "He's your father's father! You told me that when I first met him, of course, but . . . I just assumed, well . . . all you'd told me was that your father wasn't around. I don't know what I assumed. I didn't really think about it."

Chas quickly told Kate the story of how her grandfather had found her not so many years ago, and what a miracle it had been, then she shared her recently tender feelings with a woman who would understand more than most. They both cried a little, and once again Chas felt great kindness and understanding. But she still felt unsettled over the matter, and prayed that with time she could make peace with it and move on.

As the two of them went together into the house to prepare an easy supper, Chas was grateful to be surrounded by people who were so kind, and would allow her the time she needed to sort out her thoughts and feelings. In the meantime, life needed attending to and Chas was glad to see her children playing nearby while she chatted lightly with Kate and while Jackson put dishes on the table.

"Oh, look," Kate said, "it's stopped snowing."

"Good," Chas said, looking out the window to see that only a tiny amount of daylight was remaining. "We have a couple checking in this evening. I was hoping they wouldn't have any trouble with the weather."

They heard the chime that indicated someone had come through the door of the inn, and Jackson said, "I'll take care of it."

He returned fewer than ten minutes later to report that their guests had arrived and were settled into their room. According to them, the weather hadn't been so bad in Butte. They'd only seen a few snow flurries while driving the hour from the airport. And the plane had had no trouble in landing.

They all pitched in and had dinner on the table within a few minutes, but they had barely finished the blessing on the food when they heard the chime again.

"I wonder who that could be," Jackson said, and once again volunteered to take care of it.

* * * * *

Michael Westcott was hit with an unexpected swarm of butterflies in his stomach when the plane landed in Butte, Montana. He thanked the pilot and told him to take some time off.

"I'll call when I need you," Michael told him, and they exchanged a smile. He and Tony had shared many adventures of late, and Tony had become a friend and traveling companion in addition to being the man who could fly the plane to take Michael wherever his passport would allow.

"Just give me some warning, Mick. You know I have to file a flight plan."

"Yeah, yeah; technicalities."

Mick quickly had a rental car and was soon on his way to Anaconda, after going to a drive-through to get a hamburger. He thought of all the things he wanted to share with Jackson and got those butterflies again. His life had changed so much since they'd talked earlier this year. He was a different man, and he had Jackson Leeds to thank for it.

It was dark by the time Mick arrived at the inn, but it was well lit and he found it easily enough—even though he'd only been there once before. He left his luggage in the car, wondering if he should have called ahead to get a reservation. If the inn was all booked, he might have to find a room somewhere else. For now he focused on his purpose for coming.

Once inside the door, Mick noticed that the office where on his previous visit he had found Jackson Leeds working was locked up and dark. But the hall in which he stood was well lit, and he only stood there for thirty seconds before the object of his quest came around the corner. Jackson stopped when he recognized Mick. He grinned and stepped toward him, his hand extended.

"I've been wondering if you were still alive," Jackson said. "You told me you'd keep in touch."

"I've been busy," Mick said, and their handshake turned into an embrace.

"It's good to see you, kid," Jackson said as he stepped back and took Mick by the shoulders, much the way his father might have.

"It's good to see you too," Mick said.

"And your timing is perfect. We're just sitting down to supper, and there's plenty. Come along."

"I had a hamburger in Butte," Mick said, following him.

"A little home-cooked food to top it off won't hurt you a bit," Jackson said.

Mick followed him through the dining room and kitchen of the inn, into a large room that combined living, dining, and kitchen, which he now realized was a separate home attached to the old Victorian mansion. Two children were in high chairs, and two women sat at the table. One of them stood and smiled when he walked into the room. The other one didn't give him more than a cursory glance.

"This is my wife, Chas," Jackson said, motioning toward the one who was standing.

"Such a pleasure," Mick said to her as she took his hand.

"Chas, this is Michael Westcott. I told you about him. He came by earlier this year and—"

"Oh, of course!" Chas said, as if that was all she needed to hear to know exactly who her husband was talking about. "It's *so* good to meet you. Come and sit down and have some supper."

"I told Jackson I had a hamburger, and—"

"At least have a little," Chas said and hurried to grab some dishes while Jackson directed Mick toward an available chair, directly across from the woman who wouldn't look at him.

"Oh, this is Kate," Jackson said, motioning toward her. "She's a friend; she's living at the inn for the time being."

"Hello, Kate," Mick said.

"Hello," she said, finally making eye contact with him. He didn't bother to analyze why his heart quickened at the same moment. He just enjoyed the fact that it did. His next thought was that he might decide to stay at the Dickensian Inn a little longer than he'd originally planned.

"And that's Charles and Isabelle," Jackson said, motioning to the children.

"They look like you," Mick declared, then chuckled.

"Amazing," Jackson said with a mild sarcasm that made Mick chuckle again.

Chas set dishes in front of him, then his hosts were seated again and started passing the food to him. Mick couldn't resist taking some small servings, wishing he was more hungry because it all looked so good.

"So, where have you been all this time?" Jackson asked him.

"Oh, lots of places," Mick said. "I'd like to talk to you about that, but . . . later; tomorrow maybe. I don't suppose you have a room I could rent."

"We have several to choose from," Chas said eagerly, as if she were thrilled with the prospect of his staying. He really liked her.

"She's very nice," Mick said to Jackson. "It looks like you did good . . . Agent Leeds."

Kate stole another quick glance at the newcomer when she heard a clue to the connection between these two men. Apparently this Michael had known Jackson when he'd been an FBI agent. But he was much too young to have worked with him, wasn't he? Kate scolded herself for her curiosity. In truth, she really didn't care who he was or how he was connected to these people. He had a subtle air of confidence about him that she found unsettling for reasons she didn't bother to analyze. He had thick hair, blond and curly, that hung down the back of his neck, as if he'd just not bothered to get a haircut for a very long time. He wore jeans with a button-up shirt and a sports coat. Perhaps what bothered Kate most was that she knew they were *expensive* clothes. Either he was very well off or he was pretending to be. Either way, she wasn't impressed. The only incongruous thing about his appearance was a scarf he wore loosely looped around his neck. It looked foreign and well-worn. She wondered about it, but chose not to wonder too long.

"I'm glad I won't have to go elsewhere looking for a room for the night," Mick said. "If you must know, I've been looking forward to staying at the Dickensian Inn." He said it as if he'd said the White House. "But maybe I should have made a reservation."

"There are very few nights when we're completely full," Jackson said. "However, don't plan on coming on Valentine's Day without a reservation. Although, for you . . . we'd let you sleep on the couch if we were full."

Mick grinned. There was something strangely comforting in having Special Agent Jackson Leeds sharing his supper and offering his couch. All in all, that would be a far cry above most of the accommodations he'd experienced during the past several months.

Kate couldn't decide if she felt annoyed by this man simply because he'd intruded on the usual comfortable little gathering, or if there was something about him that she simply found irritating. She was wondering how to pinpoint the problem when Jackson said to him, "I assume that private jet of yours is at the airport in Butte."

"It is," the newcomer said, and Kate bristled. *He was rich.* She loathed young, rich men who had no comprehension of life outside of their posh little world. She'd dealt with them all her life, and she had no desire to deal with this one. It was no wonder she felt annoyed. She just hoped that he wouldn't be staying long, and that he stayed out of her way in the meantime.

"And the pilot?" Jackson asked.

"He's enjoying some rest and relaxation somewhere in Butte. I'm sure he'll be fine while I hang out here for a while."

Mick became distracted by the children. They really were adorable, and they were each making a terrible mess. He asked how old they were, and he enjoyed hearing their parents tell him a little about both of them with such parental pride. His own parents talked about him like that. He suddenly missed them.

After some trivial small talk, Mick had to admit he felt intensely curious over the other guest at the table. But he didn't want to single her out in the conversation. Instead he spoke to Jackson's lovely wife.

"Chas. What an interesting name. I don't believe I've ever heard it before."

"It's actually the abbreviation for Charles," Chas explained. "Given that my being born a girl denied my grandmother the privilege of naming me after her hero, Charles Dickens, she did the next best thing and named me Chas."

"What a delightful little story," Mick said. "I assume your grandmother's passion has something to do with the theme of the inn."

"Very good," Chas drawled with a smile and a wink. He smiled back. He really liked being with these people, and he'd only been here about seven minutes.

Turning his attention to the only person besides himself who wasn't a member of the family, he asked, "Is your name just Kate? Or is it short for something else?"

Kate was startled to realize he was talking to her. She made no effort to hold back her curt tone when she said, "It's Catherine."

"Is that Catherine with a *C* or with a *K?*"

"It's a *C,*" she said. "Are you always this annoying?" She tried to say it lightly enough that she didn't sound offensive, but she caught the subtle glance of confusion that passed between Jackson and Chas. She didn't want to offend her hosts, but neither did she want to talk to this man.

"Not always," Michael Westcott said as if such a question meant nothing to him. "But usually." He said it as if being annoying was a trait to be proud of. "So you go by Kate with a *K,* short for Catherine with a *C*. What is it about nicknames? I guess that's not unlike someone named Robert going by Bob. But it's very strange. I'm Michael but I go by Mick."

"I didn't know that," Jackson said, and Kate was surprised. The two men seemed to have some kind of deep bond. But how could they if Jackson didn't even know such a simple thing?

"Yeah, well . . . my dad is Michael too. It's confusing. Of course, saying 'I'm Mick' when I meet someone doesn't always sound so dignified, but my friends and family call me Mick. You people should all call me Mick. We're all friends now."

"We certainly are," Chas agreed eagerly.

"But how do you get Mick from Michael?" Mick said. "It's a *c* and an *h* in the middle of Michael. According to the rules of the English language, it shouldn't be pronounced *Michael* at all. If there was any consistency, *much* would be *muck,* but those are different words."

"This is all very fascinating, Mr. Westcott," Kate said. Then to Chas, "I hope you'll forgive me if I bow out early tonight. I'm not feeling well. I hate to leave you with the dishes, but—"

"Don't you worry about it," Chas said. "Just get some rest and I'll see you in the morning. Call if you need something."

"Thank you," Kate said and stood. Chas stood to give her a quick hug.

"I hope you sleep well," Jackson said to her as she left the room.

"You too," she said over her shoulder and hurried out.

Mick pretended to be entirely focused on the food he was stirring around on his plate. He simply hadn't expected the woman he'd felt intrigued with to be significantly pregnant. She hadn't been wearing a ring, but that didn't necessarily mean anything. In today's world, commitment came in many varieties. It was silly for him to think that she wasn't either married—or attached. Obviously there was *someone* significant in her life. He just hated the way he felt so deeply disappointed.

Once he knew she was gone and Jackson and Chas were continuing with their meal, Mick asked, "Is she okay?"

Chas was surprised to hear Mick's question echo her own thoughts. "The pregnancy has been very hard on her," she said, not bothering to explain that it was more of an emotional difficulty than a physical one. Perhaps that could explain why Kate had been mildly rude to Mick.

"I hope she feels better tomorrow," Mick said, dying to ask why Kate was staying here at the inn, and if her significant other was anywhere nearby. Or maybe the father of the baby was out of the picture. There were all kinds of reasons why a woman could end up pregnant and on her own. He wasn't sure why he felt so intensely curious—and intrigued—by a cantankerous pregnant woman. But he did.

CHAPTER 5

Mick enjoyed visiting with Jackson and Chas and their children for a while after supper was over. He tried to help with the dishes but Chas scolded him and refused to allow it. After the children had been washed up and freed from their high chairs, they became a great source of entertainment. Mick had spent months observing children in many countries, in many situations—most of them deplorable. It was nice to see children well fed and healthy, safe and sheltered.

Not wanting to wear out his welcome, Mick admitted to feeling exhausted, and Jackson took him back to the office where he officially registered him as a guest. Mick went out to the car to get his luggage, and Jackson locked the outside door of the inn after he came in. He explained that there was a key on the same ring as his room key that would open the outside doors if he needed to go out after the inn was closed up for the night. Jackson took one of Mick's bags and led him to a room on the third floor.

"I hope you're okay with the third floor," Jackson said. "The stairs are great exercise, but there *is* an elevator if you would prefer."

"No, this is great," Mick said.

"I'm giving you one of my favorite rooms; I hope you like it."

"Anything will be great," Mick said, but he was pleasantly surprised by the simplicity and beauty of the room where Jackson set down Mick's bag and handed him the keys.

"Breakfast will be in the dining room. You can eat anytime between eight and ten; just tell me when you want it ready."

"Oh, you don't have to—"

"It comes with the room," Jackson said. "What time do you want breakfast?"

"How about nine?"

"Nine it is," Jackson said. "Get some sleep and we'll catch up tomorrow."

"I'm looking forward to it," Mick said. Jackson smiled and closed the door.

Mick stood where he was and turned slowly to examine his surroundings, while the memories of places where he'd slept over the last several months filed through his mind. He felt almost guilty for being surrounded by so much comfort. But he intended to devote the rest of his life to alleviating that guilt. And he knew that the first step was to talk to Jackson Leeds about how the man had changed his life—again.

* * * * *

Kate entered the dining room at two minutes to nine and stopped. She'd put a fair amount of effort into trying *not* to think about Mick Westcott and the way he reminded her of so many pathetic dating experiences of her past, most of them initiated and prodded by her mother. He probably played polo and tennis, and he likely had no actual occupation beyond spending his parents' money. She was considering the possibility of taking a plate to her room when Mick peered over the newspaper he was reading, as if he'd sensed that he was not alone.

"Good morning, Kate," he said brightly, as if they'd been friends for years.

"Mr. Westcott," she said, barely nodding in his direction as she headed toward the sideboard to pour herself a glass of orange juice from a carafe there.

"So formal!" he said. "I don't know that *anyone* calls me *Mis-ter* Westcott. If you prefer it that way, I suppose I could call you Miss . . . or Mrs. . . . or Ms. . . . whatever your name happens to be. I'm afraid I only know you as Kate. Or Catherine. I could call you Catherine."

"Kate will be fine," she said and turned around to see Chas enter the room, carrying two lovely bowls of fruit.

"Good morning," she said to Kate. "Did you sleep well?"

"Yes, thank you. And you?"

"Isabelle slept through the night again, and for that reason, yes." Chas set both bowls on the table where Mick was sitting, not seeming to find it at all awkward when she said, "It's nice that the two of you ordered breakfast at the same time. You won't have to eat alone."

Kate didn't comment. Chas went back into the kitchen. Mick Westcott looked like a mischievous little boy. Kate again resisted the urge to take her food to her room, not wanting Chas to pick up on the negative vibes that Kate was feeling. She decided that for now, being gracious would be best.

"That *is* nice," Mick said, folding the paper to set it aside. Kate sat down and started eating. "What brings you to the Dickensian Inn, Kate?" he asked.

Kate thought about that while she chewed, and she couldn't think of a way to answer that question that wouldn't come too close to her own current issues. She swallowed and said, "What brings *you* to the Dickensian Inn?"

"I asked you first." Mick pointed his fork at her and winked.

"There's no need to flirt with me, Mr. Westcott," she said, and he looked alarmed.

"Is that what I'm doing?" He chuckled. "You don't know me well enough to know whether or not I'm flirting. I don't know *you* well enough to know if I *should* be flirting with you."

"And the likelihood of either is not very high."

"What? Of getting to know each other? It would be if you'd be willing to engage in a civil conversation. I don't know what exactly I did to tick you off, but I must have done it in the first five or ten minutes after we met. Actually, it was before that. Is it men in general you dislike? Or was there something about me that you surmised, based on first impressions, that makes you wish you were sitting anywhere but here?"

Kate felt cornered. He was sharp and perceptive. And assertive. But he was also spoiled and rich. And she wanted nothing to do with him. The absurdity of the situation occurred to her, and she felt the need to point out what should have been obvious. "Mr. Westcott, if you—"

"Could you please just call me Mick? I don't even know *your* last name, and—"

"My name is Catherine Fitzgibbons. Now, as I was saying, Mr. Westcott, it should be obvious to you that I am significantly pregnant and . . ."

Kate heard a noise to indicate that Chas had come from the house into the kitchen of the inn, and she didn't want to be overheard.

"Yes, I did notice that," Mick said. "I'm not blind, if that's what you're implying. And yet, here you are, staying alone at a remote inn. Where, I wonder, is *Mis-ter* Fitzgibbons?"

"There is no *Mis-ter* in my life, Mr. Westcott."

"A significant other, then?"

"No," Kate said with a quiet harshness that she hoped would silence this increasingly annoying conversation. When he *didn't* comment, she glanced up to see a quizzical look in his eyes. But it was the compassion she saw mixed into that look that made her heart quicken.

Chas appeared with two plates of hot waffles and bacon. The smile on her face implied that she'd not overheard any of their conversation, and Kate was glad for that.

"Thank you," Kate said. "I really haven't gotten used to your waiting on me."

"It's part of the package," Chas said brightly. "Bed and breakfast."

"It looks wonderful, Chas," Mick said. "Thank you."

"You're welcome," Chas said. "Oh, Jackson is busy with a few things this morning. He asked me to tell you that he'll be available later this morning, and the two of you can catch up."

"I'll look forward to it," Mick said.

Chas went back to the house, and Kate took the opportunity to say what she needed to say to put a halt to this ridiculous inquiry. "Mr. Westcott," she said firmly, "the reason I'm pregnant and the presence or lack of a man in my life is quite simply none of your business. I'm certain you're well accustomed to getting your own way wherever you go, and having women fall at your feet, but I'm not one of them."

"Whoa!" Mick said, looking stunned. "Was it something I said? Or just who I am? Although, it's evident that you have absolutely no idea who or what I am. If you did, you wouldn't be telling me that I—"

"I know your type well enough."

"My *type?* I'm to be condemned for being a *type?* Is that my blood type, or—"

"I know a spoiled little rich boy when I see one, and I'm *not* impressed."

Mick could hardly believe his ears. This morning he'd awakened with the realization that he felt attracted to this woman. Now he was questioning his own sanity. His relief over knowing there was *not* a man in her life was coupled with a stark astonishment at how cruel and insensitive a woman could actually be. Knowing how wealth had affected his life, he had to bite his tongue to keep from saying that such an accusation hurt him more deeply than he could ever put into words. He thought of his experiences of the last several months, and the changes in him became evident. The old Mick might have thrown back hurtful words, determined to treat her as cruelly as he was being treated. But he'd learned a great deal about human behavior of late. He'd learned that fear and anger were often the result of pain and misery. And he'd made close friends of both ends of that spectrum. He wondered what kind of pain and misery Kate Fitzgibbons had endured. With a sincere desire to find out, he kept his voice calm and even. He wanted to make his stand perfectly clear, but he didn't want to alienate her further.

"Wow," he said after moments of grueling silence. He noticed that neither one of them had even taken a bite of their waffles. "I can't dispute *rich,* Ms. Fitzgibbons, but I will hotly defend *spoiled.* You know absolutely nothing about me. I don't know what your aversion is to my *type,* but your hypocrisy is readily evident. Your speech. Your manner. Your snobbish reticence. I'd wager a great deal that you've come from a fair amount of money yourself. It's not my fault that I was born with a silver spoon in my mouth, but I've spent most of my life resenting the fact. It's not my fault that you were hurt and abandoned by someone of my gender and left to face this pregnancy alone. But since there was a time in my life when I might have been that kind of man, maybe I deserve your disdain—perhaps by some kind of delayed proxy. If you feel the need to tell me off some more and get it out of your system, I'd be glad to help."

Kate was so astonished she couldn't speak. She imagined herself grabbing her plate and huffing up to her room to eat her breakfast in solitude. But she felt as immobile as she felt speechless. She wanted to hurl angry words at him. But *his* words were so genuine, and his eyes so kind, that she was completely disarmed. *Had* she been judgmental? Hypocritical? Obviously, yes. *Was* she taking out her anger over what had happened on the only unsuspecting single male she'd encountered in months? Perhaps. Whatever might be going on, she felt suddenly overwhelmed and embarrassed and desperate to be alone. She rose abruptly to her feet, knowing she should say something apologetic or humble, but she feared she would not be able to speak at all without crying. She turned and left, realizing only when she got to her room that she'd forgotten to take her breakfast with her. She'd just have to sneak downstairs and get something out of the snack fridge later on. For now, her hunger was counteracted by a strange lack of appetite. She closed the door and leaned against it, recalling the exchange between herself and Mick Westcott. And she felt utterly humiliated.

* * * * *

Chas came into the kitchen of the inn just in time to see Kate leave the dining room abruptly. She had come to see if Mick and Kate had everything they needed in order to enjoy their breakfast. When she approached the table to speak to Mick, she noticed that Kate's breakfast was untouched.

"Was Kate not feeling well?" Chas asked, startling Mick from deep thought.

Mick weighed the option of simply glossing over this with these people whom he hardly knew, but his concern for Kate and his desire to be forthright prompted him to tell Chas the truth. "I'm afraid it's my fault. I don't think she likes me very much."

"How could that be the case when she hardly knows you?"

Mick's chuckle was more ironic than humorous. "Apparently what she *does* know rubs her all the wrong ways."

Chas recalled Kate's abrasiveness the previous evening at dinner and wondered if Mick *did* rub her the wrong way. Was it as simple as that?

Feeling the need to unburden himself, Mick added, "She called me a spoiled rich boy."

"She didn't!"

"She did."

"It's not true!" Chas said.

"How do you know it's not true?" Mick asked. "You don't know me any more than she does."

"Of course I do," Chas said, sitting in the chair Kate had been using. "Jackson told me all about how the two of you met . . . and became close. And he told me about your conversation when you came here before."

"You're very kind to give me the benefit of the doubt, based simply on that information, but I'm concerned about Kate's feelings more than my own. Forgive me if I'm being presumptuous, but I've undergone a great deal of therapy in my life. I would like to think it's taught me something. I don't get the impression she's normally so . . ."

"No, she's not," Chas said. "At least not that I've seen while she's been here. Pregnancy can make a woman's emotions go kind of haywire; maybe that's all it is. Perhaps I should go talk to her."

"I don't want to make a bigger deal out of this than it is, Chas. Truly, I just want to know that she's all right. And if she would prefer that I just stay out of her way, I will."

"I wouldn't imagine that we need to resort to such drastic measures," Chas said. "Don't worry. I'll talk to her. You finish your breakfast; I'll reheat this for Kate and take it up to her." She stood up and added, "I hope you'll be staying a few days, at least. I know that Jackson would like that."

"He would?"

"Of course. He was thrilled to have you show up . . . both times."

Mick thought for a moment of how his plan had been to come here, have a good conversation with Jackson and a good night's sleep, and then head home and make good with his parents. Now he felt compelled to stay longer. He wasn't sure if that had anything to do with his fascination with Kate or not, but he didn't feel eager to leave. Although, if his presence aggravated her, he'd do well to just move on—for her sake. "I'm just taking it one day at a time," he said, figuring that covered every base.

"We'd love to have you stay as long as you like," Chas said. "And plan on having supper with us again this evening."

"I'd like that," he said, wondering if Kate would eat in her room to avoid him. "Thank you."

Chas nodded and left him to eat, but before he could pour syrup on his waffles, she came back and picked up his plate as well. "Let me heat it up a bit."

He could hear the microwave beeping in the next room, and she brought it back to him warm. A minute later she went past him with Kate's plate on a tray, and he wondered what their conversation might entail.

* * * * *

Chas went up the stairs to Kate's room, knowing that Jackson was watching the kids while he paid some bills at the kitchen table. She'd warned him that she might be gone more than a few minutes. She felt confused over what might have spurred Kate to feel this way about Mick. She wondered if she should just mind her own business, but she also knew that Kate had no one else to talk to. Chas knew well enough that pregnancy hormones could make a woman more prone to extreme emotions, and Kate had other reasons on top of that which could certainly make her cranky. But she didn't believe that such behavior was consistent with what she knew of Kate's character.

Kate heard a knock at the door and hurried to blow her nose and wipe the tears from her face. She wasn't surprised to see Chas with a breakfast tray, but she was disconcerted to see evidence of concern on Chas's face.

"Are you okay?" Chas asked. She stepped into the room and closed the door.

"You've been talking to Mick," she said with a tone of accusation.

"Yes, I have." Chas didn't apologize. "But you also left your breakfast, and I can tell you've been crying. What did he say to upset you?"

"I don't know," Kate snarled and sat down.

Chas set the tray on the little table in front of her. "Eat. I've already heated it up once."

"Oh, I am hungry!" she said and hoped the waffles and bacon would ease her sour mood.

She was both relieved and disappointed when Chas sat down as well, making it evident the conversation would continue. Her desire to come clean about her unkind treatment of Mick battled with a preference for ignoring the whole thing.

"What did he say to upset you?" Chas asked again, and Kate realized she was being given the benefit of the doubt. Chas didn't ask why she'd been so snappy with Mick; she was assuming there had to be a reason.

Kate couldn't think of a reason that didn't sound trite, but she said it anyway. "I don't know, Chas. He just . . . rubs me wrong."

"Because he's rich?"

"Maybe."

"That's certainly not something to condemn a man over. I know you have some issues with it, but . . ."

"But that's not his fault, I know."

"He's not what you think he is, Kate," Chas said.

"You don't really know him that well."

"No, but I know he isn't what you're accusing him of being."

"And what is that exactly?"

"Spoiled rich boy. Isn't that what you called him?"

"He told you!"

"Since he was a part of the conversation, I think he has the right to discuss it."

"I suppose he does," Kate said and kept eating.

"I believe he's struggled with the effect of wealth on his life, just as you have—even though it's for different reasons."

Kate stopped chewing for a moment. "Now you've got me curious," she had to admit.

"Well, you're going to have to talk to Mick if you want to satisfy your curiosity."

"I'm not *that* curious!" Kate insisted, and Chas chuckled. "What's so funny?" Kate asked with her mouth full.

"You're attracted to him!"

"I am not!" Kate countered vehemently, but Chas chuckled again.

"What's wrong with admitting that you are?"

"Because I'm not!"

"I don't know," Chas said. "Sometimes a lack of indifference toward someone is simply an indication that you're feeling something that you can't see or you don't want to look at. When I met Jackson, I was trying to line him up with a friend of mine. When he figured it out, he was furious. He could see what I couldn't at first. I'd gone so long without being attracted to *any* man that I don't think I knew what was going on."

"Well, that's very sweet, Chas, but it doesn't mean that . . . that . . ."

"Look at yourself! He *flusters* you."

"Yes, *look* at myself!" Kate said, holding her arms up for emphasis. "I'm more than six months pregnant. I have never felt *less* attractive in my life."

"That's usually how women feel, but it's not necessarily true—to someone who is seeing you through different eyes. You're a beautiful woman, Kate. Pregnancy doesn't change that."

Kate stopped to recount the course of this conversation and groaned. Was her *lack of indifference* some kind of admission that she *was* attracted to Mick Westcott? Tears stung her eyes as if to answer the question.

"What is it?" Chas asked gently.

"Maybe I *am* attracted to him. But what am I supposed to do about it? This is not a situation a woman usually finds herself in. Most pregnant women aren't *dating*. The very idea is ludicrous."

"Is that why you felt agitated the minute he walked in the door last night?"

Kate was shocked by a fluttery inner sensation at the memory. Was *that* what had happened? One glance had alerted her to some level of attraction, and she'd slammed the door on the very idea because of her present situation? The thought tempted her to slam that door once again. She left it open, but she knew she needed some time to process all of this.

"I think I have way too much to think about," Kate said.

"Of course. You know where to find me if you need to talk."

"But is Mick going to be there too?"

"I know he's planning to spend some time with Jackson, but it's a big place. We can work around them. Just call me; I'll come up here if you need me to."

"Thank you," Kate said.

Chas gave her a hug and took the tray with her, since Kate had finished eating. Kate knew it was a ridiculous time of day to take a nap; she hadn't been up all that many hours. But she felt exhausted and laid down, wondering if it could be true. Was she really attracted to Mick Westcott? But even if she were, what could she do about it? He probably wouldn't be around long, and she was pregnant, for goodness sake! And maybe he *was* a spoiled rich boy. Chas had said that he wasn't. Perhaps with time she would learn more about him, and perhaps she wouldn't. Perhaps this was nothing. Either way, it took some adjustments in her mind to accept that her feelings certainly were *not* indifferent toward this man. But he was nothing like the man she'd always dreamed of marrying some day. She imagined herself teaching school, married to an average, middle-class man. Together they would work hard and budget to make ends meet and raise a family. Mick Westcott didn't fit the bill.

* * * * *

Once Mick had finished his breakfast, he went across the long hall of the inn to the lovely parlor situated on the other side. Jackson had told him when he'd officially checked in that the parlor was there for guests to enjoy. There was Internet access on a computer that looked like an anachronism on the antique desk, in Victorian surroundings. He looked out the windows, then sat on one of the couches and made himself comfortable, wondering when Jackson might be available to talk. He felt both eager and nervous to have a conversation that he'd imagined for months. He noticed Chas coming down the stairs with the tray, but she didn't see him as she turned to go through the dining room—into the house, no doubt. He wondered about Kate, but even more so, he wondered why he cared what she thought of him. He'd grown accustomed long ago to not caring what *anyone* thought about him or his actions. So why her? Why now?

Mick was lost in his thoughts when he heard footsteps and looked up to see Jackson approaching. "How was the bed . . . and the breakfast?" he asked with a subtle upward twitch of his lips.

"Both divine," Mick said. "Compared to where I've been lately, it's heavenly."

"Where *have* you been lately?" Jackson asked, sitting on a different couch to face him. "That *is* what you wanted to talk about, isn't it?"

"That's part of it," Mick said and shook his head. "I've been wanting to talk to you so badly, but now it's hard to know where to begin."

"At the beginning," Jackson said. When Mick hesitated he continued, "The last time I saw you, you were telling me that your life had no purpose. Dare I say that you seem like a man who has found some purpose?"

"Oh, I have!" he said with all of the passion he felt. "Thanks to you, I found a way to apply myself in ways I'd never dreamed possible. Do you remember what you said to me?"

"In theory."

"I remember it well," Mick said. "You said, 'Have you ever considered how many people in a third-world country could be supported for a year with the cost of a hot car?' And you said that a man with my resources ought to be able to find all kinds of philanthropic opportunities, if I just started digging."

"You must have started digging."

"I did," Mick said. "You also said that the possibility of what I could do put a whole new twist on wondering why I didn't die twelve years ago." He laughed at the thought of how much his perspective had changed in a matter of months. "I think I've healed more since I last talked to you than I did through all those years of therapy."

"Tell me about it," Jackson said, and Mick wondered if this was how it might feel to have an older brother. Being an only child, he had no idea. Jackson was technically old enough to be his father, but what they shared was more brotherly, in Mick's opinion.

Mick launched into reciting the details of his journeys to five different areas of the world where he'd never before ventured. Until Jackson's suggestion, he'd never considered going anywhere that didn't hold the appeal of some kind of tourist attraction. He told Jackson of the reams of red tape he'd had to cut through in order to get into some of these places and remain safe. He told Jackson stories of seeking out humanitarian groups and projects that were already present in these places, but lacked sufficient funds and could always use more helping hands. Mick had eagerly given away the generous allowance his father had always given him that had accumulated in the bank. He had even more eagerly become involved in digging wells, planting crops, and teaching better sanitation. He'd assisted American and European doctors as they'd immunized children and offered free medical treatment where needed. He'd played with children who didn't speak the same language, and he'd lived among people who had nothing. Their lives focused on a daily effort for survival. A day's food to feed the family was the result of a day's labor. Mick had come to see everything differently as he'd come to see it through the eyes of these people. His ability to help, even a little, had humbled him in a way that he couldn't describe, but he got teary in the attempt.

Mick told Jackson how he had kept in touch with his parents through a weekly phone call that had let them know he was okay, but he hadn't told them where he was or what he was doing. He was waiting to tell them face-to-face, and along with that, he wanted to propose a plan to his father that might give Mick an opportunity to actually *work* with him and grow beyond the lost and wandering young man he'd been for years now.

Jackson listened and commented occasionally, but he didn't have to say anything for Mick to know that he was pleased. And that alone was gratifying. This man had saved his life. It meant something to Mick for Jackson to know that doing so might have left a positive mark on the world.

"I'm really proud of you," Jackson said when Mick ran out of things to say. "And your parents will be as well; I'm certain of it."

"Yes, I believe they will," Mick said. "It's nice to think of making them proud. I mean . . . they've always loved me no matter what; they've always thought the best of me, even when I was so messed up for a while there, but . . . this will be good."

"You must be anxious to get home, then."

"Not *too* anxious," Mick said. "If it's okay with you, I think I'd like to just hang out here for a few days."

"It's more than okay with me. It's about time we got to know each other better." Jackson glanced at his watch. "How about some lunch? I've got a couple of stupid errands in town. If you want to come along, I'll give you a tour and we'll get a bite to eat."

"I'm in," Mick said, standing up.

Jackson left for a minute to tell his wife he was leaving, then he took Mick to the office to introduce him to Polly. She was holding her baby, who accompanied her to work, and Mick liked them both. In the car, Jackson told Mick that Polly had been Chas's best friend for years, and now she was married to a man that Jackson had worked with in Virginia.

"That is a great story!" Mick said. "Is it anyone I know?"

"I think he came on after you and I crossed paths."

"I only remember you and Agent Ekert; mostly you."

Mick enjoyed the driving tour of Anaconda, and he enjoyed sharing lunch with Jackson in a little place with zero atmosphere but great food. Mostly he enjoyed the feeling of joy and fulfillment that still lingered with him from his journey out into the real world. For the first time in his life, he felt like he'd made a difference, and he was going to continue making a difference—even though Kate Fitzgibbons considered him a spoiled rich boy.

CHAPTER 6

Kate drifted off to sleep and woke up feeling hungry again. She realized it was past lunch time and wondered if she could sneak downstairs and get something to eat without Mick seeing her. The reasons she preferred to avoid him felt different now than they had earlier today, but she still needed some time to sort out her own feelings on the matter and to gather enough courage to offer a sincere apology.

She went into the bathroom, and the phone in her room rang just as she was coming out. It was Chas telling her that Jackson and Mick had gone into town and would likely be gone a few hours.

"Come have some lunch with me," Chas said. "I could use the company."

Kate hurried downstairs and enjoyed her time with Chas, as she always did. She especially enjoyed not having the subject of Mick Westcott come up at all. Kate wasn't ready to talk *about* him any more than she was ready to talk *to* him. Before the men returned, Kate was holed up in the project room, busy with the sewing machine. She knew it was a good place to avoid Mick. She stayed there a couple of hours, then sneaked up to her room and rested for a while. When it came time for supper, she still didn't feel ready to face this man who had upset her routine—among other things. She phoned Chas and pleaded not feeling well. Chas graciously brought up a supper tray and left her to rest and to ponder.

After eating, Kate got out her cell phone and turned it on, just as she did occasionally to see if she had any messages. The *only* messages she ever got were from her father, and that was only about twice a month. They'd talked about that often since she had come here, but he'd not said a word about the pregnancy, and he'd not inquired over her whereabouts or her condition, other than simply asking how she was doing. Kate had just told him she was fine and they'd talked of meaningless trivialities. At least he called, she thought, which was a far cry above the absolute absence of evidence that her mother had any awareness of her whatsoever.

There were no messages on the phone, so Kate turned it off and got ready for bed, making herself comfortable with a book—as comfortable as she could get with a baby kicking her from the inside. Occasionally she stopped to wonder what gender it might be, and what kind of person it might be when it grew up. But she always stopped such thoughts from loitering in her mind too long. This was someone else's baby. It had to be that way. It was the only possible option.

* * * * *

Mick thoroughly enjoyed supper with Jackson and Chas and their rambunctious little toddlers. He inquired over Kate's absence, and Chas told him she wasn't feeling well. He suspected that she was simply avoiding *him,* but he didn't comment beyond saying, "I hope she feels better soon."

Over the supper table, Jackson encouraged Mick to tell Chas about some of his recent experiences in his world travels. She actually got tears in her eyes a few times as he shared the dire circumstances he'd become aware of, and the contrast of the good things he'd seen take place that had made a difference. Sometimes, it was impossible to make much difference, if any, and it had often been very discouraging. But he chose to focus on the positive experiences, and how they had changed *him.*

Mick insisted on helping rinse the dishes and put them in the dishwasher, telling them that his mother would be disappointed in him if he didn't. He also asked if they might let him cook for all of them the following evening. It was something he enjoyed doing, and he'd not had a real kitchen to cook in for quite some time.

"I'm not going to argue," Chas said.

"Sounds good to me," Jackson added.

"We've got all the usual ingredients on hand," Chas said, "but if you need something, then—"

"Oh, I'll just go to the market in the morning," Mick said. "If there's anything you'd like me to pick up, since I'm going anyway, just give me a list."

"I might take you up on that," Chas said, and Mick enjoyed the possibility of making even a tiny contribution to the lives of these good people during the short time that he would be here. It wasn't difficult to imagine being friends for life with Jackson and his family. He hoped they might feel the same way.

Mick found it difficult to sleep that night while his mind kept straying—almost against his will—to Kate, *aka* Catherine Fitzgibbons. He almost disliked her for how much she made him think of her. He couldn't decide whether he was attracted to her, or just fascinated with her for some reason. Or most likely, just irritated because she didn't like him. Perhaps he considered her dislike of him to be some kind of primal male challenge. Maybe if he could get her to see the real Mick, he might feel like he'd accomplished something on behalf of his own personal evolution in life. It didn't completely make sense even to him, but it was an intriguing thought.

* * * * *

Kate came awake following a night filled with restless sleep and strange dreams. Her thoughts went immediately to Mick Westcott. She hadn't come to any conclusions one way or another in regard to his character or whether there was any truth to Chas's suspicions about her possible attraction to this man. The only thing she knew for certain was that she owed the man an apology. And it was going to take some courage to offer it, mostly because she'd behaved so badly and made such a fool of herself. But she'd brought that on herself by jumping to conclusions and allowing her own issues to taint the conversation—issues that had nothing to do with him. She wanted to blame her behavior on pregnancy hormones, but she knew that had very little to do with it. Mick was right: it wasn't his fault that someone of his gender had hurt her. But she wondered if she had some subliminal fears in that regard. It was certainly possible, when the entire trauma surely had to exist somewhere in her subconscious brain. She wondered if it would always stay locked away there, or if it might trickle out through the course of her life and always taint her perspective of the world and the people she encountered. Not wanting to give that kind of power to the man who had done this to her, she decided that she could certainly have control over what she knew in her conscious brain, and she could be adult enough to remedy her own bad behavior, no matter what might have triggered it.

Kate had done well at avoiding Mick the previous day, but today she knew she just needed to face him. Since this mess had all begun at breakfast, she hoped that she could find him in the dining room at the same time he'd been there yesterday. A glance at the clock let her know that she needed to hurry. After a quick shower, she rolled and twisted her wet hair into some clips that held it in place. She liked keeping her hair long, but she didn't necessarily like having it in the way. This was the easiest way to deal with it, and it took no fussing with a blow dryer or any other hair appliance.

Kate checked her appearance one last time and took a deep breath before she headed down the stairs at two minutes to nine. She stopped in the doorway of the dining room, relieved to see Mick sitting there just as he'd been yesterday, reading a newspaper, his ankle crossed over his knee. Today his clothes were more average looking. His jeans were wellworn and looked like they'd been his favorite for a long time. He was still wearing that scarf. Her heart quickened, but she credited that to nerves, knowing what she needed to say to him. She drew courage and stepped into the room, knowing that once she did he would become aware of her and there would be no turning back. He peered over the paper, immediately smiled, and set the paper aside.

"Good morning, Ms. Fitzgibbons," he said with genuine politeness. "I heard you were under the weather. I hope you're feeling better today."

"I believe I am, thank you," she said. The evidence that he held no malice toward her, in spite of how she'd treated him, certainly made a statement about his character. The spoiled rich boys she'd associated with in the past would have used it as fodder to feed their ego and encourage her to feel guilty.

"Dare I ask if you'll join me for breakfast?" Mick said.

"I'm not going to snap at you like I did yesterday, if that's what you're asking."

He smiled again. "I was more concerned that you'd simply decline. Chas told me that pregnancy can make a woman's emotions go haywire. I just assumed you were having a bad day."

"You're very kind to give me the benefit of the doubt."

"That's *exactly* what I told Chas about her kindness toward *me.*"

"The thing is," Kate said, "I should have given *you* the benefit of the doubt. I *was* being hypocritical and judgmental. I want to apologize for my behavior, and . . . I was hoping we could just rewind twenty-four hours and start again."

Kate saw his smile brighten and his eyes sparkle, initiating that fluttery feeling inside her again. She credited it to relief. All things considered, attraction was simply out of the question. He just wasn't the kind of man with whom she would ever consider having a serious relationship. She felt intrigued enough with him to enjoy his company, but she considered herself too disciplined to encourage feelings within herself that wouldn't lead her to the life she wanted to live.

"By all means," he said and stood up to help her with her chair. He was a gentleman, she thought.

Once they were seated across from each other, Kate hurried to finish saying what needed to be said. "I owe you an apology, Mr. Westcott."

"Please call me Mick," he said.

She smiled and glanced down before drawing courage to look at him again. "I was unkind and unfair. I hope that you can forgive me."

"Of course," he said and leaned back in his chair. "The thing is," he added, seeming mildly nervous, "I have to admit that there have been times in my life when your description would have been accurate. I was pretty messed up for a while. I did a lot of drinking in college, which means I don't remember half of it. I finally realized what a fool I was being, and I quit drinking altogether. Maybe I resented your calling me spoiled because I knew it had once been true, but I can honestly say that I've worked very hard to *not* be spoiled—for what it's worth."

"I'm glad to hear it," she said, feeling like even more of a fool for having said what she did.

"I would assume you have some reason for disliking *spoiled rich boys.*"

"I must confess that my mother, who is all about money and social status—one being a result of the other—has tried to match me up with a few of them. And I haven't been impressed. But obviously that has nothing to do with you."

"Is there anyone in particular?" he asked, and Kate sensed that his curiosity over that was more than just for the sake of making conversation. She wondered if he was flirting with her; she'd unkindly accused him of it twenty-fours hours ago. But maybe this was simply his personality, and she was reading something into his attitude that wasn't there. She decided to just take the question at face value.

"According to my mother, there is. She's had her sights set on Henry as a possible husband for years. *She* keeps encouraging him, assuring him that I'll come around and realize what a great catch he is. I feel like I'm in a Jane Austen novel and my parents are trying to manipulate a good marriage to a rich man, offering a suitable dowry as bait."

"I've never read Jane Austen, but I've seen a couple of movies. Don't they have happy endings?"

"Yes," she had to admit, "I suppose they do."

"I think they usually get the money *and* the person they love."

"I'm more concerned with the latter than the former," she said and saw him smile. It felt a little awkward to be discussing love and romance, and she wondered how they'd gotten here. Not wanting to lead him on—even a little—she quickly took the conversation back to her aversion to her mother's matchmaking. "Henry is *very* much about money and appearances. He plays polo . . . and golf. He treasures his membership in the country club. He works at the family company *just* enough to be able to legitimately claim that he has some involvement. He's stuffy and arrogant, and I don't like him. But my mother is hoping that he'll be willing to forgive the indiscretions that got me pregnant, and that once this is over, he'll still be willing to marry me and we can get on with our perfect, fairy-tale life. Well, life with Henry is *not* my idea of a fairy tale; it would be way too grim, if you'll pardon the pun."

Kate saw Mick smile again and became suddenly self-conscious as she realized how quickly she'd just become an open book with this man. She felt mildly insane at her own erratic behavior. Yesterday she had been throwing accusations at this man; now she was sharing personal matters. Before she could think of a way to change the subject, he asked, "May I ask what your idea *is* of a fairy-tale life?"

Before she could answer, Michelle came in to serve the first course of breakfast, which was always some kind of fruit. Today it was sliced strawberries mixed with plump blueberries and accented with a mint leaf.

"Thank you, Michelle," Kate said.

"Hello, Michelle. I'm Mick."

"Hello," she said. "Chas told me you were a friend of Jackson's."

"Something like that," Mick said, and Kate was reminded of her curiosity over the connection between these two men. But she preferred to save that conversation for another time.

"Where is Chas?" Mick asked.

"Oh, she only serves breakfast on my day off—which was yesterday."

"I see," Mick said. "Well, it's nice to meet you, Michelle."

"Enjoy your fruit," she said. "I'll bring the rest in a few minutes."

"Thank you," Kate said again.

Mick watched Michelle leave the room, then he looked around at the cozy and quaint decor. "What a great place!" he said, looking across the table at Kate. He imagined sharing a meal with her while sitting on the ground, surrounded by curious, dark-faced children who lived from hand to mouth. His heart quickened at the thought. She would be beautiful no matter what her surroundings might be. But all in all, she certainly enhanced the loveliness of the Dickensian Inn. Considering the change of climate in her attitude, he wondered if staying longer than two or three days might be a good thing. He was going to have to think about it and weigh his options, but he certainly didn't feel any inclination to be in a hurry to leave. His impatience to talk to his parents had become overshadowed by a desire to just be in the same room with this woman.

"Yes, it is," Kate agreed, and they ate in silence for a few minutes.

"May I ask where you're from?" Mick asked.

"Maine," she said and sensed his disappointment in getting a one-word answer.

She expected him to ask *where exactly,* or *what was it like there,* but instead he said, "What's your favorite thing about Maine, Kate?"

She smiled at him, glad he'd stopped calling her *Ms. Fitzgibbons.* She hated that name!

"The lighthouses," she said without having to think about it. "Whenever I needed to get away, I could drive less than an hour, choosing different directions according to my mood, and find a lighthouse. I just loved to sit on the rocks and watch the ocean."

"And the ocean looks better when you're near a lighthouse?"

"Yes, I believe it does," she said thoughtfully. "Maybe it's the *concept* of a lighthouse I like. They are very picturesque, but there's a . . . simplicity about them that I like. And their purpose is . . . alluring."

"Tell me," he said, as if she might spout off life-altering wisdom.

Kate shrugged. "Just . . . the way their presence is meant to keep people at sea from getting too close to the rocks. It's a wonderful concept."

"It *is* a wonderful concept," Mick said.

"And where are you from . . . Mick?" Kate asked.

Mick grinned at her. They'd come far in a very short time. He was enjoying her company and hoped she wouldn't be opposed to spending more time with him.

"Virginia," he said.

"That's where Jackson is from."

"That's right."

"How is it exactly that you know Jackson?"

Mick's mood darkened, but he fought to cover it. He didn't really want to bring *that* up in the midst of such a pleasant conversation. It was inevitable that she would discover the truth if she was going to know anything about him at all. It was a huge part of his life, and who he was. He didn't care if she knew. He just didn't want to talk about it now. Then a better idea occurred to him. "Maybe you should ask Jackson that question."

Kate was intrigued by an air of mystery that seemed to hover around the connection between these two men, but she had also felt a prickly sensation from the way he'd responded, alerting her to the possibility that the history between them wasn't necessarily all good. Her curiosity was piqued even more.

"Maybe I will," she said, and they finished their fruit in silence.

Kate was surprised when he took both of their empty bowls into the kitchen, and she could hear Michelle telling him that he didn't have to do that. He lightly argued with her about being capable of clearing a table and serving food. He came back with two plates and set one in front of Kate before he set his own down and sat to eat.

"I must confess," he said, "I like watching the ocean myself. I'm sure the beaches are much different in Virginia than they are in Maine, but there's a continuity in the ocean that I like. No matter how long since you've been to see it, the waves are still coming in and going out, and they haven't even missed you."

"I've had exactly the same thought," she said.

They finished their breakfast while talking about oceans and beaches and lighthouses. Interlaced into the conversation Kate heard evidence of tender and positive memories of visits to the beach with his parents.

"Do you have any siblings?" she asked.

"No, it's just me," he said. "I had a brother who was born with some birth defects and died very young . . . before I was born."

"That must have been so hard on your parents."

"Yes, I'm sure it was," Mick said, diverting his gaze. Kate wanted to ask why such a comment triggered an emotional response in him—however subtle. "What about you?" he asked, looking at her directly again.

"I'm an only child as well. I think one was all my parents could handle."

"I would think having more children like you would be a great contribution to this world."

Kate heard a compliment in the statement, but she also felt some comforting validation that he could never understand. She could hear her mother's voice in her head telling her that with as difficult a child as she had been, it was no wonder she didn't have any siblings. As if her parents' decision not to have any more children was entirely Kate's fault.

"And your parents didn't want any more children like you?" she asked lightly.

"I think they would have *liked* to have had more," he said. "But my mother had trouble with that sort of thing. They call me their miracle baby." He chuckled and tipped his head, facetiously pretending to be embarrassed. "Yes, they still call me their baby."

Kate took in the implied message as well as the spoken one. And she was overcome with deep feelings of envy. It was evident that Mick

Westcott felt loved by his parents. She couldn't even imagine how that might feel. But she also had to consider that this was contrary to another point of prejudice she'd held on to. She'd always equated being raised with money to being raised without love, as if it were impossible to have both. She knew practically nothing about this man—except that, according to Jackson, he'd arrived in Montana on a private jet.

Kate realized she'd become unusually silent. Mick didn't seem alarmed. He just smiled and took their empty plates into the kitchen, where she could hear him thanking Michelle. Kate followed his example and picked up their empty glasses and took them in as well. Then she went through the open door between the kitchen of the inn and the common room of the house.

"Is it okay to just come in here?" Mick asked, following her.

"During business hours when the door is open," she said. "At least it is for me. I can't vouch for you." She said it lightly and was gratified to hear him chuckle.

Kate quickly surmised that Chas was standing at the sink. Charles was playing in the middle of a typical scattering of toys. Jackson was cleaning Isabelle's face and hands with a wet washcloth. She'd apparently just finished her breakfast as well, and she was about to be taken out of the high chair.

"Is it okay if I come in here?" Mick said to Jackson. "Kate told me the rule about the door and all. I just wonder if it applies to me too, because Kate's implying that—"

Kate elbowed him, and he laughed. Jackson smirked at both of them. "As long as you mind your manners," he said.

"That's dubious," Kate said, but she said it lightly, and Mick liked this side of her that was manifesting itself.

Kate moved into the kitchen part of the common room where Mick noticed she quite naturally started helping Chas clean up the breakfast mess while they chatted. Jackson sat on the floor with his children, and Mick decided to join him. He thought of the many beautiful dark-skinned children he'd sat on the ground to play with during the previous months. A part of him missed that, and he hoped to go back to such places before too much time passed.

"How's it going?" Jackson asked him.

"Great! And you?"

"I'm good," Jackson said. "It's hard not to be when life is like this." He glanced toward his wife, then his children, then he smiled at Mick. How could Mick not envy such a life? He liked being around these people, and he believed he could learn much from them about the really important things in life. Which brought him naturally around to a question he wanted to ask Jackson.

"Hey, would you have a problem with my staying more than a few days?"

"You are welcome to stay as long as you like," Jackson said. "The inn has good weekly and monthly rates, and I know you can afford it."

"I'm glad the inn is open to long-term guests, but . . . that's not really what I'm asking. I don't want to intrude on your family life, or cause any problems. I promise not to be a pest or anything, and . . . I don't want to wear out my welcome. I just . . . would like to hang around for a while."

"You're welcome to stay as long as you like," Jackson said. "If you're intruding, I will tell you. I'm not going to hold back to spare your feelings, if that's what you're asking."

Mick grinned. "If I know you'll be straight with me, then I'm going to stay."

"I thought you were anxious to see your parents."

"I am, but . . . I talk to them regularly. I'll tell them where I am. They'll understand. And . . . well, the other can wait."

Jackson leaned closer and said more softly, "Your desire to stay wouldn't have anything to do with Kate, would it?"

Mick felt guilty for a moment, then he saw Jackson's pleasant smile and teasing eyes. "I should know better than to think you couldn't see through me."

"I pride myself on my investigative skills," Jackson said with mild sarcasm. "But it doesn't take much skill to see that you're attracted to her. And she seems a little more warmed up to you today than she was yesterday."

"Yeah, I think that's a good sign. If—"

A chime sounded, and Jackson jumped to his feet, calling toward Chas, "I've got it."

Mick realized that someone had come through the door of the inn, and Polly hadn't arrived yet. He just remained on the floor, playing with the children, until Jackson came back in and said to Kate, "You have a visitor."

It took Kate a moment to realize he actually meant her. Mick noticed her astonishment and jumped to his feet.

"Who on earth would be here to see me?" Kate asked, wondering if it might be her father.

"A man," Jackson said, increasing her hopes. "About your age," he added, immediately dashing them.

"Henry," she said with disgust. "I don't want to see him. Tell him I'm not here."

"I already told him you were," Jackson said. "And even if you weren't, he would know you were coming back. Seeing that he came all the way to Montana, I suspect he would wait until he could talk to you."

Kate made a disgruntled noise and glanced helplessly at Chas, as if she might have some great plan on how she could avoid this encounter.

"Why *is* he here, do you think?" Mick asked, moving past the couches to stand closer to Kate.

"My mother sent him, obviously. No one knows where I am but her. But she wouldn't have sent him here without telling him that I was pregnant. I thought she didn't want him to know."

"Is he the father?" Mick asked, hoping it didn't sound too obnoxious.

"No!" Kate insisted, but she didn't sound offended by the question. "Heavens no! Never!"

"Do you want me to handle him?" he asked nonchalantly.

He expected Kate to tell him no, to assure him that she needed to take care of it. He'd perhaps expected his offer to inspire her to her own ability to do so. But she looked intrigued by the idea, thoughtfully pondering it, biting her lip in consideration. "What do you mean by 'handle him'?" she asked.

"I can either tell him you don't want to see him, or I can fluster him up a bit before you talk to him."

Kate had no idea what he meant by *fluster him up*. But the idea definitely piqued her curiosity. Getting rid of Henry permanently intrigued her even more. She wasn't concerned about Mick embarrassing her or making Henry angry, because she just didn't care. Her mother would be angry, but what difference would that make?

Sensing Kate's need for some direction, Mick said, "How about if I go talk to him? You can wait in the dining room where you can hear, then come in whenever you feel ready. I can keep him talking for a *long* time."

He waited while he could see Kate weighing her options, then she nodded and he went through the door into the inn, with Kate behind him. He turned to look at her once where she settled quietly to the side of the dining room door, out of sight to anyone in the hall. She nodded again, and Mick went into the hall. He almost laughed out loud to see this guy. He looked as if he'd just stepped off of a yacht where he might have been doing a photo shoot to advertise almost anything that would be sold for a high price. He had model good looks, was perfectly groomed, and dressed in a way that overtly advertised money.

Mick stepped forward with a big grin and an outstretched hand. "You must be Henry."

"I am," Henry said with pride, shaking Mick's hand.

"I've heard so very much about you," Mick said. "I don't suppose you go by Hank; some people named Henry go by Hank."

"No," Henry said, insulted, "I don't go by Hank."

"I'm Michael, by the way, although I go by Mick . . . because my father is Michael too, so it's confusing. Although, he goes by Mike sometimes."

"That's good to know . . . Mick," Henry said. "Is . . . Catherine Jane around?"

"Catherine Jane?" Mick laughed. "Do you call her that? Really? All the time? That's how many syllables? Four? Wow! Catherine Jane. I think she prefers Kate, really. At least that's what she told me. But maybe she told you differently. Maybe she likes . . . different names when she's around different kinds of people."

"Maybe," Henry said. "Is she here?"

"Oh, she'll be along soon. She knows you're here."

"*How* does she know I'm here?"

"Because Jackson—that's the man who runs the inn; you just met him—told her there was a man here to see her who was near her age. She said it could only be Henry. And so it is. Mystery solved."

Kate listened to the conversation and had trouble not giggling. She very much liked Mick's version of *flustering him up*. She felt more relaxed about facing Henry, and was more determined than ever to just be completely straightforward and be rid of him, once and for all.

Mick then purposely fell silent so Henry could comment. When he didn't, Mick just smiled at him as if the negative vibes he was getting from this guy didn't exist. If *this* was Kate's perception of a *spoiled rich boy*, it was no wonder she wanted nothing to do with men who came from money. Henry had a distinct air of arrogance. His very presence in the room implied that he considered himself to be of a status high above anything or anyone around him. He glanced around at the lovely decor of the inn with complete indifference. That alone left Mick feeling defensive on behalf of Chas and Jackson. But he just smiled again and asked, "You've obviously come a long way to see Kate. She must really be important to you."

"She is," Henry said, as if it should be taken for granted.

"But the baby isn't yours. That must irk you."

Kate bristled slightly from the comment, until she heard Henry's response and realized that Mick was gauging where Henry stood on the matter. Of course, Mick knew nothing about the reasons for her pregnancy—unless Chas or Jackson had told him. She had no problem with Mick knowing. She just had an aversion to talking about it. She listened carefully to the ongoing conversation, wondering what Henry might say when he had no idea she was nearby.

Mick felt pleased with the flint in Henry's eyes that indicated it *did* irk him. But he coolly said, "Catherine Jane has been struggling to find herself. It was a mistake to let her go off to college like that, on her own. I'm certain that once this is all cleared up, she'll come to her senses and want to settle down."

"Cleared up?" Mick countered. "It's not a bank error, Hank." He could see that calling Henry that was an insult. That's how he wanted it to be. Henry's arrogance was appalling. Knowing that Kate had never shared any kind of actual relationship with this man, his implications were even more appalling. "It's a baby, you know," Mick went on. "Perhaps *Catherine Jane,*" he said her name with sarcasm, "will feel differently about . . ."

Kate took a deep breath and walked into the hall before she lost her nerve. She gravitated to Mick's side. In the last few minutes he had leapt onto a pedestal for her with the way he had so neatly put Henry in his place. Now she just had to finish the job and send him on his way.

"Ah, there you are," Henry said to Kate. But Mick noted that his tone was not consistent with being glad to see her, which was further evidenced by the way he immediately added, "Who *is* this man?"

"A friend," she said and surprised Mick by taking his hand.

Kate smiled at Mick and gently squeezed his hand, expressing silent appreciation for his intervention on her behalf. Then she looked directly at Henry, whose astonishment was almost humorous. She got right to the point. "I don't know why you've come all this way. You could have called."

"Your mother felt it would be good for me to visit."

"I hope that you realize by now I'm not impressed with the way that you're so eager to do whatever my mother suggests."

Henry made no acknowledgment of the comment, which Kate realized was typical of him. If he didn't want to hear it, or he had no answer for it, he just ignored it. Her mother was much the same way. It was no wonder they were conspiring with each other. And Kate knew it was time to make it clear that she would no longer be caught in the middle of their conspiracies.

"Your mother told me you'd gotten into trouble," Henry said. Mick bristled at the way this sounded so condescending. Obviously Kate being unwed and pregnant was far from ideal, but the way that Henry spoke to her made Mick want to give him a fat lip.

"Is that how she put it?" Kate asked, sounding angry.

"Something like that."

"And was it her hope that you might be willing to forgive me for my terrible choices and still be willing to be seen with me once this mess was cleaned up?"

"*Cleared* up," Mick said more to Kate, as if she'd not been eavesdropping. "That's how *he* put it. He said that once it was *cleared* up, you would come to your senses and settle down."

Henry brutally ignored Mick's comment and Kate's visible anger. "Your mother didn't put it exactly like that, but—"

"But that's what she meant," Kate said. "You're welcome to believe anything my mother says, Henry, but she couldn't possibly be honest with you when she won't even be honest with herself about what happened."

"What*ever* happened, darling, I *will* forgive you; of course I will."

"Darling?" Mick echoed. "I can't see that she's ever been a *darling* to you."

Henry looked agitated. Kate gave Mick a brief glance of approval and he winked at her. It gave Kate the final surge of courage she needed in order to get this over with. She faced Henry directly and took a deep breath. "I could never accept your forgiveness, Henry; never. It's not that I'm against forgiveness. But I did nothing wrong, therefore your forgiveness is meaningless."

Henry looked confused, but his voice had an edge when he nodded toward Mick and asked, "Is *he* the father?"

Mick was willing to take the blame if it would help Kate get rid of the jerk. He wondered how he might give her some cue about that, but she blurted with a firmness in her voice that would have never let on to the way he felt her hand begin to tremble. "Don't be a fool, Henry. Do you honestly think I would be standing here holding hands with the man who had raped me?"

Mick felt an immediate pain in his gut, as if he'd been stabbed. A tremor radiated out from the pain through his entire body, and he turned to see Kate look at him as she felt it reach his hand. He saw the truth of it in her eyes. He saw the courage and strength there that were barely masking the pain and shame. It took all his self-control to remain expressionless, to pretend he already knew, and to keep his own breathing from becoming audible. He barely knew this woman. But he liked her. And he knew that *no* woman deserved such a fate.

Mick was brought back to the conversation when Henry let out an annoying, awkward chuckle. Mick expected some expression of compassion or concern for her. What he heard made the temperature of his blood rise.

"Your mother told me you would attempt to offer that as an explanation. You need to know that it's all right if you made a mistake, darling. There's no need to fabricate this story to cover your sins."

"My *sins?*" Kate echoed. She'd expected this, but she was surprised at how unprepared she felt to actually hear it. Her mother's anger and appalling behavior came rushing back, and she feared not being able to hold herself together long enough to tell him what she thought and get him to leave. She tightened her hold on Mick's hand, wondering how she could feel more bonded with him in the last hour than she'd felt with Henry in years. The answer was as obvious as the arrogant, uncaring nose on Henry's face. She took a deep, sustaining breath and let loose. "If having a drink at a party is a sin, Henry, then you have a great deal of confessing to do. I did nothing to bring this on. *Nothing!*

My mother is as delusional as she is insensitive. She saw the hospital records and the police report, but she would prefer to banish me and place the blame at my feet rather than acknowledge that something so horrible could happen to *her* daughter. You're as big a fool as she is if you think that coming here trying to curry *her* favor is going to get you anywhere with me. I'm sorry you wasted the trip. I have absolutely nothing more to say to you." She blew out a long sigh. "You should go now."

"Go?" Henry echoed. "I just got here. Surely we could at least—"

"What?" Kate said. "Discuss my sins? Talk about me coming to my senses?" His eyes stated clearly that she was right, and she added, "You need to go . . . now."

Henry just stood there, looking as if no one had *ever* disagreed with him. Mick said in a voice that was far more civil than he felt, "The lady asked you to leave." Henry still didn't move and he added, "The Dickensian Inn is a private establishment. They have the right to refuse business to anyone. That means you're trespassing. The police station's not far. I could make a quick call, and—"

"You're going to regret this, Catherine Jane," Henry said as if he might secretly be in the mafia and could put a hit out on her.

"No, I don't think so," Kate said. Henry turned with a huff and left the inn.

CHAPTER 7

Kate stood where she was, her hand in Mick's, while Henry stormed out and slammed the door. She started to shake before she heard his car screech out of the parking lot. She began to tally how many steps it was between her room and where she was standing, and the amount of strength it would take to get there. She looked up at Mick, searching for a way to excuse herself and get away before she completely crumbled. She was startled to see a glisten of moisture in his eyes—compassionate eyes. She was grateful to feel his arms come around her, knowing that at least for that moment, she didn't have to come up with the strength to do *anything*. Her embarrassment over crying in the arms of a virtual stranger only lasted a moment. His genuine kindness and caring radiated from him. He put a hand to the back of her head and urged her face to his shoulder. She cried as hard as she had when she'd first discovered that she was pregnant. Except that then she had been completely alone. She didn't know what it was about Mick Westcott that made her feel the need to vent every bit of her sorrow and pain right then and there, but once the floodgates opened, it seemed there was no stopping them. But she sensed no impatience from him; only a complete willingness to do whatever she might ask if it would ease her pain.

Kate heard the back door of the inn open and gasped, suddenly self-conscious.

"It's Polly," he whispered and guided her into the parlor, where they sat close together on one of the couches. He settled his arm around her and gently urged her head back onto his shoulder. "I've got all day," he said in a soft voice, but a few minutes later Kate was able to compose herself. She felt in no hurry to move away from the security of being near him this way, and she remained there in silence for many more minutes.

"I didn't know," he said in little more than a whisper. "Maybe you'd prefer that I *didn't* know. I'm not sure if you planned on telling him, or—"

"It doesn't matter," she said. "I don't have a problem with people knowing. I'd prefer that people know the truth, as opposed to thinking that I'm promiscuous and irresponsible—which I'm sure is what you must have thought."

"Actually, I didn't."

"What *did* you think?" she asked, finally lifting her head to look at him.

"I assumed someone had taken advantage of you . . . broken your heart, perhaps."

"There you go, giving me the benefit of the doubt again." He shrugged, and she added, "You were great . . . with Henry. Thank you."

"I'm glad I could help. With any luck, we've seen the last of him."

"Yes," she said with chagrin, sitting up straight. "Now I can only hope that my mother won't come personally to straighten me out once she finds out how *unfairly* I treated Henry."

"Maybe I should stick around until that happens."

Kate smiled at him. "Maybe you should." She chuckled tensely and added, "I mean . . . it's silly for you to stick around just to protect me from my mother. If she *does* show up, I'm certain I can handle her."

"I'm certain you can, but . . . I've already talked to Jackson about staying a while."

"How long?" she asked, wishing she hadn't sounded so eager.

Mick shrugged again. "I don't know. We'll see."

"Forgive me," Chas said from the doorway, and they both turned toward her. "I don't want to interrupt, but . . . I heard the dramatic exit of . . . whatever his name is, and then . . . Polly said you looked upset. I just wanted to make sure you're all right."

"I'm fine," Kate said. "Mick was like a knight slaying a dragon."

Mick snorted a sarcastic chuckle. "Taking on Polo Boy isn't such a big deal. Now, when your mother comes to visit . . ." He feigned a shiver of fright that made Kate laugh.

"Is your mother coming?" Chas asked with *genuine* fright.

"I don't know; I hope not. I just . . . wouldn't be surprised. She really has her sights set on my marrying Henry, even though I have *never* encouraged it. In fact, I've made it very clear that I'm not interested. We've never spent *any* time together except for when my mother invited him over and he followed me around like a bad penny."

"If she comes, we'll handle it," Chas said.

"Thank you," Kate said. "I don't know what I ever did without such good friends."

She smiled at Mick, and he felt warmed to be included in such a statement, but he didn't know how to tell her that he wanted to be much more than friends—even though there was nothing but this intense attraction he felt to base such desires on. Still, he was willing to give the matter time and careful consideration. The bond they seemed to have gained in the last little while strengthened his hope, but his hope was laced with a slew of emotions in regard to her confession. He didn't even know how to compute such a thing. He couldn't even imagine what it might be like for a woman to be in such a situation, to be hurt so cruelly and end up pregnant as a result. He just hoped that she would continue to trust him to help share her burden. And if she needed a friend, he was happy to be at the head of the line.

"I think I'll go lie down for a while," Kate said.

"Is there anything you need?" Chas asked.

"No . . . thank you; really, I'm fine. Don't worry about me. I'll see you later."

Mick was surprised by the way Chas stayed in the room until Kate had gone up the stairs and they heard a door close in the distance. "Is she *really* okay?"

"She had a good cry, which was probably good for her. Don't they say a good cry is good for you?"

"It certainly can be," Chas said. "I've felt like she was holding a lot inside . . . emotionally, I mean."

She seemed hesitant to say too much, so he assured her, "I was standing next to her when she told Henry what happened to her."

Chas nodded. "She's certainly not trying to keep it a secret. How did he take it?"

"Much the same as her mother, apparently." Chas bristled visibly, and he added, "It's difficult to believe a mother could treat her own child that way."

"Yes!" Chas said with vehemence. "It certainly is. What *little* I've spoken to her personally was . . . well, I wasn't impressed."

"But Kate has you."

Chas smiled. "She's been every bit as much of a friend to me as I've been to her."

"How long have you known her?"

"Since she came to stay at the inn . . . some weeks ago. I've lost track."

Mick felt surprised. Kate seemed almost like a part of the family. But perhaps that made more sense of their instant acceptance of him. Maybe they were just that kind of people.

Chas went on to explain. "Apparently as soon as her mother found out she was pregnant, she got online looking for some remote place where she could send her until it was *over.*"

"*Cleared up,* is what Henry said. But . . . there's a baby."

"It will be placed for adoption," Chas said, and something tugged at Mick's heart. He wasn't sure he would do differently if he were in that position. Being a man, he never would be. But it certainly was a dilemma.

"Is that what Kate wants?"

"It seems to be what she knows is expected of her," Chas said, then cleared her throat. "Perhaps you should ask *Kate* these things."

"Perhaps I should," Mick said. "But since we've only been on friendly terms for a couple of hours, maybe I should take it a little more slowly."

"Defending her against a dragon counts as the equivalent of several dates, I would think." Chas winked at him, then tilted her head. "I can tell you like her. And Jackson tells me you're staying longer."

"So, I'm transparent. What can I say?"

"It's a pleasure to have you here, Mick. Your being here means a great deal to Jackson."

"It does?" He felt genuinely surprised.

"Yes, it does," she said. "I'll leave it at that. As soon as I get back to the kids, he'll be out in the garage doing whatever it is that men do. Maybe you could go keep him in line."

"I think I'll do that . . . for a while at least. I need to go to the market so I can fix dinner tonight."

"I know. I can't wait."

"Did you need me to pick up anything?"

"I'll check and see before you go." She turned to leave and turned back. "Oh, and . . . make yourself at home. I mean it."

"Thank you, Chas," he said, and she left the room.

* * * * *

Once she was alone in her room, Kate had another good cry, amazed at the flow of tears that had been opened up. After getting it all out, she pondered her encounter with Henry. She cringed at the thought of having admitted to him what had happened, and felt even more chagrined at his cold attitude about *everything*. She felt sick to think of the conversations her mother must have shared with him, and conversations they would yet share. But then Kate recalled the things Mick had said to Henry, and the way Henry had been put so neatly in his place. Kate smiled to herself, then she actually chuckled. Even the idea of facing her mother again with the results of this didn't seem quite so severe when she thought of the way that Mick had stood by her side.

With thoughts of Mick, Kate had to stop and analyze where she stood with him. She wondered if it was her imagination that he had some romantic interest in her. Whether or not he did was irrelevant, however, when she considered the present state of her life. But even if she wasn't significantly pregnant, he just wasn't the kind of man she wanted to marry. That aside, he had proven to be good friend material, and she could certainly use a friend. Even in friendship, however, she needed to know that she could trust him. In her mind, she replayed every interaction with him, and her observations of his interactions with Jackson and Chas. She felt confused especially by his relationship with Jackson. It was almost as if they shared some kind of secret. They seemed close, and yet not.

And then there was the issue of attraction. Kate couldn't deny that she found Mick Westcott attractive, but she was far too practical to make that any kind of priority in assessing the situation. Focusing more on gathering information, she recalled Mick suggesting that she should ask Jackson how the two of them were connected. She resolved to do just that, then she drifted into a pleasant nap.

* * * * *

Mick sat in the parlor for a long while trying to assimilate all he'd just learned about Kate, and the strange familiarity he felt here at the Dickensian Inn that made him want to be here, for reasons beyond the woman he'd come to feel so strongly about in so short a time.

He stirred himself to get up and go find Jackson. The garage was more a workshop of sorts, with tools and workbenches. Jackson had mentioned that it was up to him to keep up any necessary maintenance on the inn. If there was a job he couldn't do, he would hire someone and make sure it got done. Obviously much of the work Jackson did himself took place here. The only vehicle in the garage was an ATV with a snow blade on the front. Mick felt sure *that* got a great deal of use in the winter months when the Montana snows had to be moved from the driveway and small parking lot of the inn.

"Very quaint," Mick said when Jackson turned to see who was there, then he turned back to the attention he was giving to sharpening some kind of tool.

"Chas calls it my man cave. Maybe she's right."

"Whatever works, I guess. Can I do something to help?"

"Nope," Jackson said and motioned to a chair that Mick imagined had once been behind a desk in the inn, and had now been replaced by something newer and in better condition.

"Don't mind if I do," Mick said. A minute later he realized Jackson wasn't going to initiate small talk. *He* could initiate it himself, or he could get straight to the point.

"I know now what happened to Kate."

"I didn't figure it would be long before you did."

"Yesterday she didn't want anything to do with me. How could you have—"

"I knew she'd come around," Jackson said, remaining focused on his work.

"You know her well, apparently," Mick said, "even though she hasn't been around all that long."

"She fit in quickly; she feels like family." Jackson finally looked up, just for a second. "Not unlike you."

Mick was stunned. "You really mean that."

"Yeah. Why wouldn't I? It's great having you here, and I want you to know that you're always welcome."

"How do you know I won't take advantage of you and make a nuisance of myself?"

Jackson chuckled. "First of all, after years in the FBI, I consider myself a pretty good judge of character, and I've seen enough of yours to believe that you would never do that. Secondly, if you *did* ever start doing either of those things—or anything else that disrupted my family or my business—I would tell you to hit the road. So, we're good."

"I really like you, Special Agent Leeds."

"I hate it when you call me that."

"I like it," Mick said. "In my mind, it kind of puts you at hero status. Batman. Spiderman. Agent Leeds."

Jackson made a skeptical noise. "You're holding on to childish delusions, Mick. Have you discussed this with your therapist?"

"Haven't talked to a therapist since last year sometime. A very good friend of mine told me a while back that maybe I was getting the wrong kind of therapy. He told me that the best way for me to heal was to forgive the people who had hurt me and my family."

Jackson stopped, set his work aside, and turned his full attention to Mick. He knew that Mick was referring to a conversation between the two of them earlier this year, the same conversation that had prompted Mick to venture out into the world with the goal of making a difference.

"And?" Jackson said.

"And what?" Mick said. "You were right. I prayed. It's not something I've done much of in my life, but I asked God to help me forgive, to help me find peace. It took a while, but it happened one night when I was trying to fall asleep on the ground, in a structure that could barely be called habitable. I'd spent the day digging ditches to irrigate a field that would grow a meager amount of corn, barely enough for a family to survive. Needless to say, those experiences made me realize how very blessed I am. But something happened in *that* moment. My heart changed. The pain left me. I'd never felt happier. I'm still happy."

"I can see that," Jackson said.

"It's as if . . . all those years of therapy . . . and all my life's experience . . . all came together in that moment, like something warm and miraculous and wonderful just cemented it all together. It's like all the darkness was removed and replaced with light."

Mick noticed that Jackson looked as if he might cry. Mick added in a softer voice, "You know that feeling."

"I do," Jackson said.

"That's why you told me . . . when we talked . . . that the most important thing I could do was to forgive."

"That's right."

"Well, you were right, Jackson. I can't even tell you how grateful I am for your advice. On that point, and other things, I've become a different man; a better man."

"I can see that."

"I've wanted my parents to be pleased with what I've done; I wanted them to believe that my life could have some purpose. Of course, I still feel that way. I look forward to that conversation, but . . ."

"But?" Jackson pressed.

"Some time since I got out of bed this morning, my priorities have shifted. My goals and desires are the same. But I feel this . . . instinctive need to just . . ."

"What?" Jackson had to prod him again as his thoughts rolled through his mind at lightning speed, and his heart seemed to be shouting that everything he was thinking and feeling was right and good.

"I want to be there for Kate. I want to make a difference in *her* life. I want to make this struggle of hers easier, somehow."

Jackson smiled and said, "I think you want a lot more than that."

Mick chuckled. "The eternal investigator. Sometimes I feel like I'm in an interrogation room and you can see right through me."

"Oh, I can see through you, but if you were being interrogated, you would definitely feel the difference."

Mick chuckled. "I can only imagine. The thought of that experience will keep me an honest man."

"I don't think you need *that* thought to keep you honest."

"Probably not, but it sounds good. Yes, Jackson, I think I want a lot more than that. But it's so . . . *crazy*. How can I feel that way about a woman I just met?"

"I felt that way about Chas . . . right off the bat."

"You did?" Mick asked eagerly. Such validation felt soothing to his spirit.

"Of course, I let time take its course. No matter how you feel about someone, it takes spending time together and careful examination to be certain they're the right one. Even if the way you feel about her now is for the sake of making a difference in her life when she needs someone, you can both come away with something of value; you can help each other become better people. And . . . if you *do* end up together, I want to be at the wedding."

Mick chuckled at the thought. *"Be* there? If I marry Kate, I'm thinking we should get married at the Dickensian Inn." Jackson chuckled as well, and Mick added, "Do you *do* weddings here?"

"It's where I married Chas. Polly and Elliott got married here as well. But I think you need to exhibit some patience and keep things in the right order."

"Of course," Mick said. "But it doesn't hurt to dream."

"No," Jackson said, returning to his work, "it doesn't hurt to dream."

They chatted about trivial things a while longer, then Mick reiterated that he needed to go grocery shopping so he could get his dinner preparations underway. He went into the house where he found Chas folding laundry on the big dining table, while the children played nearby.

"I'm off for groceries," he said. "You need anything?"

"I need a dozen eggs, and a gallon of milk—two percent."

"You got it," he said. "And . . . where exactly do I find a market?"

Chas gave him simple directions, then a thought occurred to him. "Do you think Kate might want to go with me, get out for a while maybe?"

"I don't know. Why don't you ask her?"

Chas pulled a cordless phone out of her apron pocket, dialed a couple of numbers and handed it to him. "That's her room."

"Hi, it's me," he said when she answered. "I'm going into town. You want to come along?"

Her silence implied she was considering it, but she said, "It sounds nice, but . . . I really am very tired."

"Rough morning."

"Yeah, I guess it was. Can I take a rain check?"

"You can," he said. "And it doesn't even have to be raining for you to redeem it."

Mick ended the call and handed the phone back to Chas before he drove his rented car to the market and not only bought everything he needed for tonight's dinner, but also some snacks and foods that he'd missed while he'd been out of the country. Back at the inn, he told Chas what he'd done, and asked if he could store a few things in her refrigerator and freezer. She told him that the one in the kitchen of the inn always had lots of space, and he was welcome to use it. He promised to share his booty, and told her that anyone was welcome to what was there at anytime. He liked feeling like a part of the family, and hoped it would continue throughout his stay.

* * * * *

Kate watched from her window as Mick drove away from the inn. She hoped this might be an opportunity to talk to Jackson without the possibility of Mick finding her doing so. She asked Chas where her husband might be, and she found him in the garage, fixing a piece of damaged baseboard from one of the rooms of the inn.

"Well, hello," he said. "What can I do for you?"

"You've been very kind to me while I've been here, Jackson. I want you to know that I could never express how much it means to me to feel like I'm a part of your family."

"It's a pleasure, Kate. You know we love having you here. I don't think you came out here to tell me that."

"No, but I just don't ever want you to think that I take your extra efforts for granted."

"It doesn't take any extra effort, Kate. You more than compensate for our efforts by all the help you give us in return. We really are glad to have you here."

"The feeling is mutual."

"And . . ." Jackson prodded when she was silent a long moment.

"And . . . I want to ask you something, and I hope you won't think I'm being too nosy or . . . inappropriate."

"Just ask me, and I'll let you know if it's either."

"Okay. I wonder if you could tell me, Jackson, how exactly is it that you know Mick? Because as comfortable as the two of you seem to be around each other, you hardly know anything *about* each other." Jackson lifted his brows as if he sensed her reasons for asking. She felt no need to hold back; she was way beyond any desire to play games. "Beyond any logic I can come up with, he seems to be interested in spending time with me. I just . . . want to know what he's really like. But I'm not sure that even *you* could answer that question."

"I know some of the most important things," Jackson said, "but you're right, we don't know each other all that well."

"And yet there's a bond between the two of you. I'd like to understand it, or . . ."

"Or what?"

"It feels like he's hiding something, and . . . well . . . it also feels like the two of you share some kind of secret."

He looked surprised, and she wondered if it was because her assumptions were completely off base, or if she was right on and he didn't want the secret getting out—whatever it might be.

"I confess that I have some trust issues," she added, "and I really don't want to spend time with a guy who can't be completely honest with me."

"Then you need to be asking *him* these questions. It's up to Mick whether or not he's ready to tell you the truth about his past."

"His past? If you mean that he had his wild college days, half of which he can't remember, I already know about that."

"No, that's not what I mean," Jackson said gently. "You need to talk to him, Kate. Just ask him."

"He told me that I should ask you."

Again Jackson looked surprised. "Maybe he was stalling; maybe he wasn't ready to talk about it yet. Either way, he needs to be the one to tell you. Simple as that."

Kate was a little stunned to realize that whatever it was that had bound these two men together was no small thing. She almost felt afraid, as if she were opening a can of worms that might be better left closed. But her curiosity—and her need to gauge Mick's character—overpowered any concern.

She thanked Jackson for his time and left the garage, wondering if she was blowing this all out of proportion. It was ludicrous to be taking this whole thing so seriously when they hardly knew each other. She was in no position to be considering a romantic relationship, and even if she was, it wouldn't be with a guy like Mick. He simply wasn't what she was looking for. And maybe she was being just plain presumptuous to think that *he* had any romantic interest in *her*. It was all so *ridiculous*.

The only conclusion Kate could come to that made sense was to follow Jackson's advice. Perhaps the results of that conversation could give her enough information about Mick's character to be able to move forward—or not. And secondly, she had to make it perfectly clear to Mick that for her, moving forward meant simply being friends. She hoped he was okay with that. He was just going to have to be.

* * * * *

Mick borrowed an apron and set to work in the kitchen of the inn to prepare the food he had in mind. This kitchen was more streamlined and spacious, and best of all he didn't feel like he was in Chas's way, going in and out of the kitchen area of the house while she cared for her children. He was sure they could have managed, but this was easier. Chas came in a couple of times to check on his progress, and to ask if he needed anything. He assured her that he'd found everything he needed, and she told him that whatever he was doing certainly smelled good.

"Hey, since you're going to so much trouble," she said, "maybe we should eat in the formal dining room."

"You have a formal dining room?"

"We *do,*" she said with playful pride. "This *is* a Victorian mansion, after all." He followed her into the guest dining room where she opened a door, turned on a light, and said, "Ta-dah!"

"Oh, it's magnificent," he said, noting the long table and elegant chairs that were likely original to the house. There was also an impressive fireplace with a couch near it. Chas pointed out a beautiful china closet and said, "The really nice dishes are there, and there are linens in the drawers. If you want me to help set the table, I'll—"

"No, thank you," he said. "I'm sure I can manage. If I can't find something, I'll let you know."

"Just bear in mind, if you use those dishes, you have to help wash them. They don't go in the dishwasher."

"Oh, I get it. My mother has her *special* dishes. Now, you go hang out with your kids and let me do my job."

"You don't have to beg me," Chas said and left him to his resources. He had so much fun preparing the table *and* the meal that he could hardly keep from chuckling to himself. For all the great experiences he'd had wandering around in the third world, he'd missed such niceties and relished this opportunity.

* * * * *

Kate returned to her room before Mick came back from town. She read for a while, checked the lack of messages on her cell phone, then made up her mind that she needed to talk to Mick. The drama she'd shared with him earlier made her feel an emotional connection with him, but she didn't want him getting the wrong idea, any more than she wanted to encourage a relationship of any kind—even friendship—with a man she couldn't trust.

She went downstairs more than an hour before supper was usually served. She'd asked Chas earlier if she wanted help this evening, and she'd said it was all taken care of. It seemed a perfect time to talk to Mick, if she could find him. She wondered if she should have just called his room from her own. Maybe he was there.

Not seeing anyone in the parlor, she walked through the kitchen of the inn on her way into the house. She stopped in the kitchen when she saw Mick putting something into the oven. He was wearing an apron that she recognized as being borrowed from Jackson.

"What *are* you doing?"

"You've never seen anyone cooking before?"

Kate rolled her eyes. "Okay, let me rephrase that. Why are *you* cooking?"

"I volunteered," he said. "I love to cook, but I haven't had a real kitchen to cook in for a while."

Kate felt mildly curious over that last comment, but she was more fascinated by a man who had full access to a private jet and was actually cooking. She thought of how her own mother had never let her cook, never wanted her to learn, believing it was demeaning. She'd learned many kitchen skills in the weeks she had been helping Chas, but she didn't even know where to start in satisfying her curiosity over Mick's knowledge and obvious passion for cooking. As if he knew the questions she wanted to ask, he said, "My mother started teaching me at a very young age. Sometimes Dad would help in the kitchen as well."

"You didn't have a cook?"

"We did," he said. "But Mom worked with her a lot of the time. And she made it clear that I couldn't rely on other people to take care of me for the rest of my life." He showed that wide smile that she was realizing came easily for him, then he added a wink. "I can even do my own laundry. Are you impressed?"

He'd said it facetiously, but Kate had to admit, "Actually, I am. My mother wouldn't let me learn to cook, even though I wanted to learn. It was *demeaning.*"

"No kidding." He laughed softly. "Everybody has to eat. I would think if human beings need to eat, they need to know how to make something edible."

"That's exactly what I told her," Kate said, and it was the first time in her life she could laugh at her mother's absurd behavior.

"You want to help?" he asked.

"I'd love to," she said. "Chas has taught me some things since I've been here, but I don't know that I'm very proficient at actually putting things together. I'm great at chopping, shredding, and stirring, however."

"And there's plenty of that to be done," Mick said, grabbing an apron that was hanging on a nearby hook; it was obviously there to be used by whichever employee might be preparing food for the inn's guests. While Kate put on the apron, he added, "Cooking classes were the only ones I actually got decent grades in, what little I went to college. I learned a few gourmet dishes that I enjoy eating as much as I enjoy preparing them."

"My mother wouldn't let me *take* cooking classes."

Mick pointed to a variety of fresh vegetables, a cutting board, and a couple of different knives that were set out. "You can be in charge of the salad," he said. "Everything's already been washed."

Kate set an English cucumber on the cutting board and picked up a knife at the same moment. "Maybe it's time to cut that umbilical cord, Kate," Mick teased.

"I'm sure you're right," Kate said and whacked that cucumber right in half.

CHAPTER 8

"If you don't want to tell me," Mick said while they worked side by side in the kitchen, "you certainly don't have to, but . . ."

"What?" Kate said. "Just ask me, and if I'm insulted by the question I'll be sure to let you know."

Mick smiled at her. "That's just it, Kate; you're not afraid to put me in my place, and you stood up to Henry very well. You're intelligent, you're beautiful, you know your own mind."

"That sounds like you're buttering me up for something," she said lightly. "I think you'd better get to the point."

"Everything I said was true. It's just . . . with all those things about you so evident, I don't understand *why* you even have a relationship with your mother, if she's as deplorable as what I'm hearing." Kate sighed and glanced at him, and he wondered if she would answer him. He added for the sake of clarification, *"Is* she as deplorable as I've heard?"

"Probably worse," Kate said. "She is surely one of the most arrogant and difficult human beings on the planet."

"Then you must surely be a miracle."

"What do you mean?" Kate asked, pausing in her work for a moment.

"How does a woman like that raise a daughter like you?"

Kate let out an ironic chuckle and continued cutting cucumbers for the salad. "I've wondered that myself a thousand times. I *never* felt comfortable with my mother. Thankfully, she was the kind of woman who relied on nannies and governesses, and most of them were relatively decent. But she was always scolding them—and me—for things not being exactly how she believed they should be. She's controlling, cynical, and sometimes just plain . . . cruel." Her voice cracked on that last word.

"And dare I say she was most cruel of all in regard to your present situation."

"Yes, that's true."

"So, why do you put up with it?"

"It was only in the last year or two that I realized how she's managed to keep me utterly dependent on her. She's discouraged independence all along the way. I didn't get my driver's license until I was eighteen, because she kept putting off the things *she* had to do to make that happen. She was horrified that I wanted to attend college out of state. It was the only battle I ever really won, but she'd never allowed me to have a job, or have any money of my own. The truth of the matter, Mick, is that I'm reliant on her for everything. Once I have this baby and get through college, then I can get a job and support myself. Until then, I don't know if I have any options." She chuckled with no sign of humor. "At least she's banished me to this wonderful place where I am surrounded by such great people. Jackson and Chas have taken very good care of me. I don't know what I would have ever done without them."

"Another miracle, perhaps."

"You believe in miracles?"

"I do," he said eagerly, followed by a delighted little laugh. "Don't you?"

"When you put it that way, I suppose I must."

"If you believe in miracles, you must believe in God." Mick said it as if her answer to this question was perhaps more important to him than any other.

Kate dumped the diced cucumbers into a bowl and looked at him. "Organized religion has never been a part of my life, but yes, I believe in God. There are too many things that could never make sense without the acknowledgment of a supreme being."

Mick grinned broadly, and Kate realized that he smiled a lot. She had to acknowledge while looking at him in that moment that it was a very nice smile. Impressionable and brilliant. And it made her stomach flutter.

"What?" she asked, looking away. She picked up a red pepper and cut it open to clean out the seeds.

"That is *exactly* how I would describe my beliefs. I love it when things like that happen."

"Like what?"

"Well . . . when you start talking to someone and you realize that you feel exactly the same way about something like that. I just think it's . . . remarkable . . . that human beings can come together like that."

"That's a nice thought," she said, then expounded a little further on her original thought. "If you study the arguments against God's existence, as opposed to the arguments for it, I could never accept that all of this is an accident. If there *was* a big bang, then I think God pulled the trigger."

Mick chuckled. "What a marvelous way to put it."

A comfortable silence settled around them while they worked. Mick's mind began to wander to his attraction to this woman. He could see easily enough that it wasn't just a physical thing. He felt as if their minds were programmed similarly, and their spirits were somehow drawn together. He could never put it into words, but neither could he deny that it was true—at least for him it was. He had no control over Kate's feelings or her perceptions of them. But he'd always been straightforward in nature, and he was finding it difficult to not acknowledge the way he felt—if only a little. Perhaps he needed to test the waters just a bit.

"Perhaps *this* is a miracle," he said.

"That I'm cooking, you mean?" she asked lightly.

"Maybe," he said in the same tone. Then he stopped working and turned toward her, saying more seriously, "Maybe . . . you and me . . . ending up here at the same time . . . with so much in common. Maybe that's a miracle."

Kate's heart began to pound. She glanced at him but had to look away, startled by the sincere intensity in his eyes. She'd suspected this might come up, and she'd already evaluated her own place in this equation. Still, declaring her stance on the matter was not going to be easy. She took a deep breath, steadied her voice, and said with easy nonchalance, "The way you were there for me today with Henry feels like a miracle. You've been very kind to me, and I appreciate it."

"We've come far in a day, have we not?"

"Yes." She tossed him a quick smile. "We certainly have. It's nice to have a friend . . . with so much in common."

Mick put a hand over hers to stop the way she kept slicing that pepper. Kate looked at his hand, then up at him, hoping her eyes didn't give away her true reaction. This intense attraction she was feeling didn't necessarily mean what either of them might think it meant. She had to be practical. Didn't she?

"We are so much the same, Kate. Don't you see it? Can't you feel it?"

Kate looked away. "We *do* have a great deal in common, which makes the prospect of remaining friends a great thing, but . . ."

"But?" he demanded gently.

Kate couldn't answer. She felt disarmed and exposed. And she knew that he sensed it. She could hear herself breathing when he took a step closer, then he touched her chin and lifted her face. She feared he would try to kiss her, and she wondered what she would do. But he only looked into her eyes, as if he were searching for something. Then he smiled, as if he had found it, leaving her all the more disarmed.

"But?" he repeated, more softly.

"It's . . . only been a day since I . . . decided I didn't hate you."

Mick chuckled. "I am *so* glad you made that decision, Kate. Don't get me wrong. I *want* to be your friend. I want to be the best friend you have ever had. I believe that really great relationships always start with being really good friends."

"What are you saying?" Kate asked, if only to stall and sort her own thoughts into some possibly comprehensible words.

"I am not naive, Kate, nor am I prone to rash decisions. Not anymore, at least. I consider myself a fairly sensible and practical person, but I've also learned to trust my instincts and follow them. Doing so has brought some very good things into my life. And I'm not going to stand here and pretend that my instincts aren't screaming from the inside out, demanding that I acknowledge what I'm feeling."

"Mick." She turned her eyes down even though he kept hold of her chin. "This is . . . ridiculous."

"Why?"

"Look at me," she said, turning her head farther away, out of his grasp.

"I am," he said, and she glanced up to see him gazing directly at her face, his admiration completely unmasked. Her heart quickened anew, and she looked down.

Kate stepped back. "You're either blind or a fool. I'm pregnant, Mick."

"That doesn't change who you are. Your mind, your spirit—they're still the same."

"I'm not so sure. Perhaps they're severely damaged. I *feel* damaged."

"You'll heal with time."

"How can you know that? I've researched this, you know. Some women never recover."

"You're stronger than that."

"How can you know *that?*"

"Your inner strength is one of the first things I noticed about you." He took hold of her hand, which made it impossible to hide the fact that she was trembling. She chose to keep her focus on the floor. "Listen to me, Kate. I'm not suggesting we do anything rash or impulsive. Of course we need time; we need to get to know each other better. Maybe it will come to something more than this; maybe it won't. I'm not standing here proposing marriage, but neither am I going to pretend that it hasn't crossed my mind."

Kate looked at him then, astonished at what he was saying as much as she was by her own reaction. She'd put a great deal of energy into convincing herself that this attraction she felt was nothing more than that. She'd believed that she had her future husband carefully mapped out in her head, and that Mick Westcott could never fit those requirements. Then what could explain the inimitable tremor that had instantly reverberated from her heart at the words he'd just uttered?

While she stood there, dumbstruck and completely immobile, he leaned in closer and said with quiet passion, "I don't want to know if you feel the same way, Kate, or if you believe it could be possible. Not yet. I want us to give the matter some time. I want to help you through this. I want to hold your hand when it's hard. I want to be your shoulder to cry on. I want to be the one you can talk to about anything, no matter how sweet, or strange, or ugly. And when some time has passed, when you come past this situation in whatever way you feel is best for your life, we can reevaluate and decide where to go from there."

His words melted her pride, her fears, her misconceptions and misjudgments—of herself as well as him. Recalling what he'd said about trusting his instincts, she realized that she needed to trust her own. And there was nothing inside of her that didn't feel completely good about everything he'd just said. Recalling the security and peace she had felt earlier with his arms around her, she stepped in close to him again, not giving herself time to think about it and talk herself out of it.

Mick experienced a relief that almost made him dizzy when Kate wrapped her arms around him and rested her head on his shoulder. He returned the embrace and held her tightly, praying that this would be the beginning, that it would last forever.

"Are you saying," she asked without relinquishing her comfortable position, "that you will stay here . . . at the inn . . . until after the baby is born, and . . ." She couldn't finish that sentence. She couldn't even imagine life beyond that day.

"I will be here as long as you want me to be here, Kate. I've wasted so many months and years of my life on meaningless endeavors. To be here for you now is the best and greatest thing I could ever do with my time . . . and my life."

Their tender moment ended when he remembered the food he'd left in the oven, and he suddenly feared he had burned it. They both laughed as he pulled it out and heaved a sigh of relief that it had been spared. They both got back to work, and within a few minutes the intensity of all they'd just exchanged settled comfortably into small talk. She became fascinated with his culinary skills as she watched him do things with food that she'd only seen done on cable television. She'd had such things served to her in fine restaurants, but she'd never seen them prepared right before her eyes. Chas's cooking was more homey and down to earth. Kate liked that, and she liked the basic skills that she'd learned from Chas. But it was obvious that Mick treated cooking as more of an art. Occasionally she would divert her attention from the food preparations to just watch the man. Her heart quickened as she recalled his convictions regarding his feelings for her. She was relieved by his reassurance that they would allow time to guide them through what they were feeling, but she wondered if it would make any difference. She wondered if he'd been able to see—or sense—something in her own feelings that she had missed in her neat analyses and predetermined plans for the future. She reminded herself that she didn't need to figure it out tonight. She had plenty of time to be in his presence and gauge his character. Watching him spread clams in the shell into a hot pan, she couldn't help smiling. Life had definitely taken a turn for the better since Mick Westcott had shown up. Being in this beautiful place with people as good as Chas and Jackson, she had believed that she could hope for no better circumstances to help her get through the challenges facing her. But she'd been wrong. It *was* better. And she was glad. Maybe it *was* a miracle.

"What?" Mick asked when he caught her watching him.

"Nothing," she said and looked away. "I love clams. I haven't had them in forever."

"I bet you've never had them like this," he said, but they left them to heat and went into the formal dining room to put the finishing touches on the table. Kate had been in here a number of times, but she'd never eaten here, and she'd never imagined the table set so finely. There was a fire in the fireplace, and the atmosphere was perfect. The babies' high chairs had been moved here for the meal, and it was the only hint that this was not going to be an opulent and formal event.

With the dining room all set, Kate helped Mick prepare the food for serving. There was a chicken dish that looked like a work of art, along with wild rice that had been simmered with savory herbs and a tang of lemon. The clam shells had now popped open and she helped Mick top each little clam with a chopped mixture of something he'd taken out of the fridge. She had no idea what was in it, but it smelled heavenly. He pulled broiled asparagus out of the oven and arranged it on a serving dish, and Kate gave the salad ingredients a final toss in a pretty bowl. Mick had some kind of homemade vinaigrette that had also been in the fridge. She went to get the family while he made the table look just the way he wanted it.

Chas and Jackson were *very* impressed with the meal, as was Kate. Everything tasted as magnificent as it looked. But Mick took in the compliments with humility, giving the credit to his mother, or to his spoiled college days when he'd flunked his math and English classes while he'd been cooking. He told them how he'd grown up with a family tradition that one night a week he and his parents would cook an exquisite meal, but it had to include at least one thing they'd never tried before. After dinner they'd play board games and have root beer floats and popcorn.

"It sounds heavenly," Kate said, envying such simple family togetherness. It made her realize that she didn't have to marry a poor man to create a good home. The thought surprised her as she connected it to Mick. But then, a lot had taken her by surprise today. While Jackson was telling some funny stories about life in the FBI, it occurred to Kate that she'd not had the conversation with Mick that she'd intended to have when she'd come looking for him earlier. The conversation they'd had instead made her fluttery to even think about. But she still needed to talk to him about his connection to Jackson. For some reason it felt important. She wasn't accustomed to quibbling with such feelings; she just acted on them. She wondered if that was the same as Mick's reference to trusting his instincts.

When they had all eaten more than their fill, Kate left Jackson and Chas to clean up after their children, while she helped Mick clean up the meal.

"These dishes have to be washed by hand, you know," Mick said.

"I'm up for it," Kate said and carefully carried a stack of fine china plates to the kitchen.

They worked together to clear the table and see that the dining room was in order, then to put leftovers away and clean the dishes. Neither of them had much to say until they were both standing at the sink, while Mick hand-washed each fragile dish and handed it to Kate for drying.

"Why so quiet?" Mick asked.

"A lot to think about, I suppose."

"Yes, that's true. But I get the feeling there's something on your mind . . . something that didn't come up earlier."

"I admit there is, but I . . ."

They were interrupted when Chas came in to see if they needed any help. They insisted that they didn't, and she suggested that as soon as they were done, maybe they should uphold Mick's family tradition and play a board game.

"What a great idea," Mick said. "We'll be there shortly." After Chas left the room, he said to Kate, "I guess we'll have to talk later. Okay?" He said the last as if he feared she would choose not to bring up whatever might be troubling her if given some time to think about it.

"Okay," she said.

A short while later the adults were gathered around the table in the common room of the house, setting up a game of Monopoly. "Oh, you people don't know what you're in for," Mick said, then he laughed diabolically.

They all had a wonderful time being ruthless with each other over rent and properties. When Chas and Jackson took a break to go put the children to bed, Kate started picking up the toys, as she'd done many times, and Mick pitched in to help her. When she yawned, he said, "That talk might have to wait until tomorrow."

"It might," she said and yawned again. "It seems I'm always tired. Pregnancy does that to you, apparently."

"How about we do this?" he said, pausing on his knees with a toy horse in each hand. "After breakfast tomorrow we could drive into Butte together. We could get some lunch, maybe take in a museum or something, and talk about whatever you'd like—or need—to talk about."

Kate had to admit, "I think that sounds nice." She knew she *did* need to talk to him, about more than one topic. While a part of her wanted to put it off, she knew it needed to be addressed—*especially* after the tender moments that had transpired between them earlier. To have some time alone with him, where they could talk without interruption, seemed the perfect plan. "I'll look forward to it," she said.

They finished picking up the toys, but Chas and Jackson weren't back yet. Mick started organizing the toy closet, and Kate chuckled. "You're OCD, aren't you?"

"A little bit." He laughed. "Not to worry. It doesn't control me or anything. I just . . . get the urge to clean or organize sometimes."

"So do I," she said, and he smirked at her. She could imagine him making a mental list of all the things they had in common. The problem was that she couldn't argue the point. Or maybe the problem was that she didn't *want* to argue the point. Somewhere between breakfast and dinner, she seemed to have lost her mind. Or maybe it was her heart. The possibility was as thrilling as it was frightening. But for the moment she felt inclined to enjoy her time with this man and make the most of it. If he actually got down on one knee and started making lifetime proposals, she'd have to face it. For now, one step at a time was enough.

Chas and Jackson returned with two baby monitors on separate frequencies in order to hear the children if there was a problem. They continued with their game, and the men both went bankrupt within minutes of each other. They stayed at the table and cheered for the women as the competition became intense. In the end, Kate won the game, but the minute they were done and the excitement was no longer present, she started yawning again—over and over.

"I think I'd better get to bed," Kate said while they were putting the game back into the box.

"It's *very* late for you," Chas said.

"I'll walk you up the stairs," Mick said, and Kate noticed a subtle amused glance passing between Chas and her husband.

Jackson and Chas hugged each of them, and thanked Mick profusely once again for a lovely meal. They left the house and went into the inn, closing the adjoining door. Kate was surprised when Mick took her hand, but she liked it. She couldn't be any more surprised than he surely must have been when she'd taken *his* hand this morning while they'd faced off with Henry. That seemed like a week ago now. It truly had been a long day.

They went up the stairs together while Mick said, "I had a nice evening, Kate. Thank you."

"Why are you thanking me? I didn't do anything."

He paused on the landing and turned to face her. "Oh, yes you did," he said with one of those heart-stopping grins, and she thought of their conversation in the kitchen. "I'll see you in the morning," he said and went up the next flight of stairs, turning back once to wave at her. She waved back and went into her room, looking forward to a day out with Mick Westcott. If not for the sensitive conversations she needed to have with him, she couldn't think of anything she'd rather be doing.

* * * * *

Kate was glad to get downstairs a while before breakfast, and before Mick showed up to eat. The door into the house was open and she found Chas there, scrambling eggs for the kids.

"Good morning," Chas said. "How did you sleep?"

"Very well, thank you. And you?"

"The same," Chas said.

"I wanted to let you know that I'm going to Butte with Mick for the day . . . right after breakfast."

"Really?" Chas drawled with a mischievous smile. "The two of you seemed very comfortable with each other last night, but I didn't expect *this*. Is it an official date, or—"

"Yes, I believe it is," Kate said. Recalling Mick's allusions to marriage, she certainly couldn't imply that there was nothing romantic about their spending time together.

"And apparently you're okay with that."

"No one is more surprised over that than I am," Kate said, "but yes, I'm okay with that."

They talked a while longer, and Kate shared a few important points about her apology to Mick, and the things he'd said last night in the kitchen. Chas seemed very pleased, which Kate figured was a good sign. Chas wouldn't have been pleased if she had any reservations about this man.

Chas noted the subtle glow in Kate's countenance as she talked about her budding relationship with Mick. She felt more gratified than she could express. When it was time for Kate to have breakfast with Mick, Chas told her to have a wonderful day, and to call if she wasn't going to make it home for supper.

Mick had only been sitting at his usual table in the guest dining room for about a minute when Kate came through the kitchen. He wasn't reading a newspaper today. He'd just been waiting for her to appear, determined to catch her immediate reaction. He wondered what her mood might be after she'd had time to sleep on his bold declarations. The moment their eyes met she stopped, she smiled, she locked her gaze on his and didn't look away. She was as glad to see him as he was to see her. It was a miracle!

"Hi," he said and stood up to help her with her chair.

"Hi," she said in return.

Over breakfast they talked about the inn, their hosts, the fun evening they'd had the night before, avoiding the serious topics that would come up later. Mick wondered what she wanted to talk to him about. He had his suspicions, but he would be glad to have the air between them cleared completely.

After they had eaten and cleared the table for Michelle, Kate went up to her room for one more trip to the bathroom and to grab her coat and her purse. She met Mick at the bottom of the stairs where he helped her into her coat and guided her out to his rented car. She smiled at him when he opened the door for her, and once he was seated himself he asked, "You seemed surprised when I opened the door . . . when I helped you with your chair. Is Polo Boy not that kind of guy?"

Kate laughed at his reference to Henry, which she considered perfect. "I don't think I've ever associated with a man who was that kind of guy. I thought chivalry was dead. I mean . . . I've seen it in the movies, but . . . this is my first experience with *real* chivalry."

"Chivalry?" Mick chuckled as he pulled the car out onto the road.

"Yes, I do believe you're the most chivalrous man I've ever met."

"I think that's probably the greatest compliment I've ever been given—coming from you, anyway. Maybe if someone else said it, it would be different."

"You were *very* chivalrous with Polo Boy yesterday."

"Ah," he said humbly, "I was just flustering him up a bit."

"Well, if my mother comes to visit, I might need you to fluster her up a bit as well."

"I'll look forward to it," he said as if he really meant it, and Kate felt less concerned about facing her mother about *anything* than she'd felt in years.

During the drive to the city, they shared childhood stories that illustrated the dramatic differences between their parents. Kate envied his upbringing and told him so, but he seemed a little bristled by the comment. She chose not to call him on it, thinking they'd be able to have that long talk later on. She simply said, "I would very much like to meet your parents."

"I'm counting on it," he said. "And I think I would very much like to meet yours."

"I have much more to look forward to than you do."

Mick noticed her putting her hand abruptly to her belly. "Are you okay?"

"Oh, yeah," she said. "It just . . . kicked me."

"You can *feel* that?" he asked, and she chuckled.

"I take it you've never been around a pregnant woman before."

"Actually, no. Forgive my ignorance, but you can really feel it . . . kick you?"

"Frequently."

"That is so cool," he said.

Kate didn't comment. She hoped he wouldn't notice how such a comment affected her, but he took her hand and said, "Is it taboo to talk about the baby?"

"No, of course not. It's just that . . . I'm trying to stay emotionally detached . . . as much as possible, anyway."

"I would think you couldn't help but be emotionally attached . . . when you're physically attached."

"I'm certainly attached," she said. "I can't deny that, but . . . I'm just an incubator, really. This baby is for someone else."

"Is that your final decision?" he asked, and she looked at him sharply, reminding him of when he first met her.

"Yes," she said, "it's the *only* option."

Mick didn't press the matter any further, but he did say, "I think you're selling yourself short. You're much more than an incubator, Kate. Whether this baby is raised by you or someone else, you are its mother. I have a cousin who was adopted. His birth mother is a deeply admired person in their family. She's practically a legend. She gave my aunt and uncle the greatest gift they ever received."

Mick saw the brittleness in her eyes melt into a surprised warmth before they filled with moisture and she turned to look out the window. He squeezed her hand. "You don't have to hide your tears from me, Kate. Just because I'm driving doesn't mean my shoulder isn't available—metaphorically, at least."

Kate sniffled and said, "Sometimes I think you're just way too nice."

"Is that based on having spent your life with people who are mean and stuffy?"

She turned to look at him while wiping at her tears. "Maybe it's simply that you're just a nice guy."

He chuckled, slightly embarrassed. "My parents wouldn't tolerate anything else."

"You weren't allowed to get angry?"

"I was allowed to feel whatever I felt. I've dealt with a lot of anger in my life. I just wasn't allowed to ever take it out on anybody else."

"Did they practice what they preached?"

"Absolutely," Mick said. "I've seen my parents angry, but they were never unkind to me."

"Then that explains it," she said. "That must be why you're so nice."

"Yeah, well . . . you barely know me. Give it a few months and we'll see if you *still* think I'm a nice guy."

"Okay, you're on."

Mick smiled at her reference to some degree of a future between them. She smiled too, and that made him feel even happier.

After arriving in the city, they drove around a little bit, and with the help of the car's navigation system, they found a mall. Kate insisted that they first find a ladies' room, then they wandered around while they talked and laughed and held hands. Kate couldn't recall ever having a relationship with anyone that included just being together, holding hands. All of the men her mother had lined her up with were too stuffy for that kind of thing. She'd dated a little in college, but she'd never felt this relaxed and comfortable. She told him when she was starting to feel hungry, knowing she had to eat frequently if she wanted to feel well throughout the day. They found a variety of eating places at the mall and finally settled on one they could both enjoy. Mick luxuriated over the his steak sandwich, which was loaded with peppers and melted cheese.

"I haven't had one of these in forever," he said with his mouth full.

"Why not?" she asked.

"I've been out of the country," he said and left it at that.

After eating, they wandered around a little more, then Kate asked if they could find a place to sit for a while. Mick located a comfortable little couch in a department store. After they'd sat there for a few minutes, they realized that they were hardly seeing any other sign of human life, except for an occasional customer or salesperson from a distance.

"How about that talk?" Mick asked.

"I guess now's as good a time as any," Kate said, but she still felt nervous. She decided to just dive in headfirst. "It might not sound like that big of a deal, but for some reason it is. When I asked you how you know Jackson, it was obvious you didn't want to talk about it. You told me to ask *him*. Well, he told me to ask *you*. Obviously there's a story here, and clearly you are sensitive about it for some reason. I just feel like I need to know."

Kate saw his shoulders go back and heard him draw a deep breath, as if he were preparing to be struck. When he hesitated, she tried to strengthen her case. "It's evident you and Jackson share some kind of bond, but on the other hand, you hardly know each other. And I also get the feeling that you're keeping something from me. I can't help wondering if one has something to do with the other. So, first of all . . . I'd like to know how you and Jackson met." When he didn't speak, she added, "I've been an open book to you, Mick. You can't expect it not to go the other way."

"I know," he said. "I don't have a problem with your knowing, other than . . . it's still difficult to talk about." He chuckled tensely. "You'd think with all the years of therapy that I would have gotten over that by now. I mean . . . I've put it behind me; I've made peace with it. But the memories are difficult; I guess they always will be."

Kate realized this was something much deeper and more significant than she'd been imagining. The problem was that she couldn't begin to imagine what he might be talking about. He looked down and chuckled tensely. It was the first time she'd seen him truly nervous. "We . . . uh, we . . . met through his work. But it was a long time ago. I looked him up earlier this year. We hadn't seen each other since . . . the incident . . . twelve years ago; well . . . now it's almost thirteen."

Kate put pieces together in her mind and stated the obvious. "He worked for the FBI."

"Yeah."

"You were . . . just a child."

"Eleven," he said and lifted his eyes to meet hers. The residue of anguish there put the final piece in place. She didn't know exactly what had happened. But there was a short list of possibilities that would put an FBI agent and an eleven-year-old boy together in a bonding situation. And whatever had happened, it was still difficult for Mick to talk about. Years of therapy, he'd said.

"What happened?" she asked gently.

"Well," he said with a mild flippancy that defied the hovering sadness in his eyes, "it's that 'too much money' thing. My parents were *very* rich and *very* proud of it. I mean . . . they're great people; they really are. But they live large." He became more serious. "After my dad had let some employees go from his company, apparently for some kind of questionable activities, a couple of them decided they could get rich *and* get revenge."

"Oh, no!" Kate said and pressed a fist to her mouth. Her heart quickened wildly, and her stomach began to tighten as she suspected what was coming.

"Kidnapped for ransom," he said and chuckled with no hint of humor.

When he said nothing more, Kate had to ask, "And Jackson . . ."

"He killed the man who had a gun to my head." Kate gasped and put one hand over her mouth, the other to her stomach. "You aren't going to puke, are you?" Mick asked, sounding more like himself. "Because if you're going to puke, then—"

"No, I'm not going to puke. Just tell me what happened."

"I wasn't supposed to see their faces, but I did. They kept me locked in a bathroom for five and a half days. They always locked the door, except for once, and I peeked out, hoping to escape. They saw me and realized I'd seen them. After they got the money, they were going to kill me. Jackson's timing was . . . well, it was a miracle." He looked hard at Kate. "There. That's the answer to your question. That's how I know Jackson. And that's why I believe in miracles. He never let me out of his sight for a second until I was back with my parents. I've thought about him every day of my life since then. I guess that would constitute this weird bond we seem to have."

Kate nodded. "Yes, it certainly makes sense." She took his hand. "Thank you for telling me."

He shrugged. "You asked. I'll tell you anything you want to know."

"But you didn't *want* to tell me."

"I was hoping to get to know you a little better first," he said. "It's not what I want to be known for. I prefer having people get to know me before I'm labeled *victim of violent crime.*"

As soon as it came out of his mouth, Mick realized what he'd said. The way she wouldn't look at him made it evident that she related far too strongly to the comment. Rather than ignoring it, he said, "Forgive me, but . . . I told you we had a lot in common."

She turned back to look at him with a searching gaze. "So we do."

CHAPTER 9

Kate drew courage enough to finish clearing the air between them.

"Speaking of violent crimes," she said. "I want you to know . . . what happened . . . to me. Whether anything comes of this relationship or not, Mick, I can't spend a lot of time with someone and not have them know the truth. So, let's talk about it and get it over with. I've been to some therapy myself, and I'm okay with talking about it . . . even though it's hard."

"You tell me whatever you feel comfortable with," he said, tightening his hold on her hand.

"I was at a party. Some guy was getting real chatty and he got me a drink. I remember feeling a little light-headed, and the next thing I knew . . . I woke up in my own apartment, in my own bed, but . . ." She looked down and cleared her throat quietly. "It was evident what had happened. I realized that my keys and driver's license had been in my purse; that's how he knew where I lived."

"Did you go to the police?"

"I went to the hospital, and *they* called the police. There was Rohypnol in my blood. They did the usual tests . . . exams. The problem was that I couldn't give a very good description of the guy, and no one at the party knew who it was. Either that, or someone was covering for him. There was no one to match the DNA to. I got so paranoid that I moved in with a friend, and I never went anywhere alone. Thankfully, I had a couple of good friends, or I don't know what I would have done. But I didn't tell my parents. I knew my mother would find a way to twist it and use it against me. She'd been opposed to my going to college out of state anyway. I did *not* need an excuse for her to make me come home. My friends were supportive; I'd done all I could do. I was getting some counseling through the college. I just thought it would go away and they would never have to know. I managed to pull myself together enough to finish the term, then I packed up and went home. It worked out well because my parents were in Europe for three months. That's when I realized I was pregnant, and I fell apart all over again. By the time my parents got home, I was starting to show." She sighed loudly. "And here I am. My mother got online and found a place to toss me within an hour, and I was on the plane two days later."

"How can she not see that this was out of your control? Surely she could come up with *some* kind of compassion."

"It's like I told you, she didn't believe me," Kate said, and Mick felt decidedly angry on her behalf. "My therapist told me she just can't handle the very idea of such a thing happening, so she has to pretend it didn't. And the only way to do that is to accuse me of being promiscuous, and careless at that."

"Unbelievable!"

"Yes, it is. It really is. I've struggled with my mother's attitudes for years. I've hated the lifestyle, and I counted down the days until I could go to college away from home. But I still had a grudging respect for her, and I believed she had the same for me. But this . . . this is just unconscionable. I don't know how I can ever have a civil word with her again."

"You shouldn't worry about your mother right now. You should take care of yourself and focus on healing."

"That's what my therapist said."

He chuckled. "Where do you think I got it? I couldn't come up with sensitive, profound advice like that on my own. I guess therapy is something else we have in common, although I've got years over on you."

He chuckled again and she asked, "What's funny?"

"Do you know how nice it is to talk to a woman—or anyone for that matter—and be able to talk about therapy? I was in therapy when I was eleven. Other kids my age couldn't relate."

She smiled, but it was a sad smile. He touched her face and asked, "May I ask how you're doing with that? The healing?"

Kate sighed and shrugged. "It's hard to heal from something you don't remember. Of course, the evidence is undeniable. But I wonder sometimes if I remember subconsciously, or if I've just imagined how it happened from what I know. Either way, it's . . . disturbing. My therapist told me I'm handling it well, better than most. But I'm afraid it will jump up and bite me someday. And there are times when I don't feel like I'm handling it well at all. I'm told it's okay to curl up in a corner and cry hysterically once in a while, but it doesn't feel very sane."

"Then we'll be insane together," he said, squeezing her hand. "I confess that I know what *that* is like as well. Years after the fact, I would panic for no reason. Or the helplessness would come back to me and I'd cry like a baby."

"Is it possible to *ever* heal from something like that?" Kate asked as if she truly expected him to answer.

"Jackson thinks it is."

"What does he know about such things?"

"He gave me some advice once about healing. Initially I was put off by it, but when I could see how at much at peace he was, I had to take it seriously. When you consider what he's been through, you can't deny that he must know what he's talking about."

"What *has* he been through?" Kate asked.

Mick gave her a sideways smile. "I guess it wouldn't fly for me to tell you to ask *him.*"

"Not unless you think he wouldn't want me to know."

"I don't think that's the problem. I only know the one-sentence version, anyway. He told me that he'd been held hostage in South America for a few weeks, and it had taken him a long time and a lot of therapy to recover."

Kate felt stunned. Jackson was so happy and seemed to have it all together. She'd practically been a part of his family for many weeks. She never would have guessed that he could have had something so . . . *damaging* . . . in his past. "It's difficult to imagine," she said.

"Yeah, it is."

Fascinated by what Mick had said about how much at peace Jackson was, she had to take the bait and ask, "What was the advice he gave you . . . about healing?"

"He told me that I needed to forgive."

"What?" Kate snapped as if she'd heard him wrong.

"That's exactly what I said . . . and that's about how I said it. But he told me that I might think I had a right to be angry with the people who had done this to me. He was right about that. I *was* angry. These evil men with their greed and vengeance had almost killed me. I can't count how many hours I spent wondering what it would have been like for my parents if that had been the outcome. Especially after they'd already had a child die. Nevertheless, the trauma we were all left with was indescribable. I think that whole cooking dinner together and playing games routine was a result of this mass paranoia we had about going out in public. I was a wreck. I spent years believing I was irreversibly damaged and I might as well live that way, which only broke my parents' hearts even more. I didn't realize until later that they were blaming themselves for this; they thought my behavior was their fault. Thankfully we got that straightened out, and we reached a point where we were all doing better. But I felt compelled to find the agent who had saved me, to thank him to his face for what he'd done. I hadn't expected to come away with such insight and wisdom. But I sure got it. We only talked for, I don't know, half an hour maybe. And I walked out feeling like something had changed in me, or at least the seeds of change had been planted, and I wanted to follow through."

"And that's what he told you . . . to forgive."

"That's right. He said that anger is something you certainly have to work through, but eventually you have to let it go. He told me that holding on to negative feelings toward the people who had hurt me was like carrying around a backpack full of rocks. He said you get so used to carrying it that you don't feel it anymore, but it's weighing you down and holding you back. He admitted that he'd resisted forgiving. He even told me that he'd argued with his therapist about it, and he'd argued with Chas. But in the end, he said it was forgiveness that healed him. And he said something about not only having to forgive his captors, but having to forgive someone in his family. He didn't expound on that; he said it was personal. But I think he probably has a lot more understanding—and empathy—for people like you and me than either of us could ever understand."

"Perhaps that explains why he's been so kind to me."

"Oh, I think Chas and Jackson are just naturally kind people."

"But they understand."

"Yes, I think they do," Mick said.

"Did you know that Chas is the product of a rape?"

Mick was astonished. "No, I didn't know that."

"I feel like we're gossiping about them."

"I don't think they'd mind, but if you're worried, we can come clean when we see them again."

"Maybe we should," Kate said and sighed. "After I told Chas what had happened to me, I sensed that it disturbed her. Of course, it *is* disturbing. But after some time passed, she just always got very quiet whenever it would come up. She finally admitted that was the case. Her father died in prison for what he'd done to her mother, and her mother died in childbirth, which is why she was raised by her grandmother."

"Unbelievable!" Mick said.

After a minute or two of silence, Kate said, "But . . . how *do* you forgive something like that?"

"I took Jackson's advice . . . very seriously. On all counts."

Kate looked at him firmly. "What *else* did he suggest you do?"

"He told me to get outside of myself, so I've spent the last several months wandering around the world trying to find myself, and at the same time, pondering forgiveness every hour of every day. Forgiving the men who had kidnapped me was one thing, but he also suggested that I might need to forgive my father as well."

"For what?"

"He suggested I might be holding a grudge against him for being *that* rich. I was stunned. First of all, that he was right, and secondly that he seemed to know something I'd never dared say aloud, even to any one of a number of therapists. Not one of them ever brought up the concept, so I just figured there was something wrong with me to hold that against my father. But when I started looking inside myself for how I *really* felt, I had to admit it was true. If my father hadn't been one of the wealthiest men in Virginia, living large and visibly and overtly showing the world the evidence of his wealth, it might never have occurred to his disgruntled ex-employees to steal his son."

"And you've forgiven him?" Kate asked, bristling inside to think of her own bitter feelings toward her parents. Her resentment was aimed more toward her mother, but her father had been passive and emotionless and had stood by countless times, allowing her mother to be cruel and unfair.

"I have," Mick said with no hesitation.

"And the men who—"

"I've forgiven them, too." He shook his head. "It wasn't easy. It took a lot of time and soul searching, and it took a lot of prayer. I'd never prayed much before. I'd always believed in God. I remember praying a *lot* while I was locked in that bathroom for five days. And I remember thanking God at least once a day for being alive. But I'd never *really* prayed beyond that. But Jackson suggested that there was a reason God saved my life that day. So, I started talking to Him about it. I just . . . had these silent conversations in my head with God—a lot of them. At first I told Him that I didn't know how I could let go of it, and then I remember how I started to feel the weight of that burden Jackson had talked about, and I wanted to be free of it. I started begging to be able to let it go. I ended up having the strangest conversation with a stranger. And somehow forgiveness came up, and he just said to me, 'That's why Jesus Christ did what He did. If you believe that's true, then you have to believe He will take away the burdens that we carry.' I was blown away. It was like God had told him to say it to me or something. I started changing the way that I prayed, and it wasn't many days later that I felt it happen; I felt something change."

"And the pain is gone? The anger is gone? Just like that?"

"Well, not just like *that*," he said. "As I just told you, it took some time and sincere effort. But . . . the pain and anger are gone, yes. That doesn't mean I don't still have difficult memories, and sometimes I can feel . . . sad over the losses in my life. But . . . I'm a different man. Jackson's advice changed my life."

Kate looked into his eyes and saw the evidence of what he was saying. She'd not known him before, so she couldn't compare. But the Mick Westcott she'd become so comfortable with in so short a time was a man completely at peace with himself. His confidence came from a source she didn't understand. Perhaps that's why she initially felt uncomfortable around him, and why she now just wanted to be in his presence every minute. And it only took a moment for her to conclude, "It would probably be wise for me to take Jackson's advice as well, because I certainly don't want to carry all of this around for the rest of my life."

"All of this?"

"You know what I'm talking about. Are you just trying to get me to say it?"

"Maybe."

"Okay, I'll say it. I'm the victim of a violent crime, even if I can't remember it. And I feel more hate than love for my parents. Or maybe it's that I want so desperately for them to give me some evidence that they love me, and I can only feel hateful that they don't come through."

"And maybe when you stop expecting them to do something they're not capable of doing, you can forgive them and find your own life."

Kate looked at him again, amazed at his wisdom and insight. And his empathy. If she wasn't falling in love with this man, she would be a fool. Or, more accurately, she probably needed to acknowledge that she *was* falling in love with him. The thought quickened her heart, as if it meant to tell her that she *would* be a fool to believe she could ever find a better man than this, and she should trust what her deepest instincts were telling her.

Kate realized she was staring at him the same moment she realized he was staring at her. If only to avoid having him ask her the reasons—which would make it necessary to explain herself—she asked him first. "What are you thinking about now?"

"You really want to know?"

"Will it scare me?" she asked playfully, but at this point, she didn't think that anything he could tell her would put her off.

"Maybe," he said. "But if it does, you can tell me."

"Out with it."

"I want to kiss you," he said. Kate gasped. It didn't scare her, although it did take her off guard. But it only took a moment to know that she wanted him to. And she certainly didn't have any reason to oppose the idea. That recently familiar fluttering inside forced her to acknowledge that she was intensely attracted to this man. But she wasn't *only* attracted to him with this budding desire she felt to be close to him. She was attracted to his peace, his strength, his compassion, and his sensitivity. She became so consumed with a myriad of feelings that she had to look away or she feared she might get light-headed and she'd have to blame it on her pregnancy to keep from embarrassing herself.

Feeling the need for some casual conversation to help maintain her balance, she said, "If you kiss me here, someone might see us."

Mick looked around. "There's not a person in sight."

"Regardless, we are in public together. People will believe you're the father of my baby."

"Should I be concerned about what perfect strangers think about *anything?*"

"No, but . . ." She looked at him again. "What about . . . in general? Do you really want to be romantically involved with a woman in my condition?"

"I don't care about your *condition,* Kate. And the only people whose opinions matter to me are my parents. They would be *very* disappointed in me if they thought I was the father of your baby. They would want to know why I hadn't married you and made it right. But they're not here; no one is here. And you're avoiding the question."

"Was it a question? I thought it was a statement."

"Do you want me to ask?"

"No," she said, smiling, "I just want you to kiss me."

Kate had been kissed before, but not much. And she'd *never* felt like *this* before. She already felt like a cube of butter in a microwave even before he tilted his head and closed his eyes. When their lips met with gentle sincerity, Kate felt no fireworks bursting inside of her, and she didn't hear violins playing in her head. But it was likely the sweetest moment of her life—so far. Even with the slightest possibility of Mick becoming a part of her future, the possibility of more such moments was easy to imagine. She opened her eyes to find him looking at her, his face so close that she could see every detail in the color of his eyes. He pressed his nose to hers and chuckled, then he tilted his face and kissed her again. Before it was over, Kate put her fingertips on both sides of his face, not with enough strength to hold him there, but just enough to let him know that she didn't want it to end. She felt the tiniest hint of passion creep through his affection before he eased back and smiled. Such a brilliant smile. Only then did it occur to her that after what had happened to her—even though she couldn't remember it—she had felt some fear that a moment such as this might be marred by subconscious memories. But she felt nothing negative at all, only a hope that this was not too good to be true, and that she might have truly found the man who could make her happy for the rest of her life.

They sat together in silence for a few minutes, as if there was nothing to say that might not dilute the magic of the moment. He put his arm around her, and she put her head in that comfortable place on his shoulder that she'd discovered just yesterday following Henry's visit. It seemed a week ago—or a month.

He stood up with no warning and held out a hand for her. "Come along," he said. "Let's go find a museum or something. I need a distraction. Although," he winked, "I don't think we can find anything so fine to look at that will *really* distract me from such beauty."

"If you keep saying things like that, you'll never get rid of me."

"Then I'll keep saying things like that." He chuckled and put his arm around her shoulders as they walked. "Does that mean you might possibly consider me as husband material?"

"I might consider it," she said lightly. "Although, I might have preferred someone who was more . . . average."

"Average?" He sounded insulted.

"You know . . . average, working, middle-class kind of guy."

"Oh, you want a man who has to work for a living, so he'll appreciate the value of money."

"Something like that."

"What a relief," he said. "By average I thought you meant dull. I try very hard not to be dull."

"That's not a problem."

"As for the other, I'm done being a spoiled rich boy. I am even now secretly preparing to offer my father a proposal that I'm hoping he won't be able to refuse. With any luck he'll finally put me to work with a *real* job and your wish could come true."

Kate made a noise to indicate she was intrigued. "Secret, huh? Does that mean you're not going to tell me?"

"I need to talk to my parents first. If it goes awry, I'll be less embarrassed that way."

"I see. And when are you going to talk to them?"

"Soon, I hope. I'll keep you up to date on that."

"Okay," she said. "I'm hungry."

"Again?" he laughed.

"Just take me to a drive-through somewhere on the way to the museum, and I'll be good until dinner."

"As you wish, my lady," he said and took her hand to kiss it.

* * * * *

Mick found what he said appeared to be a museum with the potential to distract him from Kate, but while they wandered around and perused many beautiful things with historic significance, Kate often found him looking at *her*. If Henry had looked at her that way, she would have wanted to slap him. But that's because she knew that Henry's reasons for doing so would have been phony and pretentious. Then it occurred to her that someone like Henry would have *never* looked at her that way. He might be prone to consider his own reflection in a mirror with such adoration, but never *her*.

Kate had to sit down at regular intervals when her lower back began to hurt—as it often did when she was on her feet too much. But Mick was completely patient, and they sat together holding hands and talking in between their explorations. When Kate felt hungry again, she used Mick's cell phone to call Chas and tell her they wouldn't be home for supper. Mick took her out for a nice dinner, and they sat across a candle-lit table and talked long after the dishes had been cleared away.

By the time they got back to Anaconda, the inn had been locked up for the night, and Mick had to use the key he'd been given to get in the door. He held her hand as they moved quietly through the dimly lit hallway and up the first flight of stairs. On the landing, near the door to her room, Mick thanked her for a perfect day. He touched her hair before he kissed her good-night, then he went up the next flight of stairs to his own room.

Kate was so tired she could hardly find the energy to get ready for bed, and once she did she doubted she could sleep while memories of her *perfect day* played over and over in her mind. Mick Westcott had changed her life. He'd made her believe in miracles.

* * * * *

Kate woke up in the night to use the bathroom, then she went back to sleep and didn't wake up again until the room was filled with daylight. She glanced at the clock and gasped. She'd missed breakfast! It had happened on occasion, but she'd especially been looking forward to breakfast with Mick. As always, when Kate missed a meal, she found a note that Chas had slid under her door.

Mick thinks he must have worn you out yesterday. I can't wait to hear about that! As always, your breakfast is in the fridge whenever you want it. Mick told me to tell you he had some errands and he'd see you later. You know where to find me. Chas

Kate grabbed one of her hidden snacks to tide her over, then she hurried to shower and go downstairs, anxious to share all of her newfound feelings with Chas. They had a good visit while Kate ate her breakfast, then she took the opportunity to play with the children while Chas accomplished some tasks without interruption. The two women continued their conversation while Kate helped Chas fold laundry.

Jackson came in and took one look at Kate before he said, *"You* sure look happy."

"Do I?"

"Is romance in the air?"

"It certainly is!" Chas said. "You know, when we both had those impressions that people would come to our inn and find healing and peace, I don't think we foresaw matchmaking in the mix."

"We're just getting to know each other," Kate said. "I don't think any of us should be jumping to conclusions."

"No, of course not," Chas said. "But it worked for Polly and Elliott."

"They met here?" Kate asked.

Chas nodded and said, "Maybe it's the magic of the inn."

"It worked for us," Jackson said, winking at his wife. Then he looked at Kate. "Whatever happens between you and Mick, I'm sure the two of you can make a positive contribution to each other's lives. That's what's important right now."

"I would agree with that wholeheartedly," Kate said. "I think we're both very sensible, and . . ."

"And they're also head over heels in love," Chas said. "Don't let her fool you."

"We'll just give it some time," Kate said, but she felt herself blushing and knew it didn't go unnoticed.

A while later Kate went to the project room and quickly found something to occupy her time. She knew Jackson or Chas would tell Mick where to find her when he came back. She hoped it wouldn't be too long.

* * * * *

Mick stopped at a few places in town to get some things he needed, consciously getting a feel for the layout of the city since he was planning to settle in here for a while. Once his errands were completed, he found an out-of-the-way place to park his car so that he could make a phone call and not be interrupted or overheard. Calculating the time in Virginia, he hoped that this was a typical Saturday and someone would answer the phone. He always called his parents at least once a week, and it had been exactly that long. When he heard his father say hello, he actually laughed before he responded. "Hey, Dad."

"Mick!" his father said with enthusiasm. "What a nice surprise." He then said more faintly, "It's Mick," and Mick knew he was telling his mother.

"I bet I know what you're doing," Mick said. "You're lounging around in your P.J.s and cooking a ten-course brunch."

"Just ate it," Mike Westcott said. "Although it was more like five courses. Don't exaggerate."

"I bet I can guess what you ate," Mick said. "Hash browns, sausage, poached eggs, muffins, and . . . a fruit smoothie."

"It was bacon, not sausage. And how did you know that?"

"It's a process of elimination. I know what you ate the last two Saturdays, and you do this rotation thing."

"So, we're predictable. *You're* not. Where are you now? Or are you still going to be cryptic about that?"

Mick chuckled, recalling how he'd made a bit of a game out of his travels these last several months. He'd told his parents he was trying to find himself, and he was searching the world. He'd assured them that he was safe and he was being good. But he hadn't told them anything else. He wanted to save that for the carefully planned conversation that had been brewing in his head. "Actually," he drawled, "I'm back in the country. No more guessing games. I'm in Montana. I'm staying at that bed-and-breakfast I told you about . . . the one now owned by Agent Leeds."

"How *is* Agent Leeds?" Mike asked with fondness in his voice. Jackson Leeds was practically a legend in their family.

"He's great, although I don't think he likes being called an agent anymore. He's been very kind to me; but you'd expect that."

"Yes, I think we would," Mike said. "And when do we get to see you again? It's been months. I wouldn't be much of a father if I didn't tell you that we miss you dreadfully."

"I miss you too, Dad; both of you. That's what I wanted to talk to you about. Can you put Mom on too?"

"Just a second. I'll get her on the extension."

Mick could hear his father quietly telling his mother that their son was back in the States and staying with Agent Leeds. Even from what little he could overhear, he could tell she was pleased. A moment later he heard her say into the phone, "Okay, I'm here. How are you?"

"I'm great, Mom. How are you?"

"Oh, it's so good to hear your voice," Joy Westcott said. "And you *sound* great."

"I really am. It's nice to hear your voice too. Are you there too, Dad?"

"I'm here," Mike said.

"Are you both sitting down? Because I want to talk you into something."

"Something fun, I hope," Joy said.

"Oh, *very* fun," Mick replied with a chuckle. "The thing is . . . I was planning to stop here to talk to Jackson—formerly known as Agent Leeds—and then I was going to come home. But there's been a little cog in my plans, and I'm going to stay here at the inn for a while . . . months maybe."

"Months?" Mike asked. "May we ask why?"

"There're two reasons, but . . . they're kind of the same reason. Maybe there're three reasons, but—"

"Just get to the point, son," Mike said.

"First of all, it's wonderful getting to know Jackson and his wife; they're incredible people. And the inn is great. But the really important reason is that . . . well, it's a girl. There's a remarkable young woman staying here, and quite frankly, I'm . . . well, I don't know for sure, but I think she might be the one."

"Really?" Joy said, completely thrilled, not at all concerned.

"We need to meet this woman," Mike said.

"Yes, you do!" Mick said with enthusiasm. "The thing is . . . she can't fly at the moment, or I'd bring her there. This is the sitting down part. She's pregnant." He heard gasps, and quickly added, "It's not mine! I promised I would give up that kind of thing until I found the right girl. And I have. Honest. I think her due date is in January, and I just met her, so I'm not to blame. Promise."

"Okay," Joy said. "I'm glad of that, but—"

"Let me finish before you ask, and then I'll answer your questions. Her mother sent her to stay at the inn until the baby was born; she's planning to put it up for adoption. She was raped."

Mick heard his mother gasp and his father make a noise of concern. Mick went on. "She's handling it very well, from what I can see, but there's definitely something good between us, and I feel like staying here and helping her through this is probably the best thing I could be doing with my time right now . . . if you're okay with that."

"Of course we're okay with that," Mike said. "You know we're okay with whatever you choose to do. You've come a long way, and we know you'll do what you feel is best."

"I just have to keep checking," Mick said. "You guys really are the greatest. So, the thing is . . . I want you to meet her, and I really want to see you guys, and I want to tell you what I've been doing, so . . . would you consider coming here for a few days? The inn is beautiful! And Jackson tells me there are plenty of rooms available. Even on the weekends there's at least one room open. You couldn't spend your money on better lodging anywhere in the country. What do you think?"

"I think it's a wonderful idea!" Joy said with overt enthusiasm. "I've been trying to get your father away from all that dreadful business for months. We could use a little vacation."

"Dad?" Mick asked.

"I don't see why not. If I go into the office on Monday, I can finish up a couple of things and make some assignments. We could leave on Tuesday, I think."

"Oh, that's great!" Mick said.

"I assume the plane is in Montana with you."

"Yeah, Tony's hanging out in Butte."

"Well, why don't you send Tony here to pick us up."

"I'll do that," Mick said. "I'll e-mail you the address of the inn and all that. Let me know when to expect you."

"We'll be in touch," Mike said.

"Tell us more about this girl," Joy said, and they spent nearly half an hour talking about the fine qualities of Kate Fitzgibbons. Mick told them a little about the situation with her parents, and they were both astonished. They also thought the common ground between the two of them was rather remarkable.

"You know," Mike said, "I don't believe in arranged marriages, but I do believe that when you're matched up with someone with a similar background, it can prevent a lot of challenges—as long as you have the same beliefs about the important things."

"I know, Dad; so you've taught me."

"Are you in love with her?" Joy asked.

"I believe I am," Mick said, "but since I haven't admitted that to *her* yet, we should probably let that be our secret for the time being."

"You let us know when you spill the beans," Mike said, "and if she loves you too, then we'll have some good things on the horizon."

"Yes, we will," Mick said, very much liking that idea.

CHAPTER 10

Kate took a break from her sewing when she heard Chas and Polly laughing in the office. She entered the room, saying, "Can I crash the party? Or is this an exclusive gathering?"

"The more the merrier," Chas said.

"Hey." Polly batted her eyelashes exaggeratedly. "I hear that love is in the air."

"Well . . ." Kate said, "let's just say there's some really strong 'like' in the air. But I can't help hoping."

The phone rang and Chas picked it up, saying, "Dickensian Inn. May I help you?"

"I certainly hope so," Mick said, and Chas laughed.

"It's your boyfriend," Chas said to Kate without even trying to lower her voice.

"Ooh, I'm her boyfriend?" Mick said. "Tell her I'm honored."

"He says he's honored," Chas said to Kate.

"That's so sweet," Polly said loudly enough for Mick to hear.

"What's going on there?" Mick demanded. "Are you people getting any work done?"

"None whatsoever," Chas said. "And who are you to talk?"

"Okay, okay," Mick said. "Well, this is a business call. My parents are coming to stay next week."

"Really?" Chas's excitement was evident.

"Jackson told me there were rooms available, but I want to make an official reservation. They're coming Tuesday if my father can get the business under control."

"Okay, it's done," Chas said, writing in the reservation book while they spoke. "How many nights?"

"I'm guessing three or four, but I'm not sure."

"It doesn't matter. I'll keep a room open over the weekend, just in case."

"Thank you," Mick said.

"I'm looking forward to meeting them. I'm sure Jackson will be thrilled to meet them as well."

"Jackson already has," Mick said.

"Oh, of course," Chas said, "but it's been a long time. This will be a nice reunion. We'll make sure to plan some meals together . . . if you want, of course."

"I was hoping for that," Mick said. "We'll work out the details. Thank you, Chas. Tell Kate I've got one more errand, and then I'll be home."

Mick smiled as he said the word *home.* The inn felt more like a home away from home than any place ever had.

"I'll tell her," Chas said and ended the call.

"What was that all about?" Kate said.

"His parents are coming to stay at the inn next week," Chas said.

"Oh my," Kate said and put a hand to her heart.

"Are you nervous?" Polly asked.

"A little, maybe," Kate said. "But he's told me they're wonderful people."

"Then I'm sure it's nothing to worry about."

"Except that his girlfriend is pregnant. I wonder if he warned them about that."

"Just ask him," Chas said. "I'm sure everything will be fine."

"What was that about . . . a reunion?" Kate asked.

"He reminded me that Jackson has already met his parents, but it's been years, of course."

"Oh, of course," Kate said. "Then that will be a *poignant* reunion."

"Yes, I suppose it will," Chas said. "Oh . . . he said to tell you he has one more stop to make, and then he'll be *home.*" She smiled and raised her brows comically. "Apparently he likes it here, and I think it mostly has to do with you."

"The inn is a wonderful place to stay," Kate said on her way out of the room.

She went back to her sewing, anticipating Mick's return. And she had to admit that she was looking forward to meeting his parents.

While there was some nervousness involved, she had no reason to believe it wouldn't be a positive experience. With everything he'd told her, she imagined them to be all that she'd wished her own parents could be. She just hoped they were okay with the pregnancy thing.

* * * * *

When Mick pulled the car into the parking lot of the inn, he felt an unexpected quickening of his heart at the thought of just seeing Kate. He practically ran inside, where he found Polly in the office.

"Hey," he said to her, "how are you?"

"I'm great. How are you?"

"The same. Do you know where—"

"The project room," Polly said with a knowing smile.

"The *what?*" Mick asked.

"That's what it's been dubbed. Kate's been making good use of it." She pointed. "Across the hall and down a little. The door's open. You can't miss it."

"Thank you," Mick said and entered the *project room* to see Kate with her back to the door, sitting at a long table. The sound of his coming in was lost in the noise of the sewing machine she was using. Mick glanced around the room at tables filled with an odd variety of items, and packing boxes spread over the floor. There were piles of fabric and packing supplies. He couldn't begin to imagine what kind of project she was involved in, but he felt a warm chill rush over him as he took in the contents of the room once more before focusing on the woman who consumed his thoughts every waking minute. Even from behind she was beautiful

"Boo!" he said, and Kate jumped slightly before she turned and glared at him for startling her. "Sorry," he added, and her countenance warmed immediately, then brightened. She stood and turned to face him. He couldn't resist hugging her, and she accepted his embrace eagerly. It felt so good to hold her that he didn't let go right away. As he eased her closer, her pregnant belly prevented him from holding her *too* close. He glanced down and said somewhat mischievously, "It's like a little chaperone."

Kate smiled and said, "I didn't take you for the kind of guy that would need a chaperone."

"No, but . . . it's kind of funny."

"I suppose," she said and stepped back, but not before she gave him a quick kiss. "I missed you," she admitted. Kate noted her own behavior and hoped she wasn't being too forward—or gullible. She realized that in a very short time she had completely opened herself to him. She had no desire nor intention to play games, or to pretend to feel anything different than what she felt. She just hoped that she wasn't setting herself up for a fall. Looking into his eyes, she believed he would never hurt her. She hoped her instincts were on track.

"I missed you too," he said. He looked around the room again. "What *are* you up to in here? It's like some kind of mini warehouse."

"Something like that," she said and felt some excitement at sharing with Mick what she'd been doing. "You sure you want to know? It might seem kind of strange."

"Of course I want to know. One of these days—very soon—I'm going to share my secret project with you. It'll put a whole new slant on *strange.*"

"When?" she asked.

"I'm working on getting it all put together to share with my parents when they come. I can share it with all of you at the same time—if you're okay with that."

"Of course," she said. "Chas told me they were coming. Should I be nervous?"

"Not even a *little* bit. I told them all about you and they're already in love with you."

Kate wondered about the implication of that word *love* coming up, but she skipped over it to address her most prominent concern. "Did you tell them about the pregnancy?"

"I did," he said. "Better to tell them over the phone than have them walk in and wonder if I've been a bad boy or something."

"Yes, of course," she said, looking down.

"Hey," he said, taking hold of her chin. "There's nothing to feel ashamed of . . . or guilty for. They know the reason, and they were nothing but concerned for you."

"My mother could take a lesson."

"Yes, she could," Mick said with compassion. "So . . . tell me what you're doing."

"Well . . ." Kate looked around, wondering where to begin. "When I first came here, I was bored out of my mind. I asked Chas if there was something I could do to help, but as you well know, everything around here runs perfectly smoothly without any intervention from me. I'd always wanted to learn to cook . . . and to sew . . . but my mother never approved, as I've told you before. Chas told me she had committed to hemming some little blankets for a church project, and she asked if I would like to do it. She taught me how, and I did it. I enjoyed it so much that I went to buy more fabric and kind of went crazy with it."

Mick noticed some folded blankets on one of the tables, but stated the obvious, "There's a lot more in here than just blankets."

"That was just the beginning," Kate said, and he noticed a light of excitement in her eyes that he'd never seen before.

"Chas told me that the blankets were to put into little kits that were being shipped to third-world countries for a humanitarian project."

Mick coughed in an attempt to disguise the little gasp that jumped out of his throat. His heart began to pound, but he fought to keep a straight face. She could never know what this meant to him. She couldn't have even an inkling of understanding the depth and breadth of what was going on inside of him. And now was not the time to tell her. Already he felt so emotional he was afraid he might burst into tears and cry like a child. He just kept his mouth shut and nodded while he listened with growing amazement.

"I asked Chas if I could come with her to the church the day the ladies were putting the kits together, or if there was some rule about outsiders attending." She laughed softly. "Chas said she would be thrilled to have me there, so I went, and the ladies were working on other kinds of kits, too. I got so excited about the whole thing that I just couldn't stop. Chas guided me to a website where they have very specific instructions for different kinds of kits—what to make, how to pack them, all that stuff. Chas taught me some more about sewing, and I've been making these little baby nightgowns to go in the newborn kits. And there are hygiene kits, and education kits."

She motioned toward the tables full of items waiting to be bagged up, and boxes waiting to be filled and shipped. She looked at him again and shrugged as if it were nothing. "So . . . that's what I've been doing with my time."

Her silence prompted Mick to the realization that he should comment. He coughed again, hoping to get the lump out of his throat. His voice still cracked a little when he said, "It's truly remarkable, Kate. Truly." She didn't seem to notice the emotion he was trying to hold back, and he was grateful, but there was so much he wanted to know, and he couldn't squeak out a question without letting on how affected he was. He felt his phone vibrate in his back pocket, and he was immeasurably grateful for a brief reprieve. "Oh, sorry," he said, his voice more steady with the distraction. "I'm expecting a call. I'll . . . be back in a few minutes."

Mick answered the phone as he headed toward the stairs to his room. It was Tony, responding to a message that Mick had left for him. He gave Tony instructions to fly to Virginia and get his parents, and return with them next week. Tony was a wandering spirit who loved his job, but he *did* have an apartment in Virginia and he said it would be nice to get back there and check on things.

"My parents will probably only stay a few days," Mick said, "but I'm staying a while; a few months maybe. So when you fly them back, you can just stay there for a while. Maybe Dad will need something. We'll see."

"Whatever you say," Tony said. "I'll just keep enjoying my cushy job."

"Cushy?" Mick retorted with mock astonishment. "All that sleeping on the ground and digging ditches with me was hardly cushy."

"It had its fringe benefits."

"Yeah, it sure did," Mick said, recalling some of the great experiences they'd shared. Then his mind went to Kate and her *project,* and he felt that urge to cry again.

He wrapped up his call with Tony and slumped onto the edge of his bed, glad to be alone as the feelings he'd been trying to suppress rushed to overtake him. "We are so much the same, Kate," he said to the empty room. "We are so much the same."

* * * * *

Kate returned to her sewing while Mick went upstairs to take his phone call. She had no reason to think that he wasn't pleased with what she was doing, but since he'd had to leave so quickly, she really had no idea if it might hold some interest for him or not. As passionate as she'd become about making a difference in far-reaching places through her minimal efforts, she would like to think that the man she was growing to care for might understand her passion, even if he didn't fully share it. She was picking out a little segment of bad stitching when she looked up to see him standing in the doorway.

"Sorry about that."

"It's not a problem," she said.

"Now, where were we?"

"I was done," she said. "You asked what I was doing, and I told you."

"I'd like to know more," he said and seemed sincere.

Still, she had to say, "There's no need to act more interested than you are just to make me feel validated or something."

"Kate," he said with an intensity that took her off guard, "I am genuinely interested in what you're doing, and I'd like to know more."

"All right," she said and stood up.

"May I ask where exactly you are sending these . . . kits?"

"The distribution warehouse is in Salt Lake City. From there they go all over the world, wherever there are needs."

He hung his head for a moment, and Kate wondered if he was okay. When he looked up he seemed fine. "That's . . . amazing," he said. "And do you know exactly how many of these things you've put together yourself? Have you kept track? It certainly seems like you've been working very hard." He looked around. "And you have a lot of stuff here."

"Yes." She smiled and looked around as well. "I'm not sure my mother would approve of how I'm spending the money she sends me, but what she doesn't know won't hurt her."

"I should say not," he said vehemently. "She should be *thrilled* to know what you're doing with the money. I know *I* am."

"You are?"

"I am. I doubt there is little in life you could be doing that could have more meaning. It just makes me love and admire you even more."

Kate looked at him abruptly, wondering if he realized what he'd just said. Her heart quickened and she couldn't keep herself from calling him on it. "Do you know what you just said?"

"I said that I love and admire you even more."

"More than what? More than a few days ago when we didn't even know each other?"

He looked at her intently, and she knew that whether or not the words had slipped out, he meant what he'd said. "More than a few days ago when I first saw you and could hardly keep from staring. More than when you were angry with me for being spoiled and rich but I couldn't stop thinking about you anyway. And more than yesterday when every moment I spent with you felt like one moment closer to having my every dream come true."

Kate couldn't speak until she consciously took a deep, sustaining breath. "Are you always so articulate?"

"Not usually, if you must know. I think you inspire me to such thoughts . . . and the ability to express them."

"So . . . what are you saying exactly, Mick? I don't think I want any room for doubt."

He took a deep breath but didn't break eye contact with her. "Yesterday I was falling in love with you. Today . . . I love you. I know it sounds crazy. But it's so right . . . it's the greatest thing I've ever felt." He laughed gently and shook his head in disbelief. "We are so alike, you and I. And I look forward to every new day unfolding where we can continue to discover how very much alike we are."

"We might discover that we're very different as well."

"That just makes life more exciting." Silence settled in and became mildly awkward before he added, "You don't have to say it back, Kate. I don't want you to say it just to make things even. If you feel it . . . when you feel it . . . you let me know."

"Oh, I feel it," she said. "I just have trouble believing it's real. And I must confess that . . . sometimes I fear that it's too good to last. I fear that . . . pouring my heart out to you will . . . backfire somehow."

Mick took a step toward her and touched her face. "There is no need for such fear. If you want me in your life, I will always be there."

"How can you promise such a thing when we know so little about each other?"

"We know enough to make a marriage work, if we decide to make it work."

"Are you proposing?"

"I'm speculating; I'm hypothesizing. I stand by what I said the other day. When the baby is born and you've come to terms with it, however you choose to handle it, we'll reevaluate."

"Okay," she said and eased closer with a silent invitation for him to kiss her. He had no trouble picking up on the hint. "Maybe I should get back to work," she said after he'd kissed her again.

"Maybe you should," he said, but he kissed her once more before he cleared his throat and said, "I was asking if you know how many kits you've sent off."

"Yes," she said and crossed the room to open a journal. He stepped closer to see meticulous lists with numbers and an occasional note. He glanced through it and was once again overcome with the temptation to either cry or let out a whoop of joy. He so desperately wanted to share his secret with her, but he preferred to wait. He wanted the moment to be just right. And he really felt that simply inviting her to join him while he shared it with his parents would be the best way to handle it. For now he held the thrill of his own related experiences close to his heart, and commented on the enormous amount of work she'd done, and his certainty that she had made a tremendous contribution toward making the world a better place.

A thought occurred to Mick that made his heart pound again. "Did you say this was a *church* project?"

"That's right."

"And this is the church that Chas and Jackson go to?"

"Yes, of course."

"And . . . this is the same church . . . where you are shipping these things . . . to Salt Lake City?"

"Yes, Mick."

"The Mormons," he stated with certainty. He laughed and shook his head, putting his hands on his hips. "Chas and Jackson are *Mormons?*"

"Yes," Kate said, confused over his apparent delight. "Is that significant?"

"Yes, I do believe that it is. I met some Mormons a while back, and they left quite an impression on me. I knew from that life-changing conversation I had with Jackson that he had some spiritual convictions, but I had no idea he was a Mormon. Boy, if it isn't a small world!"

"Yes, I suppose it is."

Mick chuckled again. "He and I are going to need to have a little talk."

"Let me know how it goes," Kate said.

Mick looked around the room again and asked, "What can I do to help?"

"Really?"

"Of course. It looks fun."

Kate showed him how the contents for a large number of hygiene kits had been laid out over a long table, and they had to be assembled into plastic bags. She showed him the specific instructions, and they started a little assembly line, talking nonstop while they worked together to make a difference.

Kate and Mick took a break to make some sandwiches for lunch and eat them, realizing then that Chas and Jackson had driven to Butte, taking the children along to visit Chas's grandfather. The two of them went back to the project room to do a little bit more before Kate declared that she was feeling tired, and she generally felt better throughout the evening if she took some time to rest in the afternoon.

"Then you should rest," he said. "I've got some phone calls to take care of, and a few other odds and ends. So I'll see you later."

"Okay," she said, and he kissed her quickly, as if they'd been kissing for years. "If I don't show up for dinner, wake me."

"I will," he said, and they went to their separate rooms.

* * * * *

Mick made some phone calls and spent some time organizing photos on his laptop until late in the afternoon. Wanting to talk to Jackson, he wandered downstairs to see if Jackson and Chas had returned. The adjoining kitchen door was open, and Mick could hear the children playing. He knocked on the open door, pleased to see Jackson turn from where he was sitting on the couch, reading a book.

"Hey there, kid," Jackson said. "What have you been up to?"

"This and that," Mick said. "Am I interrupting?"

"Not at all. I'm just in charge of the little bugs while Chas is taking care of some stuff." Jackson lifted his brows mischievously. "And how is Kate?"

"Kate is resting, and the last I saw her she seemed to be quite well." Mick sat down across from Jackson, so that he could clearly gauge his expressions. "She showed me her projects." Jackson's smile was mildly conspiratorial. "You knew," Mick said. "You knew when I told you what I'd been doing, that Kate was involved in very similar things."

"Yes," Jackson said. "I knew you'd figure it out. I'm not playing matchmaker here, Mick. If the two of you have common interests and enjoy each other's company, that has nothing to do with me."

"Okay, I get that," Mick said, "but Kate also told me something that's left me rather stunned."

"And what might that be?" Jackson asked nonchalantly.

"You're a Mormon. Is it true? You're actually a Mormon?"

Jackson chuckled. "It's not a big secret, Mick. We're not some kind of clandestine cult. I figured it would come up sooner or later. How much time have we actually spent in conversation, Mick? In the whole of our being acquainted? What was I supposed to say? In the middle of reminiscing, 'Oh, by the way I'm a Mormon'?"

"So, you really are. You're a Mormon."

"Do you have something against Mormons, Mick? Does this make you uncomfortable for some reason? Because if it does, we should talk about it."

"Exactly the opposite, if you must know. I told you about that experience I had . . . where I was able to forgive and let go, and I felt healed."

"Yes," Jackson drawled.

"What I didn't tell you is that one of the key elements that led up to that experience was a conversation I had with a Mormon missionary." Jackson's eyes widened but he didn't comment. He didn't need to. His expression perfectly portrayed his amazement. "The whole

. . . connection here is just . . . blowing me away, Jackson. I'd spent some time in this village, mostly feeling utterly helpless because there was so little we could do to help. You can't buy for them what isn't available to purchase. Next thing I know, these missionaries show up, and they're distributing these . . . kits; the same kind of thing that is being made in the other room by the woman I'm falling in love with." He chuckled and shook his head. "Maybe the kits I saw distributed were actually made by her. Not likely, but in principle . . ."

"Whether or not they were is irrelevant. Regardless of anything else, it can't possibly be a coincidence."

"My point exactly," Mick said. "It's like some . . . huge, magical force is at work in my life."

"It *is* huge, Mick, but not magical. Miraculous, perhaps."

"Exactly!" Mick pointed a finger at him, then he reached into the back pocket of his jeans. "There's something I want to show you. I carried this notebook around while I was traveling. It's not a journal, but sometimes I'd make notes of things to remind me of what I wanted to write in my journal."

"You kept a journal?"

"I did. Anyway, this notebook is full of all kinds of lists and random notes. After I had that healing experience I told you about, and I was starting to feel like it was time to come back to the States, I felt like I should make a list of the most important things I should do when I returned. Read this." He stood up to hand the open notebook to Jackson, then he sat back down.

Jackson took a moment to adjust the distance of the book so that he could read it without finding his reading glasses. He noted the date at the top of the page was a little more than a month ago. Before he read on, he took a moment to consider the strong feelings he'd had about having this young man under his roof. He considered the things that he'd not even begun to share with Mick, things that could change his life.

The conversation of the last few minutes had prompted a subtle trembling inside of Jackson, as if forces were at work here that he couldn't begin to comprehend. Feeling somewhat emotional, he was a little disconcerted when Mick said, "Read it out loud. This is important."

"Okay," Jackson said and cleared his throat. "Number one. *Visit Jackson.* Subheadings: *Share experiences. Express gratitude.*" Jackson looked up at Mick. "You've done that."

"Okay, but I want to say how important it was for me to let you know what your advice led me to. And if I learned nothing else through wandering among the poorest people on the planet, it was the importance of expressing gratitude. I just want to be clear on how grateful I am for *everything* you've done for me, and help you understand that I'll never take your presence in my life for granted."

"I appreciate the principle," Jackson said. "And for the record, you're welcome. We've already talked about this."

"I know, but . . . well, go on."

"Number two. See my parents. Subheadings: Share experiences. Express gratitude. Propose business plan." Again Jackson looked at Mick. "They're coming next week. So, this one will get taken care of."

"That's right," Mick said, "and I'd like you and Chas to be there when I share my experiences with them."

"It would be an honor," Jackson said.

"Okay, finish the list. There's not much more."

Jackson noted only one more notation. He cleared his throat again. *"Number three. Find . . ."* Jackson couldn't even finish as an unexpected wave of emotion stole his voice. He read it silently. He looked at Mick. He cleared his throat once more and resigned himself to not being able to hide his emotion. But maybe Mick needed to see it. *"Number three,"* he said again in a cracked voice. *"Find the Mormons. Subheading: Do whatever it takes . . . to become one."*

Jackson looked again at Mick, unashamed of having tears on his face. Mick nodded and chuckled and wiped tears from his own face. "Imagine," Mick said, "if I'd not figured this out, how you might have felt when I asked you if you knew where the closest Mormon church might be. Because I *was* going to ask."

"I'll give you a ride," Jackson said and chuckled. "I'll even baptize you . . . when you're ready, anyway."

"You can *do* that?" Mick asked, astonished and delighted.

"I can . . . if you want me to. It doesn't have to be me. It could be—"

"Who better than you?" He leaned forward. "What do I have to do?"

"I think you need to attend church, for starters. But we can contact the local missionaries and set up appointments for them to come and teach you. They'll know what to do. That's what I did."

"How long have you been a Mormon?" Mick asked and immediately added, "This is what changed you, isn't it. When you said that your process of forgiveness was a spiritual matter; this is what you meant."

"It was certainly a big part of it. For me, accepting the Atonement of Jesus Christ as the true source of healing was a huge step. The other step was to know beyond any doubt that *this* is His true church on the earth. Chas made it clear all along that she didn't want me joining for her sake, or for any other reason beyond knowing for myself that it was true. I was pretty stubborn initially, but I came around."

"So, it was her. That's how you found it."

"I'd never known anyone like her," Jackson said. "But I didn't credit that to her religion as much as I should have. I agreed to be supportive of her beliefs, and be involved in them enough to raise our children with them. I made it clear I was not interested in joining. But after my PTSD had nearly destroyed me—and our marriage—I began to look at things differently. When I realized it was true, it changed my life. Last February we went to the temple together, and—"

"What's that?" Mick asked.

Jackson let out a delighted little laugh. "Oh, my friend. You have so many wonderful things yet to learn. In the temple, ordinances are performed that make it possible for families to be together forever."

Mick's heart quickened at the implication, but he didn't understand. "Explain . . . *forever.* I mean . . . I know what *forever* means, but . . . I hear it all the time. I've always just assumed it was a figure of speech; people falling in love and being together forever."

"I think that out in the world it *is* just a figure of speech. In reality, marriage ceremonies end with that final blow . . . that this is only until death. But when two people are married—or sealed—in the temple, the vows go beyond death. It's forever—literally."

Mick felt stunned. He'd been so thrilled and consumed with how the power of the Atonement had changed his life, he couldn't imagine that more blessings could be in store. He considered his growing feelings for Kate, and the possibility of such affection not ending at death gave him a thrill beyond description. He was completely enthralled as Jackson continued.

"In the temple, these ordinances can also be done for our loved ones who are deceased, who did not have the opportunity to have the gospel in their lives while they were living. Chas and I take one day a month and travel to a temple in Idaho where we are slowly doing work for our family members who can't do it for themselves."

"Is that where the two of you were . . . what did you say?"

"Sealed. We were married here at the inn; I wasn't a member of the Church then. We were sealed in Washington, DC. There are more than a hundred temples all over the world. They all work the same."

Mick took it in. He chuckled. He shook his head. "I don't even know what to say."

"Why don't you just give it some thought, and I'll get hold of the missionaries. I have a spare copy of the Book of Mormon if you want to start reading it and—"

"Oh, I've already read it. The missionaries gave me one. I'm almost through it a second time." Jackson smiled, and Mick added, "But if you have an extra one, I'd like to give it to Kate."

"What an excellent idea," Jackson said. "But let me offer a word of caution. Her life's experiences are different from yours. If she's not initially receptive, don't let that discourage you, and don't let it come between you."

"Very good advice," Mick said, and Jackson shared more about his own conversion, and how patient Chas had been with him. The children played so well while they visited that it almost seemed they had some sense of the sweet spirit in the room.

Mick was able to candidly share with Jackson the way he was feeling about Kate, and he felt gratified that Jackson's advice to simply be patient and cautious settled well with the attitude that Mick had already established within himself, and in the things he'd said to Kate. But in his heart he knew she was the one, and he knew he was on the life path that God wanted for him. He just prayed that it would all come together without too many glitches.

CHAPTER 11

Mick saw movement from the corner of his eye and turned to see Kate standing in the doorway.

"Well, hello," he said, standing to greet her. "Did you get some rest?"

"I did, thank you," she said. He took both her hands and kissed her cheek. "What have you been up to?"

"Jackson and I are just shooting the breeze," Mick said. "Have a seat."

"I was coming to see if Chas needed help with supper, actually."

"Oh, she's helping Jodi with something," Jackson said, glancing at the clock. "She said she'd be home at six-thirty, and she's bringing pizza with her, so we're good."

"Pizza sounds heavenly," Kate said and sat down next to Mick. He put his arm around her and they exchanged a smile. "So, what have the two of you been talking about, really? Or is it a secret?"

"Not at all," Mick said. "We've been talking about Mormons."

"Really? You told me you and Jackson were going to have a little talk. It went well, I take it."

"I believe so," Jackson said. He pointed at Mick. "Maybe you should show her your list."

"You think so?" Mick asked, sincerely wondering if he should. Then he wondered what he had to be afraid of.

Jackson clinched a very important point when he said, "If you like her as much as you say you do, she should know about your list."

"I'm sure you're right," Mick said and took the notebook out from where he'd returned it to his pocket. "I told you," he said while he found the right page, "about having a conversation with some Mormons that left an impression on me."

"Yes, I remember. Which obviously makes it an amazing coincidence that Jackson and Chas *are* Mormons."

"Have you been to church with them?" Mick asked, the prospect exciting him.

"I haven't," Kate said, and he covered his disappointment. "They've invited me, but . . . well, going to church was never really a part of my life, and . . . I just haven't. Why?"

"If I go to church with them, will you come with me?"

While Kate was thinking about it, Mick held his breath. Her attitude about these desires he had in regard to religion could make a huge difference in their relationship. He knew from what Jackson had told him that such differences could be overcome, and two people could still have a good marriage in spite of them. But sharing such things with Kate could make the journey all the more thrilling. She shrugged and said, "I don't see why not. Maybe it would be good for me . . . especially considering all that stuff about forgiveness we were talking about."

Mick laughed with relief and held out his notebook, but he held onto it while he gave a brief explanation. "This is where I kept some random notes and lists while I was traveling. This is the list I made of the most important things I needed to do when I got back to the States."

"Okay," Kate said and took the book, looking at the page it was open to. Mick watched her closely, waiting for a reaction. She looked at him, then at Jackson, then at him again. "This is so . . ."

"Miraculous?" Mick said.

"Yes." Kate smiled, and Mick's heart quickened with relief. "It surely must be."

Their eyes met again, and Mick sensed that she had many questions, but just then Chas came in with two pizza boxes. Jackson stood up to help her, and Kate hurried to put some dishes on the table. Mick stood up to help Kate, but Chas tossed her car keys at him and said, "There's a box from the bakery in the car. Could you get it for me and make sure the car is locked?"

"Sure thing," Mick said and did as she'd asked.

A few minutes later when they were all seated and ready to eat, including the little ones in their high chairs, Jackson offered the blessing on the food. For Mick, it wasn't the first time he'd shared the experience, but now that he knew *which* religion these people lived, everything felt different to him. Jackson expressed appreciation for having Mick and Kate in their home, and for the wonderful discovery that Mick had made in his travels, and he asked that God would continue to bless him—and Kate—in their journeys.

Following the amen, Chas said to her husband, *"What* discovery?"

"Show her the notebook, kid."

Mick chuckled. "My private list has sure become public today."

"We're not public," Kate said. "We're all practically family."

Mick loved the way she said it, even if he knew she was referring more to the closeness they all shared, as opposed to any implications in regard to the future. Still, he loved it. He loved feeling like a part of Jackson's family, and he couldn't imagine what divine providence had made it possible for Kate to be here when he'd arrived.

Mick got out the notebook, found the page, and gave the same explanation to Chas before she read it. There was no hiding her tears, and she didn't apologize for them. Kate seemed a little confused over the reasons for them, but certainly more intrigued than put off. The word *miracle* came up in the conversation a few times after that, and Mick was glad to hear Chas and Jackson talking about the stories of their conversions to the gospel. In his heart he absolutely knew it was true, even if he knew very little about it. But he appreciated more than he could say this opportunity for Kate to hear about it from someone besides him. He wondered why it hadn't come up before, with Kate spending so much time with them. But he knew that Jackson and Chas were not pushy, overbearing people. And perhaps they'd had intentions of sharing what they knew, knowing that Kate would still be with them for a while yet.

When dinner was over and cleaned up, Jackson left for a minute and came back with a copy of the Book of Mormon, which he handed to Kate, saying quietly, "Mick told me he's already read it. We've wanted to share it with you, but we were waiting for the right time. We'd love for you to keep this, and we hope that you'll read it, and if you have any questions, you can ask us anything."

"Thank you," Kate said and seemed to mean it. Mick hoped she *would* read it without too much coaxing, and it might give them something to talk about. She smiled at Jackson, then at Chas who was looking on. "You've been so kind to me; you're such wonderful people. How could I not be curious about what makes you that way?"

The children disrupted the moment with an argument over a toy, but Mick figured it was probably just as well left at that. The adults all sat down to visit while the children played. Mick loved the way Kate sat close to him, and he was even more pleased when she held his hand. He was surprised when she said, "We have a confession to make." Mick wondered what exactly this confession might be until she added, "We've been talking about the two of you. We hope you don't mind, but . . . some of the experiences you've shared with each of us at different times have had meaning for us, and it . . . just kind of came up."

"We don't have any secrets," Chas said. "If there was something we didn't want repeated, we would certainly have said so."

"And the same goes for me," Kate said. "Just so we're clear."

"Glad we got that out of the way," Mick said.

A mildly awkward moment of silence preceded Kate saying, while she looked at Jackson, "Mick told me about the advice you gave him . . . specifically about forgiveness; how it was the key to truly healing. He said it worked for him. You told him it worked for you. I've been thinking about it . . . well, it's only been hours since he told me, but it's still been on my mind. I hope it's okay to just . . . talk about anything here, because I—"

"Of course it's okay," Chas said. "I thought that was well established. The kids are too young to understand *anything* we're saying."

"I know, but . . . this is a little more sensitive. I know that you've talked to Jackson about what happened to me, but we haven't discussed it much when we were all together, and . . ."

"I was in the FBI, Kate," Jackson said. "I don't think there's much in regard to your circumstances you could say that would embarrass or shock me."

Kate felt Mick tighten his hold on her hand in silent encouragement, and she forged ahead with thoughts that had been with her since she'd awakened from her nap. "The thing is . . . I don't think it would be that difficult for me to forgive the man who . . . did this to me. Maybe it's because I don't even know who he is; perhaps it's because I don't remember. Or maybe I'm in some kind of denial. I think what's bothering me more is the idea that I need to forgive my parents for a *lot* of things; especially my mother. I know I need to. I know it's a burden I'm carrying around. But it just feels so *hard.*"

"I think it *is* harder when it's a family member," Jackson said. "I had issues with both of my parents, especially my father. And I had a *very* hard time letting go of them. I think one of the most difficult things for me was believing that a parent should love and nurture a child, not damage them with cruelty and abuse."

"Boy, that's for sure," Mick said. "My parents have always been so great, I can't even imagine being treated that way. I might have to work on forgiving Kate's parents too."

"Why?" Kate asked, looking at him.

"Because I've seen how much they've hurt you; *especially* your mother."

The cordless phone on the coffee table rang; the line for the inn. Chas and Jackson looked at each other, as if in silent debate, until Jackson said, "Fine, I'll take care of it." He stood up as he answered, "Dickensian Inn," and immediately walked out of the room, as if he knew he would likely have to go to the office to take care of whatever might be needed.

Chas said to Kate, "I think before you can forgive someone, you need to acknowledge what they've done to hurt you. I know that for Jackson, he had to define exactly what the issues were. Since the issues with your father are less severe than with your mother, perhaps you should start there."

"I think I'm most angry with my father for his passiveness. I don't think he's a bad person. He just . . . stands back and lets her manipulate me and verbally abuse me, and he makes no effort to step in and solve the problem. I think he knows her behavior is out of line, but he just won't stand up to her. I've always wanted him to be my hero, to be on my side, even a little. But he just . . . seems to not care. I know he *does* care, but not enough to put some effort into showing it."

"So, he's never hurt you," Mick said, "but he's allowed you to be hurt."

"That's exactly right," Kate said. "And if my mother—"

"Speak of the devil," Jackson said, coming back into the room. He chuckled and added, "I don't think using that particular cliché has ever been more appropriate—at least not when I've said it."

"Get to the point," Chas said.

"That was Kate's mother. She just made a reservation."

"No!" Kate said, squeezing Mick's hand so hard it nearly hurt. "When?"

"Tomorrow night, and the night after. She didn't say exactly what time she would be arriving tomorrow."

"No," Kate repeated. "I can't believe it."

Kate felt on the verge of erupting, either with sobbing or anger—or both. She looked around at these people she'd come to care for so dearly, people who had proven that her mother's atrocities were even more atrocious. As much as she'd told them how horrible her mother could be, the idea of them actually having to be in the same room with her made Kate feel more nauseated than she'd felt since the nausea of her pregnancy had settled down several weeks ago. Not knowing what to say or how to handle this, she simply stood up and said, "Forgive me, but . . . I need to be alone. Thank you for dinner."

After Kate had left the room, the silence was startling. Mick finally cleared his throat and said, "I, uh . . . don't have a lot of experience with women. Do you think she *really* wants to be alone, or do you think I should . . ." He couldn't finish the sentence. He was hoping Chas might fill in the blank.

"I have no idea," Jackson said with exaggerated chagrin.

"Give her a little time," Chas said, "then check on her and ask *her* that question."

"Okay, well . . . maybe I'll go work on some stuff in my room while I . . . let her have some time alone." Mick picked up the Book of Mormon that Kate had left behind. "I'll see that she gets this. Thank you for everything."

Jackson nodded and said, "We leave for church at 10:40."

Mick thought about that for a second. "With the dragon lady coming, we might need to rethink that. I'll talk to Kate, but . . . if she's not up to it, maybe I should stay here and . . ."

Chas said, "We understand. There's always next week. We're glad you're here to take care of her."

"I think the two of you were managing just fine without me," Mick said.

"Or maybe not," Jackson said.

"I think she needs you," Chas added.

"I hope so," Mick said and left the room.

He paused on the landing of the second floor, near Kate's room, wondering if he should knock on her door now. He decided to wait. Since he still had a couple of hours before she might normally go to sleep, he figured he had some time to give her the space she needed, and still check on her before bedtime. He went up another flight of stairs to his own room, feeling angry toward Kate's mother, and reminding himself that he needed to stay calm over the matter. He had made a conscious decision to actively live his life as a good Christian. He couldn't renege on that now just because he already didn't like the dragon lady—at all.

* * * * *

"Tomorrow should be an interesting day," Jackson said, once he was alone with his wife and the children were engaged in some kind of activity that involved baby dolls *and* dinosaurs. But at least they were playing together and being polite to each other.

"She really didn't give you any idea when she would be arriving?"

"Nope. I asked, and she wouldn't tell me. It's almost like she *wants* Kate to be on edge, waiting for her to come."

"So, she knows that Kate knows she's coming."

"She asked me to 'inform her daughter of her pending arrival.'"

"And that's it?" Chas couldn't help sounding angry. "She's not so much as given her—or us—a call to check on her daughter the entire time she's been here, and now she's—"

"I don't know if it's wise for you to get all worked up over this. It's appalling, but we can't fix it. We can only do our best to help Kate through it."

Chas took a deep breath. "I know you're right. It's just so . . . astonishing how badly some people can behave."

A long moment later, Jackson said, "Speaking of people behaving badly . . ."

"What about it?" Chas asked, sensing he was trying to get to an important point.

"You know what Kate was saying earlier about forgiveness?"

"Yes," she said, wondering what he might be getting to.

"It occurred to me—rather strongly, if you must know—that perhaps forgiveness is the key to what's been bothering *you.*"

It took Chas a moment to figure out what he meant, and when she did, she almost felt angry again. Jackson knew more than anyone how she'd been struggling with ill feelings toward her father—or, rather, the man who had fathered her. In this situation, there was a huge difference. The very idea of the solution being based on simply *forgiving* him for what he'd done to her mother almost felt like a slap in the face. But memories of other conversations between her and Jackson came back to her even before he brought it up.

"Chas," he said, taking her hand, "when I was struggling to come to terms with . . . so many things, *you* were the one who told me I needed to forgive. I was angry. I resisted it. And in the end, it was the key. I don't know why one of us didn't think of it before now. It seems so obvious."

"Maybe," Chas said, then wished it hadn't sounded so spiteful.

She attempted to stand up and leave the conversation, but Jackson took hold of her arm to keep her from doing so. "Wait a minute," he said. "Is this hypocrisy I'm hearing?"

"Maybe," she said. More humbly she added, "Obviously it's a lot easier in theory than it is in practice."

"Is that supposed to be a revelation to me?" he asked, and Chas felt like a fool when she considered all he had been through in his life, and so much of it at the cruel hand of others. And he had made peace with it. There was no one more qualified to talk about forgiveness than Jackson. But she still felt unprepared to apply the principle to her own uneasy feelings in regard to what had happened to her mother.

"I need some time . . . to think about it," Chas said.

"Do you *really* need some time," he asked facetiously, "or should I . . ." He stopped when she glared at him. "Fine. Take all the time you need. You know where to find me if you need to talk about it."

"Okay," she said and started picking up a day's worth of scattered toys.

* * * * *

Mick waited more than an hour before he could no longer keep himself from knocking on the door to Kate's room. She opened it just a little, and he could see that she'd been crying.

"I know you said you needed to be alone," he said, "but I'm just wondering if you're okay."

"You're very sweet," she said. "But . . ."

"What I want to know is if you *really* need to be alone, or if you need a friend to talk to."

Kate stepped out into the hall and hugged him tightly, loving the way his embrace filled her with something she'd never known before in her life. He cared for her without any conditions or expectations, and she could feel it by simply being with him.

"Thank you," she said, "but . . . I really do think I need sleep more than anything." What she omitted saying was that she was certain she would cry herself to sleep, and she preferred to expend the majority of her tears in private. "I'm sure that in the morning I'll be able to think this through more reasonably."

"Okay," he said.

"I'll see you at breakfast?" she asked.

"Of course," he said and kissed her brow. "Just call my room if you change your mind."

Kate nodded. "Thank you, Mick. I'll see you tomorrow." She closed the door and leaned against it, wishing with all her heart that all of the wonderful things she had found here at the inn were not about to become tainted by Avis Fitzgibbons. She felt as if she'd opened the door for a plague to enter in and wreak havoc. And she felt sure these people she'd grown to love would never see her the same again.

* * * * *

Kate was grateful to have slept well, in spite of her concerns. Perhaps all that crying had helped. A few minutes before nine, when she was accustomed to going downstairs for breakfast, she felt suddenly afraid of even stepping outside of her room for fear that she might run into her mother. A knock at the door startled her, and then her heart pounded with fear. Had her mother already arrived? Had someone told her which room Kate was staying in? She hardly dared speak, and felt angry at the power her mother had over her.

"Kate, are you there?" Mick called, and she heaved a deep sigh.

"Yes," she said, and opened the door. "I was afraid it might be someone else."

"I thought you might like an escort down to breakfast," he said. "I've already checked in with the chief, and your mother hasn't come yet."

"I hate to admit how much I do *not* want to face her," Kate said.

"It's okay to admit that, but maybe we should talk about how you *can* face her and get over feeling this way. I hate seeing how she affects you. I think you're a lot stronger than you think you are."

"Except when it comes to my mother."

"Maybe we should figure out why that is," Mick said.

Kate looked at him, taking in the perfect confidence he had in her. She touched his face and smiled. "I can't think what made you come along when I needed you so very much. I didn't *know* I needed you, but it seems I do—for many more reasons than helping me stand up to my mother."

"One thing at a time," he said. "Come along," he held out his arm. "I'll make sure the coast is clear."

Kate took his arm and closed the door to her room, tucking the keys into her pocket. They crept quietly down the stairs partway, then Mick went ahead of her and peeked in both directions down the hall. "Make a run for it," he said with comical exaggeration.

"Like I could run in this condition," Kate said, hurrying past him and into the guest dining room.

While they were sharing the breakfast that Michelle had served, Kate admitted to Mick that she simply didn't feel up to going to church today. "Perhaps next week," she said. "But I don't want to keep you from going, or—"

"I'll stay here with you," he said. "We'll go next week."

"Okay," Kate said, pleased that he was willing to stay with her, even though she hadn't wanted to ask him to.

Before they were finished eating, Jackson found them, and Mick told him the reasons they wouldn't be going to church today. He was very understanding, and even said, "I suspected that might be the case. Either way, Michelle will be covering the inn while we're at church. If any guests arrive while she's on duty, she will take care of getting them checked in. She's been warned about your mother's personality, and she assures me that she can handle it. If you prefer to not see her right off, the two of you can hang out in the house while we're gone, and Michelle can truthfully tell her that you are not at the inn right now."

"Oh, I like that idea very much," Kate said. "Thank you."

"And when we get home," Jackson said, "we'll see what we can do to help . . . manage the situation." He said the last with a gentle smirk, and Kate appreciated his attitude more than she could ever say.

"Thank you," sounded trite, but he seemed to understand.

A while later, Kate found Chas preparing a chicken dish that would bake at a low temperature while they were at church. While the men and the children were elsewhere, Kate said, "I'm well aware that you have all the help you need around here, but I just have to ask if . . . well, I've realized that my mother's biggest control over me is the money, and I don't want her to have that control anymore. I just have to ask if . . . it might be possible for me to do something to at least earn my room and board until—"

"We would be more than happy to have you stay with us as long as you need," Chas said, almost sounding offended by Kate's suggestion. "If your mother were not—"

"Hear me out," Kate said. "Once the baby is born and placed with the right family, I will be able to find a job and start to take care of myself. I just have to know if, in the meantime, you would let me help you in some way to—"

"Listen to me," Chas said, putting a hand over Kate's, "if your mother truly does cut you off, you will never be homeless. You have friends who care about you, and you have nothing to worry about. If you feel you need to help, we'll figure something out. But I don't want you to worry about it."

"Okay," Kate said, "thank you. I think just knowing that I *can* live without her will help me face her with more . . . confidence."

"I'm sure you're right," Chas said. "And you're a lot stronger than you think you are."

"That's what Mick said. But it's different with her. I just want to change that."

"And today might be a good step in the right direction," Chas said.

* * * * *

When Chas and Jackson left for church, Kate's mother still hadn't shown up. Once Kate and Mick were alone, she appreciated the way he took her hand and told her that her value as a human being was not measured by her mother's opinion of her, or her treatment of her. He talked of having learned this principle through his observance of his mother's relationship with her sister. Eventually Mick's aunt had become so controlling and difficult, trying to be far too involved in the lives of her sister and her sister's family, that Mick's mother had gotten some advice from the therapist who had been helping Mick at the time. It had been hard for Mick's mother to stand up to her sister and declare her boundaries, but it had alleviated a great many problems in the long run. Mick talked to Kate about how she needed to do the same with her mother.

"You can't have a relationship with someone who is so toxic to you," Mick said. "If she wants to have a relationship with you under terms that are mutually respectful and kind, then that's a different matter. But if she continues to behave this way, you need to make it clear you won't tolerate such treatment. Does that make sense?"

"I think so," Kate said, but they talked about it some more, and Kate appreciated his insight, as well as his support. She felt better prepared to face her mother, but was still dreading it with all her soul.

When Chas and Jackson returned from church, Avis Fitzgibbons still hadn't arrived. They all shared a nice Sunday dinner together and cleaned it up, and still she hadn't come. Kate began to wish she'd just get to the inn so they could all get it over with. Feeling that she needed some kind of plan, her mind played over the possibilities until her head ached.

"I still can't believe she's coming here," Kate said. "I don't want to see her. It will be *nothing* but a disaster. There's no hope for it to ever be tolerable." She looked at Mick, then at Jackson, then at Mick again as an idea occurred to her. Mick had done great with handling Henry, and Jackson had been an FBI agent. "I need the two of you to help me. I need you to . . ."

"Protect you from the dragon?" Mick asked facetiously.

"Exactly!"

"And how exactly do you think we should go about that?" Jackson asked.

"Just . . . waylay her when she gets here . . . before she sees me. I can assure you that it will only take a minute for her to say something offensive enough to give either of you just cause to put her in her place. Will you do that for me?" she pleaded. Looking at Mick, she said, "Just fluster her up a bit. Isn't that how you put it?" She turned to Jackson. "Will you let her know that this is not a place where she can throw her money around and intimidate people?"

"I can do that," Jackson said. "Should I check her in first, and give you some time to—"

"Now that it's this late in the day, I think I'd just rather get it over with. Maybe she'll get really ticked off and she won't *want* to stay here. I'm ashamed to say I'd be thrilled with that." She got a little teary and groaned. "Oh, here come those hormonal tears again."

"What's going on?" Chas asked gently. "Is there something more to this?"

"It's just that . . . I love this place. It feels like such a refuge from my home . . . from my former life. I feel like she's going to walk in and contaminate it. She's going to bring her arrogance and bigotry with her. Unless people have wealth and power and . . ." she took on a snobbish accent to mimic her mother, "good breeding and proper manners . . ." she returned to her normal voice, "they're just not worthy to be seen as her equals, and she treats everyone as if they are in her servitude. She would have done marvelously well living in Georgia in the early nineteenth century."

"It's going to be okay," Mick said.

"If she's too difficult," Jackson said. "We'll just . . . hide you away and refuse to let her see you."

"You'd do that?"

"Oh, yeah," Mick said, and Jackson smiled. Kate was amazed at how loved and safe she felt, in spite of the impending doom.

When they heard the chime that indicated someone had come through the door of the inn, Chas said, "I'll go do the initial greeting. I can't wait to meet this woman."

Chas said it as if it would be fun, but Kate had knots in her stomach. Chas returned a minute later and said, "Okay, she's in the parlor. I told her that I'd tell Kate she was here. She doesn't *look* very scary. Well . . . no more so than Cruella de Vil."

This made Kate laugh as Mick stood up, saying, "My turn to meet her. I'll just . . . fluster her up a bit."

Mick walked into the parlor with his hands in his pockets, nonchalant and carefree. His first glimpse of this woman showed a kind of perfection in appearance he might have expected. Her blonde hair was sleek and cut in a short style that implied she was trying to be a teenager. Her clothes were expensive, as were her purse and shoes. She wore too much makeup and jewelry, and she looked too thin. She was sitting on the couch with an attitude that implied that the entire minute she'd been kept waiting was trying her patience.

"So," Mick said, trying not to sound *too* sarcastic, "I finally get to meet the famous Mrs. Fitzgibbons."

"And who are *you?*" Avis Fitzgibbons asked snidely.

"I'm Mick," he said, holding out a hand, and was not surprised when she only looked at it but made no effort to offer her own. He put his own hand back in his pocket and sat on the other couch in order to face her. "Kate and I have become friends while we've both been staying here. She's a remarkable young woman."

"Yes, she is," Mrs. Fitzgibbons said in a tone edged with warning. "What *kind* of friends?"

"Oh, *very good* friends," Mick said proudly.

"I hope you're not implying anything romantic," Mrs. Fitzgibbons said. "I don't know how that could be the case when she's in such a condition. But just so we're completely clear, *Mick*"—she said his name as if he were a drug dealer or a convicted felon, while she examined his attire with disdain, as if his clothes told her everything she needed to know about him—"my daughter will not be getting romantically involved with anyone who is not of her caliber."

Mick shook his head and chuckled. "She told me you were like this, but I thought she had to be exaggerating—at least a little bit. I can see now that she was right on."

"I don't know what you're talking about."

"That makes it good for both of us, because I'm going to explain it to you. People like you who wear your money like it gives you some kind of aristocratic title are so pathetically transparent. You think your money gives you power to govern your child's life—and anyone else who will jump to the flashing of your bankroll. She's better than you, and she deserves better than to be manipulated into living some kind of puppet's life with you holding the strings."

Mick loved the way Avis's mouth fell open enough to catch flies, and her eyes widened into perfect circles. He could tell her face had been given Botox injections by the way it didn't wrinkle with her astonished expression. "You have such a nerve, young man."

"Yes, I do," he said proudly. "Someone's got to stand up to you. I'm not afraid of your power *or* your money; and by the way, you wouldn't have any power if you didn't have any money. In my opinion, that's the true mark of a person's character—whether or not they are the same person with or without money."

Mrs. Fitzgibbons shook her head as if he were pathetic, and she chuckled as if he were nothing to her. "You are going to regret this."

"I don't think so," he said as if *she* were nothing to *him.*

"Whoever you are and wherever you came from, you will not get away with any further association with my daughter. I will make sure of it."

CHAPTER 12

"And how are you going to do that, Mrs. Fitzgibbons?" Mick asked, wondering if this woman might actually be his future mother-in-law. The thought was truly humorous. He doubted she would share his sentiment.

"Are you aggravating our guests?" Jackson asked, coming into the hall according to the little plan they'd devised.

"Yes, he is," Mrs. Fitzgibbons said indignantly. "I'm Avis Fitzgibbons, and I've come to see my daughter. If you could tell her I'm here. Tell her I want to see her immediately, and I want this . . . cretin," she motioned toward Mick, "to go away."

Mick saw the astonishment on Jackson's face before he said, "My wife has already let Kate know you're here. I run the inn. I don't take orders."

Mrs. Fitzgibbons made a disgruntled sound that was very unflattering, and Jackson headed toward the office. "I will remove my daughter from this place," she threatened, and Jackson turned back to look at her. "And I will cease payment of your services immediately. I've never encountered such insubordination, or—"

Mick saw Jackson's impatience turn to anger as he stepped toward Mrs. Fitzgibbons and looked at her squarely. "For there to be any insubordination, Mrs. Fitzgibbons, you would need to have some authority over me, and you do not. You won't send your daughter anywhere else because she can't travel at this stage of her pregnancy, and she needs us to help her get through this. Someone's got to. I'm assuming you still want to use the room you reserved for yourself tonight. If so, I'll take care of that. But remember, I have the right to refuse service to anyone. As for your daughter, she is an adult and she can decide whether or not she's staying."

"I won't pay for it."

Jackson shrugged. "I'm sure we'll manage." Jackson glanced toward Mick. "He'll pay for it."

Mrs. Fitzgibbons laughed. "*If* I were going to accept charity on behalf of my daughter—which I would not—I wouldn't be—"

"Make up your mind, Mrs. Fitzgibbons," Jackson said. "Are you going to pay for her to stay here or not?"

She glared at Jackson, ignored his comment, and focused on Mick. "*If* I allowed someone else to pay my daughter's bills, it would not be someone who . . ."

She hesitated at Mick's glare. "What, Mrs. Fitzgibbons? Tell me what you've assessed about my character in these few minutes."

"You're rude and disrespectful."

"And *you* are a hypocrite," Mick said, and she gasped. "*You* are rude and disrespectful," Mick said, but it was matter-of-fact and calm. "The Dickensian Inn is supposed to be a happy place, a place where people treat each other kindly and with respect. You just don't really seem to fit in. Maybe you should stay somewhere else while you're in Montana."

"I came to see my daughter, and you are not going to stop me."

"Oh, you can see her," Mick said, "but if you say anything to upset her, I will escort you out of the building myself and call the local authorities to report trespassing and disorderly conduct.

"Is that a crime?" he asked Jackson, then he said nonchalantly to Mrs. Fitzgibbons. "He's former FBI. He knows these things."

"Something like that," Jackson said.

"I've never imagined such atrocious behavior!" Mrs. Fitzgibbons said.

"You and I are in complete agreement over that," Mick said. "Perhaps if—"

"Hello, Mother," Kate said from the doorway. Jackson smiled at her and slipped away. Eavesdropping on the things that had been said so far had given her an unexpected surge of courage—and perspective. She'd never felt less intimidated by her mother. And most of all she felt indifferent. As hurt as she'd been by this woman—more times than she could count—she was now overcome with a gentle calm that let her know she didn't need this woman in her life to survive. And she was never going to get her to change and provide for Kate the love and validation she'd always sought. To let go of hoping for those things felt suddenly liberating.

"Catherine Jane!" Avis said in a tone that held no hint of being glad to see her daughter after all this time. It was more in preparation for some kind of scolding. In lieu of saying something more, she took in Kate's pregnant figure with overt disgust in her expression, as if she might have hoped that the reasons Kate had been banished here weren't really true.

"How are you, Mother?" Kate asked.

"I'm terribly upset, if you must know," Avis said, as if she might need smelling salts at any moment.

Kate ignored her mother's predictable drama and sat down on the same couch as Mick, but she kept some distance between them. Mick smiled at her, then they both looked at Avis.

"What did you want to talk to me about, Mother, that couldn't be done with a phone call?"

"I would prefer some privacy."

"And I would prefer that Mick stay. Just say what you need to say and get it over with."

Avis eyed Mick with disdain, cleared her throat, and focused directly on Kate with scolding eyes. "Henry tells me you were very unkind to him."

Kate wanted to tell her that she had no right to criticize *anyone* for being unkind. Kindness was foreign to Avis Fitzgibbons—except in the way *other* people were expected to treat *her.*

"Henry is delusional, Mother." Kate wanted to add that her mother was as well. "I made it clear to him before I came here that I had no desire to ever see him again. His interest in me was never something I encouraged. *You* encouraged it, in spite of my making it clear to *you* that I was not interested."

"He's a good man, Catherine Jane. He has all of the qualities you could ever want in a husband, and you must accept that—"

"He has *none* of the qualities I want in a husband, Mother. And if you'd paid even a little bit of attention to what I've had to say on the matter, you would have known that a long time ago. His coming here was a waste of time. I was not unkind. I was honest and forthright. If he can't get it through his head that there's nothing between us, that's his problem. And if your coming here was simply to scold me about Henry, then your trip was a waste of time as well."

Avis looked stunned, and Kate took advantage of the silence to say more of what she wanted to say. "Notice how many minutes you've been here and you haven't asked how I'm doing. You haven't asked if I'm feeling all right, if I've had any problems, if I've missed you and Dad." She took a deep breath and dealt the final blow. "I don't want you to even stay here, Mother, if you can't be kind and appropriate."

"If I pay for accommodations, I have a right to receive the best possible service, and—"

"This isn't about what you pay for, Mother. These people are my friends. They deserve respect. If you can't give it, then I don't want you to stay here."

"I will not listen to such—"

"No, you *will* listen, Mother. You traipse in here like some kind of self-proclaimed queen, and you toss around your toxic debris, completely oblivious to how you poison people with your arrogance and impudence."

"I cannot believe that you would speak to me that way, or—"

"Be quiet and listen to me, Mother," Kate said in a firm voice that lacked anger but overflowed with a quiet strength that got Avis's attention.

"I deserve better than that from you, and these people who have done more for me in a matter of weeks than you've done for me in a decade, deserve better than that from you as well."

"I have done more for you than anyone could ever—"

"Again, I am not talking about your money. I appreciate the way you have provided for my needs, and even many of my wants. You have been generous with your money, and I thank you for that. But it's come at too high a price. I won't be your puppet. I won't be your scapegoat. I'm done with that. If we can't sit down and have a civil conversation, like two adults, then you need to leave; you need to stay somewhere else."

Avis began ranting with an anger that was not at all a surprise to Kate; she'd seen it many times before. She was more surprised by how unaffected she felt. Perhaps the Dickensian Inn *was* a magical place. It had changed her—in the best possible ways.

Kate was just wondering how to interrupt her mother's ongoing diatribe and get her to leave when Mick said, "I think you need to go."

Avis looked even more astonished, if that was possible. But before she could comment, Kate added, "He's right. You need to go."

"I *refuse* to leave you here with people like this, Catherine Jane. I—"

"Oh, cut the 'Catherine Jane' baloney," Mick said. "She hates it and you know she hates it."

"I know no such thing!"

"Only because you don't listen to me," Kate said. "I've told you many times I don't like it."

"I suppose you prefer the ridiculous nicknames your father uses."

"Yes, actually, I do. But Kate is a lovely name, and I'm quite content with it."

"It *is* a lovely name," Mick said, as if they were drinking tea as opposed to throwing out Kate's mother. He then turned to the source of aggravation and added in the same tone, "You need to go. You need to go now."

"I will cut off your funding here," Avis threatened.

"Dad will send what I need," Kate said. "And as soon as I have this baby, I'll find a way to make it on my own."

"You'll never be able to do it," Avis snarled, as if she'd love to see her daughter groveling in the streets, if only to prove herself right.

"I appreciate your confidence in me," Kate said with light sarcasm. "I believe I can do anything I set my mind to. I'm not trying to extinguish our relationship, Mother, but I want it to be based on the fact that we're family, not that my decisions are controlled by your money. I'm done with that."

"You'll be ruined!" Avis said, as if she'd not heard anything about *relationships* in Kate's plea.

"No, she won't," Mick said. "She'll be able to make it no matter what happens. But at the moment, she's got a rich boyfriend, and he's not going to leave her high and dry."

"*What* rich boyfriend?" Avis demanded.

Mick leaned forward. "What? You think because I don't dress like Polo Boy that I couldn't possibly have good breeding and a proper upbringing?"

"What are you saying?" Avis asked as if knowing he had those things—and money—would change her opinion of him immediately. And it made him want to puke.

"I'm saying, Mrs. Fitzgibbons, that your prejudice is revolting. You have no idea who or what I am. But you're dying to know, aren't you? Would you consider me the perfect choice for a son-in-law if you learned that I was filthy, stinking rich? Would you like to know that my father inherited a family business worth billions of what it is you prize so dearly? Would you be thrilled to know that my mother collects precious stones and expensive clothes, and my father collects cars—only the best of the best?"

Avis made a scoffing noise. "You're just toying with me, and I don't find it amusing."

Mick felt angry now, but he kept his voice in check. "My name is Michael Preston Westcott, the third. I am the sole beneficiary of Preston Westcott, Incorporated, of Virginia. Go ahead. Google me. I dare you. And then you can eat crow. But while you're assessing the value of me and my family, bear in mind that there's one huge difference between mine and yours. My parents *love* me and they make sure that I *know* they love me."

"How dare you imply that I don't love my daughter!"

"Take note of that last part. Try to make a list of things you've done or said in the last ten years to let Kate know you love her. The pen will dry out while you're thinking."

Avis made another of those astonished noises and turned to Kate. "Are you going to let him talk to me like this?"

"It's about time *somebody* did. I think the biggest regret of my life is not telling you how I really felt all these years. But you're not an easy person to tell anything to if it goes against what you want to believe."

Avis was stunned into silence. Mick took advantage of it to say, "You need to go. How fortunate that your luggage is still in the car."

"Catherine Jane," she said. "I cannot abide this kind of—"

"Call me one of these days, Mother," Kate interrupted, "and when you can call me by a name that I feel belongs to me, we might have something to talk about."

"You need to go," Mick repeated.

Avis looked at Kate, at Mick, at Kate again, then she stood and huffed out of the room as if she'd been deeply insulted by a bad waiter in a restaurant. After the front door had slammed, Kate looked at Mick with tears pooling in her eyes. "I think that's the most noble and heroic thing anyone has ever done for me."

Mick shrugged. "I just say what I think, you know. It's gotten me into trouble many times."

"Well, today it made you my hero."

Mick smiled and took her hand. "My mother told me that my annoying traits would serve me well one day if I learned to use them wisely. Maybe she was right." His smiled widened. "You were great! I don't know what you were worried about. You handled her marvelously!"

"It was all that coaching you gave me earlier," she said. "I never could have done it without you."

"And how do you feel now?"

"I feel great, actually," Kate said. "Potentially destitute, but great otherwise."

"I meant what I said, Kate. I won't leave you high and dry."

"I know that Mick, and I'm grateful. But I don't want *our* relationship to be based on your being able to meet my needs. *If* we decide to make this permanent, that will be different. For now, I need to consider other options. I've already talked to Chas about what I can do to earn my room and board, if the need arises. And after the baby is born, I can find a job. I'm actually capable of working hard, and I have some skills that make me fairly competent."

"Oh, I'm not worried about that," Mick said. "You were right in what you told her. You *can* do anything you put your mind to, and I'm absolutely certain that you are capable of surviving in this world on your own merits. But right now your health is most important. You need to take care of yourself."

"And I will," Kate said. "Truthfully, I don't think she'll cut off payment. And if she does, I really do believe my father will help me . . . until I have the baby and . . . move on."

"And what about me?" Mick asked, affecting a hurt expression. "You're talking as if you're planning on going forward completely on your own. Should I be offended?"

"No, you should be patient. We both need to be patient and give this some time. If it works out between us, nothing could make me happier. But it needs to be for the right reasons, and at the right time. You understand."

"Of course I understand," he said. "I wouldn't want it any other way."

"Then we should go find some ice cream," Kate said. "Suddenly I really need ice cream."

* * * * *

Kate was amazed at the happiness she felt to no longer be living under the cloud of Avis Fitzgibbons. Twenty-four hours later, her mother hadn't tried to call—which was no surprise. And when Jackson ran Avis's credit card number to do the standard weekly fee, it went through with no problem. Kate counted her blessings and focused on more important things.

Mick told her he had a lot to do on Monday and he probably wouldn't see her much. He said he was preparing some things he wanted to share with his parents—and her—and he had a great deal of work yet to do on the project. Kate continued working on her own project, played with the children, helped Chas here and there, and felt more relaxed about her life than she had in years—if ever. She found it funny that even in facing the reality that she was pregnant—for abhorrent reasons—and all the associated complications, she still felt an unfamiliar inner calm. She knew it was the combined influence of Chas and Jackson, and Mick. She also knew that having faced her mother in that way had cut some ties that had been holding her back and damaging her in ways she'd not realized. The therapist she'd worked with not so many months earlier had also suggested the need to break free from her mother. But at the time she hadn't believed it could be possible. That advice, added upon by the support of her new dear friends, had finally made it possible to take this step.

That inner calm she was feeling was enhanced when she decided to start reading the book that Jackson had given her, the same one that Mick had been so enthused about. Initially her biggest motivation was that she should become more familiar with it, if only to be able to show an interest in something that people she cared about were interested in. But she'd barely read twenty or thirty pages before she recognized a special something about the book that she couldn't quite pinpoint.

Kate became distracted from the book and *everything* else in her life when Tuesday arrived and they were officially counting down hours until Mick's parents arrived. Mick had talked to Jackson about wanting to do some kind of slide show, where he could project pictures from his computer. Jackson told him this issue had come up with previous groups staying at the inn who had wanted to do presentations or slide shows. He had a large screen that attached to some discreet hooks in the ceiling of the formal dining room. Mick was going to purchase a projector that would work with the computer, but Jackson already owned one, and between the two of them they had it set up in no time. Kate knew that Mick had asked Jackson if he and Chas would like to be present for the grand event, and Jackson said he would arrange for a sitter for the kids so the adults could all enjoy it without noise or interruptions.

Kate noticed that Mick was a little nervous, but his excitement far outweighed any nervousness. He was obviously thrilled with the prospect of seeing his parents. And while he was somewhat secretive about what exactly his project entailed, he told her more than once, "I hope you love it."

She assured him that she would, but after it had come up the third time, he said with more soberness, "Kate, I need you to know that all of this was in my head long before I met you."

"I know that," she said.

"But . . . I don't want you to think that I'm just . . . trying to impress you, or—"

"I don't think you're that kind of person."

"I'm not, and I believe you know that, but . . . we really *haven't* known each other that long, and . . . some of this might seem kind of strange. Some of it might even seem kind of personal; I mean . . . in some ways it *is* very personal—between me and my parents—because my life was pretty messed up at some stages, and they've been worried about me, and these months have changed me. Some of what I say to them and share with them . . . is . . . well, I just hope you won't be put off by it. I want you there. I really feel like you should be there. I just hope that you'll keep an open mind, and . . . later, or tomorrow, or when the time is right, we can talk about it some more. I just want you to understand where I'm coming from."

"It's okay, Mick," she said and kissed him quickly. "I'm not going to jump to any conclusions, and I promise to give you the benefit of the doubt. I'm sure that whatever this great plan is of yours, it will be wonderful."

"I hope so," he said. "I guess we'll see. I'm glad my parents are very forgiving people."

"You think there's something they'll hear today that will require forgiveness?"

"Only my keeping it from them this long. Everything else, everything from the past, is stuff we dealt with a long time ago. That stupid teenage stuff I did—that's all forgiven."

"Then everything will be fine," Kate said and hugged him.

Mick drew in the comfort and strength of her embrace and knew she was right. She pulled back and asked, "You're sure they're okay with this pregnancy thing?"

"Absolutely," he said.

"And me? Are they okay with me . . . being in the middle of whatever you're doing?"

"They can't wait to meet you."

"Okay, but—"

"Don't worry," he said. "They'll love you."

He took her hand to walk into the other room, and she tugged on it to stop him. "What?" he asked.

"There's something I need to say, and I want to say it before they get here. I'm sure there will be more commotion with them here, and . . . I just have to say it."

"Okay," he said, turning more toward her but keeping her hand in his.

"I just want you to know that . . . I love you too, Mick. I really do." She saw him smile, but more importantly she could see in his eyes that this was no small thing to him. "I don't know what the future will bring for us, but I want you to know that . . . right now, right here, I'm so glad that you're in my life. And I love you. Whether we part or stay together forever, the impression you've left on my life is deep."

"And vice versa," he said and kissed her with a slow meekness that fully expressed how he felt. But he added for good measure, "I love you too. And I'm voting for together forever."

"Let's just give that some time. Right now we need to see if Chas needs any help in the kitchen. She's in more of a frenzy over putting on a nice supper for your parents than you are over presenting your secret project."

"Then we'd do well to help her," Mick said and led the way.

After Mick had assured Chas that there was nothing to be concerned about and that his parents would be impressed if she served tuna sandwiches, he and Kate each took on some tasks, and everything was well under control long before the anticipated arrival. Polly arrived with her baby to watch the kids, and they visited with her for a few minutes while Chas went to change her clothes. Jackson was out on an errand but was expected to return soon. Chas and Jackson came into the common room at about the same time, and Chas gave Polly instructions while Jackson sat down to play with the kids. Mick and Kate went to the parlor of the inn and sat close together on the couch. When there was nothing more to do but wait, Mick glanced at his watch and said, "Did they say they'd be here by five?"

"It's only 4:45," Kate said and laughed at him. He laughed as well, but it was a nervous laugh. "Hey," Kate said to distract him, "I started reading that book."

She was amazed at how quickly the comment shifted his entire focus to her. "Did you?" he asked with a sparkle of curiosity in his eyes.

"It's . . . fascinating," she said. "I'm barely getting started. We'll have to talk about it . . . later."

"Why not now?" he asked, glancing again at his watch.

"Okay, what do you want to talk about?"

"I'd just like to know your impressions so far."

"Well . . . other than a theology class I took that focused on certain sections of the Bible, I've never really studied scripture before. In a way it seems easier to follow than the Bible; the language is more . . . direct, I suppose."

"Has anything stood out to you so far?" he asked, as if the answer were very important to him.

Kate shrugged. "Not in the text particularly, but . . . I've just really enjoyed my time reading it. There's this kind of . . . calm, peaceful feeling that comes with it. I've felt that way sometimes when I've read really great works of fiction; the classics, the powerful stuff. But it's more than that; more defined than that. And yet, very difficult to describe."

Kate realized he was staring at her, and the curiosity in his eyes had merged into a warm satisfaction. "I was praying you would feel that way when you read it; that you would feel the same way I felt. We have much to talk about. I'm so—"

They heard the outside door open, and Mick shot to his feet. "I hope that's them," he said with a delighted chuckle.

Kate hung back a little as Mick went into the hall. She knew immediately that it *was* them by the way they all laughed when they saw each other. Mick's mother had short dark hair, and the same smile that had been bestowed upon her son. His father had the same blond, curly hair that Mick had, even though it was showing signs of gray. He was near Mick's height and build, with a mild hint of the thickness of middle age. They were both distinguished and nice looking, and Mick was a perfect combination of their physical features.

When Mrs. Westcott saw her son, she dropped her purse and practically ran the few steps toward him. "Oh, my little boy!" she said and wrapped him tightly in her arms. The irony of her calling him that was not lost on Kate, since she was a petite woman who barely came to Mick's shoulder. He laughed and hugged her in return, almost swallowing her up in his embrace, then he lifted her off the floor for a few seconds in a way that seemed common and comfortable between them.

After setting his mother down, he turned to accept a handshake and a hug from his father. "You look great, son," Mr. Westcott said, taking Mick's shoulders.

"So do you," Mick said. "Both of you." He smiled at his mother, who was beaming with pride and adoration. Kate couldn't recall either of her parents *ever* looking at her like that. "It's great to see you!" Mick added. "I'm so glad you were willing to come."

"Of course we would come," Mrs. Westcott said, removing her coat.

Mick helped her and hung it on one of the hooks near the door, while his father removed his own coat and did the same. Kate's heart quickened when she saw Mick's mother turn and notice her there. Mick turned as well, saying eagerly, "Mom, Dad, this is Kate. Kate, these are my parents, Mike and Joy."

Kate stepped forward, expecting perhaps a handshake, or a friendly nod. But Joy hugged Kate with only a little less enthusiasm than she'd given Mick. She took Kate by the shoulders, looked at her with sincere, kind eyes, and said, "It is so good to meet you, my dear. Mick has told us so many good things about you."

"The pleasure is all mine," Kate said. "He's spoken nothing but praise of his parents."

"What a sweet boy," Joy said, winking at Mick. "Did you hear that, Mike? Isn't he a sweet boy."

"Mostly," Mike said with a teasing chuckle.

Joy kept hold of Kate's shoulders and said more softly, "Mick told us what happened to you, and about the baby. I hope that's okay."

"Of course," Kate said.

"We don't want to make you uncomfortable, but perhaps there's less chance for awkwardness if we just talk about it."

Kate could see where Mick got his straightforward approach, and once again she said, "Of course."

Joy's countenance expressed perfect compassion when she said, "Are you doing all right, my dear? Is there anything we can do to make this easier for you?"

Kate couldn't help wondering what it might have been like if her own mother had offered a greeting even half so kind. She fought back the sting of tears that accompanied the thought and smiled at this dear woman. "I'm doing well, thank you. And my every need is being met. But you're very kind."

"You dear, sweet thing," Joy said.

"Mom," Mick nudged her, "you're making it awkward by trying not to make it awkward."

"Nonsense," Joy said and moved to stand beside Kate, putting an arm around her. Kate couldn't remember the last time her mother had hugged her or touched her in any way. "We've cleared the air now, and it's all good."

With Joy having said that, Mike Westcott stepped forward with an outstretched hand. Kate took his hand, then Mike wrapped both of his around it. "You must really be something, my dear," he said, "to have Mick going all mushy like that."

"Is he?" Kate asked teasingly, glancing at Mick.

"He sounded more mushy on the phone than he's ever sounded over *any* girl," Mike said with a wink that was very much like his son.

"Now you're embarrassing me, Dad," Mick said, but he didn't seem to mind. Kate considered the fact that this man was enormously wealthy, and in light of what her life's experience had been with wealthy people, she found it difficult to believe. They were both dressed very nicely, and Joy was wearing some jewelry that looked expensive, though not at all gaudy. Beyond that, they seemed quite ordinary and down to earth, and contrary to what Mick had said, Kate didn't feel at all awkward. The countenance of these people was completely different from that of her own parents, and of their friends and associates.

"Come and sit down," Mick said, motioning toward the parlor. "There are no other guests here tonight, so we have the place to ourselves. Jackson and Chas will be along shortly."

"Oh, the inn is *very* beautiful," Joy said, looking around as they moved into the parlor and were seated. Mike and Joy sat on one couch, and Kate and Mick sat on the other one, facing them. "Didn't you say," Joy went on, "that Agent Leeds married a woman who grew up in this house?"

"That's right," Mick said. "Chas and her grandmother turned it into a bed-and-breakfast, and Jackson came here to stay, and now they're a family."

"What a precious story," Joy said.

They heard footsteps and Mick said, "That's probably them." Everyone stood as Jackson and Chas entered the room.

"Agent Leeds," Mike said, giving him a hearty handshake. "I didn't know if we'd ever see you again, but I'm sure glad for this opportunity."

"It's good to see you as well," Jackson said. He let go of Mike's hand and Joy threw her arms around him.

Jackson looked a little taken off guard, and a moment later everyone realized that Joy was crying. She stepped back and sniffled, dabbing moisture off her cheeks with her fingertips. "Forgive me," Joy said. "I didn't know if we'd ever see you again, either. But I always hoped that we would. I know I told you that day there was no way to express our gratitude for what you did, but . . ." Joy's emotion overcame her, and Kate felt a little choked up herself, considering the story behind this reunion. Mike put a comforting arm around his wife. "Every day with Mick alive and well and a part of our lives has been a special gift to us, and you helped make that possible. I have thought about you every day. I just want to say how deeply, deeply grateful I am—as a mother—that you were in the right place at the right time. You were surely an instrument in God's hands to answer our prayers."

"That's exactly it, Mrs. Westcott," Jackson said. "The matter was in God's hands. I was just doing my job."

"I think it was more than that," Mike said.

"That's what I told him," Mick added.

"I've heard you were very good at your job," Mike said.

"I tried to be," Jackson said, glancing down. "I'm just glad it all turned out so well."

"And now we're together again," Joy said, regaining her composure, "after all these years. And this must be your sweet wife."

"Yes," Jackson said, feeling more comfortable now that the attention wasn't focused on him, "this is Chas."

"It's such an immense pleasure to meet you, Chas," Joy said.

"This is my mother, Joy, and my father, Mike," Mick said. "Now you've met Chas. And you need to call Jackson by his name. He gets offended if you call him Agent Leeds."

"Not offended," Jackson corrected lightly. "It's just not true anymore."

They all sat back down and Chas said, "Dinner will be ready in a short while."

"That's very kind," Joy said, "but you shouldn't have gone to any trouble for—"

"This is a great occasion," Chas said. "Mick and Kate pitched in, and Jackson took good care of the children."

"Mick said you had children," Mike said.

Chas and Jackson talked about their kids and mentioned they had a sitter for the evening so they could relax, but Mike and Joy could meet the children tomorrow. The Westcotts had lots of questions about Jackson's life since the day he'd rescued their son. They were horrified to hear a very brief account of Jackson's own hostage situation, but thrilled to hear how well he'd come to terms with it. They spoke openly of these horrible events, and the struggles of making peace with them. Mick's parents seemed surprised when Mick boldly declared that *he* had made peace with it, but he preferred to share details with them later.

Since dinner was ready, they all moved to the formal dining room, while Mike and Joy asked questions about the inn and its history. Kate and Mick helped Chas and Jackson put the meal on the table, and Jackson surprised Mick by asking him if he would offer the blessing on the food. Mick was taken off guard for a moment, but Jackson gave him an encouraging nod, and Mick was surprised at how easily he was able to do it after sharing so many meals—and prayers—with Jackson and his family. In the prayer, Mick expressed gratitude for having his parents there, and for being gathered with good friends and loved ones. After the amen, he discreetly glanced at his parents, noting that they both seemed pleasantly surprised.

The conversation picked up and lightened as Jackson and Chas shared the story of their meeting and becoming a family. Then Chas prodded Mike and Joy to share the story of *their* family. When they were finished eating, Jackson insisted that Mick and Kate give their guests a tour of the inn while he helped Chas clean up. They all ended up back together in the parlor, all chatting and laughing comfortably as if their familiarity had been in place for years. Kate loved the way that Mick held her hand. She noticed that his parents often held hands as well. Apparently he'd had a good example in such things. Kate couldn't recall her parents ever showing *any* affection for each other. She watched Mick closely while they all continued to talk. He caught her looking at him and smiled. She wondered if it could really be possible that she could spend the rest of her life having him by her side, and being a part of a family that actually knew how to love and be loved. Oh, how she *wanted* it to be possible!

CHAPTER 13

"We're still waiting to hear what you've been doing all these months," Mike Westcott said to his son. "We've worried and wondered, and you told us if we came here you'd tell us everything."

"Are you going to keep us in suspense?" Joy asked. "Do we have to wait until tomorrow? You sounded pretty excited about it on the phone."

"If you had other plans for this evening," Mike added, "it's okay. We don't want to intrude with your friends. We just—"

"Now's as a good a time as any," Mick said. "And I've asked them to join us, anyway. I confess that I've talked a little bit with Chas and Jackson about what I've done, but I've kept Kate in suspense."

"He's keeping secrets from the ones he loves most," Jackson said, but Kate noted he looked pleased. In Jackson's opinion, whatever Mick had shared with him was apparently something good.

"I'd like to show you some of the pictures I took while I was traveling," Mick said and stood up. "I say 'some' because I took several hundred. I've picked out the best ones and put together kind of a slide show . . . back in the dining room where we ate."

"How delightful," Joy said, and they all stood up.

While they walked across the hall, Mick said, "I just thought I could tell you a little bit about what I've been doing while we look at the pictures." He chuckled nervously. "I think it's true that a picture really is worth a thousand words."

In the dining room, Jackson rolled down the screen that the men had hung from the ceiling earlier, while Mick moved a little table from a corner that held the laptop computer and projector, and he turned them on. Mick and Jackson then turned the couch near the fireplace in the other direction, and they also moved a few of the chairs from around the dining table. Mick sat in a chair next to his computer. Chas and Jackson took two chairs, side by side. Mike and Joy sat together on the couch, and Kate ended up on the couch next to Joy. When everyone was settled, Mick turned off the lights, and a projection of the desktop on his computer lit up the room. He made a couple of adjustments, then a picture of Mick and another man next to a small jet came up on the screen.

"That's Tony," Mick said. "My parents know Tony, but for the rest of you, Tony flies the plane. Tony kind of got roped into going on this adventure with me, because I needed him to get me where I was going. He's kind of a loner and he likes his job, but I don't think either one of us knew what we were in for. Once I made the decision to embark on this adventure, I decided that I needed to document everything with pictures, and that meant we needed a picture of us by the plane. That's at the airport in Butte, Montana, by the way—the same day I came here to talk to Jackson. Our conversation was very brief that day, but it changed my life. He gave me two pieces of advice, and I was determined to heed both of them."

Mick changed pictures to show him and Tony waiting in a long line of tired and impatient-looking people.

"Who took these pictures?" Mike asked.

"Oh, I just asked random people here and there—at least if I wanted both Tony and me in the picture. This is just one shot that represents a ridiculous amount of hours that we spent tangled in red tape at various times throughout our adventure. We both had passports, but obtaining the necessary papers to get into certain parts of the world wasn't always easy."

The next picture made Kate's heart pound. She'd perhaps been expecting photos of great tourist attractions throughout the world, and some explanation of how Mick had found himself among the beauties and wonders of his explorations. What she saw was Mick and Tony, both sunburned and dirty, among a group of smiling, dark-faced children, with signs of abject poverty clearly evident. Kate heard Joy gasp softly, and knew that she was equally surprised by what she was seeing.

"And so the adventure begins," Mick said. He set the computer to run through pictures at an even pace as a slide show, while he leaned back in his chair and said, "When I came here to personally thank the man who had saved my life, I hadn't expected to end up telling him that I felt like my life had no meaning. I felt like I'd spent my whole life since that horrible incident just trying to figure out who I was. He suggested that God had saved my life that day for a reason, but I certainly couldn't think of anything I'd done that was really worthwhile. And I couldn't imagine anything I might do in the future that could really leave a mark on the world."

While Mick talked, the pictures kept filing past their eyes, clearly depicting hard work and various projects in horrific living conditions among many kinds of people and different cultures. Kate's heart began to thud as she considered the quiet work she'd been doing all these weeks, making and sending her little kits to just such places via Salt Lake City. She recalled Mick telling her after he'd seen her work that they were so much the same. But she never could have imagined! She realized she had tears on her face the same moment she heard Joy sniffle, and looked over to see *both* of Mick's parents weeping openly. If they had spent years concerned about their son finding his way in this world, then surely what they were seeing was nothing short of a miracle.

Mick continued to talk while the pictures went on and on. "Jackson told me that I should get outside myself. He said that I should stop putting so much energy into wondering what was wrong with *me,* and look at what was wrong with the world and do something to make it better. He asked me if I'd ever considered how many people in a third-world country could be supported for a year with the cost of a hot car, and that a man with my resources ought to be able to find all kinds of philanthropic opportunities, if I just started digging. So I dug."

Mick remained silent for a few minutes while pictures continued to tell the story of his hands-on involvement with the people he'd searched out who were in need of humanitarian aid. And then he said, "Okay, Kate, this next part is for you."

Kate only had a moment to wonder what he meant before she saw photos that documented the story he began to tell of encountering some Mormon missionaries who were assisting in the distribution of the kind of kits that Kate had been working so hard to make. "It was one of the most amazing things I'd ever witnessed," Mick said, "and I remember wondering about the people back in the States who put so much effort into these kinds of projects."

Heat began to burn in Kate's chest, and her tears became difficult to keep silent. She met Mick's eyes across the room in the light that kept flashing off and on while the pictures changed. She saw the potential for many conversations they had yet to share, and she felt the bond between them deepen in ways that could never be put into words. She turned her attention back to the screen, not wanting to miss anything.

"Ironically," Mick said, "it was my conversation with one of these missionaries that changed my life in a different way, and made it possible for me to follow the *other* advice that Jackson had given me."

When Mick paused, his mother asked in a voice strained with emotion, "What advice was that?"

"He told me that I needed to forgive the people who had hurt me. And since he'd been through such horrible things himself, I could hardly convince myself that he didn't know what he was talking about. Throughout the entire journey, I'd thought about it, and even prayed about it, every day. And then this missionary said some things that made all the difference." Pictures came up of Mick with an older couple wearing black-and-white name tags, and then with a couple of young men with the same kind of name tags. They were all wearing big smiles that seemed enhanced by the sweat and dirt on their faces and clothes, evidence of hard work under extremely adverse conditions.

"It was after that," Mick said, "when it all came together for me, and I *was* able to forgive the men who traumatized me so badly, and nearly stole my life from me. I really have made peace with it, and now I'm ready to move on and make something of my life."

Mick remained quiet as the remainder of the pictures played out. The last one was of Mick and Tony next to the plane again, looking more tan and weathered than they had in the first picture. Mick was wearing that scarf that he wore frequently. Kate knew now that it had some significance from his experiences. A minute of darkness following the end of the slide show allowed everyone to reclaim their composure. Mick flipped on the light and moved his chair so that he was facing his parents.

"There's a couple more things I want to say," Mick said, "and then we can talk more tomorrow about any of this . . . if you want to. First of all, it's important that I formally thank you for everything you have done for me. You have given me a good life, and . . . I know that I gave you grief sometimes, and I took things for granted. But you always loved me no matter what, and I want you to know how grateful I am for all that . . ." He stopped when it became evident that his mother was crying none too softly against her husband's shoulder, and Mike had tears on his face. "What?" Mick asked.

Mike cleared his throat and spoke to his son as if no one else was in the room. "We always felt so . . . responsible . . . for what happened."

"But you weren't," Mick said.

"I'm not so sure," Mike answered. "We've talked about this before, son. If we hadn't been so flashy with the money and—"

"Listen to me, Dad, Mom . . . I admit that I felt angry over that at times. I admit there were times when I was trying to place blame and I said some unkind things. But everything's different now. You were always good parents. You always loved me and took good care of me. None of what happened was your fault. Those men were greedy and evil. But I've forgiven them, and you need to do the same."

"How?" his mother asked. "How can you?"

"We can talk about that some more, Mom, when it's not so late. For now there's just one more thing I need to say." Mick turned more toward his father. "Dad, I want a job. I want to come to work with you and start earning my way. I have some ideas that I want to propose to you; we can talk about it tomorrow. I'm hoping that you'll at least consider what I have to say."

"Of course I will," Mike said, stunned and overcome. "Nothing could make me happier than to have you come to work with me. I'm certain we can come to some agreement that will work for both of us."

"Good," Mick said, planting his hands on his thighs. "In that case, I think we've had sufficient drama and tears for one day, and the two of you are probably exhausted from traveling." He looked at Kate. "I know Kate's tired. It's past the hour when she usually turns into a pumpkin."

She comically rubbed her belly and said, "I'm always a pumpkin."

This provoked a chuckle from everyone, which eased the tension, then Jackson offered to help Mike get the luggage out of the car and take care of getting them settled into their room. Mick helped as well. When that was taken care of, everyone said good night at the foot of the stairs, and Mick's parents went up to the second floor to get some sleep.

Jackson surprised Mick by shaking his hand firmly as he said, "That was very impressive, kid. When I said what I did to you, I never imagined that you would go to such lengths. I'm proud to be your friend."

Mick gave Jackson a quick hug and said, "It's the other way around."

Chas hugged him as well and said, "We're so glad to have you here . . . and your parents; they're wonderful people."

"Yes, they are," Mick agreed, then Chas and Jackson said good-night and went to their home and closed the adjoining door.

When Mick was alone with Kate, she turned to him and said, "Now I know what you meant. That day . . . when I showed you what I was doing . . . I . . ."

"I was trying not to cry, Kate. It's just so . . ."

"Yeah," she said, as if neither of them could come up with a word.

"We're so much the same, Kate."

"Yes," she said and put a hand to his face. "I want to look at those pictures again sometime . . . and all the others you took."

"I'll look forward to it," he said and hugged her. "You're exhausted," he added. He could tell by the way she slumped into his embrace.

"I admit that I am," she said, and he walked her up the stairs. "There's so much I want to say, but I think my brain is on overload."

"We can catch up soon," he said and kissed her good-night at the door to her room. "They love you, by the way. They're enchanted by you; I can tell."

"They're wonderful people, Mick," she said, once again wishing her own parents could have been half as interested and involved in her life. "Just like you," she added and kissed him once more before she went into her room and closed the door. She leaned against it a moment, then sat down on the edge of the bed and cried, still overcome by his stories and his pictures and the uncanny coincidences. "Oh, Mick," she muttered into the empty room, "we're so much the same."

* * * * *

Kate woke up with a sense that she'd overslept. She looked at the clock and wondered if she could hurry and get herself together quickly enough to not miss breakfast with Mick—assuming he would be eating at the same time he usually did. Perhaps he'd already eaten with his parents.

Kate approached the guest dining room and heard a burst of laughter that she recognized as a combination of Mick's and each of his parents'. She entered quietly, not wanting to intrude, but smiling to see their enjoyment of each other's company. Mick saw her immediately, as if he'd purposely seated himself to be facing the door, anticipating her arrival. He stood and crossed the room to give her a quick kiss in greeting.

"Good morning," he said.

"Good morning," she replied and glanced past him to see his parents both looking on as if they were watching a romantic movie.

"Good morning, my dear," Joy said as she stood from her chair to embrace Kate. "Did you sleep well?"

"I did, thank you," Kate said. "How about you?"

"Oh, very well," Joy said.

"Wonderful bed," Mike added as he stood to greet Kate with a hug as well.

They chatted lightly over breakfast, then Mick asked Kate if she would show his parents what she had been working on.

"It's all kind of a mess," Kate said, "but that would be fine."

Intermixed with Kate explaining to Joy and Mike what she was doing and how she had gotten started, Mick told his parents the obvious miracle of this unforeseen connection in the work they'd been doing. Joy and Mike both agreed and seemed very impressed with Kate's work. Joy especially asked Kate many questions and showed such a genuine interest in her that she couldn't help but feel touched.

They left Kate to her projects so that Mick could spend some time with his parents. He'd warned her about this part of his plan, and she had wholeheartedly agreed that they needed time without a newcomer hanging around. Mick left the inn with his parents, and Kate went to find Chas, visiting with her while they folded laundry and enjoyed some time with the children. They both agreed that Mike and Joy Westcott were wonderful people.

Chas said, "If things keep going as they are, you may well be marrying into a very fine family. It could help make up for what you haven't had in your own family."

"I won't say it hasn't crossed my mind," Kate said. "We just need time."

"You don't want to do anything rash," Chas said. "On the other hand, you don't want to miss the opportunity of a lifetime just because your situation isn't ideal."

"Ideal?" Kate countered, realizing that Chas had come to know her very well. "I'm pregnant, for heaven's sake. I can assure you that with all of my girlish dreams of when and how I might meet Mr. Right, this wasn't it. And if he *is* Mr. Right, my possible future in-laws have . . ."

"Have what?" Chas pressed.

"Well, look at me," Kate said, pointing at her belly.

"I can understand why this is hard for you," Chas said. "But I don't think that *anyone* else is thinking badly of you or feeling upset over the circumstances—beyond their concern for you, of course."

"I know that," Kate said more softly. "I just . . . wish it could be different."

"It's all *going* to be different," Chas said, giving her a hug. "Pregnancy can feel eternal when you're in the middle of it. But this will resolve itself soon enough, and you can make a good life for yourself—whether it's with Mick or not."

Kate smiled at her friend and said, "You're right, I know. Just keep reminding me."

"It will be all right," Chas said, and a moment later she asked, "Are you still firm on choosing adoption?"

Kate felt stunned. They'd never talked about any other option, so she couldn't understand why Chas would put it that way. "I don't know what other choice I have," Kate said. "I'm in no position to be a mother."

"Okay, but . . . if you were . . . do you think your decision would be different?"

"I don't know. I haven't really thought about it. I've just tried to accept that it had to be this way."

"Well, maybe you should think it through more carefully, so that you won't have any doubts when the time comes."

Kate thought about that a minute. "I don't know how it's possible to make such a decision and know for certain that it's right . . . that you won't regret it."

Chas urged Kate to sit down with her, and she talked to Kate about her own beliefs in praying for guidance, and how to understand the answers. Chas was aware that Kate believed in God, even though religion had never been a part of her life. Kate couldn't deny that the things Chas said made complete sense. She thanked her for the advice and said that she needed to give it some thought. She felt a desire to talk to Mick about it, and she was glad to know that he actually had some interest in religion. She'd often thought that having *more* religion in her life couldn't hurt, but she'd never been exposed to anything that had held her attention. Mick's interest combined with all she'd observed in Chas's home had started changing her perspective, but she felt so infantile in such matters. As with everything else in her life, it seemed she just needed time.

"And how are you doing with the other?" Chas asked.

"The other?"

"With . . . what actually happened to you? I know you don't remember, but . . . I worry about how it's affected you, nonetheless."

Kate shrugged. "I think I keep waiting for something to jump out of my subconscious and freak me out. I know that some women in my position have nightmares or panic attacks—understandably so. But I can't really address what I don't feel or remember. I feel . . . fine. I just hope it isn't some form of denial."

"I'm sure you'll be able to handle whatever comes up," Chas said. "And maybe it *won't* come up. Maybe you're just a strong woman who has come to terms with it enough to move forward."

"I don't know about that," Kate said, then her thoughts shifted to Chas. "And what about *you?* I know you've been struggling with your own feelings about what happened to your mother."

Chas sighed heavily. "I'm working on it, but . . . it still bothers me when I think about it. I keep praying that I can make peace with it.

I believe I will eventually. I'm not sure what else to do, really. If I felt like I needed to talk to a counselor, I would. But it just doesn't feel that drastic."

"That's kind of how I feel," Kate said. "Sometimes I wonder if I need more time with a therapist, but then I wonder what I'd actually talk about. I've talked it through with you, so it's not like I'm holding it inside. And I don't have any symptoms or issues that are bothering me; not really. So . . . I guess we'll both just hang on and see what happens."

"Good plan," Chas said. "Now let's get some lunch. There are some great leftovers from last night."

"Sounds wonderful," Kate said, wishing she would never have to leave this place, and hoping that there wasn't some unseen monster inside of her that had yet to be faced.

* * * * *

Mick drove his parents into Butte while they caught up on many things, talking about relatives and friends and all the happenings that might have been overlooked in their weekly phone conversations. They asked Mick to tell them more details about his travels and related experiences, and he enjoyed sharing things that they'd not had the time to get into the previous evening. They had lunch at a nice restaurant where they were able to sit in a quiet booth that felt private and secluded so that they could continue their conversation. When the meal was winding down, Mick finally felt it was the right time to approach them with his little business proposition. He knew they were surprised when he opened up with some discussion over the law of tithing. He referred to the way it was taught in the Bible, even though the idea had come to him when he'd read references to it in the Book of Mormon. He then merged into a study he'd found on businesses that had applied the principle of tithing in their dealings, and how their profits had flourished as a result. Mick gave them memorized statistics and examples connected with some very successful businesses that he knew his father would recognize.

Mick noted that his parents seemed engaged by what he was telling them, rather than just being politely diplomatic. He took a deep breath and dove into the main point. He proposed that his father take on the principle of applying ten percent of his profits toward philanthropic projects and humanitarian aid, locally and throughout the world. Mick expressed his firm belief that even if it didn't expand profits for the company, with the kind of money they had, the gratification from making a difference in the world should be enough. He then took another deep breath and proposed that his father consider officially making him the head of this project, to at least give it a probationary period where they could try it and see how it worked.

Mike asked Mick some pretty intense questions, and the discussion became more like a job interview. But Mick had expected this, and he was prepared to take it on—more prepared than he ever had been. His father was a tough businessman; he'd learned that from his own father. And he didn't leave his business or his assets to take care of themselves. He was savvy about all that was going on, and he expected integrity and hard work from every one of the thousands of people he employed. Mick made it clear that he would expect no special treatment. He just wanted a job, and a chance to prove that he could apply what he'd become passionate about in a positive way.

"And you know what the ghost of Jacob Marley said to Scrooge," Mick said.

"What did he say?" Joy asked.

"He said that mankind should be our business . . . or words to that effect." His parents both smiled, and he shrugged. "I've been staying at the Dickensian Inn," he said. "I guess it rubs off."

Mick summarized his plan briefly and felt like the conversation had gone as well as it possibly could have.

"Your proposal is well thought out and has a great deal of merit," Mike said.

"Thank you," Mick replied.

"I'd like some time to think about it," his father added, but Mick had expected that as well.

"I wouldn't expect you *not* to take some time," he said. "I'll e-mail you all of the information I've gathered."

"That would be great," Mike said, and they changed the subject.

They did a little bit of shopping, mostly because Joy couldn't travel anywhere without doing *a little bit of shopping.* However, Mick wasn't prepared for the way that Joy kept talking about Kate while she wandered around the mall. It seemed that overnight Joy had taken to the idea of treating Kate like a daughter. When Mick thought of how Kate's mother had treated her, he almost felt choked up to see Joy looking through racks of maternity clothes, asking Mick if he thought Kate would like this or that.

"I don't want to be too pushy," Joy said, "but a woman enjoys something new once in a while. Do you think it's okay if I buy her something?"

"As long as it comes from the heart," Mick said, "I'm certain it's more than okay."

Joy finally settled on an outfit that looked comfortable but stylish. She took a guess at Kate's size and bought it, along with a set of rose-scented bath products.

When Joy declared that she'd spent enough money to feel satisfied, they drove back to Anaconda. About halfway there, Mick said, "I also want to tell you that those Mormon missionaries I met left a pretty deep impression on me. I've been studying their beliefs."

"I've heard some good things about them," Joy said.

Mike added, "We read an article about them a while back. We were both rather pleasantly surprised, I think. I don't believe the world perceives them very accurately, if what we read is true."

"That's exactly what I thought," Mick said, certain that what his parents had just told him was surely one more piece of evidence that God's hand was working in his life. "Ironically," he added, "I didn't know until I came back to visit Jackson that . . . well, they're Mormons."

"No kidding?" Mike said and chuckled. "That *is* ironic."

"So, you've found religion as well as a purpose," Joy said, sounding pleased.

"Yes, I believe I have," Mick said. "I hope you're okay with that."

"As long as you're not doing anything illegal or immoral," Mike said. "We just want you to be happy."

"So you've always told me," Mick said.

"And I assume," Joy said, "that you'll be staying at the inn until . . ."

"I'm going to stay until Kate has the baby, or until she tells me to hit the road. As long as she wants me around, I want to help her through this. Beyond that, I guess we'll see what happens."

"I guess that means you won't be coming home for Christmas," Joy said.

"I'm ashamed to say I hadn't thought about that," Mick said. "Let's talk about it when Christmas gets a little closer."

Mick was intrigued with the thought of spending Christmas at the Dickensian Inn with Kate, but he would miss his parents. However, it wouldn't be the first time he'd missed Christmas with them. He wondered if they would consider coming back. But that was a decision that needed to be made when the time came.

When they returned to the inn, Mike sat down in the parlor to read the *Wall Street Journal* he'd picked up in the city. Joy went with Mick to find Kate, who was in the project room, busy at the sewing machine.

"You're back," she said and stood up. Mick hugged her. "Did you have a good time?"

"Oh, we did!" Joy said and held up two fancy little shopping bags. "Forgive me, but I just couldn't resist getting you a little something. I hope you won't think it's too nervy of me, or—"

"No, of course not," Kate said, hesitating a moment before she reached out and took the bags. How could she not think of the contrast to her own mother? Kate didn't need gifts to feel loved or appreciated. It was simply the act of someone thinking of her, and going to the trouble to get her something—just because. It didn't matter what was in the bags. It was the fact that she couldn't remember the last time her mother had given her a gift for *any* reason. Even for birthdays and Christmas, Avis had always just handed Kate some cash and told her to get something for herself.

"Are you all right?" Mick asked, putting a hand on her shoulder. The question alerted Kate to the fact that she'd been staring at the bags in her hand for several seconds. She was unprepared for the tears that came in response to his question. She looked up at him, feeling helpless to explain and afraid that her emotion would ruin the moment. She saw him look confused for just a second, then perfect understanding appeared in his eyes before he put his arms around her.

Kate immediately found her way to that safe place against Mick's shoulder, and the tears burst out of her. She felt the shopping bags being removed from her hands and heard Joy say quietly, "Did I do something wrong?"

"No, of course not," Mick said gently. "I think you did something right."

"I don't understand," Joy said.

Kate struggled to gain some composure and eased away from Mick, wiping at her tears, trying not to feel embarrassed to be crying in front of Joy. "I'm sorry," Kate said. "It's just that it's been so long since . . . I mean . . ."

When she couldn't think of how to explain, she was glad to hear Mick say, "I think she means that her mother never thinks to buy her gifts, and it probably just feels good to have someone think of her and do something nice."

"Yes," Kate said, offering him a grateful smile, "that's what I wanted to say."

"It seems you know her well," Joy said and took hold of Kate's arm, urging her to sit down. She set the shopping bags aside and sat next to Kate, taking hold of her hand. "I would never want to take away a mother's rightful role in her daughter's life. However, if she's not filling that role, I am more than happy to make up the difference. You're a precious girl, Kate; that's evident—if only in the way that Mick cares for you so very much." Joy smiled at her son, then turned back to Kate. "You're everything I ever would have wanted in a daughter, if I'd been able to have one. I *do* hope it works out with you and Mick. Having you a part of the family would be so grand." She wiped her fingers over Kate's cheeks to help dry her tears, as if Kate were a little girl. They shared a smile, and Joy added, "No need to be ashamed of tears, sweetheart. Tears are good for you."

"So she always told me," Mick said. "Now, why don't you open your presents."

"We can exchange it if it doesn't fit," Joy said, "or if you don't like it."

"You're just so sweet," Kate said and looked into the bags to see what Joy had gotten for her. She loved the outfit and declared it to be the perfect size, and she also loved the bath products, admitting that long baths were one of her favorite luxuries. The two women hugged, and Kate thanked Joy for being so kind and thoughtful.

"You're welcome," Joy said, then looked around the room. "I'd love to hear more about what you're doing, Kate." She asked some specific questions and Mick hung around, mostly observing as his mother bonded with the woman he intended to marry. He knew what this meant to Kate, but he doubted that Kate could know how badly his mother had wanted a daughter, and how this would fill an empty place in *her* life.

That evening, Kate joined Mick and his parents while they used the kitchen of the inn to prepare one of their traditional gourmet meals. Kate had come to feel comfortable with Mike and Joy in the short amount of time she'd spent with them, and they had a wonderful time. Jackson and Chas joined them for dinner, and this time the little ones were present. Mike and Joy fussed over Charles and Isabelle, entertained by their antics and making comments on how delightful children were.

The following day Mike and Joy had to leave so that Mike could get back to business matters in Virginia. Kate was sad to see them go, and she couldn't help hoping that it really might be possible to be a part of their family. But she reminded herself that she had known Mick only a number of days. Turning to look at him once his parents had driven away, however, it didn't feel like days. It felt as if she'd *always* known him.

"Did everything go well?" Kate asked him. They'd hardly had a moment alone while his parents had been there.

"It did," he said.

"How did your business proposition go?"

"Fine," he said. "Dad said he needed to think about it . . . which I expected."

"Are you going to tell *me* about it?" she asked.

"I would love to," he said, and they sat in the parlor to have a long talk. After Mick shared his proposal, they talked more about Mick's travels and experiences, and they marveled once again about the passions they had in common, most especially to make the world a better place.

Mick told her about the scarf that he wore sometimes. He said it had been given to him by an elderly woman who made them, and an interpreter had helped him understand her wish that it would bring him good luck, just as his coming to their village had given help to her grandchildren. He said the scarf had come to represent all he'd learned and felt during his travels, and he liked wearing it, but he'd noticed it had started looking a little tattered, and he didn't want to wear it out. It would always be precious to him.

"That's very sweet," Kate said, thinking how wonderful it would be to have such an experience.

The conversation halted when Kate let out a gasp because the baby had kicked her. "Oh, it's getting bigger and stronger," she said, her hand pressed over her belly.

"It's such a paradox, isn't it," Mick said. "A baby is such a wonderful thing; so innocent and perfect. But to have a baby come from a situation like this is . . . strange. It must feel strange for you, especially."

"I admit that it does," she said, looking down at her hand as it caressed the mound where the baby grew. "Sometimes I'm not sure what to think . . . or how to feel. I don't know. Maybe I won't be able to fully figure that out until after it's born . . . after it's over. Oh, there it goes again," she said and laughed. "You want to feel it?" she asked.

"What? Me?" he asked. "Is that possible?"

"Of course it is," she said. "Although, it can be somewhat unpredictable, so you need to be patient. Chas has felt it a few times. Come on." Kate took his hand and pressed it over the place where the baby had just kicked a couple of times. "Sometimes," she said, "I can almost feel it roll over." She looked at Mick's stunned expression and laughed softly. "It's not some kind of alien that's going to pop out and bite you. Relax."

"Okay," he said and chuckled tensely. She pressed her hand over his and felt him relax a little. Their eyes met, and the moment suddenly felt very intimate. In the natural course of life, if two people who loved each other were sharing the experiences of pregnancy, they would also be the parents of the baby. It felt strange and surreal to be falling in love under such circumstances, but Kate was grateful for Mick's perfect acceptance and compassion, and she tried to remember that this was temporary. They would move beyond it and go on with their lives. Still, in that moment, the reality of the baby she was going to have couldn't be ignored. Mick's eyes held a sparkle of fascination as he moved his gaze to where his hand was pressed. Now that he'd relaxed a little, he tightened it more over her belly. Just a moment later, as if in response to his movement, the baby kicked beneath his fingers, and Mick laughed.

"Did you feel that?" Kate asked, even though she knew he had.

"I did!" he said. "It's so . . . enchanting."

"It is, isn't it," she said, and something occurred to her that she knew should be voiced. "Thank you."

"For what?"

"The way you . . . talk about the baby; the way you . . . seem to know how I feel. It means a lot to me. As hard as this is, I can't ignore the fact that there's a baby growing inside of me. *If* I were spending time with a man like Henry, for instance—which I would *not*—he would probably try to simply ignore the situation, as if that might make it not real. He would make the whole thing awkward. I think he'd want me to feel ashamed."

"It's a good thing you have more sense than to hang out with someone like Polo Boy."

"That's right," she chuckled. "I have the good sense to hang out with someone like you."

"I'm very glad of *that*," he said, and the baby kicked again, making them both laugh.

Their eyes met again and Mick wanted to kiss her, but he didn't want kissing her to become so comfortable that it lost its magic. He reached out tentatively to touch her face as if she were a timid animal that might bolt if he got too close.

"Kate, I know that I can't possibly begin to understand what you're dealing with, or what it takes for a woman to heal from what you've been through. But I *want* to understand, and I want to help you. I also have this insatiable desire to kiss you."

She smiled. "You don't need to ask my permission."

"I know but . . . I want you to know that it's always a choice. And I want it to always mean something." She looked surprised by the comment, but not upset, so he pressed forward. "I must confess that after I'd made some terrible mistakes with women and I came to regret my behavior, my mother told me that a kiss should be respectful; it should be a genuine expression of affection—nothing less, *ever!* She'd actually told me that years earlier, but I'd been too snotty to listen or remember or care. All of the above, maybe. I want you to know now that any effort I make to express my affection for you comes with that intention. But I know you've been hurt, and you always have the right to tell me no. Tell me if it's too much too fast. Talk to me about what you're feeling." He let out a tense chuckle. "I'm talking too much, as usual, but . . . I would never want you to misconstrue my intentions or feel uncomfortable." He paused and took in her expression, not sure where he stood. "Now it's your turn to say something."

"You're very sweet, Mick. And I appreciate your talking about it; I really do. The problem is that . . . I don't remember anything. I'm afraid that something might happen to trigger a memory in my subconscious and I'll freak out or something. If that ever happens, I just . . . well, I guess I want to apologize in advance."

"We'll just take it slow and deal with whatever comes up," he said, easing his fingers into her hair. "Is it okay if I kiss you now?"

"If I didn't want you to kiss me, I can assure you that I would let you know." She softened her voice. "Yes, Mick, it's okay if you kiss me." She lifted a hand to his face to echo her words, then her eyes fluttered closed as she lifted her face toward his, making it perfectly simple, and simply perfect. He kept his hand over her belly, and she kept her hand over his. It was a perfectly intimate moment, just the three of them. But Kate couldn't help wondering how this story would turn out.

CHAPTER 14

The Montana winter settled in deeply, surrounding the Dickensian Inn with a soft comforter of snow. Kate continued working on her projects and helping Chas with the usual tasks each day. Mick helped Kate some with putting kits together and shipping boxes. He also enjoyed helping with the children and spending time with Jackson. Kate kept watching him closely, silently assessing if her feelings for him were simply a temporary fascination, or if he truly had the character traits to be a good husband. She *wanted* to share her future with him, but she just wasn't sure if it was right.

Kate pondered the decision-making process that Chas had shared with her, and she continued reading the Book of Mormon in little snatches. She began to make prayer a part of her daily life, and she even went to church with the family when Mick was determined to go and wanted her to come along. She just took it all in and wondered if she could trust all the good feelings she had. She asked Chas again about the difference between the peace and the stupor of thought that she had described. Chas told her it was a simple difference, and while it could be subtle, there was no disputing the difference when you felt it. Kate liked that explanation, and she realized as she examined her feelings for Mick in that light, she felt nothing negative at all. She hoped he would stick around as he'd said he would. At this point, she realized he'd have to exhibit some pretty bad behavior to counter everything good she knew about him—and all that she felt. She'd spent enough time with him now to believe that he was all he seemed to be. No one could fake good behavior for that long when they were often together for so many hours a day. While they hadn't known each other long in the spectrum of time on the calendar, the amount of time they'd spent talking and sharing activities equated with many months of dating. It was Chas who had mentioned the analogy, and it settled well with Kate, making her feel more comfortable with her desire to move forward in her relationship with this incredible man. If she didn't have pregnancy and childbirth in the middle of all of this, it would be a lot less complicated.

Mick became excited when two young men who were serving as missionaries came to the house to teach Mick more about the gospel and to answer his questions. At Mick's request, Jackson had arranged for the missionaries to come. Mick invited Kate to join him in what would be weekly visits, and she was happy to do so. The missionaries were pleased to hear that she was reading the Book of Mormon, and they were able to answer some questions she had about it. She didn't feel the zeal for this religion that she knew Mick felt, but she felt enough intrigue that she had no problem with keeping an open mind and remaining involved.

Mick's parents came to stay at the inn for Thanksgiving, and they all had a wonderful time. Chas's grandfather joined them for the traditional feast and related activities, and so did Polly and her husband, Elliott. Kate and Mick had both gotten to know Polly and Elliott quite well as they'd come and gone from the inn, and they all had a marvelous time together. The day after Thanksgiving, Jackson's sister Melinda arrived from Arkansas. She'd shared the holiday with her children and grandchildren at home, but she'd wanted to spend some time with her brother's family as well. Melinda quickly bonded with the newcomers, and everyone had a great time. Kate found it difficult to believe that Jackson and Melinda were siblings. From their outward appearance, they seemed to have nothing in common. Jackson was conservative and reserved. Melinda was colorful and exuberant. But Kate quickly began to see that they were both equally kindhearted and generous. Kate and Mick both agreed that they liked Melinda very much.

On Saturday Mike and Joy returned home to Virginia, but they left some wrapped gifts with instructions to save them for Christmas. Before they left, Mick's father told him that he'd considered his business proposal and had discussed it with members of the board. They had made the decision to give the project a trial period of two years, and Mick was being put in charge. He would officially begin the first of February. Kate felt touched to realize that this date had surely been decided on because Kate's baby was due the first week of January, and by February the matter would all be taken care of. In the meantime, Mick would start doing some work by phone and online to begin making the right connections and incorporating his plans. Mick was thrilled with his father's willingness to take him on this way, and Kate was thrilled to see him so happy.

On Sunday everyone went to church together, which is when Kate and Mick learned that Melinda was also a Mormon, thanks to her brother's influence. They also learned that Chas and Jackson both had what they referred to as "Church callings," where they were given an official assignment that was their responsibility for a certain period of time, sometimes for years. Chas taught Relief Society once a month, which was the women's meeting, and it just so happened that she was teaching that day. Kate very much enjoyed her lesson, and it gave her a lot to think about. Jackson's calling was to teach a Sunday School lesson to a group of teenagers every other week. The mechanics of this church fascinated Kate, but not as much as the beliefs at its core.

Kate knew that Mick intended to officially join this church, and she was fine with that. She wasn't sure if she wanted to take that step herself, but she certainly didn't mind being involved, and she was slowly plodding through the Book of Mormon, finding that some of it was puzzling and difficult to understand, but other parts of it were intriguing. She and Mick talked about it some, but he came right out and said that he just wanted to give her time to take it in at her own pace.

The following week Mick helped Jackson haul all of the Christmas decorations out of the basement, and they all worked together to complete the daunting task of decorating the inn. Garlands were wound around the stair rails, and little lights framed every window and eave on the beautiful Victorian mansion. Live evergreen trees were erected and decorated in the parlor of the inn, and in the common room of the house. And lots of little holiday touches were added to every room. Polly and Elliott came over to help with the decorating, and they also came on specified evenings to participate in traditions of making all kinds of goodies to be enjoyed and also shared with neighbors and people they went to church with.

A week after Thanksgiving, Kate was nearly eight months along in her pregnancy, and she still felt confused over certain feelings she had. She'd expressed them more than once to Mick and to Chas, and she knew that Chas kept Jackson in the loop about anything that was pertinent, since she was practically a part of the family. She just wished she knew why she felt such an unrest over this baby. Were her feelings connected to some repressed horror over the circumstances of its conception? Or was it more to do with the baby's future—and her own? She'd made no effort to find a family that was right for her baby, and she wondered if her procrastination was some kind of Freudian way of wishing that she were in a position to keep the baby. A part of her wanted to, but another part of her that was at least as strong knew this was not how she wanted to begin her life as a mother. But one way or another, she needed to make some decisions. This baby would be coming into the world whether she was ready or not.

* * * * *

Mick finished up some work he was doing from his room, which mostly consisted of answering and sending e-mails to a number of contacts. Kate had told him she would be in her room and to come and find her when he was finished with what he needed to do. He knocked at the door and heard her call for him to come in. He liked the way the doors in the inn weren't like standard hotel room doors. They didn't lock unless you actually locked them. It made the inn feel more like a home than rooms for rent. He opened the door and peered in to see Kate sitting cross-legged on the bed, her belly filling her entire lap. She set down a magazine and smiled at him.

"How are you feeling?" he asked, leaving the door open.

"I'm okay," she said. "How are you?"

"I missed you," he said. "Am I interrupting your alone time, or do you mind if I—"

"Make yourself at home," she said. "I could use some company. When I'm alone I think too much."

Since Mick wasn't wearing shoes, he impulsively sat cross-legged on the bed to face her, taking both her hands into his. "Tell me what you're thinking about that you don't want to think about."

Her eyes turned down but he persisted. "Come on. If something's bothering you, you should talk about it."

As soon as he said it, she tightened her eyes shut and tears glistened on her lashes. "Hey," he whispered and touched her face, "you can talk to me about anything; *anything.*"

"I know," she said. "I just have trouble believing—still, after all these months—that this is happening to me. It feels surreal and . . . all wrong." She opened her eyes to look at him. "But . . . if it hadn't happened, I wouldn't have met you, and . . . it feels so right to be with you, and it feels . . ." she sobbed quietly, "all wrong to be . . . falling in love while I'm in this situation, in this condition."

"Your condition is temporary, Kate, and so is the situation. I will remind you of that as much as you need me to. What you and I feel for each other is *not* temporary. This has nothing to do with the baby or how you got pregnant."

Kate looked at him, her eyes glistening with a hope that had become more defined as time went by. Suddenly the words he'd avoided actually saying just came out of his mouth. "Let's get married," he said.

"What?" she gasped. "Are you out of your mind?"

"Actually, no; I think I'm less out of my mind than I've ever been."

"But, we—"

"Hear me out," he said, putting his fingers over her lips. "This might sound impulsive, but it's not. I've thought this through very carefully. My offer is threefold. First of all, I'm in love with you. While my feelings for you are certainly strong enough to want to marry you, I recognize that I can't base such a decision on feelings alone. Which brings me to part two. I really believe that you and I have enough in common to make a good marriage. We have similar feelings, beliefs, and goals—so the love and attraction is not at all impractical. Now the third part is a little more sensitive, so let me finish before you protest. Promise?" he asked, his fingers *still* over her mouth. She nodded, and he moved them. "Given parts one and two, if marrying you *now* would solve some problems and ease your stress, then I'm all for it. I would never consider marriage *just* to solve a problem, or . . ." he shrugged, "I don't know; maybe I would. Depends on the problem." He refocused. "I'm trying to say that if you want to keep this baby, Kate, I'll marry you and make it my own. Neither the child nor you would ever want for anything, and when I say that I'm not just promising to provide for you, I'm promising to be a good husband and father."

It took Kate a moment to absorb what this meant. "You really mean that," she said.

"I really do," he said sincerely while making firm eye contact with her.

Kate had trouble holding back her emotions while her mind raced with thoughts that were difficult to decipher. After a couple of minutes, he said, "You're not saying anything. Tell me something to ease this unbearable fear I have that you're offended by what I just said."

"Offended? No, never. I just . . . it's an adjustment to realize that I actually have a choice. Right from the start I just . . . took it for granted that I could never give this baby what it needed. And, of course, my mother would have never accepted any other option. Even though I've come to realize that I don't need to live by her dictates, I just . . . knew I was not in a position to keep the baby." She looked at him more firmly. "Given the fact that I have a choice, I think I need some time to think about it."

"I wouldn't expect you to do *anything* impulsively. I'm not going anywhere."

"Even if I say no? If I tell you I can't marry you, not now or ever, would you still be around?"

"I'm staying until you get through this, one way or another." He shrugged and nodded his head. "Then we'll . . . reevaluate, I guess. Right now, I'm staying. I think you could use a friend, but I don't want you to take that to mean that my being here is selfless, because it's actually quite selfish. I've never wanted to just . . . be in the same room with someone the way that I do with you. There's nowhere in the world I would rather be than here with you." He touched her nose with his. "And regardless of anything else, we are going to have a wonderful Christmas."

"Yes, I think we will," she said. "Even though I'll be as big as a beached whale."

"No," he said, touching her belly, "it's more like you're trying to smuggle a beach ball. But you look cute pregnant."

"Since you've never seen me any other way, that is a biased statement."

"Maybe," he said and kissed her quickly, "but you still look cute." He noted her countenance and added, "You also look perplexed."

"You just asked me to marry you. I have a lot to think about."

"Okay," he said. "Will talking about it help?"

"Maybe," she said, and went on to share the things Chas had taught her about making decisions. He told her he believed from personal experience that the formula worked. He had studied it himself in the Doctrine and Covenants, another Mormon book of scripture. He'd shared with her his feelings about the steps he'd taken in the past year, and how he could look back and know that God was guiding him through his feelings. He felt certain she would feel the same guidance as she asked for it, and she could then simply follow her feelings.

Kate shared some of her mixed feelings about the baby, and Mick completely understood. He spoke of feeling an abstract sense of responsibility in wanting to take care of the child because it was a part of her, but he also agreed that it wasn't the best way to start a family, and perhaps the baby was meant to be raised elsewhere.

Once again he pressed his hand tentatively on her belly and smiled. "I can't get over it," he said. "It's so amazing."

"What exactly do you think is amazing?"

"That there is a little life in there, but also that you're willing to nurture this life."

"Let me remind you that I'm not doing this by choice."

"No, but you chose to give the baby life. You could have had an abortion."

"No, I couldn't have," she said. "It's against my religion."

"But you told me that you weren't a religious person—before you started going to church with me, anyway."

Kate wondered how to explain this. "I was never actively religious, but I was still raised with basic beliefs, and . . ."

"I get it; really I do. I was raised much the same way. We almost never went to church, but the fear of God was definitely used as a motivator to keep me out of trouble."

"Yes, I suppose that's about it," Kate said, "except that my parents weren't worried about me getting into trouble. The fear of God was meant to inspire me to excel at everything, as if He might mete out some unforeseen punishment if I did anything less than my best."

"Was it the fear of God that kept you from getting an abortion? Do you think God would punish you for doing such a thing?"

"I don't know, but I'd rather not find out."

"Punishment or not, I think your making the choice to give this child life is a good one. I admire you for it."

Kate leaned forward and put her head on his shoulder. "Now if we can just figure out where this baby belongs."

"That decision is yours, Kate. I will support you in whatever you decide."

Kate hugged him, grateful for his love, and for him giving her a choice.

* * * * *

Later that day, Mick found Jackson in the garage, and they shared some casual small talk while Jackson was putting some things away.

"Can I ask you a question?" Mick asked.

"Sure," Jackson said absently.

"You're a religious man, right?"

"You know that I am. That's a rhetorical question."

"Okay, I know you are. So . . . do you think God punishes us for making choices that He has deemed as wrong?"

"Did you have a specific example in mind?"

"Kate and I were talking about abortion. She could have gotten rid of this baby, but she didn't. She said it was against her religion, even though she's not been religious in the typical sense. Is it your opinion that God would punish someone for making such a choice . . . if she had done it?"

"It's my opinion that God is more about preserving our happiness than He is about punishing us. I think what some people label as punishment is actually their own suffering from the natural consequences of their choices. I've never personally been close to someone who's had an abortion, but I've heard that many women have struggled emotionally from the choice. Personally, I think it would be a hard thing to live with, but maybe that's just me."

"Does your church prohibit abortion?"

"To be honest, I don't know the official stand the Church takes. I haven't been a member all that long. Maybe Chas knows."

Mick nodded and became thoughtful. A minute later, he said, "That's very profound, you know."

"What is?"

"That statement about consequences as opposed to punishment."

"I think that God allows things to happen more than He actually makes them happen. That's not to say He's not capable of rendering judgment and making something happen to punish the wicked if He thinks it's necessary—like Noah and the flood, for instance."

"Okay, I get that. It makes sense."

"According to the story in the Bible, the people were horribly, horribly wicked and God knew if they were not destroyed, the wickedness would never cease. I've seen a lot of evil in this world—working for the FBI can do that to a person. Your situation is a good example of that. What those kidnappers did to you was evil for the sake of personal gain. They were willing to take a life and make a family suffer for their greed. They're in prison and they're getting what they deserve. But I think for the most part people are just struggling through this life, not really knowing what's right and wrong, and making mistakes based on ignorance or weakness. In such cases, God would certainly not be tossing out punishment, but He's bound by natural laws and cannot hold back the consequences."

Again Mick thought about that. He was terribly impressed, and it made him all the more intrigued with this religion he was in the process of exploring. While Jackson continued to put his tools in order, Mick took some time to ponder what had been said, then he came up with another question. "How do you figure in things like that?"

"Like what?" Jackson asked.

"Like . . . innocent children getting kidnapped; innocent women getting raped. What about horrible accidents that kill people or disable them?"

"Our time on this planet is a test, Mick. And our free agency is absolutely necessary for that test. There are forces of good and evil present, and they are continually opposing each other. God can't take away the free agency of the bad people any more than He can take it from the good people. Accidents happen; bad things happen to good people. I don't claim to understand it all, but I can say for sure that

God provides a way for *anyone* to find peace and healing, no matter *what* has happened to them."

Mick thought about that, increasingly impressed. A thought occurred to him that made him even *more* impressed. "I guess you would know."

"Know what?"

"A man who hadn't suffered any serious pain in his life might not have much credibility making a statement like that—about peace and healing—but you've suffered more than most men *ever* would, and you *are* at peace."

"Yes, I am."

"For the record . . . I'm really grateful for your example in that . . . and for your advice. You've taught me more than you'll ever know."

"You've said all that before."

"I don't want you to forget."

"I won't," Jackson said. "You're welcome. Now let's go inside and see what those beautiful women are up to. I'm thinking they could use some help with supper."

"What a great idea," Mick said, and they left the garage to go into the house.

* * * * *

In the middle of supper, Jackson said to Chas, "Mick asked me what our religious beliefs are in regard to abortion."

Mick glanced at Kate, wondering if she'd be unhappy with him for being the instigator behind this conversation. But she only seemed curious.

Jackson added, "I told him I didn't know, and he would have to ask you."

Mick looked directly at Chas as if to echo the question.

"I actually know the answer," Chas said. "Ironically, I know the answer because there was a time when it occurred to me that my mother had chosen to give birth to *me,* in spite of what had happened to her." She said, speaking more to Jackson, "This was before I met you." She paused to put a forkful of potatoes into her mouth and chew them. "As I understand it, we believe that every baby has the right to life, and that even unwanted pregnancies bring children into this world who can find good homes with people who aren't able to have children. Officially, abortion is considered to be an acceptable option if the mother's life is in danger. Apparently the mother's life is considered more valuable in such a situation, which makes perfect sense. Ironically, the only other time it's considered an option is in the case of a rape, and then it depends on the personal decision of the mother. Personally, I'm grateful my mother made the decision to keep me, but I can certainly understand why, in some cases, it would be best to terminate the pregnancy. I would think that some women might not be able to emotionally handle such a situation. I think that makes women like my mother—and Kate—quite remarkable. It doesn't make a rape victim who decides to not go through with it any less remarkable; we're all just different, and we deal with challenges differently. That's my take on it, anyway."

"For the record," Kate said, "I could never regret giving this child life. Whatever I decide to do, I'm grateful to know that I gave it the opportunity to live."

The conversation shifted to plans for Christmas, including a Church party that they would all be going to. They also talked quite a bit about the annual open house that would be held at the inn, where anyone was welcome to come in and take a tour and have refreshments. Mick and Kate were both excited to be involved in helping with the event. Jodi would also be helping out, as well as Polly and the other girls that worked at the inn.

In spite of all the excitement over the upcoming festivities, Kate's mind stayed with her need to make a decision. If she was really going to place this baby with an adoptive family, she needed to be arranging that. And if she decided to take Mick up on his offer, they would have to start planning a wedding. The thought made her feel fluttery inside, but that didn't necessarily have any bearing on whether or not that was the right course.

That night Kate knelt and prayed before she got into bed, and she laid there for a long while, continuing to pray. She was surprised at how quickly she had come to rely on prayer, and she hoped that God would see fit to give her an answer to her question that would make it possible for her to move forward with confidence.

The very next day, Kate was amazed to realize that she knew the course she needed to take, and she knew it with confidence. It wasn't an overwhelming feeling, but she felt a peaceful, calm assurance that this was a decision she could live with, and that she would never look back and regret it. Now that she'd come to a decision, there was some action that needed to be taken, but the first step would be to talk to Mick. He came into the project room while she was picking out some stitches, and she asked if she could talk to him.

"Of course," he said and slid a chair closer so that he could sit to face her.

Kate set her work aside. "I told you the things Chas taught me . . . about making decisions . . . about praying."

"Yes," he said.

"I don't know that I'm very good at it, the praying I mean, but . . . I've always trusted my instincts. I think it just came naturally for me. I think it's what saved me from believing that my mother was a normal person." She took a deep breath. "Anyway, I've made some decisions, and I know they're right. I can't explain how I know; I just know. And I need to stick to them. No matter what emotions might tug at me, I have to do what I know is right . . . for me . . . and for my baby."

"Okay," Mick drawled, so nervous his heart was pounding. What would he do if she told him that one of those decisions was not having him be a part of her life? He wasn't sure he could accept it. He reminded himself not to get upset when he hadn't even heard what she had to say.

"First of all," she said, "I know that . . ." Her voice broke and she wiped at a sudden appearance of tears. "I know that . . . this baby is meant for someone else." She shrugged and grabbed a tissue. "I've known it from the start. I guess I just had to reaffirm it. I don't know how to go about finding the right family; that's something I'm going to have to deal with, so I guess it's good that I absolutely know now it's the right course. I know it won't be easy, but in my heart I know it's best. I want to be a mother, but . . . not yet. And not like this." She looked straight at Mick and took his hand. "But I want you to know what it means to me that you gave me an option. I think it made it easier for me to settle firmly on this, knowing that I wasn't giving my baby up out of desperation."

"I understand," he said.

"You're disappointed . . . about the baby."

"A little, maybe. But I'm more proud of you. I think you're an amazing woman. And I believe this decision will work out well for you. I know there are a lot of good people out there who can't have babies and want them. You can give a wonderful gift to someone. I admire you for that."

Kate nodded and looked down, pressing the tissue under her nose.

"There's more," Mick said, "and since you said you'd made *decisions,* I'm assuming that it has something to do with me."

"You've been so kind to me, Mick," she said. "It's difficult for me to believe that I ended up in this place with so much love and support. And having you show up as well just seems too good to be true. I want you to know how grateful I am for everything you've done for me."

Mick's heart threatened to explode. When she didn't go on, he said, "I sense a 'but' coming."

Kate looked astonished. "No. There's no 'but,' Mick. I'm grateful for all you've done for me. I'm amazed at how much alike we are. I think that *you* are amazing. I'm trying to tell you that I want to accept your proposal." He sucked in his breath and couldn't let it go. "Or . . . let's put it this way: I'm hoping you'll ask me again after the baby is safely delivered to its parents and we can make a fresh start."

"Oh, you can count on it," he said and impulsively went to his knees as he wrapped her in his arms. "I love you, Kate," he murmured, "and we're going to have a great life together."

"Yes, I believe we will," she said, and he kissed her. "If I can just get through the next month or two."

"We'll get through it together," he said and kissed her again.

* * * * *

Kate woke up Sunday morning looking forward to going to church. Now that her decision had been made, she felt more at peace with herself. And knowing that her relationship with Mick would not be temporary, she loved just being anywhere with him, having his hand in hers. The few times she'd been to church had been pleasant, and she felt inexplicably happy.

While the children were being bundled up to go out into the cold, Chas said to Mick and Kate, "You should know that this is the first Sunday of the month, and the meeting is a little different. We call it *fast Sunday*. We go without a couple of meals in order to help us feel closer to the Spirit, and instead of having speakers in our main meeting, members can go to the pulpit and share their testimony, or their feelings about the gospel. I just wanted to warn you, so you know what's going on."

"Yeah," Jackson said, "and we have a couple of eccentrics who love to monopolize the time. Don't take what they're saying as what we're all about."

"If you have any questions we can talk about it later," Chas added.

"Fair enough," Mick said. "Let's go."

They all got into their coats and went outside to the vehicles that had been warming up. Mick and Kate followed behind in a separate car since the baby seats took up so much space. When they arrived it became apparent that people were getting used to seeing Kate and Mick, and some were warming up a little bit. Jackson and Chas introduced them as good friends, only using their first names. After Kate was asked a number of times when her baby was due, and offered congratulations, she whispered to Mick, "People think we're married."

"I'm good with that," Mick said. "Just go with the flow."

They were barely settled onto a bench when the meeting began. Mick put his arm around Kate and loved the way she smiled at him.

About ten minutes into the testimony portion of the meeting, Chas was distracted by the children when a woman that she barely knew went to the pulpit. They had been introduced, knew each other's names, and said hi in the hallway when they passed. At the moment, Chas couldn't even *remember* her name. Since this woman served in the Primary and Chas went to Relief Society, they rarely crossed paths. The children miraculously settled down, and Chas tuned in as this woman talked about how much she loved teaching the children; then she got emotional as she talked about how difficult it had been when she'd been asked to take this calling, since she was unable to have children of her own. She briefly mentioned that after years of trying and a great deal of effort from a good infertility specialist, they'd finally had to accept that adoption was the only way, but they'd only reached dead ends with that. Chas turned in her seat to share an astonished gaze with Jackson, wondering if he could feel what she was feeling. Then she turned to find Kate watching the speaker with tears rolling down her face.

The woman concluded her testimony by saying that often when she taught her Primary class she felt a calm warmth inside that gave her hope that one day the Lord would bless her and her husband with a child. After she said amen, Chas watched her walk back to her seat, where her husband put a comforting arm around her. Chas then turned to meet Kate's gaze, and she understood perfectly. Mick's astonishment was also evident. They all knew that it was no accident that they were all sitting here today. Chas could have told Kate what she'd heard, but this was different. Kate had heard with her own ears this woman's tender plea. And yet this woman had no idea that a visitor sitting in the audience was looking for a suitable placement for her baby.

Chas moved Charles to the other side of her and scooted closer to Kate, putting an arm around her shoulders. She whispered softly, "I barely even know her. I had no idea that was an issue."

"She's the one," Kate whispered back. "I know she's the one."

Mick leaned in and whispered so they could both hear him. "It's a miracle."

Kate nodded in agreement, but then she felt a swelling of emotion rise inside that she knew could not be kept silent. She stood and eased past Mick to go out. It wasn't uncommon for her to leave the meeting long enough to use the ladies' room. Today she was glad to find it empty, and once she was alone she cried without restraint. It *was* a miracle! And Kate had never felt such joy at what was about to unfold, but at the same time she'd never felt such sorrow. She could feel the baby moving and growing inside of her, but her time with this child would be done in another month or so. And she would have to let it go. She couldn't imagine anything in life ever being so hard as this, not before, not ever again. But she knew it was right. She *knew* it, and she would not waver. She imagined this sweet childless woman, and the gift she was about to receive, and her heart gladdened with an immeasurable joy that consumed her. It *was* a miracle!

CHAPTER 15

After sacrament meeting, Mick took Kate home. She felt too emotional to sit through more meetings. Jackson took Charles to the nursery while Chas looked for a member of the Relief Society presidency and stopped her. They shared some friendly small talk, then Chas asked, "Could you tell me the name of the sister who bore her testimony . . . about wanting a baby?"

"Oh, that's Pam Tuttle."

"That's right," Chas said. "We've been introduced but I'm not so good with names. Thank you so much."

While sitting through the remainder of the meetings, Chas wondered how to go about this. She knew there were legalities that would require an attorney, but there was no reason she couldn't just talk to Pam about the situation. She was both terrified and thrilled at the prospect of that conversation, and she couldn't wait to arrange it. But, of course, she needed to talk it through with Kate first. They needed to do all of this in the proper order.

After church they had dinner as usual. The kids were actually down for naps, since church time and Sunday dinner didn't work well for their schedule. They would be fed again when they woke up, but their absence made the meal unusually quiet until Jackson said to Mick, "So, I take it you're staying for Christmas."

Mick felt a little taken off guard. He'd certainly thought about it, but he wasn't sure of the best way to handle it. He was a guest in their home, and he didn't want to wear out his welcome or intrude in any way. He also knew that straightforward communication was the best approach, and he knew Jackson would feel the same way.

Before Mick could think how to respond, Jackson went on. "We already made it clear to Kate—a long time ago—that she would be sharing our Christmas celebrations. We assume you'll be here as well."

"I hadn't really gotten to that yet," Mick said. "I'd like to be where Kate is, and my parents are okay with that. They're considering a visit to my uncle's home. But . . . you already do so much for me, and—"

"Don't even go there," Kate said. "They won't put up with it."

"That's right," Chas said. "Everything will be more fun with more people."

"You will never convince me that such a thing is *always* true," Mick said. "If you had annoying relatives you were trying to avoid, you would *never* say something like that to them."

"Okay, you got me there," Chas said. "But you're not related, and you're not annoying. We love having you here. We mean it."

"She's right," Jackson said. "You should just plan on it."

"Okay," Mick said. "You talked me into it. How could Christmas at the Dickensian Inn not be great?"

"My thoughts exactly," Jackson said. "My first Christmas here was pretty amazing."

"I'd like to hear about that," Kate said.

"Some other time," Jackson said.

"I have one problem with being here for Christmas," Mick said. "It's the whole gift thing. If we're all worrying about what to get each other and we don't want anybody else to worry about what to get us, then it just gets so awkward, and . . ." He noticed a glance pass between Jackson and Chas. "What?"

"That's exactly what I said to Chas," Jackson said, "when I decided to stay for Christmas that first time. We solved it rather nicely, I think."

"Don't leave us in suspense," Mick said.

"Ten-dollar limit," Jackson said, "which meant that the gift would either have to be silly or sentimental—or both."

"That's a wonderful idea!" Kate said.

"I would agree," Mick added and chuckled. He looked at Kate and lifted his brows comically. "I have an idea already."

"Well, that's not fair," Kate said.

"Don't worry," Chas said to Kate. "We'll figure something out, and it will be great fun."

"Yes, I believe it will," Mick said, but he was looking at Kate.

Chas felt warmed to see the love between Mick and Kate that was not at all deterred by the sensitive and challenging circumstances. She almost didn't want to bring up the miracle that had happened in testimony meeting, wondering if Kate needed more time to think it through. She was relieved when Kate opened the subject. She reaffirmed what she had felt when this woman had been talking, and she truly believed it was an answer to her prayers. She marveled that God would be so merciful when prayer was such a new part of her life.

"Or perhaps," Kate said, "this is more about answering the prayers of that dear woman. She said she'd been trying and praying for years."

"I'm sure it's for both of you," Jackson said. "Don't sell yourself short. I'm certain God is mindful of you, and of your desire to do what's best for this baby."

Kate smiled humbly, then said to Chas, "When can we talk to her? Is it all right to just talk to her?"

"I'm sure it is," Mick said. "But I'll look into it."

"Once we're sure it's okay," Chas said, "I'll call her and we can get together and talk. I was thinking it might be better with just us women; she might feel overwhelmed otherwise."

"Yes, I think you're right," Kate said.

After dinner Mick checked some things on the Internet, then he made a quick call to the home of their family attorney, who was also a family friend. With a few questions answered, he said it was fine to propose the idea to Pam. Once they were in agreement, they simply needed a local attorney who specialized in adoption to take care of the formalities. Mick had already found listings online for a few possibilities in Butte. They could make some phone calls the following day.

Chas said a prayer before she found Pam's number on the ward list and dialed it. Pam answered the phone and Chas said, "Hi, I'm not sure if you remember me at all, but I'm in your ward. My name is Chas Leeds. I run the Dickensian Inn, if that helps."

"Oh, I *do* know who you are," Pam said kindly. "What can I do for you?"

"I was very touched by your testimony today," Chas said. "I can't imagine how difficult this must be for you."

"Yes, it is," she said, "but I wouldn't want to trade problems with anyone else, if you know what I mean."

"I do know what you mean," Chas said. "Listen, I was wondering if we could sit down and talk. Would you be able to come to my home, perhaps?"

"Oh, I'd love to! Does this mean I can see the inn?"

"Of course. You'd be welcome to see the inn anytime. We actually live in a house attached to the inn, but we kind of go between all day. We could chat in the parlor of the inn, if you'd like. Would you be able to come tomorrow?"

"Well," she sounded disappointed, "I work all day, and I have a dentist appointment right after work, and then we have plans with my husband's family. Are you busy this evening?"

"Oh, that would be great!" Chas said, her heart quickening to think of this happening so quickly. "You tell me what time you can be here, and I'll be ready."

"Can I ask what this is about?" Pam asked, and Chas wondered if she had any suspicion that the comments made during her testimony were tied into the purpose of their visit.

Since she was coming this evening, Chas just said, "Oh, I just felt like I needed to talk to you about something. A prompting, I guess. We can talk when you get here."

They decided on six o'clock, and Chas told her to just come to the front door of the inn and come in; she didn't need to knock. This way Chas didn't have to tidy the common room of the house. The inn was always orderly and more suitable for entertaining guests.

When Chas told the others that Pam would be there at six, they were all pleased. And Kate became immediately nervous.

"You know this is right," Mick said, taking her hand. "Remember what you said to me? You said you knew what was right and you couldn't waver because of emotion."

"Oh, I'm not questioning that it's right," she said. "I just hope this woman feels the same way."

"I can't imagine a woman in her position not taking a baby if it's offered to her," Jackson said.

Mick said, "I would agree with that."

* * * * *

Chas and Kate were sitting in the parlor when Pam came through the door of the inn. Chas went to greet her and impulsively gave her hug. She thanked her for coming, and Pam became immediately intrigued with her surroundings. They stood in the hall for several minutes while Chas gave her some history about the home and its restoration. She invited her to come back any weekday in the afternoon for a tour of nearly every room in the house. Pam promised that she would.

Knowing that Kate was raw with nerves, Chas said, "There's someone I'd like you to meet."

They went into the parlor where Pam was momentarily distracted by the decor. Kate rose carefully to her feet and extended a hand as Chas said, "This is my dear friend, Kate. She's staying with us for a while."

"It's so nice to meet you," Pam said.

"The pleasure is mine," Kate said, and the women were all seated.

Chas knew it was up to her to get this started. She and Kate had talked about how to go about it, and they both believed the direct approach was best.

"I'll get straight to the point, Pam. Kate is not a member of the Church, but she attended the meeting with us today. She heard your testimony, and she was very touched by it. The thing is, Kate has known since the beginning of her pregnancy that it wasn't right for her to keep the baby."

Years of heartache and struggle passed quickly through Pam's eyes before tears pooled there. She moaned softly and put a hand over her mouth, sobbing behind it before Chas added, "She wants to know if you would be willing to adopt her baby."

Pam couldn't speak. When it became evident that Pam's emotions were overwhelming her, Chas came to her feet and opened her arms. Pam stood as well. Chas hugged her tightly and let her cry, then Pam turned to Kate and they hugged too, while they both cried. The two mothers of the same baby then sat side by side and tightly held hands while they shared their experiences and their present relief. When their conversation went on and on, Chas slipped out to give them some time alone and to help Jackson put the children to bed.

"What's going on in there?" Mick asked when she walked into the common room where he was watching *Masterpiece* on PBS.

"Bonding," Chas said. "No worries. It's all going beautifully."

After the children were down for the night, Chas returned to find the women still talking as if they'd known each other forever. The plans they were making on how to handle the situation were so easily agreed on that it seemed further evidence that this was meant to be.

Pam then insisted that her husband Jim come over and meet Kate and hear the news personally. She called Jim and talked him into coming without letting on to the surprise. Chas went to get Jackson and Mick and invited them to come to the parlor in order to help Jim feel less outnumbered. Jackson had baby monitors so they could hear the children, and they all settled in comfortably. The men were pleased to meet Pam and thrilled that this was all going to work out. When Jim arrived, Jackson showed him in and made introductions. They'd met briefly in elders quorum meetings, but didn't know each other very well.

After everyone knew everyone else's name and they were all sitting down, Jim said to his wife, "So what's the big surprise, honey?"

"This must seem very strange, huh?" Mick said.

"Yeah, I admit it does," Jim said.

"Honey," Pam said, looking straight at her husband, "Kate is having a baby in the near future and is putting it up for adoption. She wants to give us her baby."

Jim's tearful response made it evident that these years of trying to have a baby had been equally hard on him. They all talked while a warm, sweet spirit hovered in the room. Then Jim and Pam expressed the need to go home and hopefully get some sleep while they allowed all of this to settle in. After they left, no one seemed to want to leave the parlor, but none of them had much to say. It seemed that they too needed to let the events of the day settle in. Then Mick broke the quiet by saying, "Oh, by the way, Kate and I are getting married."

Chas and Jackson both looked pleasantly astonished, but once the surprise wore off, their expressions showed that they were both pleased. "That's wonderful!" Chas said.

"I think we all knew it would happen," Jackson added. He nodded toward Mick. "I'm glad you have the good sense not to let her get away."

"I think it's the other way around," Kate said and smiled at Mick. "I think he's a keeper."

* * * * *

The following morning Kate woke up with that calm sense of contentment settling into her more deeply. She knew more every hour that her decisions were correct, and that everything would work out the way it was supposed to. When she went downstairs for breakfast, Mick told her that he'd already spoken to an adoption attorney that he liked, and he'd spoken to Jim and given him the attorney's contact information so that everything could get worked out from both ends. Kate thanked Mick for his help and told him how grateful she was to have him by her side through all of this.

"It's a pleasure," he said and kissed her hand.

"Speaking of help," Kate said. "I have a doctor appointment in Butte tomorrow. I was thinking if you took me, we could get some lunch and start our Christmas shopping."

"What a wonderful idea!" Mick said. "We can start looking for those ten-dollar items."

"Yes, we can do that; *however,* we should send gifts to our parents, and we should probably spend a little more on them."

"Maybe," he said. "Maybe not."

As soon as Kate had eaten, she realized she wasn't feeling very well and went back upstairs to lie down. When she did, she noticed that her ankles looked quite a bit more swollen than they had. She wondered if that was anything to be concerned about, but since she would be seeing the doctor tomorrow, she would ask him about it then.

Mick came to check on her a while later and she told him she was just tired and needed to rest. At lunchtime he brought lunch for both of them to her room and she sat up in bed to eat. After he left, she took a long nap and felt a little better, but she went to bed early due to a nasty headache.

A good night's sleep seemed to help, even though the headache was still there. But during breakfast Kate felt an increasing relief to know they were going to see the doctor. She assured Mick that she was fine, but a few minutes after setting out, he asked, "Are you sure you're okay? You don't look like you feel well."

"I must admit that I'm feeling pretty lousy."

"What kind of lousy?"

"I don't know; just . . . lousy. And I've got a headache. It started coming on last night. I thought some sleep would get rid of it, but it's still there."

"Well, it's a good thing we're on our way to the doctor; he can make certain everything is all right."

"I'm sure everything is fine," she said. "It's just pregnancy. I'm almost getting used to it."

"But you feel more lousy today than you did yesterday, right?"

"I suppose. Maybe I'm coming down with something. I hope you don't get it, whatever it is."

"Let's just see what the doctor says before we worry about that."

Kate felt sleepy during the drive and was glad that the seat could recline. She adjusted it to go back as far as it would and closed her eyes, trying to relax. Acknowledging how much her head hurt, she wondered if something *was* wrong. Or maybe she was getting the flu. She was glad they were almost there, since she felt mildly uneasy. Mick was right. She felt more lousy today than she did yesterday; something had obviously changed.

At the office, Kate was especially glad that they didn't have to wait very long. When it came time for her to go in, she said to Mick, "Come with me while I talk to the doctor. If he wants me to change for an exam, you can come back out to the waiting room."

"Are you sure?" he asked. She nodded, and he took her hand. Kate felt mildly nervous and didn't want to be alone. She wasn't sure she could explain to Mick how she felt, but she was glad to have his company.

Walking down the hall, hand in hand, Mick once again felt a sensation that had recently become familiar. He wished they were married; he wished they were having a baby together. He could hardly admit how emotionally attached he'd come to feel toward this baby, and even more so toward Kate. Noting that she was walking slowly and that she looked a little peaked, he would be glad to hear the doctor tell her that everything was okay.

In the examination room the nurse asked a few questions and made some notes, then she took Kate's blood pressure. Mick happened to glance at the nurse's face while she was watching the little dial, waiting for the result. Her concern was starkly evident, and Mick's heart quickened. He didn't comment, not wanting to alarm Kate, who was oblivious to the nurse's reaction.

"Let's try that again," the nurse said calmly and started over. Her concentration was firm and focused. When the result came up the second time, she put a hand on Kate's arm and said in a gentle voice, "Your blood pressure is high, Kate. I'm going to help you lie back, and I want you to just stay here and relax. I'm going to get the doctor."

"Okay," Kate said warily, and the nurse rushed from the room the moment Kate was lying back on the exam table.

Mick saw Kate's concern and took her hand, standing close beside her, saying with a smile, "I'm sure everything will be okay. Getting uptight isn't going to help your blood pressure."

"Probably not," Kate said, but it was hard to relax when she didn't know how high her blood pressure really was. She felt sure it jumped up a few notches when the nurse returned with the doctor, and it had only been about forty-five seconds since she went to get him.

"I hear you're not feeling well," he said with a calm smile.

"Apparently my blood pressure might be the reason?" It was more of a question than a statement.

"Let's find out," he said and took the blood pressure himself. He exchanged a knowing look with the nurse, then focused on Kate as he said, "It's 204 over 107, which is dangerously high. But I don't want you to panic or get upset. We're glad you're here, and we're going to take good care of you." He looked at Mick. "Did you drive her here?"

"Yes."

"Can you drive her directly to the hospital ER? It's only a few blocks away."

"I can," he said.

"We're going to take her to the clinic entrance in a wheelchair, where you can pick her up. When you get to the ER, get her directly into a wheelchair. I'll call them so they'll know you're coming."

Mick nodded toward the doctor, then he turned to Kate, sharing the alarm he saw on her face, but he smiled and said gently, "You stay calm now; it's going to be okay."

She nodded courageously, and Mick left to bring the car around to the clinic entrance. Running across the parking lot, he was so glad he'd been the one to bring her. If something was wrong, he wanted to be at her side. But he wondered if Kate might be more comfortable to have Chas with her. It was a natural conclusion that at the very least Chas should be notified of the problem, so he dialed the inn before he put the car in reverse and backed out of the parking place.

Chas answered, and he quickly explained the situation. "I'm happy to stay with her," Mick said. "Even if she doesn't want me in the room, I'm not leaving the hospital until I know she's okay, but I thought you should know."

"I can't leave right now," Chas said. "I'm the only one here with the inn *and* the children."

"It's okay," Mick said. "I'll call as soon as I have something to tell you."

"And I'll be there as soon as Jackson gets back to stay with the kids. Give her my love."

"I will," Mick said and turned off the phone as he pulled up to the entrance. He'd only been there a moment before a nurse came through the doors pushing a wheelchair that held Kate, who was looking a little dazed and even more peaked than earlier. Mick helped her move into the car and thanked the nurse. He closed the door and hurried back to the driver's seat.

"You okay?" he asked, going as quickly as he dared out of the parking lot, toward the hospital that could be seen from where they were.

"Apparently not," Kate said.

"Okay, but . . . how are you feeling?"

"Scared," she said, "but I'm trying not to think about it."

"Good plan," he said.

She reached her hand over to take his and added, "Stay with me."

"Of course," he said. "I called Chas, but she can't leave right now."

"It's just as well. I don't want everybody making a fuss." She smiled faintly. "You're the exception to that. I think that *you* should be making a very *big* fuss, if only to prove your love for me."

"I can assure you that making a fuss comes very naturally. I'll stay with you every minute that they'll let me."

"I have no idea what to expect."

"Neither do I," he said, "but at least we know what the problem is and you're getting some help."

Mick pulled up to the ER entrance, and a minute later Kate was being wheeled into the hospital. It took him a few minutes to find a parking place, then he hurried inside and was guided to a room where Kate had already changed into a hospital gown. She was lying back on the bed with a sheet over her legs while one nurse was putting an IV into her left arm and another was adjusting the settings on a blood pressure monitor that would remain on Kate's right arm and automatically check the readings every few minutes.

One of the nurses said hello to Mick when he came in. "You must be the father," she said.

"Uh . . . no," he answered. "We're just . . . friends.

"He's my fiancé," Kate said, and he was surprised at how matter-of-factly she added, "The baby is being placed for adoption. I was raped."

"Oh, honey!" the same nurse said.

"I'm so sorry," the other one added.

"It's okay," Kate said. "I'm doing fine. Well . . . other than my blood pressure. My baby will have a good home."

"That's a great thing," the first nurse said. She then shifted to a more professional mode and explained, "The medicine you're getting through the IV is going to hopefully lower your blood pressure, and we're also giving you something that will help to prevent you from having a seizure or a stroke."

"That's possible?" Kate asked.

"Not as possible as it was before you came here," the nurse said. "We're going to take very good care of you, and everything is going to be fine. You mustn't worry, because that *will* keep your blood pressure up." Kate nodded. "The doctor will be in to talk to you in just a little while, and you can ask him anything you want. Just push the button if you need anything."

Kate nodded again, and both nurses left the room. Mick scooted a chair closer to the bed and took Kate's hand.

Kate quickly found it difficult to keep her eyes open. She felt very relaxed but didn't fall asleep. She was keenly aware of Mick's hand in hers and she felt the baby move inside of her. Evidence of its life was reassuring. She wondered how long she would have to stay here, and imagined being sent home with lots of medication and told to stay down for the remainder of her pregnancy. The thought of being in bed for the next month held no appeal whatsoever, but she knew she needed to do whatever was best for the baby, and her own health as well. She wondered if the problem was really as serious as it seemed. The very idea that she could have had a seizure or stroke felt alarming, but she tried not to think about it, not wanting her blood pressure to go up. She felt the cuff tighten on her arm every few minutes, and she always opened her eyes long enough to see the numbers come up on the monitor. They seemed a little better, but it was hard to tell. She wondered when it had gotten so out of control. She'd been doing as the doctor had suggested, checking her blood pressure every few days. Saturday evening it had been fine according to the drugstore's monitor. It had only been yesterday that she'd begun to feel unwell. Could it have jumped up so quickly? Now that she thought about it, she knew the swelling in her face and ankles had been worse. From the doctor's attention to her swelling in the past, she assumed there was a connection.

Kate's attention was drawn to a young doctor when he entered the room.

"Kate Fitzgibbons?" he asked, holding out a hand to shake hers.

"Yes," she said, her voice sounding mildly drunk.

"I'm Dr. Patterson," he said. "I'm an OB-GYN specialist. Your doctor phoned me and asked that I help you out." He turned to Mick, who was now standing. "And you are?" He extended a hand and Mick shook it.

"Mick Prescott. I'm her fiancé." Mick caught a glance from Kate and knew she wanted him to finish the explanation. "Kate will be placing the baby for adoption. She was raped."

"I see," the doctor said with compassion. He sat down, and Mick took his chair again. "Have you chosen parents for your baby yet?"

"I have," Kate said.

"That's good," Dr. Patterson said. "If you want them to be here for the birth, you should call and let them know that it will probably be tomorrow." Kate forced her eyes to stay open and reached for

Mick's hand. "You have what we call pre-eclampsia. With your blood pressure where it's at, we will only be able to get it to a safe level for a limited time, typically within twenty-four to forty-eight hours. That will be our optimal window for delivering this baby."

Kate squeezed Mick's hand tightly. "Will the baby be okay?"

"It will be fine," he said. "You're almost to thirty-six weeks. It will be a little small, and might need some extra care, but delivering at this point should present very few problems. We're going to take good care of you *and* the baby, but you're going to need to stay down completely until the baby is delivered and we get this blood pressure leveled off. No exceptions." Kate nodded again.

The doctor told them more details of what to expect and answered some questions before he left the room, promising to check on her later. As soon as he was gone, Kate said, "Will you call Chas . . . and tell her to call Pam? I'm thinking Pam might need her more than I do today. Tell her you're taking very good care of me."

"I'm all over it," he said and stepped out to make the call. When Chas answered he said, "Kate doesn't want you to come up today; tomorrow might be better."

"So, they're keeping her overnight?"

"At least," Mick said.

"It's that serious?"

"They're going to induce labor tomorrow, once they have her blood pressure at a safe level."

"Oh, my goodness!" she said.

"We told the doctor about the adoption. Kate wants you to call Pam, and she thinks you should be with *her* today. I'm betting she's got some things she'll need to take care of."

"I would think so," Chas said, sounding a little flustered.

"I'm thinking you should bring Pam to the hospital tomorrow. I'm just going to stay here tonight; Kate wants me to. There's a recliner in the room, and they said it would be okay. But I think she'll need you around when it starts to get intense."

Mick stayed near Kate and kept her distracted and entertained. She insisted that in spite of being unable to hold her eyes open, she didn't feel sleepy. In fact, when it came time to sleep, she asked for something that would help her. Once she'd taken the pill the nurse brought her, she drifted off and Mick managed to get a reasonable amount of sleep in the recliner, even though he got up more than once just to watch Kate sleep and to look at the digital numbers that were indicative of her vital signs. Her blood pressure was slowly improving, and he felt confident that she would be okay.

Mick was sitting next to Kate when she woke up, and they she gave him a wan smile before he stood and leaned over her to kiss her brow.

"Today's going to be a hard day," she said.

"Yes, it is," he said, "but I will be here as much as you need me."

"Except for when I'm actually in the delivery room, I want you here."

"I promise," he said. "Just think about how life might be in a week or two, when this is behind you and you're starting to feel better." She nodded with tears in her eyes. "Think about Christmas. We'll have such fun! And when the holidays are over, I'm taking you home with me to Virginia, and we'll plan the wedding." She nodded again, and the tears leaked into the hair at her temples. He kissed her and added gently, "It's going to be okay."

"I know," she said. "I know because God sent you into my life just when I needed you most. As long as I have you, I know that everything will be okay."

"I will always be here," he said and kissed her again.

CHAPTER 16

Kate composed herself when a nurse came in to make certain all was well. After Kate ate her breakfast, a counselor affiliated with the hospital came in to visit with Kate about the adoption. She asked Kate a great many questions about the process she'd gone through to make this decision, and her state of mind concerning this step. She seemed pleased with the way Kate was handling it, but she wanted to talk to Kate about some of the feelings she might yet experience, and to share some coping mechanisms that might make it easier to adjust. While Kate had been thinking it might be best not to even see the baby, this woman explained to her that many studies had been done that had proven it was actually better for the birth mother to spend some time with the baby before turning it over to the adoptive parents. The counselor explained that this seemed to help cement the decision more firmly, and it also helped to create better closure. Kate understood and agreed to follow this woman's advice, but she felt afraid of facing the emotions that would inevitably be a part of the process.

After the counselor spoke to Kate alone for a while, she asked that Mick come in and visit with them. Since he was her fiancé and heavily involved in this experience, he could help Kate deal with the natural challenges that would arise in the coming weeks.

"There is a grieving process that comes with any loss we experience," she told him. "It's important to be able to grieve over letting go of this baby. It's normal for her to shed a lot of tears, especially with the hormone imbalances that come with giving birth. It's also normal for her to experience some pretty extreme mood swings. If she's not improving with those things in a few weeks, it might be a good idea for her to talk to a counselor. You keep an eye on her."

"I will," Mick promised and smiled at Kate. The smile she gave him in return was weak and forced. But he couldn't expect her to be looking forward to all that was on the horizon at the moment. He was dreading it himself. He couldn't even imagine what she might be feeling.

Throughout the day Kate just rested, and Mick stayed nearby. He communicated by phone with Chas, keeping her updated. She was helping Pam take care of some preparations, while Jackson was taking charge of the kids until the ordeal was over. Between Polly and Michelle, they would make certain the inn was covered. Chas was helping Pam clean up the bedroom in her home that had been designated as a nursery for years. They had everything they needed for a baby, but much of it had been sitting and collecting dust for a long time. Pam and Chas had cleaned the room and the furniture, washed the sheets for the crib, and put all the clothes and diapers in order. The only thing they had to buy was a car seat, and Jim would be taking care of that. Chas told Mick that Pam was probably the happiest woman she'd ever seen. She was overwhelmed with excitement over the miracle taking place in their lives, but was also frequently expressing concern for Kate. After Mick got off the phone, he repeated to Kate everything he'd been told. She smiled when he told her about Pam's excitement and preparations, and he felt sure that it made her own sorrow more easy to bear.

Kate was wheeled to another part of the hospital for an ultrasound to determine the size and position of the baby. The doctor declared that everything looked as good as it possibly could. The baby was head down and in the perfect position to be born, as if it had known it needed to come now. With that done, the drug to induce contractions was put into Kate's IV, and Mick phoned Chas to say, "Labor is supposed to be starting soon. It's time to put the plan into action."

"Okay," Chas said, "we'll be leaving Anaconda within the hour."

Kate began to feel some discomfort before the women arrived. An epidural had been ordered to block the pain, and Mick could tell by the way Kate squeezed his hand and grimaced at regular intervals that she was wishing they'd hurry. When Chas and Pam arrived, Mick moved away and allowed the women to exchange their emotional, feminine greetings. Chas hugged Kate and gave her comforting reassurances, then she moved aside and Pam sat on the edge of the bed, wrapping her arms around Kate as if some magnetic bond drew them together and made it difficult to pull apart. Mick realized they were both weeping, then he looked at Chas and saw her wiping her eyes as well. Pam finally eased back from their embrace and said, "What you're going through today is something that will never be forgotten, Kate. We will be forever grateful for your sacrifice on our behalf, and this child will know that it always, and forever, will have two mothers."

Mick saw something peaceful and calm mingled with the tears that welled in Kate's eyes. She nodded, and the two women hugged again until it became evident Kate was enduring a contraction.

"Tell me what I can do," Pam said.

"Just . . . stay with me," Kate said, and Pam nodded firmly.

The anesthesiologist arrived to administer the epidural, and Mick left the room. He paced the hall until Chas came out to tell him that Kate wanted him in there for the time being. While Chas went out to sit with Jim, who was down the hall in a waiting area, Mick sat on one side of Kate, and Pam sat on the other. He could see the effect of the painkiller setting in as she became more relaxed. The contractions were being measured by a monitor, and they all watched the progress intently while saying very little. Each time a nurse came in to examine Kate to check her progress, Mick stepped out to give her privacy. But she always wanted him to come back. He sensed from the nursing staff that his leaving was unusual, since most of the time the man offering support was the father of the baby, and privacy over the intimate details was not an issue. But they all took it in stride and watched as the progress of Kate's labor continued.

When it came time to move Kate to the delivery room, Mick kissed her and told her he'd be nearby. Her hesitance to be without him was evident, but he knew this was how it needed to be. Mick traded places with Chas, since Kate had requested that both she and Pam be present in the delivery room with her. Since Chas had been through labor before, she could coach Kate through it and be her support. Pam simply needed to be there for the birth of her child. Kate had insisted that it only seemed right.

Mick found Jim pacing the waiting room, as any expectant father might. Mick encouraged him to sit down, even though he felt tempted to pace as well. He tried to distract Jim with casual conversation, glad for the way it also took his mind off what was happening. He was more and more impressed with what good people Jim and Pam were, and he knew that there couldn't have been a better choice for a couple to raise this baby. At the right moment, Mick told him that. Jim smiled humbly and asked Mick how he'd come to know the Leeds family, and how he'd met Kate. By the time Mick had shared the basics of the story, they only sat there another minute before Chas came out to find them. Both men stood, and Mick noticed that she was smiling.

"It's a girl," Chas said, "and everything is fine. She weighs almost six pounds, and she's perfectly healthy. The doctor said if she'd gone full term she would have been a big baby."

The men laughed and hugged each other, then they each hugged Chas. "Come along," she said. "Kate wants you both to see the baby right away."

They followed Chas down the hall to the same room Kate had been in before she'd gone into delivery. But on the way they stopped to wash their hands at a special sink, and they put disposable gowns over their clothes to avoid the spread of germs when holding the new infant. The second they entered the room, Pam overwhelmed Jim with a big hug while she said with excitement, "It was so incredible! I got to cut the cord, and Kate insisted I hold her first. It's such a miracle."

Their eyes all turned to Kate, who was holding the baby. She looked up at Mick and smiled, but he saw the poignancy in her eyes as she said softly to him, so that only he could hear, "She's so beautiful, Mick." As if to put perspective on the situation, she added, "But I don't think she looks like me. It might have been hard to raise a child who looks like someone I don't even remember."

"If it was right," Mick said, "we would only see *her*. But we both know what's right."

"I *do* know," Kate said in a whisper. "I know it now more than ever." She looked down at the baby and asked, "Do you want to hold her?"

"Yes!" he said as if he'd be insulted if she didn't ask, but it made her laugh.

As Kate eased the infant into Mick's arms, she saw him smile with a happiness that contradicted a subtle sorrow in his eyes. And she knew exactly how he felt. He chuckled as he took in the tiny face and hands, then he looked at Kate and said, "I want you to remember this moment, Kate. We will share this moment again. And again. And maybe again. Do you hear me? It's a promise from the deepest part of my heart."

Kate felt his promise penetrate her own heart, and her sorrow was soothed a little more. "I hear you," she said, "and I'm counting on it."

They both realized in the same moment that Jim and Pam were discreetly watching them, more than willing to give them the time they needed, but excited to see their new baby. Mick knew that Pam had held the baby, so he carefully shifted the infant into Jim's arms, then he sat on the edge of the bed beside Kate and put his arm around her. They watched together as Jim and Pam looked the baby over, both weeping openly. Mick had to wipe away a few tears of his own, and he noticed Kate pressing the sheet to her face to dry it.

"That's a beautiful picture," Mick said.

"Yes, it is," Kate agreed.

"It's a wonderful thing you've done, my love."

"I never could have done it without you," Kate said, and Mick distracted her with a kiss.

* * * * *

For twenty-four hours after the birth, Kate kept the baby in her room, and Mick stayed close as much as it was appropriate. They held the infant and cuddled her. They laughed at her funny faces and sweet noises. And they cried together over having to let her go. But they both agreed that they felt ready to face the formalities, and that it was time to move on.

Kate signed something that legally declared her absolute knowledge that the identity of the father of this baby was unknown, and she made certain that the document clarified that this was due to a rape. She didn't want her child one day seeing these records and believing that her mother had been promiscuous or irresponsible. Kate signed another document that legally and forever gave up her maternal rights to this child. She felt emotional as she signed, but that calm sense of peace she'd become familiar with overcame her in an undeniable wave, assuring her that it was right, and that she would never regret it. It would take time for all of the legalities to be taken care of, but the most important step was over. Once the papers were signed, she turned to see Mick beside her, and she found hope for the future in his eyes.

All of Kate's sorrow was balanced out by the joy she saw in Pam and Jim as they prepared to take their daughter home. According to their choice, the birth certificate listed her name as Lilian Kate. Lilian wouldn't be leaving the hospital for another couple of days, but now she would remain in the nursery and Kate wouldn't see her again. Before Pam and Jim left her room with the baby, they each hugged Kate tightly and thanked her again for such a priceless gift. After they were gone, Kate cried for an hour, and then she slept, thankfully aided by the pain pills available to her.

Mick stayed again that night in the recliner in her room, grateful that Chas had brought him some of his personal belongings, and that the hospital provided a place for him to clean up when necessary.

After monitoring Kate closely for three days following the birth of the baby, the doctor announced that her blood pressure had evened out very well, and she was released from the hospital with a clean bill of health and no need for medication. During the drive home they listened to Christmas music, and Mick talked about plans for the holidays—and for the future. It kept Kate distracted for a while, but then it became evident that she just needed to cry. He told her it was okay to cry as much as she needed, but he reminded her they had much to look forward to.

Back at the inn, Kate was greeted with an outpouring of love from her new family there. She took the elevator up to her room, where she found a huge bouquet of red roses, with a card from Mick. She thanked him with a tight hug, then laid down to rest. After a short nap, she decided to accept Chas's invitation to spend recuperation time in the common room of the house, where there were people and distractions. Every time her mind drifted to the emptiness she felt from the absence of a baby inside of her, she thought of Pam and Jim and felt a smile touch her lips.

The timing of the annual Christmas open house for the Dickensian Inn proved to be a great distraction for Kate, and she immersed herself in the preparations with great zeal. Chas's friend Jodi was around a lot more than usual as everyone pitched in to make certain the inn was in perfect condition and the holiday decorations were all pristine. A variety of refreshments were prepared, and the finest linens and dishes were brought out for serving them. On the evening of the big event, Kate enjoyed watching the faces of the many people from around town who came to bask in the lovely decor and sweet spirit of the inn. Some even drove an hour or more to participate in the tradition. Many had come before; for some it was their first time. Kate liked to show people around and answer questions. She was amazed at how educated she had become on the history of the inn, and of Charles Dickens himself, through Chas's influence.

Kate also helped keep the refreshment tables full and keep an eye out for guests that might need assistance in any way. Mick was always close by, doing the same, as were Polly and the other girls who worked at the inn. Chas and Jackson mostly mingled among their guests, while Polly's husband, Elliott, watched the children in the house. He'd made it clear he preferred to avoid the crowds.

During these few hours, Kate was able to completely immerse herself in the spirit of Christmas. The friendly chatter of guests, the low hum of Christmas music, and the sweet and spicy aromas of scented candles mingled with tasty treats galore. It was everything Kate had always imagined that Christmas could be—everything it had never been for her. She basked in the experience and gratefully pushed away any hint of emotion related to thoughts of her baby.

After the last guest had finally left, it took more than an hour for everyone to pitch in and clean up and put the inn back to its perfect order. Kate felt the magic of the evening gradually slipping away in spite of her efforts to hold on to it. When Mick asked if she was okay, she just smiled at him and claimed to be tired—which was true. She was soon off to bed where she cried for only a few minutes before she drifted into oblivion.

A week after returning home to the inn, Kate was feeling fairly well and had again become actively engaged in making little blankets and baby gowns for children in other parts of the world. It had a soothing effect on her for reasons that were hard to explain. She considered the irony of sewing baby clothes when her whole being was throbbing with a maternal ache. But it gave her peace and it kept her busy, so she worked at it as much as she felt well enough to do so. Occasionally she just had to stop and have a good cry, and then she'd get back to work, wanting to stay busy. Mick hung out with her there sometimes, and sometimes he was busy elsewhere with his phone and computer. Kate didn't sew all day every day. She eased back into helping Chas with simple chores, and they shared a number of Christmas projects and festivities.

Kate found comfort in the time she was able to spend playing with little Charles and Isabelle and helping care for them here and there. There were moments when she would hold one or the other of them close to her, and for a moment she would wish that she had a child of her own to fill this maternal emptiness in her that was trying to heal. Then she would remember the peace that had accompanied her decision, and she would force herself to keep busy.

Some excitement occurred when a package arrived from Virginia. Everyone assumed it was for Mick, since the return address was his parents' home. It was Chas who noticed and commented, "It's addressed to Kate."

"So it is," Mick said, putting the box in front of her.

Kate felt confused as Mick helped her open it. Inside she found a card signed by Mike and Joy, expressing their compassion for the current situation, and their contrasting pleasure in knowing that she would be officially joining their family. The note said that they just wanted to send a few things to help her through the transition, and they would look forward to seeing her next month. Beneath folded layers of colored tissue, Kate found some DVDs, expensive bath luxuries, and a beautiful blouse that was obviously not maternity. There was also a lovely framed photo of her and Mick that Joy had taken when they'd visited for Thanksgiving.

"They're just so sweet," Kate said, wishing her own mother would even bother to call. At least she'd kept paying the bill for the inn, she thought. And at least Kate had found a family who would love her unconditionally. She had much to be grateful for.

The next day Kate wore her new blouse, and Mick took her into the city to do some shopping. They also had a nice lunch, and Kate could feel the evidence inside of her that the future was becoming brighter, and the past was settling more peacefully into place.

Getting caught up in Christmas preparations alongside Chas made it easier for Kate not to think about the changes that had occurred in her life. But every day was still hard, and she prayed that she would be comforted in her loss and be able to fully put the past behind her.

Kate helped Mick wrap some gifts that were for his parents from both of them. They put everything together in a package, including a card from Kate where she had written a personal message of appreciation for all of their kindness, and her delight at becoming a part of the family. She went with Mick to wait in line at the post office to get it sent off, then they went out for ice cream.

In an effort to come to terms with all that had changed in her life, Kate wrote separate letters to her parents, appropriately expressing appreciation where it was due, and also stating her need to make changes in her life and move on. She told them each separately that she would love to see them whenever the opportunity arose, so long as their visits could be pleasant and that they could share a mutual respect. She sent the letters along with some simple Christmas gifts, wondering if she'd ever hear from them again. But she knew she had done her part, and she was okay with that.

Along with these ambivalent feelings and the absence of a baby, Kate felt sure she likely still had unresolved issues over the way she had been violated, and a part of her couldn't help but grieve over the present situation with her parents—especially her mother. Feeling incapable of doing anything more about any of it, she focused on the joy of the present, and her hope for the future.

* * * * *

A few days before Christmas, Mick sensed that Kate was having a difficult day. He wondered what he might do to cheer her up, or to at least let her know that he was aware of her difficulties without drawing too much attention to them. He was in the office chatting with Jackson, who was doing some paperwork, when he noticed something he hadn't seen before. He stood up to look closer at a set of shelves filled with books, cards, and a variety of simple paraphernalia.

"What is this?" Mick asked.

"How many times have you been in here?" Jackson countered. "They're souvenirs. Dickens novels. Key chains. Mugs. Candles. People come here for special occasions, and they like souvenirs."

"And these?" Mick asked, picking up a couple of cards that came with envelopes.

"Do I really need to explain?" Jackson asked, barely glancing toward him before he returned his attention to his work.

"This is a picture of the inn," Mick declared, noting the exquisite photo of the unique mansion, printed in sepia tones so that it looked like it had been taken a century ago.

"I always knew you were sharp," Jackson said with mild sarcasm, then he chuckled.

"You should be nicer to me," Mick said.

"Probably," Jackson said and kept working. "But you're kind of like the little brother I never had. Who else am I going to torment?"

"Okay, but . . . within reason," Mick said, opening the cards to see that there were a few different varieties with quotes by Charles Dickens printed inside. "He was quite profound, wasn't he?"

"Who?" Jackson asked, looking up.

"Dickens."

"How long have you been staying here?" Jackson asked. "His words of wisdom are in frames all over the house."

"I guess I should stop to read them sometime."

"Yes, you should," Jackson said.

Mick read a few that impressed him, but then he read one that quickened his heart and brought to mind such a clear picture of Kate that it almost took his breath away.

> *You have been the embodiment of every graceful fancy that my mind has ever become acquainted with. Charles Dickens,* Great Expectations

"So, you sell these things?" Mick asked.

"I should think that's obvious."

"How much for the card?"

Jackson leaned back and chuckled. "You really think I'm going to make you pay me a couple of bucks for a card? Just take it if you like it."

"I like it. Thank you. I'll make it up to you."

Mick hurried upstairs, suddenly anxious to add some of his own thoughts in the card, and to let Kate know that to him, she *was* every graceful fancy in his life. The phrase seemed so antique, but delicate and lovely somehow. It perfectly expressed what it had been like for him to fall in love with a woman like Kate, in a place like the Dickensian Inn.

Mick sat down to write his thoughts, then he sealed up the card and wrote Kate's name on the front. He went straightway to find her, loving the way she smiled just to see him with a card in his hand. He said nothing as he watched her open it and read. He bit his lip to keep from chuckling when it occurred to him that the moment was like a Hallmark commercial. Only better. She got a tiny glisten of moisture in her eyes as she read, then she hugged him tightly and said, "I love you, Mick. I really love you."

"I love you too," he said, and it was easy to imagine his every dream coming true, now that he'd found Kate.

* * * * *

The following day, Kate still seemed very down, and Mick prayed more fervently to know if there was something he could do to help her, if there was some perspective he might offer that could make this easier to get through.

At supper Mick found his mind wandering while the usual conversations were taking place at the table. He thought of the miraculous way he'd been led into Jackson's life, and made to feel so at home. Then his mind went to that fateful day when Jackson had offered his simple words of advice, and how they had impacted Mick irrevocably. Then the most powerful principle of that conversation came back to him, so crystal clear in his mind that it took restraint not to gasp aloud. *You have to forgive.*

Mick looked across the table at Kate. Her effort to look cheerful and include herself in the normal activities of life was noble, but he could see the cloud in her countenance. And now he recognized it for what it was. He recognized it because he'd lived under that same cloud for years, blaming all of his ill feelings and discomfort in life on the people who had so dreadfully traumatized him. But now he was free of that burden, and he knew the Spirit was prompting him to help guide Kate to that freedom.

After they'd all pitched in to clean up after supper, Mick whisked Kate away to the parlor where they could have a quiet conversation. Sitting near the Christmas tree just made it more pleasant.

"Kate," he took her hand, "I've been praying for you, praying for a way to help you get through this."

"You do more than—"

He put his fingers over her lips. "Hear me out. I've just had an epiphany, and I know that I'm supposed to share it with you. Every person has to go about these things at their own pace and in their own way, but . . . I wonder if . . . perhaps . . . what's holding you back from making peace with this is . . . well, have you forgiven the man who did this to you, Kate?" Her eyes widened but he kept his fingers over her lips. "I know we've talked about it, and I know you've worked at it, but . . . have you *really* forgiven him? Or . . . is it possible, that somewhere inside, a part of you is blaming him for the grief you're feeling now?" He paused a moment to let that sink in, wishing he could tell if the emotion in her eyes was surprise or alarm. "If he hadn't done this to you, you wouldn't have gotten pregnant, and if you hadn't been pregnant, you wouldn't be grieving over having to give up your baby."

Huge tears rose in her eyes, as if to confirm the truth of what he'd just said. He moved his fingers and took her face gently into his hands. "Ask the Lord to take this burden from you, Kate, and He will. I *know* that He will, because I've felt it in my own life. I can see what you're going through, because I've been there. You have a right to grieve over letting the baby go, and I'll give you all the time you need, but . . . if it's more than that, you need to figure it out and move on. You deserve to be happy. You deserve to be blessed. You have given one of the most selfless gifts that a human being can give in this world. You *deserve* to be blessed for that."

Kate felt his every word sink deep into her heart, and she knew he was right. She wrapped her arms around him and wept, and that night she prayed especially hard to be able to forgive the nameless man who had traumatized her so cruelly. Unable to remember the actual incident, the person she needed to forgive felt ambiguous and obscure. But surely that was the case with many women who had suffered her fate. It was common for women to not know the identity of the perpetrator, whether they were unconscious or not. The need to forgive was for Kate's benefit, and the special circumstances did not change that need.

The next morning she talked with Mick about it some more, expressing some confusion in facing up to the complicated emotions of such trauma, and at the same time recognizing that she could never regret coming to the inn, where she'd found friendships that would last a lifetime, and the man of her dreams. They talked a long while and she felt a little better, but she was still struggling.

That evening over supper she was surprised to hear Mick ask Jackson about priesthood blessings. Jackson explained the principle briefly, and Kate realized that Mick knew all of this. The explanation was for her benefit. Any doubt was waylaid when Mick turned to Kate and asked, "Would you be comfortable with Jackson giving you a blessing?" Kate asked some questions about it, then decided that it certainly couldn't hurt. It seemed to be a more powerful form of prayer, and she could use every bit of divine assistance that might be available to her.

After the children were tucked in for the night, another man from the Church came over and helped Jackson give Kate a blessing. Jackson said that this man knew practically nothing about the situation, but he was kind and good and more than happy to come and help. Apparently it was more proper for the blessing to be given by two men. They both put their hands on Kate's head, but it was the other man who actually spoke the words of the blessing. It was short and simple, but Kate took the words to heart. She was told that her Heavenly Father loved her and was mindful of her. And she was told that the sacrifice she had offered would be made up to her manyfold. She was promised that as she gave her burdens to her Savior, she would be blessed with perfect peace. She was also told that there was nothing to fear from events she couldn't remember; with time she would be healed and made whole. Kate felt stunned by what she was hearing, but even more so by what she felt.

Once the blessing was over, she thanked everyone involved and graciously excused herself with the explanation of being tired. But she actually laid in her bed for hours, staring upward, pondering and praying and trying to take it all in. Tomorrow was Christmas Eve, and she didn't want to feel this way while they were celebrating such a great holiday. She didn't want to be the dark cloud that everyone was concerned about. But neither could she pretend to feel differently than she did; not for long, anyway. These people she currently shared her life with were too sharp and knew her too well for her to get away with any such thing.

Kate woke up with her thoughts still running in this same vein. She immediately began to pray, sincerely expressing her deepest desire to be free of this weight she carried. The warmth she felt didn't come on suddenly, but once she became aware of its presence, it began to filter slowly through her, magnifying in intensity as it did. Tears came softly at first in response to the sensation, then they flowed into a cleansing burst of emotion that consumed her for untold minutes. When her tears finally subsided, the warmth eased into a tangible serenity that she'd never imagined possible. She had believed that such a feeling was possible, or at least she'd *tried* to believe it. Mick had described it; Jackson too. But Kate had wondered if she was somehow exempt from such an experience. But it had happened! And she'd had just enough exposure to the true principles of Christianity to understand and recognize the source of such peace. What better day for this to happen to her? Here in the midst celebrating Christ's birth, Kate had been blessed to feel the great miracle of His healing power.

Suddenly she couldn't get out of bed fast enough, and she ignored the early hour as she grabbed her bathrobe and wrapped it around her while she flew out of her room and up the stairs to the third floor. She knocked on Mick's door, wondering if he was still asleep, or in the shower perhaps. He pulled the door open immediately, dressed for the day, his hair damp, which made it a little more curly.

"Good morning," Mick said, wondering what might bring her to his door this way, adorably disheveled from sleep. Since Kate usually wore her hair twisted into clips, it wasn't often that he saw it down, but he thought she looked especially beautiful. At first he wondered if something was wrong, then he took a moment to examine her countenance just before she threw her arms around him.

"Are you okay?" he asked, hugging her tightly. It had been strange at first to become accustomed to hugging her without her pregnant belly in between them, but he loved holding her in his arms. And right now his heart quickened as he sensed that something had changed.

Kate stepped back to look at him, taking hold of his upper arms. He held to her shoulders and absorbed the light in her eyes. "It happened," she said, her voice trembling. "I've been praying so hard, Mick, and my prayers were finally answered. It happened. *Everything* feels different. It's okay. Everything's okay."

Mick laughed and hugged her again, lifting her feet off the floor. "And what better day for such a thing to take place?" she added. He laughed again and set her down. They sat together and she told him more details of her experience, and they shared a few tears over such a miraculous event.

Kate finally returned to her room to take a shower so they could get started with the day. It was going to be a *really* great day!

* * * * *

Chas and Kate worked together to get this evening's Christmas dinner prepared ahead of time so that they wouldn't be confined to the kitchen at a time when they wanted to be relaxing and enjoying each other's company. Chas listened as Kate shared her tender experience of healing, and the thoughts and feelings that had led up to it. Chas was thrilled to see the change in Kate, and she told her of how she'd once seen an equivalent change in Jackson. Chas felt genuinely thrilled for the change that had taken place in Kate. She hugged her and told her so, but Chas was left feeling almost a little cheated. She too had been praying—for quite some time—to be free of an equivalent weight that she felt in regard to her father. She wondered why Kate would have crossed this bridge so much faster than Chas, when Chas had actively lived the gospel for many years. It only took a moment's thought to realize that no two experiences could be compared, especially when it came to spiritual matters. But she still couldn't help wondering why this issue with her father continued to hover over her. In her heart she *felt* like she had forgiven him, but she also still felt so unsettled. However, it was Christmas Eve, and today was not the day to stew over such a thing. Surely it would all work out with time.

When evening settled in, everyone had such a wonderful time over Christmas dinner that Chas completely forgot about her ongoing concerns. Observing Kate and Mick together, she felt a deep sense of gratification over the opportunity to have these wonderful people in her home, and to see the impact that being here had made on their lives. Polly and Elliott were there with their sweet little daughter, and Chas felt equally grateful to see them together and so happy. Polly was the dearest friend a woman could ever ask for, and Elliott was such a good friend to Jackson. Chas loved the way that they all preferred to celebrate holidays together, simply because they all *felt* like family. Chas's grandfather was also there, and she loved the part he'd come to play in her life. He would be spending the night at the inn and sharing Christmas morning with them as well, since he'd made the decision this year not to fly to one of the places where his other children lived.

Every minute of the evening was filled with fun and a sweet spirit, reminding them all of the reason for the holiday. When it got late, Mick and Kate went up to their rooms for the night, Polly and Elliott went home, and the children were put to bed. Jackson told Chas he had a little surprise project he needed a short while to finish up, which left Chas alone in the parlor of the inn with her grandfather. The Christmas tree lights twinkled nearby, casting a magical glow over the room. Chas had been too busy throughout the day to think about the issue weighing on her. But it came back to her out of nowhere with the quiet that was surrounding them. She wasn't sure she wanted to bring it up and cloud the mood of such a wonderful evening. But the thought was strong, and she couldn't ignore it.

"Can I ask you something, Grandpa?" Chas said.

"Of course," he said, "you can ask me anything."

"Have you forgiven him?"

"Who?"

"Your son . . . my father. Have you forgiven him for all of the hurtful things he did? I know you're not a religious man, but I know you appreciate and understand the value of the principle, and I just have to know if . . ."

"I know exactly what you mean, Chas, and the answer is yes, I *have* forgiven him, but it took time, and it wasn't easy." He shook his head and sighed. "I don't understand why he was the way he was, or why he felt compelled to do the horrible things he did. But that's just it. I *don't* understand, so how could I possibly judge that? Eventually

I realized that I just didn't *want* to carry that burden anymore." He took her hand. "Truthfully, my dear, it became easier for me to let all of that go when you came into my life. As we've said before, you are living proof that good things come from bad situations. How could we ever regret your existence? That's what matters now; nothing more."

Chas nodded, appreciating all he'd said. She just wished she could be free of this ongoing weight that continued to press on her shoulders, in spite of all her prayers and efforts to be free of it. She couldn't think of anything else to say, but knowing that her grandfather *had* been able to move on gave her hope that she could as well. She just had to keep trying.

CHAPTER 17

Kate woke up on Christmas morning as excited as any child might be. She couldn't recall *ever* being so thrilled to celebrate the holiday. Her parents had always made it so stuffy and rigid. But here everything was relaxed and comfortable, and there was a perfect balance of having a great time and keeping the true meaning of Christmas at the center of everything. After the baby had been born early, she and Mick had discussed changing their plans for Christmas, since Kate would be able to travel. But they'd decided to go ahead with their plans and stay at the inn until January. It didn't hurt that Jackson and Chas were so thoroughly pleased.

They all had a wonderful time watching the children open their many gifts. Isabelle needed help, but Charles quickly figured out how to tear into the paper and make the surprises appear. Their antics inspired a great deal of laughter, and they all had a marvelous time. Kate could easily imagine one day sharing such moments with Mick and their own children. He exchanged a meaningful gaze with her more than once, and she felt sure he was thinking the same thing. After the children's gifts were all opened and the wrappings were cleaned up, the kids were set free to play with their new toys. The two little ones were well occupied while the adults exchanged gifts. There were gifts from Mick's parents that proved to be thoughtful and appropriate, and not at all ostentatious the way that Kate knew her mother would have been *if* she had bothered to send gifts, which she had not. But Kate didn't think too long about that.

The ten-dollar gifts were saved for last, and they all shared laughter and some tender moments over the different things that had been chosen in regard to the friendships they had formed in the preceding months.

Mick purposefully manipulated the gift-giving so that he and Kate exchanged their gifts last of all. It wasn't that what he'd chosen to give her was all that exciting; it had more to do with him savoring the anticipation of this first exchange of Christmas gifts between them. As Kate opened the gift from him, he thought of how far they'd come since he'd first gotten this idea. When Kate saw the little lighthouse she laughed and said, "You remembered!"

"Remembered what?" Chas asked.

"I *love* lighthouses," she said and kissed Mick. "I told him that a long time ago."

"And when you did I remembered that I had seen these in a little gift shop near my home in Virginia where I went once in a while. I asked my mother to send it a while back." He took it from her and flipped a little switch on the bottom, and it lit up right where the light would be on a real lighthouse. "It's a nightlight," he said with exaggerated triumph.

"I love it!" Kate said and hugged him. "Thank you!"

"You didn't read the note," Mick said. "The note didn't cost anything, so I'm still within the spending limit . . . unless you count the shipping."

Kate smiled at him as she opened the little card that had been in the bottom of the box. On it Mick had written, *He that ascended up on high, as also he descended below all things, in that he comprehended all things, that he might be in all and through all things, the light of truth; Which truth shineth. This is the light of Christ.* She read it and got a little teary. She looked at Mick and he said, "Don't ever forget it."

"Oh, I won't," she said and hugged him again before she let everyone read the note.

It was Nolan who said, "Oh, that's very nice."

"Now it's your turn," Kate said, handing a package to Mick. When he'd opened it and folded back the tissue, it only took him a moment to realize what it was, and another moment for his vision to blur with tears. He knew the implication even before Kate said, "With all those baby nightgowns I've been making, I thought we should keep at least one. This one will be put to good use one day . . . in our home."

Mick hugged her tightly and whispered close to her ear, "Thank you. It's perfect." He was glad that only Kate knew how emotional he was feeling.

"It's kind of a strange gift," she said softly, "but—"

"No, it's perfect," he said and smiled at her before he kissed her. "It's perfect."

With all the gifts opened, again they cleaned up the wrappings and worked together to put things in order, then Jackson said, "Oh, look. There's something in the tree."

Chas reached in to get the tiny box with a little silver bow. Kate knew by her expression that she'd had no idea it was there, but Jackson looked a little conspiratorial. Chas looked at the tag and smiled before she held it out. "It's for you, Kate."

"What?" she asked and tossed a quick glare at Mick. "We agreed that—"

"This is something I would have given you anyway. Christmas just seemed like a good time."

Kate gasped as what he'd just said coincided with the size of the box. She hurried to sit down, fearing her legs might buckle. She'd agreed to marry him, but she felt almost afraid to open the box. Mick nudged her and she did so, immediately delighted with the ring that appeared, and a little stunned to realize that it was now official.

"Do you like it?" Mick asked as he took it out and slid it onto her finger, where it proved to be just a bit too big.

"I love it!" she said and hugged him before she admired it on her hand, and the others gathered around to do the same.

"We can go have it sized later in the week," Mick said. "And you can pick something else if—"

"No, it's perfect," Kate said, "but . . ."

"But what?" Mick asked, feeling a little alarmed. Had he missed something?

"I think if it's going to be official . . . you should . . . do it . . . officially."

"Do what?" Mick asked.

"For being such a smart kid," Jackson said, "sometimes you're not very smart."

"What?" Mick laughed.

"I think you need to get down on one knee," Jackson added.

Mick laughed again, feeling a little stupid. "Of course," he said and did so. "It would be an honor to make it official." He took Kate's hand and held it tightly. "Will you marry me, Kate?"

"Yes," she said, and the others applauded.

"I have another question," he added. "When the time is right . . . after we set a date and all that . . . will you marry me at the Dickensian Inn?"

"I can't think of any place more romantic," Kate said.

"I can," Jackson whispered to Chas, and she smiled up at him, knowing he meant the temple.

"Give them time," Chas said and put her arms around her husband. What a perfect day!

* * * * *

The afternoon became very quiet while the children were down for their naps. Nolan left to go home where he would have long phone calls with each of his children and grandchildren who lived out of state. Jackson and Mick were discussing the prospect of getting leftovers from last night out of the fridge for a late lunch, since they'd had a late breakfast. Kate and Chas were discussing how they might put together a wedding at the inn when the time was right. The chime rang, indicating that someone had come in through the door of the inn. Since the inn was closed for the holiday, Jackson said, "I wonder who that could be."

Jackson left to take care of it and returned a minute later, carrying a very large, beautifully wrapped package, with a smaller one on top of it, and the two were tied together with a large gold ribbon.

"It was Jim," Jackson informed them. "He said these are for Kate."

Kate gasped as the implication settled in. He held them out toward her but she just stood there.

"They're not going to blow up," Jackson said, and she took the combined packages from him. They weren't as heavy as she'd expected. She sat down with them on her lap, and the others gathered around with curiosity.

"Well, come on," Chas said.

Kate looked at her and said, "I wonder what the baby did today."

Jackson said lightly, "She probably ate and slept and cried. That's all babies ever do."

"And the diaper thing," Chas said.

"Oh, yeah. How could I forget the diaper thing?"

"Need some help?" Mick asked, and Kate nodded, feeling a little numb.

Mick untied the sparkly gold bow and pulled the ribbon away. Kate picked up the smaller package on top and Mick moved the larger one aside. She took a deep breath and opened it to find a little scrapbook, filled with pictures that told a story. Kate cried as she looked at them, but they were tears of peace and joy more than tears of sorrow. Chas admitted that Pam had asked her for pictures, so that the story could begin before the baby was born. There were a few pictures that Chas and Jackson had taken of Kate at different stages of her pregnancy, and there were a couple of pictures of the inn. There were pictures taken at the hospital, both before and after the baby had been born, and many pictures since of precious moments with this beautiful little family. On the last page was a picture of Pam and Jim sitting by the Christmas tree, holding little Lilian, who was dressed in a funny red and white suit with a little elf hat on her head. Underneath the picture it said, *Merry Christmas, Kate. We love you!*

"Oh, it's so beautiful!" Kate said, and had to look at the pictures once more, in reverse order, before she could set it aside.

"It *is* beautiful," Mick said, looking through it with her.

Before Kate could start through the book a third time, Mick took it from her and placed the large package on her lap. Once she had removed the paper and opened the top of the box, she found a card on top of folded tissue. She opened it to read: *I made this, and several more like it, during the many empty hours I tried to fill while my heart ached with wanting a child. It only seemed right that you should have this as a reminder of the priceless, eternal gift you have given us. May it always give you comfort and warmth, and may your life be filled with all of the love and joy that you so richly deserve. With love, Pam*

Kate handed the card to Mick and said, "You should read that aloud; I don't think I can." While he was reading it, Kate folded back the tissue paper to reveal an exquisite pieced quilt, more beautiful than any bed covering that Kate had ever seen. She pulled it out of the box to see that it was likely queen-sized. Little squares and triangles of different fabrics had been sewn together to create a magnificent pattern over the top, and Chas explained that the actual quilting stitches—which also contributed to the design—had been done by hand. Kate spread it over her lap and admired it with her hands as well as her eyes. "I can't even imagine," she said tearfully, "how many hundreds of hours it must have taken."

"Perhaps as many hours as you spent making things to send to children around the world," Mick said. Kate sighed at the comparison, feeling more deeply bonded to Pam, and so grateful that she'd made the choice she had. Holding the quilt close, she *did* feel warm and comforted, but it came as much from inside herself as it did from the quilt. It spread over and around her as surely as a bright future was spreading out before her. It was the best Christmas of her life!

* * * * *

The week between Christmas and New Year's was filled with good times and the creation of great memories. The bond of friendship between Mick and Kate and Jackson and Chas deepened even further, until it truly felt like they were family. They all knew that this closeness would remain throughout their lives, simply because it felt natural, as if they would always gravitate back to each other. It was the only thing that made leaving bearable for Kate. She knew she had a wonderful life unfolding before her, and that the Dickensian Inn would always be more a home to her than the home where she'd grown up.

A couple of days after Christmas, Kate received a card from her father with some money in it, telling her to buy herself something nice. It was as impersonal and succinctly polite as if it might have been from a distant uncle. But her mother had sent nothing. She *had* continued to pay the bill at the inn, however. Kate had to accept that this was apparently the only way her mother knew to express her love.

On the first Sunday of January, Kate felt especially nostalgic about her time at the inn. She and Mick would be leaving the next morning. She hadn't been to church since the baby had been born; at first because she wasn't feeling well, and then for fear of seeing the baby there. She felt no regrets. She simply didn't want to burst into hormonal tears while surrounded by people. But when Chas offered a personal invitation for her to attend church with them one last time before leaving the state, Kate decided she wanted to go, as long as Mick stayed close enough to hold her together. She wondered as they walked into the chapel if Pam and Jim would even be there, but she caught sight of the backs of their heads as soon as she sat down. And a few minutes later when Jim put the baby to his shoulder, Kate had a perfect view of her, even though she was some distance away. Kate felt emotional for a minute and wondered if she should just leave, but she took a deep, calming breath and decided to stay. She was glad to be there when Pam went to the pulpit, tearfully expressing her joy over the great miracle that had occurred in her life since she'd stood in the same place a month earlier. She made eye contact with Kate and held it while she spoke of the great sacrifice that had been made by Lilian's birth mother, and how she would never be forgotten. Kate wept silently and thanked God for giving her the opportunity to bless this woman's life. And she was glad to be sitting there in that moment.

After the meeting was over, Kate was on her way out of the chapel with Mick's hand in hers when she heard Pam say, "Thank you for coming. I'm so glad to see you here."

Kate turned to see that Pam was holding the baby. She smiled and said, "I know you're leaving town tomorrow. Would you like to hold her?"

Kate looked at the baby and wondered if she would regret it, but she nodded, and Pam eased the baby into her arms. She was amazed at how much the baby had changed since she'd last held her, even though the pictures had given her some idea of this. And she was surprised to realize that she felt like someone else's baby. She didn't feel like a part of Kate anymore, a part that had been taken away. Kate knew that little Lilian belonged to Pam. Still, the baby seemed to look right at her, as if she meant to express some kind of otherworldly appreciation. Kate absorbed this feeling into her spirit and gave Lilian back to her mother, grateful for the moment. The two women hugged carefully, with the baby between them, then Kate turned and walked away. Once out the door, she realized that she should have thanked

Pam for the beautiful Christmas gifts, but she decided to write her a card and express *all* of her feelings over the matter when she wasn't hovering so close to tears.

"Are you okay?" Mick asked in the car.

"I am," she said, taking his hand. "I really am."

"Good," he said. "So am I."

The following morning was difficult as good-byes were exchanged, but they promised to see each other soon, and, of course, Mick and Kate would be coming back to the inn for the wedding—if not before. After sharing final words and embraces all around in the parking lot, Mick drove away with Kate's hand in his. She only glanced back once, then she focused on the road ahead. During the drive to Butte, Mick talked about how excited his parents were to have them coming home. She liked that word *home.* She wondered if she would ever think of the house she was raised in that way. Now that she'd experienced a *real* home, and *real* love, she seriously doubted it. After talking it through carefully with Mick, she'd made the decision to not even go to her own house at this time. There was nothing there that she couldn't live without. Perhaps one day they'd go and visit, but Kate would prefer to keep her distance until she and Mick were married, which would give her mother less opportunity to meddle and get up in arms about the wedding not being the way *she* had always dreamed it might be.

At the airport Kate met Tony, and she was escorted aboard the Westcott family's private jet. "*My* family doesn't have one of these," she said with mock envy when they were settling into the luxurious seats.

"I'm your family now," he said, "although I dare say we could manage with commercial airlines."

"Not with all that traveling we're going to do that goes along with your new job."

"That's true," he said. "We're going to keep Tony pretty busy."

The flight went smoothly, and the time passed quickly while Kate reflected on how it had felt to fly to Montana months earlier, with so much uncertainty in her life. Now, everything had changed, and everything was just as it was supposed to be. With Mick's hand in hers, watching the clouds float beneath them, she couldn't imagine being happier.

* * * * *

Chas felt decidedly lonely without Kate and Mick around, even though they had certainly kept themselves busy most of the time. She was grateful, as always, for Polly's friendship, but Polly admitted that she missed them too.

The morning after Mick and Kate departed for Virginia, Jackson and Chas left the children in Polly's care and drove away from the inn while it was still dark to begin their monthly trip to attend the temple in Idaho. They were slowly working to complete the ordinances for their loved ones on the other side of the veil, and today Chas would begin doing the work for her mother. While contemplating her mother's brief life, her thoughts naturally strayed to her father's place in all of this. Unlike with the father of Kate's baby, Chas knew his identity and she knew his family; she'd come to love them. It all just felt strange and a little unsettling. She shared her feelings with Jackson, even though there was nothing to say that hadn't already been said before.

While she sat in the temple, Chas wondered why she hadn't been able to forgive her father, or at the very least to let go of this uneasy feeling. She pondered this dilemma and prayed as she had many times. For a while her mind went to other things, then suddenly it jumped back to her father as if by some strange magnetic force. In her mind she could almost see him; not as a violent man who had broken lives and hearts and had died in prison, but as a spirit with the burdens of the world set aside, and the opportunity to learn and grow placed before him. But he was stuck. Then the truth rushed into her like a hot wind that took her breath away. The problem wasn't at all about forgiveness. She realized then that she'd crossed that bridge months ago, and the Spirit witnessed the truth of it to her. The problem was something else entirely. The unsettled feelings she'd been dealing with were due to the fact that her father's temple work needed to be done, and for some reason he felt anxious over it. Perhaps he feared that it would be forgotten or overlooked due to the way he'd lived his life. But Chas knew that all souls were great in the sight of God, and her father was a link in the chain of her family. He connected her to her grandfather, whom she had grown to love dearly. His work needed to be done, and she was the one to make certain that it happened.

In the celestial room, Chas felt anxious to share with Jackson the feelings she'd had. They sat down close together as they always did, but before she could say anything, he leaned over to her and whispered, "I think we need to hurry and do your father's temple work. I think that might be the problem."

Chas smiled up at her husband while tears blurred her vision. "I don't think there's a problem anymore," she said and put her head on his shoulder.

During the drive home, Chas pondered the change in her perspective, and those peaceful feelings of the temple hovered with her.

The following morning, she opened her e-mail to find a long letter from Kate. They'd arrived safely at the Westcott home, where Joy had provided a lovely room for Kate to stay in until the wedding. Kate felt pampered and loved, and Chas missed her less with the evidence of how easy it would be to keep in touch. Kate had even attached a couple of pictures that helped bridge the gap.

When Polly came in to work, Chas showed her the pictures, and they shared a long conversation about all the wonders that had taken place at the inn—not only while Kate and Mick had been staying there, but through the many years that Polly had worked so closely with Chas. They reminisced for a long while, both concluding that the really good things had begun to occur when Jackson Leeds had come here to stay, not so many years ago.

"Yeah," Chas said, "other than losing Granny, it's all been uphill since then." She sighed and stood up. "I'd better go take over with the kids so Jackson can get some work done."

"Wait a minute," Polly said. "I was leading up to something."

"Oh, I'm sorry," Chas said and sat back down.

"I want to say that you've been a good example to me in more ways than I could ever tell you, and the best of friends. And I want to say that it's been a privilege to be a part of the miracles that have taken place here at the inn. You have a way of attracting miracles, I think."

"I don't know about that," Chas said. "I just . . . try to live right and do my part."

"Well, that's part of the point," Polly went on. "What I'm trying to say is that . . . there is one aspect of my life where I've resisted following your example, but I think I've finally come to terms with that now. I haven't talked to you about it because, well . . . I didn't want to talk to *anybody* about it—except Elliott. He's been wonderfully patient, and he's finally helped me to see reason. He's finally helped me to realize that whatever I do in my life in the present should have nothing to do with the dysfunctional and false conceptions I was raised with in the past, and if I—"

"Polly," Chas stopped her, "I have no idea what you're talking about."

"I'm trying to say that . . . or to ask you if . . . well, would it be all right if Elliott and I come to church with you this Sunday? I want to take it slowly, and I still need to figure out a lot of things, but I'm thinking we might just make a habit of it."

Chas gasped, then nearly melted into her chair. Years ago she had accepted that Polly was well aware of her religious beliefs, and Chas had come to accept the fact that Polly wouldn't be swayed in her desire to avoid religion altogether. So, Chas had left it alone. She knew from things that Elliott had said to Jackson a long time ago that he had some interest in the Church, but he'd declined becoming involved, and she and Jackson suspected it had to do with Polly's overall aversion to organized religion—due to challenges in her upbringing. And now it seemed that one more miracle had taken place.

Chas and Polly both came to their feet in the same moment and hugged tightly. "That sounds like a great habit to me," Chas said, more happy than she could ever express. Polly couldn't begin to understand what this meant to her, but she had a feeling that one day she would.

* * * * *

Six months later

Summer in Montana was perfect for a wedding, and Mick and Kate both readily agreed that there was no place lovelier than the Dickensian Inn, at this time in their lives, for them to be married. Jackson and Chas had begun a romantic tradition of being married there, and they felt they could do no better than follow that example.

Jackson and Chas and their children had come to Virginia a month earlier for a little vacation, and to finalize plans for the wedding. They'd stayed in the Westcott home and had a marvelous time. And while they were there, Jackson had the privilege of baptizing Mick. Immediately following Mick's baptism and confirmation, he'd been given the Aaronic Priesthood so that he was able to then have the privilege of baptizing Kate. With their growing love of the gospel, they intended to also follow Jackson and Chas's example in making a temple marriage their most prominent goal.

Kate and Mick and his parents arrived at the inn two days before the wedding so they could pull all of the plans together at a relaxed pace. It would be a simple affair with very few guests, but they still wanted it to be perfect. Jackson's sister, Melinda, had also flown in for the event. She loved being a part of any festive occasion, and she especially loved being able to put her hostess talents to good use by overseeing the simple decorations that were added to the decor of the inn and helping with the food that would be served. Jodi eagerly got involved as well, contributing her unique baked goods to the fare.

Kate had sent a carefully written letter to her parents along with the wedding invitation. She expressed a sincere desire to have them there, even though she feared that her mother's presence might bring with it some drama. In the end, her father came to stay at the inn the night before, and Kate felt truly happy to see him. He and Mick hit it off, and Jackson and Chas made him feel completely at home. Kate had a moment of regret to think that her mother wouldn't even come to the wedding of her only child. But it only lasted a moment. She'd come to terms with all of that, and she was okay with moving on. There were other women in her life who lovingly and graciously filled the role of a mother for her. She had come to accept that she would be happier if she stopped expecting something from her mother that she would simply never get. And she would be fine.

The wedding came together perfectly. Kate and Mick wore classic wedding attire that might be expected at a huge cathedral with organ music and hundreds of guests. That's how Kate's mother would have preferred it. But everything else was sweet and simple. Every guest present was someone they knew and loved, and they were married by the local Mormon bishop, who was thrilled with the opportunity and spoke openly of the goals they'd shared with him of going to the temple together in the very near future.

Pam and Jim and little Lilian—who was crawling—attended the wedding. And Kate felt nothing but thrilled to see them. She was astonished to see that Lilian looked so much like Pam that no one would ever suspect she'd been adopted. Mick agreed.

After spending their wedding night at the Dickensian Inn, Mick and Kate embarked on a honeymoon that would begin in a remote region of Africa. The plane was loaded with everything they could possibly take into the country legally to help the people there and in other places they would visit during the coming months. They'd decided not to find a place to live just yet, figuring that when they were in the States they could either stay with Mick's parents or at the inn. After a year or so of working to lay the foundation for the work to which Mick wanted to devote his life, they would start a family and get a home of their own, traveling only when it was feasible while keeping the children their highest priority.

"Did you know," Mick said to his wife as the plane headed south toward the equator and beyond, "that Charles Dickens did some amazing things in his life on behalf of the poor and destitute?"

"I didn't know that," she said. "I knew he'd written a great deal about such things, but I didn't realize it was more than that."

"Oh yes," Mick said. "He made a difference in child labor laws, and in the way that the schools for the poor were governed. I think he'd be pleased with what we're doing."

"I'm sure he would," Kate said. "But where exactly did you learn all of this?"

Mick made a comical, deprecating noise to indicate that he was shocked and appalled by her ignorance. "My dear Mrs. Westcott," he said, "you can learn all kinds of wonderful things when you live at the Dickensian Inn."

About the Author

Anita Stansfield began writing at the age of sixteen, and her first novel was published sixteen years later. Her novels range from historical to contemporary and cover a wide gamut of social and emotional issues that explore the human experience through memorable characters and unpredictable plots. She has received many awards, including a special award for pioneering new ground in LDS fiction, and the Lifetime Achievement Award from the Whitney Academy for LDS Literature. Anita is the mother of five, and has two adorable grandsons. Her husband, Vince, is her greatest hero.

To receive regular updates from Anita, go to anitastansfield.com and subscribe.